REVENGE OF THE MONGOOSE

Joseph R. Lavers

MINERVA PRESS
LONDON
MONTREUX LOS ANGELES SYDNEY

REVENGE OF THE MONGOOSE
Copyright © Joseph R. Lavers 1997

All Rights Reserved

No part of this book may be reproduced in any form,
by photocopying or by any electronic or mechanical means,
including information storage or retrieval systems,
without permission in writing from both the copyright owner
and the publisher of this book.

ISBN 1 86106 454 3

First Published 1997 by
MINERVA PRESS
195 Knightsbridge
London SW7 1RE

Printed in Great Britain for Minerva Press

REVENGE OF THE MONGOOSE

Contents

One	9
Two	23
Three	31
Four	49
Five	55
Six	63
Seven	68
Eight	72
Nine	80
Ten	82
Eleven	87
Twelve	89
Thirteen	93
Fourteen	100
Fifteen	101
Sixteen	110
Seventeen	112
Eighteen	113
Nineteen	121

Twenty	124
Twenty-One	132
Twenty-Two	133
Twenty-Three	138
Twenty-Four	145
Twenty-Five	147
Twenty-Six	149
Twenty-Seven	153
Twenty-Eight	158
Twenty-Nine	162
Thirty	167
Thirty-One	172
Thirty-Two	175
Thirty-Three	179
Thirty-Four	184
Thirty-Five	188
Thirty-Six	194
Thirty-Seven	201
Thirty-Eight	206
Thirty-Nine	209
Forty	215

Forty-One	219
Forty-Two	229
Forty-Three	231
Forty-Four	239
Forty-Five	253
Forty-Six	263
Forty-Seven	275
Forty-Eight	291
Forty-Nine	305
Fifty	308
Fifty-One	320
Fifty-Two	328
Fifty-Three	332
Epilogue	334

Chapter One

24th May 1969

The air was suddenly filled with fire and a cacophony of sound like a devil's fireworks display. Darkness became light and, twenty yards ahead, Jennings saw his friends begin to disintegrate like the first grouse on the twelfth of August.

In what seemed a lifetime, but was only part of a second, he threw himself from the path into the wet clinging foliage. His face and body were being grasped by thin witch-like tendrils as he rolled down the slope to escape the bedlam he had witnessed.

Above and ahead of him the air calmed until the only sound he could hear was the steam hammer in his chest. The jungle was silent and the dank air seemed to crush him.

Slowly but surely his training began to take control of his senses. He rolled to a position where he had a field of fire, both ahead and above. He checked his Sterling carbine and found everything in place. He inspected himself and found no holes where there shouldn't be. He felt in his pouch, removed the nightsight and noiselessly fitted it to the Sterling.

A slight movement above caught his attention. He looked though the sight towards the sound. In the eerie haze of the infra-red he saw two shapes about forty yards ahead and above him on the bank.

He took the silencer from the weapon's pouch and soundlessly screwed it on to the muzzle of the Sterling. He peered through the red mist, clicked the weapon to single shot and took aim at the nearest shadow. His hand squeezed on the pistol grip and trigger. The Sterling gently kicked his shoulder and the apparition slumped forward.

His aim switched immediately to the second, and the exercise was repeated. The Sterling made a sound like a raindrop falling in the sea and the phantom twitched and sank into the undergrowth.

He rolled sideways and waited for the thunder of fire being returned to where he had just been lying. None came.

He moved forward, stopping, listening, then moving until, suddenly, he heard the unmistakable metallic click of an ammunition belt being removed from the breech of a gun.

Through the nightsight he scanned the area from where the noise had come. There was no sign of movement above him. Slowly he eased forward. Reaching the top of the slope, he stopped and lay still.

He heard a voice whisper. About thirty feet below him there were three figures crouching around a medium machine-gun. The weapon was mounted on a tripod.

Reaching into his pouch, he pulled out a grenade. Holding it underneath his chest, he removed the pin and released the striking lever. He heard the muffled click as the pin struck the fuse. He counted the seconds, one, two, three, and rolled the pineapple down the slope.

He saw the flash of the explosion and heard, with a strange clarity, the thuds of small pieces of metal striking flesh and bone. Then all was silent again.

Jennings lay still and quiet for another hour, the only sound being the gentle groaning of one of the three ambushers who was still clinging to life.

Moving in a circle, he approached the machine-gun post from the other side.

In the half-light he could see a grotesque picture before him. Two men lay twisted and covered in blood. The third had dragged himself away, his legs shattered and blood oozing from his chest and neck.

Jennings approached him silently from behind, put his foot on the rifle he was holding and pressed the silenced Sterling into his neck.

The head jerked around and terrified eyes stared at Jennings. He mumbled, "Help me," in a coarse Mandarin dialect.

"Who sent you here?" growled Jennings in the man's own tongue, hating him for slaughtering his friends. No answer came.

"Who sent you?" Jennings repeated, his anger beginning to boil.

Again the question was met by silence.

Jennings moved the rifle and shot the man twice in the shoulder.

Through the man's cry of pain Jennings shouted, "Who sent you, you bastard?" and shot him once through the other shoulder.

"Lee Kim, Lee Kim," screamed the man through the fire-storm of pain engulfing his body.

"Lee Kim," Jennings mouthed the name, little knowing that it was a name which would haunt him for the next three years.

The terrorist was of no use to Jennings any more. Fury seethed inside him searching for an escape. He salved his rage by emptying the remains of his magazine into the prostrate figure's head, watching with indifference as it disintegrated.

Jennings sat wearily on the bank, his emotion drained away. His mind was incapable of comprehending what he could see and why.

Slowly the robotics of military training took over and he started to look objectively at what he saw.

The machine-gun was mounted on a tripod. It was set up for firing on a fixed line. Through the sight he could see that the weapon was aimed at chest height and the traverse covered the width of the path. Anybody on the path would be engulfed by the fusillade of tracer rounds which would gush from the gun's muzzle.

In front were the shredded remains of a wall of scrub, heavy enough to hide its destructive presence at night, but not to stop the withering hail of death that would be emitted from its barrel.

Beside it he found a small box which looked like a tiny light. He followed the wire from the box, over the bank and along the side of the jungle track. The wire ran underneath the body of the second shadow, then along the bank for another twenty yards and ended by the first corpse.

The body lay there, with what looked in the darkness like a grotesque grin. The exit wound had torn away most of the lower face.

There was a small button attached to the end of the wire. Jennings took the button, stood up, and pressed it. A tiny firefly of light danced by the machine-gun.

He looked over the banking and saw the shadowy outlines of his dead comrades on the path. He did not want to accept what his mind was telling him.

This was planned.

Whoever planned it had known they were coming.

They had known when they were coming.

They had known the path being taken.

Jennings and his section had walked into a trap.

At once Jennings realised it was not safe to stay there. More men would be coming.

Clambering down to the track, he moved towards the remains of the team of which he had once been a part. They looked like rag dolls who had been fought over by a class of three year olds.

Going through their pouches, he closed his mind to the fact that these had once been his friends. Whilst these were men who would have died for each other, they were no longer part of his mission.

He collected spare ammunition, extra rations and Captain Butcher's binoculars, compass and map. He looked at the stricken body. Butcher should not even have been on the patrol.

The identity tags of each man were removed and put in his pocket, along with the captain's pips from his epaulettes. Corporal Hennessey's stripes were also stowed away.

Dawn would soon be upon him and he needed to be hidden and away from this scene of annihilation.

He moved noiselessly up an escarpment to a point three hundred yards away, from where he could watch. He knew there would be more players in this grisly script. He knew not who, he knew not when, but he knew.

With the dexterity of a jungle veteran he pushed and pulled the undergrowth to make a hide from where he could observe without being seen.

Patience and attention to detail were prerequisites. The previous year he and three others were given an observe and arrest mission in Armagh in Northern Ireland. A cache of arms had been discovered and they were to watch and take the terrorists when they came to collect their weapons of doom.

For three days and nights they had lain, still and silent, in camouflaged burrows near the cache. On the fourth night five men had appeared to retrieve their collection of Kalashnikovs. One of Jennings's number had disturbed his cover and a fire fight had erupted. All five of the bandits had been killed and two SAS members had been wounded.

The political repercussions of that night still reverberated in the media. Before a shoot-to-kill policy had been unknown. After that night it had become the rallying banner of the Republican press. One trooper's mistake had so damaged the political reality that his squadron was withdrawn from the province.

Jennings checked his field of vision, field of fire and the escape route should it be needed. He settled down to wait for the next act to start, hoping he would be an bystander not a participant. The sun would rise behind him in a couple of hours.

He fell into a fitful sleep with images of the ambush interspersed with memories of better times with his dead colleagues.

Jim Murphy was striding up a ridge in Brecon, semi-shrouded in the syrupy Welsh mist, shouting, "Come on, Allan! If we don't make it home before those other bastards, I'll lose twenty quid."

"Lose your twenty quid, you dozy sod, I'm knackered," he heard himself bawling back.

Murph had carried him through these last six days, cajoling, threatening and even pleading with him to keep up the murderous pace. Murph, most definitely, wanted to lord it over the rest in the bar at the Battle School tonight.

The picture in his dream changed to Murph's body lying on that jungle track, his arm shot away and his face unrecognisable.

Then, without warning, he was at base camp. Colonel Herne was briefing them.

"This, gentlemen, is a straightforward meet, collect-and-return mission. The rendezvous is on track B147 somewhere between paths S22 and S23." He stabbed at the map with a pointer. "The two men you are to escort back will make themselves known to you. This is a bandit area but we do not expect any trouble as the people you are collecting will know the bandits' movements." He tossed the map to one side.

"Finally Captain Butcher will lead this patrol, as your platoon commander, Lieutenant Starkey, has been attacked by some sort of virus. Any questions?"

"Yes, sir," said Hennessey. "Why, if the job is so easy, don't you send a patrol of penguins rather than us?"

"If it is your opinion that this mission is too menial for the SAS, Corporal, I suggest that you complain to the area commanding officer. Meanwhile, *your* job is to take orders and mine is—"

Jennings was jolted out of his sleep by a noise below. Down the slope on the path, figures were moving and shouting.

He rubbed his eyes before raising the binoculars to them. The sun had been up for about an hour.

Through the 8×40 wide-angled lenses he could see about fifteen men in camouflage gear. Four were by the machine-gun and the others ahead along the track.

A voice from the front shouted in Mandarin, "There are only six, Lee Kim. There should be seven."

"Look up and off the track," came the reply.

Some of the group moved up the track and others to the side over the bank.

There was a shout of, "Lee Kim, come!"

A Chinese, taller than the rest, with jet-black hair, ran from the machine-gun towards the voice. He got to where the voice had called from, as did several others of the group. Voices spoke quietly for a while and then Lee Kim started to give orders. These were not shouted but spoken only for his men to hear.

Jennings only caught the odd word such as 'escaped' and 'killed'.

The men below spread out into defensive positions along each side of the bank, apart from Lee Kim and two others, who were studying the slope with binoculars.

Jennings prayed that his camouflage was as good in daylight as it had looked in the dark.

They studied the slope for forty minutes before Jennings caught the words 'gone' and 'escaped'. He carefully raised his head and saw that the men had stood down.

What followed was beyond Jennings's comprehension.

Below they began to photograph the scene of the ambush. They spent about half an hour photographing the dead SAS men. The other terrorists posed among the bodies, holding up the dead men's weapons, equipment and their own National Party flag.

When this was all completed, they proceeded to bury the bodies of the fanatics Jennings had slain and placed the bodies of the British into containers. When this was completed, the party took the containers along the path to the west, in the direction of the Chinese border.

Jennings was undecided. Should he follow the bandits or return to base and report? But what could he report? The ambush which had been planned well before their arrival? That they knew there should have been seven bodies not six? The photographing of the results of the ambush? The removal of the bodies?

He could make no sense of any of it.

Lee Kim knew that one man had escaped the trap. The operation was so well planned that the demise of all seven troopers was probably a requirement. If this was so, there would soon be patrols searching for him. They would concentrate their search to the east to stop him making it back to base.

He considered following the enemy patrol. The idea was dismissed. There would be no benefit in following the party towards the border.

He got out the map and spread it in front of him. To the south the jungle was nearly impassable. To the north it was passable, but the terrorists were active in that area. If he took that route he could expect no help from any of the villages. All the villagers either sympathised with the terrorists or were terrified of them. Whichever way, the end result was the same.

South would be safe but slow, north quicker but unsafe.

Overriding all this was the knowledge that the enemy knew the British's plans, route and timing. Other patrols could suffer the same fate as his own, so speed was essential. The slower his return the greater the danger to others.

It had to be north.

Jennings packed away the map and donned all his equipment. The extra ammunition and food he had taken weighed heavily on his shoulders.

He took a compass bearing to the north. He could not see through the jungle for more than fifty yards. He moved laboriously a few yards at a time.

Stop, take a bearing, move and stop again.

All day he struggled through the undergrowth until the light began to fade, all the time trying to leave no trail behind him. Jennings was one of the best jungle men in his squadron. He could simply disappear in the jungle and suddenly appear behind a man like a ghost. His time with the Gurkhas had been well spent.

Deftly he built a hide for the night and settled down to await the morning.

Although physically tired from the exertions of the day, sleep would not relieve his brain. Images appeared, dragging him back from the wonderful unreality of sleep.

Lee Kim. Who was he?

Why the photographs of the slaughter?

Why bury their own but take the bodies of the SAS men?

How did they know there should have been seven bodies?

He was jolted from his fitful dozing. There was movement below and to his left. Through the nightsight he could make out three or four figures huddled around a small pack. As his eyes focused better he could see that the pack was a radio. He could hear the tinny sound of a message being passed. The odd word drifted across in the still night.

'Ambush!'

'Success!'

Then, as though a red-hot knife was driven into his brain, 'Jennings'.

The word seemed to echo inside his head: 'Jennings... Jennings...'

Why was his name reverberating from this enemy radio in the Asian jungle?

He tried to hear more, but could make no sense of anything. Now he was Jennings instead of the survivor of seven.

He was now a prisoner of the urgency to pass on this knowledge, rather than a servant. If the leak of information was accurate to a name, without identification tags, who and where was the source?

He lay motionless, watching the men below. Would they move away or would they rest?

Jennings watched and waited. Patience was his only leverage.

The four men started to look around. They selected a suitable place and started to make shelters. They were hardy jungle veterans and did their jobs well. If Jennings had not been watching, the shelters would have merged into the background.

Waiting for them to complete their task, Jennings noted every detail of their construction. The entrance, the escape route and the alarm system each man used.

One used bent twigs which would crackle if moved. The second lay down, a string attached to his finger so that any movement would be felt. The third appeared not to bother, but Jennings could not be sure. The fourth would be the nightwatchman.

Jennings dug his hand into the mud and replenished the blacking on his face and hands. He drew the *kukri* and placed it between his teeth. The familiar feel of the cold steel comforted him like a baby's dummy. Silently he eased himself out of his shelter.

He moved around the slope to come up behind the sentry. Moving like a cat stalking its oblivious prey, he eased up behind the guard. Jennings reached out and crushed the windpipe in his left hand while cutting through it with the knife. The blade had been satisfied. A Gurkha would never draw the *kukri* without its tasting blood. He laid the body down silently and moved away towards the apparently unprotected shelter.

He examined the surroundings and found the escape route unprotected. His cutting edge moved; another set of lungs would take in no more air.

One of the last two was needed alive.

Jennings cut the string while leaving the gentle pressure for the resting man to feel. He rolled a grenade into the hide and ran to his left, jumping into the other shelter. The sheer force of his landing emptied the lungs of his unsuspecting quarry. He rolled the body over, forced the face into the foliage, and made his prisoner aware of the presence of his *kukri*.

The grenade exploded and number three was no more.

The curved blade was at the terrorist's neck. He grabbed the shoulder and roughly turned his next victim over. He looked at the face. His breath caught in his throat. He was looking into the most exquisite dark hazel eyes. Her face was smooth and round. She had a soft beauty which clashed violently with the harsh surroundings of the jungle.

Her eyes were glazed with the shock of his sudden appearance. They slowly cleared and fear took over from shock.

"Don't kill me," she whispered in Mandarin.

"Who was on the radio?" Jennings snarled, regaining his control.

"Lee Kim," she answered, perplexed to be addressed in her native tongue.

'That name again. Who is this man?' thought Jennings.

"He gave my name. Why?" Jennings asked in a cold voice.

Those bewitching eyes opened even wider. "*You* are Jennings?" Her voice croaked the question, terror paralysing her larynx.

He nodded.

"We must try to take you alive."

"Why?"

"You are propaganda – you shouldn't have escaped our trap."

Jennings pressed the *kukri* on to her throat and whispered, "How many others are looking for me?"

She had seen the aftermath of a Gurkha attack – the bodies dismembered by this terrifying curved weapon.

"Four other patrols." She would tell him everything just to avoid the feel of that evil blade.

"Where are they?"

Her voice was shaking and her body trembled with dread. "Three to the north and one in this sector."

"Are you in radio contact?"

"Yes."

"How often?" he said, forcing a tone of menace into his voice.

"Every two hours," she said.

Jennings looked at his watch and estimated that it was about an hour and three-quarters since their last radio message.

"Who calls? You or them?" He spat the words at her.

"We call in to report progress; we are only called with orders." She was now totally quiescent.

Jennings thought about his next course of action. He had to get back as soon as possible to report what he knew. Most important was the fact that he had to get back.

"When do you next report?"

"0200 hours," she mouthed.

'Ten minutes,' thought Jennings.

He cast his eye around the shelter and saw some twine in the top of her backpack. He turned her over, roughly, and tied her hands and feet. He leant down and said in her ear, "If you make any noise, I will cut your throat, slowly."

The menace in his voice and the sight of the unsheathed weapon sent a shiver of fear down her spine.

He went to the other shelters. The radio was in the second. He checked it and all appeared undamaged. Jennings went back to where the petrified girl lay and propped the radio upright. He then turned her over and sat her up. "Now you will radio in and report that all is quiet. One false word and it will be your last."

He undid the binding on her hands and watched as she expertly tuned the frequency, which he noted, and started to repeat a call sign. The radio crackled with a reply. She reported that nothing had been found. She was ordered to rest for two further hours and then resume the search in their area.

He knew that if he left her alive she posed a threat to his objective, but could he destroy something so exquisite? Could he extinguish the light of life in those ethereal eyes?

No matter what his training told him, he could not execute her in cold blood.

She was a woman, and he was trapped in the Western image of womanhood and the role of the weak woman: a woman should never be harmed.

Damn the result – he could not kill her!

He retied her hands, gagged her and checked the binding on her feet.

"If I hear you, I will come back and you will die slowly and in pain." He patted the *kukri* to add weight to his words.

He could see the terror in her eyes confirming that she would be silent until she was sure he was far away.

Packing the radio away, he left her to be found by someone, some time.

He moved in an easterly direction.

Every hour he stopped and tuned in the radio to hear positions and orders being exchanged. He knew that eventually the frequency would be changed but until then he had an edge.

For two days he made good progress towards the safety of his own side. After six hours he lost the radio contact but those hours allowed him to plot his escape route in order to avoid the pursuing patrols.

On the third morning he studied the map and estimated that another full day of travel, uninterrupted, would take him into the areas where the British regularly patrolled. He packed his equipment and waited for the time to reach the hour. He would scan the frequencies just in case he picked up the bandit patrols.

On the hour he turned the radio on, tuned to the first frequency. The radio hissed into life and he immediately recognised the call sign of Lee Kim.

"All patrols to return immediately to base," the voice crackled. "The detention of Jennings is no longer required."

Jennings sat for a moment and mused.

Was this a genuine order?

Was it meant for him to put him off his guard?

He had seen so many things he could not explain that logic could not be trusted.

He searched the frequencies for other instructions but could find nothing.

He had to move on and assume the message was false. He loaded the pack and radio on to his back, picked up the Sterling and set off towards the hope of safety and answers to many questions.

Late that afternoon he came across signs of British patrols. They were the sort of signs a soldier of his training would not leave, such as cigarette ash and an impression in the mud of the butt of a self-loading rifle. Some group of half-trained imbeciles had sat in a war zone and had a smoke and a chat.

'Bloody stupid penguins,' thought Jennings to himself. This jungle war had been bloody and long, and as he surveyed the signs around him he knew why. If Jennings had his way, no badly trained crap-hat cannon fodder would have ever been allowed out of the UK.

He knew from the signs that this area was regularly patrolled and that his best option would be to await a patrol and go in with them. The problem he faced was how to attract the idiots' attention without getting shot by some trigger-happy terrified amateur.

He looked around and took in the surrounding land. The ground rose above the path and offered plenty of concealment, but how could he attract the patrol's attention? He searched around and found several large stones. He then cut a number of switches from the undergrowth well away from the track. He set the switches out on the path in the shape of the Union Flag and the word 'stop'. The stones were put into a neat pile in front of the sign.

He moved up the slope and found a point with a good view of the message, which also had cover in case the next patrol were adversaries not friends. He checked the three escape routes unseen to those on the path.

Satisfied, he settled down and waited.

Night fell and he dozed in a light dreamless sleep.

The sun playing on his eyelids awoke him. The sign on the track was undisturbed.

By noon he was beginning to doubt he had made the right decision. As the afternoon wore on he started to plan other strategies. He was on to his third possible option when the sound of movement below focused his attention on the track. The sounds came closer until a lone soldier came into his vision.

Jennings could see clearly that the soldier was British.

The man below saw the sign. Jennings was impressed by what happened next.

The soldier signalled to the rest of the patrol to take cover and in the same movement dived from the path. Jennings heard him land in the undergrowth and then roll. 'Very professional,' thought Jennings to himself.

Everything was now silent.

'Now for the dangerous bit,' thought Jennings.

In a whisper loud enough only for the man below to hear he said, "Sergeant Jennings, 22nd Special Air Service. The rest of my patrol were ambushed and I am returning to base."

He heard the rustle of movement.

A voice said, "Show yourself with your hands and weapon above your head."

Jennings stood up with his hands above his head, the Sterling in his right hand.

"Move down to the path by the stones," was the next instruction.

Jennings moved carefully down the slope and stood by the stones.

"Lay the weapon on the floor."

He obeyed.

"Move away ten feet and spreadeagle yourself on the ground."

Jennings did exactly as he was told. He felt a rifle muzzle in the back of his neck and hands searching him for other weapons. The Browning pistol, grenades and knife were removed.

"Stand up with your hands on your head," he was ordered.

He stood and found himself facing a stocky ruddy-faced man of about twenty-five. The pips on his epaulette showed that he was a lieutenant.

"I am very glad to see you, sir," said Jennings. "My patrol ran into an ambush and were all killed apart from me."

He heard a voice from behind say, "Why don't we just shoot the bastard now and piss off, sir?"

"Shut up or I'll have your balls off," the lieutenant hissed.

He turned to Jennings and said, "I have orders, if I find you, to take you directly back to the Pai Ling Base Camp. You are officially under protective arrest. You are not allowed to communicate with any of my men."

He turned and commanded, "Corporal Gates, you will be responsible for the prisoner."

"Leave the bastard to me, sir," came the gruff reply.

"What's going on here, sir?" Jennings asked.

"I have my orders, you have my instructions and that is all you need to know," he replied, adding, "If you do the least thing untoward, Corporal Gates will shoot you. Clear?"

"Yes, sir," whispered Jennings.

"Prisoner second in line of march, rest as before."

Jennings was pushed roughly into a position in front of Gates, who clearly looked as if he hoped Jennings would do something untoward.

The patrol moved off and marched hard for the next two hours. They eventually came to the edge of a large clearing. The officer spent five minutes on the radio and returned to where Jennings sat.

"A helicopter will be arriving to take you away and you will be off my hands, thank God."

"What's happened, sir? I don't understand all this," Jennings blurted out.

"Just shut up before I lose my temper," was the terse reply.

Twenty minutes later a Wessex helicopter arrived. Four men emerged, all wearing the insignia of the military police.

"Is this the prisoner?" said the officer, a major.

"Yes, sir," replied the lieutenant.

"What equipment has he got?"

"Sterling, Browning, grenades, knife and this, sir." The lieutenant placed the weapons and the bandit's radio in front of the senior man.

"That's an interesting piece of equipment," muttered the major, picking up the radio. "Bring him along and all this gear," he snapped to his subordinates.

Jennings was grabbed and roughly pushed towards the helicopter by the largest of the policeman while the other two carried his equipment.

As the Wessex took off, Jennings's mind was in total turmoil and he could not resist the thought that he had actually died and was now in hell.

Chapter Two

The flight was short and no one spoke. Jennings clearly sensed an animosity towards him but knew not why. They bumped to a landing. 'Army pilots were never a match for the RAF or the Navy,' Jennings thought. He was manhandled from the Wessex and into the back of a closed one-tonner. The officer seemed pleased to travel in the cab rather than have to share any more time with Jennings.

The lorry stopped and, as he was pulled from the lorry, Jennings saw a sign: PAI LING MILITARY POLICE.

He was taken inside, searched and locked in a small cell.

For the next two hours he was alone, the only sounds muffled conversations from somewhere outside his cell.

Jennings's mind replayed the events of the last few days again and again, trying to put a line of rationality into what was happening. No logic came to the rescue, only panic and despair at his predicament.

His mind moved again over the events. What had he done to engender this treatment?

The ambush – he was lucky, he escaped.

The second terrorist patrol – why the photographs?

Why bury their own yet take away the troopers' bodies?

Why were they looking for seven and how did they know how many to look for?

Why send so many patrols to look for him?

Why, suddenly, did they no longer want him?

The British patrol – why the obvious hate?

Why was he being treated like an enemy, not a friend?

He had no answers, too many questions and he was exhausted.

He lay down and slept, hoping that dreams would take away the fear gnawing at his brain.

"Allan, I am so proud of you. Only once before have a father and son won the Sandhurst Sword of Honour," said Brigadier Sir Charles Jennings. He wanted to hug his son but he knew that officers did not show that sort of emotion. "The Lancers have another Jennings to be proud of, son."

Allan Jennings looked uncomfortably at his father, a proud man with a deep feeling for family history. "I am not joining the Lancers, Father," he stated quietly and waited for the explosion.

"You're not what?" bellowed his father. "There has been a Jennings in the Lancers for over two hundred years and you will carry on that tradition, you hear me?"

Jennings looked at his father, who had changed in a microsecond from a loving father to a frenzied commander about to lose a good potential officer. He could see why his father's nickname was Thunderbolt and it had little to do with speed of foot.

"Father, I do not intend to incarcerate myself in a reinforced tin can and have myself blown up by squaddies with rockets squirted out of tubes."

"Bloody tin cans! You self-opinionated little sod – a little bit of training at Sandhurst and you think you're an expert at it all," raged his father. "I've been at it twenty-nine years and I'm still learning, you arrogant young shit."

"Father, I have a choice of any regiment and have made up my mind that I want to join the Gurkhas."

"You're not a bloody curry muncher. All your life you've been brought up a Lancer. Tank warfare is in your blood."

"Perhaps that's why I want to be a curry muncher," said Jennings through clenched teeth.

Both men were now boiling with a fury which would arrive, explode and die in the laughter that would follow.

"You're too tall to be a curry muncher," barked the Brigadier.

"Then I won't fit in one of your tin cans, will I?" retorted Jennings, trying now to hold back the laughter he knew was coming.

"They wouldn't want you in a tin can if you'd been curry munching. Poison gas is contrary to the Geneva Convention," his father spluttered as he was overcome by the need to collapse in laughter.

They both broke into fits of laughter and the tension was gone.

Jennings knew that this was only a truce. Whenever they fought, they always ended laughing and always doing what the Brigadier wanted. This time would be different.

Jennings awoke with a start, just as a large MP kicked his bed.

"You're wanted," grunted the man as he pulled Jennings to his feet.

He was taken to a room slightly bigger than his cell furnished with a table and two chairs. The chairs faced each other across the table like two protagonists across a boxing ring. He was pushed into the room and the door closed and bolted behind him. The room was oblong, about 10 feet by 12 feet, with white walls and one light suspended above the table.

Jennings had been in many rooms such as this during training to withstand interrogation.

Why should he be interrogated rather than debriefed?

He heard the bolts clatter back and the door opened. A short man with a goatee beard entered. Jennings snapped to attention as soon as he saw the three pips on the man's shoulders.

"Captain Harris. At ease, please sit down, Sergeant," the man said amicably.

"What is all this about, sir?" asked Jennings.

"In due time, in due time," came the reply.

"Name, rank and number first." His tone was both friendly yet carried authority.

"Jennings, Sergeant, 23738959," Jennings replied.

"You are with the 22nd Special Air Service, is that correct?"

"Yes, sir."

"You went on a routine collect-and-return mission with a section of seven men, including you, Sergeant, and to date you are the only one to return, and without the bodies you were supposed to bring back.

"In your own words, Sergeant, can you explain to me what has happened?"

"Can I ask you, sir, why am I being debriefed by military intelligence rather than my own commanding officer?" Jennings asked.

"We can take over any debriefing we wish to and we have taken over this one. Now answer my question."

Jennings related all the events accurately without any questioning or comment. Captain Harris made copious notes, occasionally stopping Jennings to have a point clarified. The only part Jennings missed out was leaving the girl alive.

"Thank you, Sergeant," said Harris. "Just one or two more points to clarify."

"You say you took the dog tags of the rest of the patrol before the arrival of the second terrorist group – is that correct?"

"Yes, sir," he replied.

He was starting to become nervous for the debriefing was beginning to seem like a cross-examination.

"These are the dog tags you are referring to, Sergeant?" Harris pulled some identification tags from his pocket.

Jennings took them and examined each one – Butcher, Hennessey, Murphy, Wilde, Potter and Crafts.

"They appear to be, sir." He was now becoming very uneasy at the line of questioning.

"It's a simple question, Sergeant. Are they or are they not the tags you removed from the bodies of your patrol?"

"They are the same names, sir, but I have no way of knowing if they are the same tags," he replied.

"We're a little bit defensive, aren't we, Sergeant?"

"No, sir, I am trying to be factual," Jennings retorted.

"Factually, do those tags bear the names and details of the other members of your patrol? Is that better, Sergeant?"

"They do, sir."

"Right then. So you confirm that these or identical tags have been in your possession from the time you took them to the time they were passed to my men, is that so?"

"Yes, sir."

"Good. Now did you check all the bodies for any other form of identification and remove it?"

"Yes, sir."

"There is no way that the members of your patrol could have been identified by a third party to whom they were unknown – is that correct?"

The 'is that' end to each question was beginning to grate on Jennings.

"That is correct, sir," Jennings mouthed without hiding his growing anger.

"All pockets were thoroughly examined and all insignia of rank removed – is that so, Sergeant?"

"That is so, sir," Jennings clenched his teeth to try and keep his control. If he lost his self-discipline, the interrogator would win.

Harris stood, walked to the door and tapped it with his stick. He turned to Jennings and said, "That will be all for the moment, Sergeant."

The door opened and Harris said, "Take him back."

Two burly MPs took him back to the first cell, pushed him in and slammed the door shut.

Jennings sat on the bed, closed his eyes and tried to make sense of the questioning.

In his polite barrister's way Harris had been accusing Jennings of something – but what? It was standard to remove all identification from anyone killed in action. There was nothing wrong with that, but the questioning seemed to imply there was.

Jennings sat for what seemed hours, his mind in turmoil, trying to fathom what was happening to him. He knew not whether it was day or night.

The door banged open, he was ordered to his feet and marched to what he now knew to be the interrogation room.

He stood to attention in front of an officer he had not seen before. The crown on his epaulette showed that the level of inquisition had progressed from captain to major.

"Sit down, Sergeant. I am Major Lawrence."

Jennings sat, his unease growing.

"Now, Sergeant, I would like to know a little more about the radio you had in your possession when the patrol found you."

"Yes, sir."

"How did you obtain this radio?"

"It's in my statement, sir. I took it from an enemy patrol," he replied.

"Ah yes, you ambushed an enemy patrol, killed them all and took their radio. Why did you take the radio?"

"As they were looking for me I thought that if I could listen in on their transmissions I could avoid capture, sir."

"Very James Bond, Sergeant. How would you know their frequencies?"

"They had just been transmitting, sir, and I guessed that they would not change for twenty-four hours."

"Is that standard practice for small patrols in the British Army, Sergeant?"

"No, sir."

"Why did you think their practice should be any different from ours, Sergeant? You've been fighting them for some time, and you and I know they are professionals."

"I probably did not think, sir." Jennings was now becoming very uneasy.

"You – top recruit at Sandhurst, three commendations for bravery and one of the best SAS men – didn't think. With your training it is *impossible* not to think! How did you come by that radio?"

Jennings felt his hackles rising, which he knew was what the interrogator wanted. He forced his anger back down and replied, "I have told what happened, sir."

"I would like you to think very carefully on your next answer, Sergeant," Lawrence said, in a tone so even that it was menacing.

"You say your patrol was a simple collect-and-return. You say your patrol was ambushed and the way the ambush was set up it appeared that they knew you were coming. Am I right so far, Sergeant?"

Jennings nodded agreement.

"You were tail-ending the patrol and were out of the line of fire, correct?"

Again Jennings nodded.

"You, single-handedly, killed the ambushers, and the next day saw another patrol arrive and take away the bodies of your patrol. You then left, ambushed another patrol, took their radio and returned to your own lines. Is all that right?"

"Yes, sir."

"You also say that the enemy knew that the patrol should have been seven strong and that you heard your name being used over the enemy's radio, yes or no?"

"Yes, sir."

Lawrence looked up at the guard and said, "Take him back."

Jennings was ordered to his feet and double-marched back to his cell.

The door slammed and he was left in a world where nothing seemed real.

He slumped in his cell with his mind scanning the past few days. Nothing seemed to make sense. Why was he banged up in jail instead of receiving a commendation for bravery?

After two days the door crashed open and he returned to the interrogation room.

"Sit down, Jennings," said Captain Harris, all pretence at courtesy gone.

As Jennings sat he noticed Major Lawrence in the corner of the room.

"Now, Jennings," continued Harris, "let me run through parts of your story. You say that you were ambushed on 24th May and that the ambush was set up knowing you were coming. Correct?"

"It appeared that way, sir, yes."

"You subsequently knocked out the enemy ambush and took all the identification tags from your own patrol."

"That is correct, sir."

"How do you explain this, then?" said Harris, throwing a newspaper on the table.

Jennings took the paper and read the headline.

SAS DESTROYED BY FREEDOM FIGHTERS screamed at him from the page. He read the story of the ambush but there was no mention of the terrorists' own losses. He felt an icy hand grip his heart as the names of the dead troopers sprang out at him from the body of the report, each accompanied by a grisly photograph of the shattered remains.

"If you removed all identification, how does this communist propaganda rag know not only the names but the ranks of the rest of your patrol?" Harris whispered.

"I don't know, sir."

"They've put the right names to each photograph. Look at them, you bastard," Harris barked.

"I don't know! In God's name I don't know!" Jennings slammed his fist on to the desk in frustration.

Harris said nothing as he walked around the desk. He picked up the newspaper and held it in front of Jennings.

"This story was published while you were still in the jungle, and a subsequent story was written thanking you for your help in the ambush. You sold the lives of your own men, you bastard."

"That's not true," snapped Jennings, clenching his fists until he could feel the nails cutting into his palms.

"How do you explain the transfer of £20,000 into your bank account from a numbered account in Basle?" Lawrence interjected from behind him.

Jennings turned to look at his accuser. "I don't know what you are talking about, sir. Apart from anything else, my family is wealthy enough that £20,000 means nothing."

Lawrence stood, walked across to Jennings and said, "You, Sergeant, are an arrogant, greedy traitor of the worst kind and a cold-blooded murderer. I intend to see you rot in prison for the rest of your miserable life, which I hope will be very short." He walked to the door and shouted, "Get this murdering bastard out of here!"

The guards came in and manhandled Jennings back to his cell.

That evening his cell door was thrown open and the order, "Attention," was bellowed.

Lieutenant Joe Starkey told Jennings to sit. "I've been told the full story by the intelligence people, Allan. I don't believe a bloody word of it. I promise you that I will do everything in my power to get you out of this mess. I should have been on that patrol, and my guts turn every time I think about what happened." They talked for another hour before Starkey left, promising to do whatever was necessary to help Jennings in his predicament.

Jennings did not know why, but he felt more uneasy *after* Starkey's visit than he had *before*.

Chapter Three

Two days later Jennings was taken under escort to the military airfield and flown back to Abingdon RAF Base. Overnight he was held in regimental police barracks. The next day he was transferred to the military police headquarters in Huntingdon.

He was interrogated for three more days. The same questions were asked and the answers repeated. The terrorists' newspaper and its pictures haunted his dreams. Every night he saw the swaggering figure of Lee Kim.

On the fourth day he was taken to the interrogation room, where he expected to have to repeat the whole story to yet another officer from the intelligence unit.

The door opened, and suddenly Jennings was face to face with Sir Charles Jennings.

"Dad! Thank Christ you are here! I don't know what the hell is happening."

"Joe Starkey contacted me. You appear to be in very serious trouble, Allan," said his father. "The allegations made by the intelligence people are that you sold information on your patrol and were involved in setting up the ambush on your own men."

"But that's a load of bloody rubbish! Why should I do that? They were my mates."

"Look, Allan," said his father, "they have some very strong evidence against you. I know you, and I know that you would not have done what they are saying, but they will be charging you and you will have to defend yourself."

"For fuck's sake we were ambushed! Some bastard arranged it, but it was not me."

"I know that, but you have got to prove it to a court," his father replied. "I have asked Stuart Rittle to come and talk to you, and act for you if it comes to a court martial." He turned and called through the open door, "Come in, Stuart."

Stuart Rittle QC was a short, tubby, slightly effeminate man with half-moon glasses perched on the end of his nose. He reminded Jennings of the toad he had kept as a pet when he was a boy. He bustled around the desk and placed his attaché case on the floor.

"Allan," he said, "I am afraid that we will have to go through the whole story from start to finish and then I will look at what evidence will be presented against you." He produced a large notepad from the depths of his case.

For the next three hours Jennings related the whole saga from the first briefing to the present. Rittle made copious notes and interjected numerous questions.

When the tale was fully told, Rittle sat back, twirled his glasses between thumb and forefinger and said, "I think you may have been fitted up, my boy. That can be the only explanation other than your being guilty."

"Who the hell would want to do that and what the bloody hell for?" said Sir Charles. "If Allan had not been tail-end charlie, he would have been dog meat with the rest of the sodding patrol!"

"Look," said Rittle, "there are too many things in here which cannot be explained. How did the communists get hold of names and ranks when Allan had removed all the identification? How did the patrols in the jungle know his name and why did they write that second report implicating Allan? The only reason can be that Allan must, for some reason, be discredited. His story cannot be seen to be acceptable to anyone. I must look closely at the evidence against Allan before I can go any further."

With that he folded his papers, stood and shook hands with Jennings and his father, and left.

Sir Charles turned to Jennings, "Look, son, there are too many things I don't understand here. I intend to find out exactly what is happening. Until then, do not say anything further without Stuart or myself being there."

With that he shook hands stiffly and left.

Jennings was left alone to ponder his impending fate. He had to try and make sense of what was happening to him and why.

Rittle visited each afternoon for the next three days asking many questions but offering no answers to the questions which were tormenting Jennings.

4th June 1969

Rittle arrived while Jennings was picking at his lunch of unrecognisable meat and overcooked vegetables. His arrival was in time to stop Jennings from having to decide what to do with the alleged ginger pudding and the yellow mush that surrounded it.

Rittle sat for what seemed an hour, but was probably only five minutes, studying the bundle of papers in front of him. Jennings wondered why all barristers tied their documents in bundles with pink ribbon. He supposed that if you wore a wig to work, it hardly mattered if your papers were festooned with pink embellishments.

Finally he looked up and said, "Allan, my boy, I am afraid that you are in very deep trouble. The military have not fully decided on the charge to be presented against you but the most likely will be murder or conspiracy to murder. They are also considering charging you with espionage. These charges would, of course, take the matter out of the military courts and into the civil courts."

"What evidence have they got to sustain it?"

"Firstly," he continued, "you are the only survivor of the ambush. Secondly, the ambush was set up with the terrorists appearing to have advance knowledge. Thirdly, you appeared with an enemy radio in your possession. Fourthly, there are the two reports in the communist propaganda paper naming names and implicating you. Fifthly is the transfer of the money to your bank account from an unknown source. Finally, and I only heard this yesterday, the bodies of the rest of your patrol have been recovered, partially decomposed, from the ambush site. All the evidence is circumstantial but it adds up to a very strong case against you."

"But the bastards took the bodies away. How were they recovered at the ambush site?"

"You tell me, Allan, you tell me," replied Rittle. "That is not all, I am afraid," he continued. "I have been trying to look for a credible and workable defence. This is quite possible as all the evidence is circumstantial and they could have problems with reasonable doubt in front of a jury. However, to do this I must have access to all the information surrounding the patrol, the people you were supposed to collect and the reasons why such a straightforward job was given to the SAS. I have tried to obtain this information and have been denied access, as release of such is contrary to the national interest. That instruction can only come from the attorney-general's office. Someone very important wants the lid kept on this. They want you discredited and they want the whole matter hushed up."

"Why?" snapped Jennings, smashing his fist on the table. "What have I done to them?"

"I honestly think that your sin was to survive the ambush and come back. The whole patrol was meant to go – no survivors – that is my opinion," mused Rittle.

"Where the fuck do we go from here then?"

"I think there may be one possibility, but before I pursue it I must have your agreement. It is obvious to me that someone wants this whole thing hushed up. If that is the case, whoever it is would prefer a court martial, *in camera*, rather than a case in open court. In court I could defend the likely charges, but the result would, to an extent, be a lottery and you could end up with life imprisonment. Alternatively I could try to make an arrangement in which you plead guilty to a lesser charge and accept a short sentence in a military establishment. If we chose the alternative, I would propose a guilty plea to a charge of 'lack of moral fibre', which would probably mean between six and twelve months in jail and discharge from the army."

"What choice do I have?" said Jennings bitterly. "The bastards have got me by the balls."

"Okay, leave it with me and I will see what can be done." Rittle was rising to leave but he stopped and turned to Jennings. "Allan, don't let your father dig into this through any of his connections. I believe that that could put him in danger." With that he left.

The following day Jennings's father arrived with Rittle.

"Stuart has told me what you are proposing to do, Allan, and I can tell you that I am against it. This family has been an army family for over two hundred years and I will not have the family stained with a charge of cowardice when the whole bloody thing is untrue," barked Sir Charles. "I have enough connections in the establishment to dig out the whole truth and that is exactly what I intend to do, do you understand?"

"I don't like the situation any more than you do; in fact, I like it a bloody sight less. Stuart has told you the level of people we may be dealing with and I want you to stay out of it, Dad."

"I will do no such bloody thing. If you are not prepared to stand up for yourself, *I* bloody well will." The fuse on his father's temper was now burnt out. "I will not have the family name tarnished for no reason."

He stormed out of the room, attempting to drive the door through the wall as he left.

"For Christ's sake, Stuart, you have got to stop him doing anything stupid," Jennings pleaded. "I love that bad-tempered old sod and he may get hurt."

Rittle said in his barrister's calm voice, "I will talk to him, but we both know how stubborn he can be. Don't worry, I have spoken to the prosecuting officer and he has agreed to the charge proposed. The court martial will be in two days' time. Once that is over, I hope Charles will accept what has happened and drop the matter. Do you agree?"

"I have to," sighed Jennings.

Two days later the court martial was convened *in camera*. The charge was read and Jennings duly pleaded guilty. The circumstances of the offence were presented to the court, but they bore no resemblance to the reality of 24th May. Rittle pleaded eloquently in mitigation, citing Jennings's exemplary record and his citations for bravery. Lieutenant Joseph Starkey was called as a character witness.

"I have known Sergeant Jennings since he transferred from the Gurkha Regiment. As the court has been told, he won the Sword of Honour at Sandhurst and subsequently resigned his commission in order to volunteer for the Special Air Service. He has enormous ability and several of his compatriots owe their lives to his courage. He has recently been recommended for a commission in the regiment, which, as the court knows, is an honour not lightly bestowed."

The court thanked Starkey and retired. Twenty minutes later it reconvened.

"Sergeant Jennings," the senior officer said, "you have pleaded guilty to a most serious offence in an active zone. If this had been in a situation of a declared war, the charge would have been cowardice in the face of the enemy and the punishment a firing squad. This court sentences you to be reduced to the ranks and to serve two years' detention in Colchester Military Prison. At the completion of your sentence you will be dishonourably discharged from Her Majesty's service. Take him away."

Jennings stood stunned at the sentence. He looked at Rittle, wondering if the sentence was a surprise to him. Rittle did not return his look.

"Prisoner and escort, left turn," bellowed the escort commander. "By the front, quick march."

Jennings was marched back to his cell and ordered to collect any belongings he wanted to take. The escort returned and he was marched, in double-time, to the waiting transport. He was locked into the transport and with a judder the journey to Colchester, and whatever it held in store, began.

The journey seemed to drag on for ever. At last the lorry stopped. The back was thrown open and Jennings and his escort disembarked into a yard. He looked at the high wall, with its crest of broken glass, and despair gnawed at his intestines.

"Prisoner and escort, left turn. By the front, at the double, quick march, left, right, left, right."

They double-marched into a small office and were ordered to halt in front of a desk which was too large for the office. Behind the desk was a short stocky man with huge hands and a crown on the forearm of his uniform.

"Prisoner for transfer, sir," shouted the escort commander.

"Thank you, Corporal, I have been looking forward to having Mr Jennings as one of my guests." The man's quiet menacing voice sent a shiver of apprehension down Jennings's spine.

The escort about-turned and double-marched from the office. Jennings noticed two other military police inside the door of the office.

"Jennings, I am Sergeant-Major Bonner. For the next two years I am going to be your conscience. For what you have done, you murdering bastard, you are going to pay. One foot out of line and you will suffer. I intend to make two years seem like twenty."

Bonner turned to the corporal by the door. "Corporal Hyde, have we arranged the accommodation?"

"Yes, sir," replied the corporal. "All the arrangements are made. He will be sharing with Swift."

"Take him out then," ordered Bonner.

Jennings was double-marched to another area where he was issued a uniform and all his belongings taken away and stored.

He was then taken to the showers, where he showered and donned his prison garb. It appeared that everything in Colchester nick was done at the double with the escort bellowing at the top of his voice.

"At the double!" screamed Hyde, and they entered the main confines of the prison. They doubled along a lengthy corridor with steel doors set every dozen or so feet and military police guards lounging against the walls armed with pick handles.

"Halt!" the order came about halfway down the corridor. The door to the left was opened. "Prisoner and escort, fall out." The three executed a right turn and Jennings was pushed into a cell about the size of the one he had previously occupied. The door slammed behind him.

The cell was dimly lit and it took a while for his eyes to adjust. As they became accustomed to the gloom he saw bunk beds on the right-hand wall and a table and chair on the other side. Jennings could make out the shape of a huge man lying on the lower bunk. Jennings was over six foot tall but this man would dwarf him. 'Swift,' thought Jennings.

He said to the man, "My name's Allan Jennings," and proffered his hand. Swift lumbered to his feet, ignoring Jennings's hand, and said, "I know all about you, you yellow-bellied murdering bastard. That's why you're here. I intend to teach you a fucking lesson."

With that he launched himself across the cell at Jennings. Swift had size on his side but apparently little or no finesse. Jennings ducked under the first rush and turned to face the aggressor. He was poised on the balls of his feet, his fists tightly closed with the middle knuckle protruding.

Jennings remembered his first lesson in unarmed combat: no matter how big they are your leg will always be longer than their arm. Swift lunged again. This time Jennings was prepared. He leaned back and struck out with his right leg. His aim was true and his heel struck the big man's kneecap. Jennings heard the patella shattering. Swift staggered forward, losing his balance. Jennings swayed to one side and drove his clenched fist into the nape of the giant's neck. He crashed face down on the stone floor, and again Jennings heard the sound of bones cracking. Swift lay motionless on the floor.

Jennings pounded the cell door. He knew that Swift now needed attention from a doctor. Nothing happened for ten minutes despite Jennings hammering with all his strength. Above the din he could hear the groaning of the incapacitated man, who was lying like a rag doll on the floor, blood seeping from his broken nose.

After ten minutes he heard the lock being opened and one of the guards threw the door open. A look of total surprise crossed his face when he saw Jennings standing next to the prostrate body of Swift.

He shouted, "Get a medic and a stretcher," and pushed past Jennings.

"Don't move him," Jennings said. "He may have spinal injuries."

The guard turned. "You bastard. Ten minutes and you are already starting trouble."

The medic arrived, as did the stretcher. Swift was fitted with a neck brace and taken off, presumably to the hospital. The cell door was locked and Jennings was left alone.

So this was to be prison. It seemed that everyone in the place already knew about Jennings. They all knew a story, but was it the right story or was it a story planted in the hope that he never made it out of Colchester? If that was the case, he had two savage years ahead of him but, by Christ, they weren't going to break him.

An hour later the door clanged open. "On your feet, at the double." He was double-marched back to Bonner's office.

"One hour you have been here and already I have a prisoner assaulted."

"He attacked me, sir, I was acting in self-defence," snapped Jennings.

"Shut up. I don't want to hear your opinion. Twenty-eight days' solitary. Take the bastard away."

Jennings was double-marched to another part of the building, a cell door was opened and he was half pushed, half thrown through the door. This cell was even smaller, maybe six foot by eight. The only contents were a straw palliasse on the floor and a slop bucket.

Jennings sat on the palliasse. He was here for two years and he now knew that for those two years trouble would follow him as a heat-seeking missile follows a jet engine. He had to stay fit and strong. He must train harder and become more formidable than he had ever been, just to survive. In his mind he planned a training routine. Circuit training without moving.

Every day he aimed to improve on the previous day. Once a day he was taken out for thirty minutes' fresh air in the exercise yard. This consisted of donning a heavy canvas overall and doubling around the yard carrying an old Lee Enfield rifle, either above his head or at arms' length in front of him. After the first week the rifle was replaced by a sandbag. Bonner thought he was giving Jennings grief but he was actually helping him.

He had been in solitary confinement for three weeks when the cell door was thrown open at the wrong time. "Attention." Jennings snapped to his feet. "The commanding officer wants to see you. At the double, quick march."

They double-marched along several corridors and halted outside a heavy oak-panelled door. The sign on the door said MAJOR F.M.A. PARKER. The corporal knocked and a surprisingly gentle voice said, "Come in."

Jennings was marched into the room and ordered to halt in front of a large mahogany desk. The man behind the desk had dark brown hair, greying at the sides. His eyes were dark green and set beneath bushy brown eyebrows.

"Thank you, Corporal, that will be all. Please wait outside." The corporal about-turned and marched from the office.

"Stand at ease."

Jennings stood at ease.

"I think you had better sit down, Jennings. I have some rather bad news for you."

*

Lunch at the Wig and Pen Club had been excellent and washed down with a particularly fine claret.

"You seem distracted, Charles," said Stuart Rittle. "What's troubling you?"

"What the hell do you think is troubling me? Bloody Allan is shut up in Colchester for something I am sure he did not do and I cannot find out a damned thing about the whole affair! I don't know who authorised the mission, what was the purpose of the mission or whom they were supposed to collect. I can't get access to any documents or bloody information about that patrol. All the response I get is that I don't have the security clearance."

"Don't make too many waves, please, Charles. I have a bad feeling about this," Rittle whispered.

"Make bloody waves? I intend to do more than that. I have already told those arseholes at the ministry that unless I get the right answers I intend to go to the press. Let's see what they have to say about that. I intend to get to the truth even if I have to kick every arse in Whitehall until its nose bleeds."

That evening the telephone rang at Sir Charles Jennings's flat.

"Jennings speaking," he barked into the handset.

"Is that Sir Charles Jennings?" said a softly spoken voice.

He thought he recognised it but did not know from where. "Yes."

"I may have some information you need about the mission your son was on. I think we should meet somewhere private."

"Where do you suggest?" said Sir Charles, his voice showing positive interest.

"Near your country home in Woldingham. Go down Chalkpit Lane and park in the lay-by just before the M25 bridge."

"When?"

"Ten o'clock tonight."

"I will be there."

It was 9.45 p.m. when Sir Charles Jennings turned into Chalkpit Lane and down the hill towards the motorway bridge. He parked the Jaguar in the lay-by.

It had been a long day and Sir Charles had not slept properly for some time. He leaned back into the soft leather of the Jaguar seat and closed his eyes. The dream was of better times. His son was being presented the Sword of Honour and he was trying to force back the tears of pride. His heart was saying, 'This is my son in whom I am well pleased.'

He neither heard nor saw the tipper truck round the corner behind him and accelerate.

Suddenly he felt the Jaguar being driven forward and he saw the front of the car being crushed into the bridge, the glass from the shattering windscreen raining on him like a fiendish hailstorm. The steering wheel attacked his chest. He felt the searing heat of flames as though Hades was manifesting itself on earth. Then he felt no more.

*

"There has been a motor accident," said Major Parker. "It seems that someone stole a tipper truck and was in collision with your father's car. I am afraid he is dead."

Jennings's mind became blank as though it could not accept the information it was receiving.

Parker droned on, avoiding eye contact. "The funeral is in two days' time and arrangements have been made for you to be released into Mr Rittle's custody tomorrow afternoon. That is all, Jennings."

"Attention ! About-turn! Left, right, left, right, left, right."

Back in his cramped cell Jennings broke down and wept. The brigadier had been more than just a father: he had been a big brother, a confidant and a shoulder to cry on. What shoulder could Jennings use now?

Slowly he regained control of himself. The gods had dealt him a nefarious hand to play, but play it he had to. He resolved to be intractable in his pursuit of the truth, no matter what the consequences to himself or others.

The next day Stuart Rittle arrived after lunch and Jennings was released into his custody.

"Allan, I have serious doubts about Charles's so-called accident," Rittle said grimly as he gunned the BMW along the M25.

"What do you mean?"

"Your father was beginning to make a lot of noise in the wrong places about you and the mission you were on. He put people's backs up, both at the MOD and MI6. I had lunch with him the day he died and he was talking about going to the press."

"What had he got to go to the press with?" asked Jennings, puzzled.

"I don't know, but whoever heard of a joyrider stealing a tipper truck?"

"Look, Stuart, do not do anything yourself. I intend to get to the bottom of the whole bloody thing once I am out of that stinking dump. I don't care how long it takes or how much it costs – I will get to the truth. It has cost me two years of my life and perhaps my father his life. This is personal."

"Any help I can give you, you know where I am," Rittle said, more to placate Jennings than to offer assistance.

They arrived at the family home in Woldingham at about four that afternoon. Jennings felt as though he were in a dream.

The house and gardens nestled in the south face of the North Downs. The view on a clear day was spectacular. The countryside rolled away towards the South Downs and every colour known to man was exhibited in the panorama. The summer flowers danced among the rich green grass. Fields of wheat were changing their hue to a golden tan. Butterflies displayed and birds sang out their praises of summer. Above, the sun smiled on the vista its warmth had created.

Jennings went into the garden and his skin was caressed by the warm afternoon effulgence. He looked across East Surrey and West Kent and felt a gleam of satisfaction. Even the squat, round gasometer in Oxted was not ugly that day. His happiest times had been spent here. As a child this garden had been a wonderland. One day it had been the Wild West, the next the desert, and then the jungle. He and his friends had played out all their childhood fantasies in this place.

Then he looked to his left, where he could see clearly the motorway bridge over Chalkpit Lane, and his guts tightened in a simmering rage. He turned, went in and poured himself a stiff Glenfiddich.

That evening they drove down the lane through Oxted to The Haycutter on Broadham Green. The bar was warm and friendly, as Jennings always remembered it. The locals sat to the right and newcomers to the left, exchanging the normal banter across the U-shaped bar. Jennings and Rittle sat in the centre as the teasing passed across the bar.

"I am so sorry about your father's accident, Allan." The voice came from behind his right shoulder.

Jennings turned and saw the familiar face of Tony Hacker. He was tall but slightly built yet had an air of authority which was of great value for a chief inspector of police.

"Thank you, Tony," said Jennings. "I am only just beginning to accept it myself."

"Look, I can tell you one thing. He must have died instantly because the car was smashed beyond recognition."

"How do you know that, Tony?"

"Well, I attended the scene myself. The accident was reported when I was on duty."

"What actually happened?" Jennings enquired.

"The truck hit your dad's car from the back and they both caught fire, but that is really all I know."

"But, if you were the attending officer you would be preparing the accident report, wouldn't you?"

"Normally that would be true," mused Hacker, "but in this case, presumably because your dad was a bigwig, the whole thing was taken out of my hands. In fact some of the people did not even look like coppers to me."

Jennings had a few more pints of Friary Meux, exchanged some stories, and then he and Rittle finally left just before closing time.

The funeral service, at St Mary's Church, was both sombre and uplifting. The craggy old Norman church added to the grandeur of the dignitaries attending. The vicar had known Sir Charles for many years and his eulogy came from his heart not his notebook. Jennings had not cried since he was a child. He wept tears of grief and anger.

At the interment all the luminaries made sure that an acceptable distance was maintained between them and Jennings.

Jennings and Rittle did not attend the Ministry of Defence booze-up at The Old Bell as Jennings would have been an obvious embarrassment to some so-called family friends.

Back at the house in Woldingham, Jennings got drunk, introspective, morose and then collapsed into sleep. The next morning brought a hangover and the reality of a return to Colchester.

Rittle stopped at The Haycutter for Jennings to enjoy a pint or two, which would have to last him for the next two years.

Back in the prison, matters took up from where they had begun. For the next year and a half Jennings was the object of various assaults. Mostly he won the battle, sometimes he lost, but the end result was the same – solitary.

If he lost solitary followed the prison hospital, and if he won solitary followed immediately.

Jennings forced himself to work harder during each confinement, with his body and mind fixed on the objective of finding the truth and righting the wrong done to him and his father.

Then, with only six months of his sentence remaining, everything seemed to change.

Jennings was taken back to his cell after yet another period in solitary. As his eyes became used to the semi-gloom of the cell he saw that the other bunk was occupied. Jennings was used to a new cellmate on each return. He walked over to the man, who was prone on his bunk, and snarled, "You want it now or are you going to try later when my back's turned?"

The figure on the bunk stood and faced Jennings. He was not a big man, probably three or four inches shorter than Jennings and about the same measurement narrower.

"What the hell are you talking about?" the man replied.

"Look, pal, for the past year and a half every time I've come back there's been some so-called hardcase put in here to do me over. Do you want to try now, or later when I've got my back to you?"

"I don't know what the fuck you are on about! I've just arrived to spend six months in this shit-hole just because I smacked some dozy captain in the mouth. The last thing I want is to thump you. Have you got some sort of persecution complex?" the man snapped back.

"Forget it," said Jennings.

"Look," the other retorted, "I suggest we start again. My name is Jim Cross. I was with the Green Jackets in Belfast when this arsehole of a captain wanted me and my section to go and poke about in a building that was supposed to be booby-trapped. I told him to fuck off and he started pushing me so I smacked him one. Now I'm here for six months before being dishonourably returned to civilian life."

"Nice speech," murmured Jennings. "Best introduction I've heard for a long time. I could almost believe you."

"Go fuck yourself," snapped Cross.

The next two weeks passed with both men wary of each other, unwilling to make the first move to break down the wall between them. The only words exchanged were the minimal courtesies which only the English would bother to exchange in such a situation.

Then one afternoon three long-termers decided it was their turn to have a go at the yellow bastard from the SAS. They cornered Jennings in the latrine. Jennings was just holding his own but running out of steam, when Cross came to his aid. The two of them dispatched the long-termers into starry-eyed oblivion. As usual, as soon as the rough-house was over several guards appeared, grabbed Jennings and marched him off to receive the pleasantries of Sergeant Bonner.

"You're like a fucking yo-yo, Jennings. Have you got an elastic band tied to you and that cell in solitary?" Bonner snapped. "What's your story this time, hero?"

"No story, sir." The last word was mouthed as an insult. "Just the same as always, sir."

Bonner's neck muscles tightened as he fought to control his growing rage. He had tried to break this bastard but Jennings seemed to get stronger not weaker.

"Twenty-eight days' solitary, double exercise morning and afternoon. Take him out."

The punishment ordered, Jennings about-turned and was double-marched by his escort to the tiny cell which had practically become his second home. Jennings knew that double exercise meant two hours, morning and afternoon, of being dressed in the canvas overall, carrying a sandbag and being abused by a psychopath with the brains of a newt and the cruelty of a crocodile in a military police uniform.

After two days the cell door was thrown open at the wrong time. Jennings was only halfway through his own private circuit training session so formal exercise was not due for at least another hour. He was ordered to his feet and double-marched to the commanding officer's quarters. He stood rigidly to attention in front of Major Parker, who was studying or pretending to study the documents on his desk.

Parker looked up. "Stand at ease," he ordered in a quiet voice. He turned to the guards and dismissed them. "Jennings," he said abruptly, "since you have been with us you have been in and out of solitary on a regular basis. You seem to have the ability to attract trouble to yourself. However, at the request of Cross, who I believe witnessed this latest incident, I have made further enquiries into this matter."

Jennings shuffled uneasily. What was this leading to? Did they have some new idea to try and break him?

"It would seem", Parker droned on "that this latest *fracas* was not, in fact, your fault. Cross has made a statement to me that you were assaulted and were simply defending yourself and that he came to your aid. Consequently I have decided to quash your punishment.

"Corporal!" Parker shouted through the door.

The door flew open and the guard commander burst into the room. He looked distinctly displeased to see that Jennings was not attacking the CO, and he lowered the pick handle he was brandishing.

"Corporal, take Jennings back to his cell and then ask Sergeant-Major Bonner to come and see me."

"Jennings is due for exercise within the hour, sir – shall I take him there first?" barked the corporal.

"Not back to solitary, you stupid oaf!" snapped Parker. "Back to his cell. Do you understand?"

"Yes, sir."

"Then move your arse, and get Sergeant-Major Bonner down here at the double."

Jennings was double-marched back to his cell, tossed in and left.

Cross returned to the cell at about six in the evening. He had been working in the library, a job he had been allotted when he first arrived at Colchester. This was much to the aggravation of many inmates as this was seen as the ultimate in cushy jobs and one which shouldn't go to a new boy. This had actually made Cross nearly as unpopular as Jennings.

Jennings looked up at Cross and said, "I believe I owe you thanks and an apology." Jennings detested having to do this. Both he and his father were arrogant, and to admit a lack of judgement was a major assault on their ego.

"What for?" asked Cross casually.

"The thanks for helping me with those apes and for telling Parker the truth. The apology for acting like a shit since you arrived."

"Three to one weren't too good a set of odds, although you were standing up quite well, and telling the truth isn't exactly medal-winning heroics, is it?" Cross replied, smiling.

"All right, let's start again. My name is Allan Jennings. I've been here a year and a half," Jennings said. "I pleaded guilty to LMF, even though it wasn't true, but if I hadn't I could have been in even deeper shit."

"I know what you are supposed to have done, but what I don't know is what actually happened. You are reputed to have arranged to have your patrol ambushed and made a nice lump of cash out of it. Is that true?"

Jennings looked into Cross's eyes and could see no malice or deviousness there. For eighteen months he had had no one to confide in, no friendly ear in which to pour his anger and frustration. He decided, although he knew little of this man, there was so much built up inside him that it had to be released, and Cross was there. He started at the beginning with the ambush and told the whole story as he knew it up to his father's death. He knew Cross could only listen, but just to tell the saga aloud punctured the ball of tension he had carried in his guts since his father's death.

Cross waited for him to finish. He sat for a while, mulling over Jennings's story.

"Look, there's one thing I don't understand. Why should someone go to so much trouble to set up a sergeant in the SAS? Could it have something to do with your father?"

"I don't fucking know, but, by Christ, I will find out or die in the bloody process."

They sat, Jennings brooding on the tale he had just related and Cross pondering the facts.

"What about the money?" said Cross. "Where did it come from?"

"All I know is that it was from a numbered account in Basle and it was put into my account at Coutts after the ambush. I don't know where it came from."

"How much was it?" Cross enquired. "You didn't say."

"£20,000, that's all."

"Bloody hell, that's enough! It would see me through a few good times," Cross retorted.

"My family is one of the richest in the south of England. Money is of no great relevance to us. I came into a trust fund worth a quarter of a million pounds when I was twenty-one, and now my father is dead I'm probably worth several million, even after the leeches have sucked the death duties out of it." It was a simple statement of fact given without any hint of pretension.

"Lend us a few bob then, will you," Cross said with a broad smile on his face.

The comment broke the pall of gloom that had slowly descended on Jennings.

"I might be rich, but I'm *not* fucking stupid," Jennings laughed back to the man who was slowly becoming a friend.

The next few months were as though Jennings had found the Land of Oz. There was no trouble. Both guards and inmates, who in the past had seemed to be out for his blood, treated Jennings and his cellmate with unexpected deference. Jennings knew not why but enjoyed the sensation rather than looking for the reasons.

Jennings and Cross talked for hours about their futures, both their fears and desires. Cross had many ideas for the rest of his life, most of which revolved around how much money he could make. Jennings was impressed by the ideas, flair and unbounded enthusiasm which poured from Cross. He remembered his Uncle George, the city banker, saying, "If a man has a hundred ideas for making money, one of them might be good, but if he only has ten it's ten to one against a good one." Cross was most certainly in the hundred ideas bracket.

By the time their sentences were nearing completion they had decided that they would work together, using a combination of Cross's ideas and enthusiasm and Jennings's level-headedness plus, of course, Jennings's money.

Cross was released two days before Jennings. They arranged to meet at the house in Woldingham after Jennings's release.

Jennings was released on 26th June 1971.

Chapter Four

London,
25th June 1971

"Unfortunately he seems to have survived Colchester. It is vital that a lid is put on this once and for all. What is the situation as it stands today?" The speaker was dressed in a three-piece pinstriped suit which was obviously from an extremely expensive tailor.

"My agent is quite close, sir, and will make sure that we are fully apprised of any developments. If there are any adverse developments, remedial action will be taken."

"Good. I want you to make sure the matter is either dead or that he is led along a trail going nowhere. I want this whole thing closed."

"It will be, sir, one way or another."

Colchester,
26th June 1971

The air tasted clean and fresh. Jennings had not tasted the air of freedom for two years and gulped huge draughts of it into his lungs. He wanted to dance in the street, but the English don't do that type of thing.

He looked across the street and saw Stuart Rittle semi-perched on the wing of his Solent blue BMW. Jennings suppressed a smile when he realised that Rittle looked as though, with small encouragement, he would hop across the road to meet him. Jennings remembered *The Wind in the Willows* and wondered whether Kenneth Grahame had modelled Mr Toad on one of Rittle's ancestors. Both Mr Toad and Rittle could be described as slightly camp.

Jennings crossed the road, enjoying the simple pleasure of walking and not being pursued by someone screaming, "At the double!"

The two men shook hands warmly.

"I thought I would come and meet you, Allan. I've made some arrangements for you. The house is opened and has been scrubbed from top to bottom. There is a very pleasant lady ensconced there whom I've employed as a housekeeper for you. If you don't like her, she is only on a month's trial."

"For Christ's sake, Stuart, I've had two years of being organised, and the last thing I want today is for you to carry on where those bastards in there left off," Jennings snapped somewhat unfairly and then immediately felt sorry for the outburst.

"All right, sorry, let's be on our way."

The BMW's 3.5 litre engine purred just loud enough to be heard as Rittle pushed it round the M25.

"Straight home then, Allan?" Rittle asked.

"Sod off, Stuart, The Haycutter first, home second."

"okay, but I'll have to leave you at the pub as I must be at a conference in the Temple this afternoon. You can get a taxi home, I presume."

"If you give me some money, I can."

"Of course," muttered Rittle. "Stupid of me. You don't get paid in there, do you?" He took his wallet from his jacket pocket and tossed it in Jennings's lap. "There's a couple of hundred pounds in there I got out for you. Oh, and this as well..." He passed across a cheque book. "Current account in your name. I will have to ring you to sort out all the other paperwork."

"What paperwork?"

"While you have been in detention, I have been acting as your trustee, in accordance with the requirements of your father's will. I will have to rescind all my signing rights and give up a couple of directorships and transfer them to you. I will ring you to fix up a convenient time."

"I know all this crap has to be done, but give me a few days, please, just so I can get my bearings," Jennings sighed wearily. All he wanted was to drink a few beers and then sleep in a comfortable bed.

The BMW eased smoothly off the M25 and on to the A25. Rittle turned off at Tandridge and took the back roads to Broadham Green. The Haycutter sat invitingly at the far end of the green.

"I'll ring you in a couple of days," Rittle shouted as the BMW eased away.

Jennings pushed open the door of the pub and was immediately greeted by the landlord. He sat on one of the bar stools and ordered a pint of Friary bitter. His first gulp demolished half of the contents of the glass.

"Long time no see," said the landlord.

"I've been away for some while," Jennings said quite truthfully.

Just then the door opened behind Jennings and he heard a familiar voice say, "Allan, it's good to see you."

Rittle had telephoned Hacker the evening before to tell him of Jennings's imminent release. Hacker had telephoned the station and told them he was ill, knowing that Jennings would probably appreciate some company.

Jennings turned and shook Tony Hacker's hand warmly. He ordered another couple of pints. Hacker sat on the stool next to Jennings, raised his glass and said, "Here's to the future. Let's hope it is long and happy."

"I'll drink to that."

They sat there for over an hour just reminiscing on the old days and the good times they had had together. The topics flitted from school to the football and cricket clubs, and of course their various conquests. The only one not mentioned was Jennings's conquest of Penny, who was now Hacker's wife and mother of his two children. Hacker had asked her to help welcome Jennings back to the real world, but she had a prior engagement which could not be cancelled.

Eventually the subject that both had been so energetically avoiding had to come up.

"You attended after my father's accident, didn't you," Jennings stated rather than asked.

"That's right."

"Well, what actually happened then?" Jennings felt huge guilt about his father's death. He knew that in some way it was connected with his own problems, but he did not know why or how.

"It appeared that your father was parked in the pull-off just before the motorway bridge. Someone – we don't know who – stole one of the dumpers from the lime works and must have lost control coming down the hill. The dumper went into the back of the Jag and pushed it into the bridge. Whoever it was must have been doing some speed because the Jag was smashed to pieces. That's basically all I know."

"But what the hell was the old man doing there? There's no reason for him to be parked up there," Jennings snapped.

"God only knows," Hacker replied gently. "All police inquiries after the accident were taken out of my hands. The final report simply recorded it as a hit-and-run accident and the inquest returned an open verdict. The dumper driver was never found."

"Do you think it is as simple as that?" Jennings retorted.

"Well, there are a few matters that don't actually fit too well into the logic. Firstly I've never come across a joyrider in a lime works dumper truck and I've never known of a case where a dumper truck has been nicked to sell on." Hacker's remarks were offered in a matter-of-fact way. "Also the chalk pits are a bit off the beaten track for a passing opportunist, and I can't imagine why anyone would plan to break into the yard and steal only a dumper truck."

"What if the reason for the theft was exactly what happened – the truck was nicked for the sole purpose of smashing up my father's car with him in it?" Jennings felt a flood of relief that, at last, he had unbottled his suspicions.

"As a thesis that would answer a lot of the questions, but why would someone want to kill your father? Would he have been a target of some foreign government?"

Jennings thought that perhaps he had already gone too far, considering Hacker was a policeman, but his growing anger overcame his reticence. "No! But maybe for some bastards in this country. He had been making a lot of noise in the wrong places about my problems. There seems to be some connection between all the events from the ambush onwards."

"Ambush?" queried Hacker.

"I'll tell you what, Tony, let's order some lunch and I'll tell you a story."

Both ordered the liver and bacon option which came with onions and a mammoth portion of thick chunky chips. Jennings remembered the so-called food he had been getting for the last two years and began to devour the pub lunch as though it were his first meal for weeks. In between mouthfuls of liver soaked in rich onion gravy he started to relate events from the ambush to his father's death.

Hacker interjected occasionally when he wanted something clarified. "Who was your father making the wrong noises to?"

"So every time there was trouble in prison you took the rap whether it was your fault or not.

"The change in attitude – was it connected with Cross or was it just a coincidence that it happened at the same time he arrived?"

Jennings answered the questions as far as he could. He finished his story, and Hacker was silent for a while.

Finally he looked Jennings in the eye and said very quietly, "Either there are an awful lot of coincidences or for some reason you have upset someone with a lot of power who wants you silent. If I were you, I would put the whole bloody thing in the past and get on with the rest of your life."

"That's all very well but it's not your old man in the bloody cemetery," Jennings retorted, his anger now clearly showing.

"I was telling you what a sensible man would do, but I know you're a pig-headed dickhead. Is there any way I can help?" Hacker picked up the empty glasses and took them to the bar to give Jennings time to decide on an answer. He ordered two more pints, which arrived with the froth running down the side of the glasses. He carried them back to the table, placing one in front of Jennings.

Jennings studied the contents of his glass. He watched the head of the beer slowly disappear and took a draught from the glass.

"Can I trust you, Tony?"

"We were like bloody brothers when we were young, you arsehole. If you don't trust me, don't trust any bastard," Hacker snapped the answer. He clenched his fist under the table, trying to suppress his anger until his fingernails cut into his palms.

"I'm sorry, Tony. I don't know who or what to believe. I've been in the nick for two years for doing my job, my father's dead and I don't know who is on my side and who is against me." The anguish Jennings was suffering proclaimed itself through his eyes.

"You can take it I'm on your side. Just think on a few things. One, I don't think you were supposed to survive the ambush."

"That's exactly what Stuart Rittle said," interjected Jennings.

"Don't interrupt me when I'm thinking. Two, someone did not want your old man sticking his nose in too deep. Three, be careful of this bloke Cross."

"Oh no, he's straight," Jennings interrupted.

"He is too much of a coincidence, and as a copper I don't like coincidences," Hacker retorted calmly. "Four, and most important, do you really want to chase this or do you want to start the rest of your life? You're rich and you can do whatever you want."

Jennings sat for a moment, his brow furrowed. "You're bloody right. I *am* rich and I can do what I want and I can afford to do it. What I want to do is find who knocked off my old man and return the compliment."

"As a police officer I did not hear that; as a friend I agree with you." Hacker held up his hand to stop any response from Jennings. "If I were you, I would start at the beginning and work forward. Find this guy Lee Kim, find out his part and who he got his orders from. Find the next guy and do the same. Keep going down the line and eventually you'll find an answer which you probably won't like. Once you've got an answer, don't do anything without thinking seriously about the consequences." Hacker's voice carried both the authority of his occupation and the understanding of a friend.

"How the fuck do I go about finding the bastard - advertise in *The Times*?"

"You employ someone to do it for you," Hacker retorted, now realising that perhaps the Friary was beginning to work after two years of abstinence. "Look, I'll phone for a taxi and take you home. Get a good night's sleep and I'll phone you tomorrow." He walked across the bar to the phone and dialled Jack Martin's number.

When Jack Martin's taxi arrived, Jennings lumbered rather than walked to the car, with Hacker supporting him when needed.

"Don't go up Chalkpit Lane," was Jennings's last comment before he lapsed into sleep.

Chapter Five

The dream returned. The dream which had tortured him in Colchester. He could hear the incessant crack of the machine-gun and the dull thud of high-velocity bullets gouging into flesh. He could see the fireflies of tracer rounds skimming through the night air. Then the silence, the terrifying tranquillity of the jungle totally devoid of any form of life. Then he was walking among the dead. The bodies of his friends had been tossed about by a typhoon carrying fire and lead. Then he realised that there were seven bodies not six. The seventh was scarred by fire, the clothes now only ashes burnt on to the skin. The only recognisable features of this lifeless mass were the brigadier's crown and three pips on each shoulder. This charred smouldering heap was all that remained of his father. He tried, desperately, to remove the insignias of rank from the shoulders, but they were red-hot. He heard himself shouting, "If they know who you are, they will kill you!"

Jennings started into wakefulness, beads of sweat running down his face on to the pillow. He looked around, but there were no bars, no solid metal door, no slop bucket and no guards. All he saw was the room in which he had grown from a small boy to his current adult torture.

He went to the window and drew back the curtain. It was a dark night with no moon. He could see the street lights in Oxted. Things which looked like great cat's eyes were chasing each other along the M25. He could hear no sound other than the wind rustling in the tree outside his window; the tree which had often been his escape route to a new adventure when he was a child.

He looked around the room, his eyes now accustomed to the gloom. Little had changed in twenty years. The bed, soft and enveloping, the school pictures, football, cricket and boxing, in all of which he had excelled, and the deep leather armchair where he had read and dreamed of the future. He thought, ruefully, that his present was not a dream but a nightmare. This room, *his* room, was a sanctuary from the world. A sanctuary from the ache that tore at his heart. It had always been thus and would always stay so.

He went back to his bed and the mattress, pillows and blankets cocooned him till he fell into a deep dreamless sleep.

Jennings awoke early in the morning. The sunlight poured through the window and his eyes blinked involuntarily at the brightness. He looked around the room as his focus slowly returned. For two years he had awoken to bare walls and bars, but now he was in a warm, comfortable room which was his home. The anguish which had accompanied consciousness for the last two years evaporated. He sat up and realised that his head was telling him yesterday had been too good a day. His mouth tasted of something foul that was deep in his memory. He felt true pleasure. It might be a hangover to others but it was freedom to choose for Jennings – a freedom he had not had for too long.

He wandered rather than walked into his bathroom. Shower or shave first? It was the sort of decision he had not made for two years.

Shower!

The needles of warm water stabbed at his torso as though massaging the blood around his entire body. He stood under the shower for an age, allowing the fresh water to wash away the stink of two years in the pit called Colchester Military Prison. He turned the shower to cold and immediately felt the glow of his metabolism fighting the assault on his basic structure. He switched off the shower and dried himself vigorously on the rough towel the brigadier had always insisted were good for a real man. He thought that the first change he made in the family home would be the towels.

He moved across to the basin. The mirror behind showed his body lean and hard. It also showed his eyes. It wasn't just the Friary which made his eyes look older than the body that contained them. They showed the grief he had suffered.

After shaving he donned slacks and a polo shirt. He realised then that he was both ravenous and had a thirst which could have been brought on by a week in the Sahara.

He strode across the upper landing, noticing that one of the guest rooms showed definite signs of occupancy. He went down the two flights of stairs, across the lobby and into the kitchen. The kitchen was warm and smelled of fresh cooking. His senses were assaulted by the smell of freshly baked bread. Across the room was a woman of comfortably generous build in deep concentration on the contents of the sink. She seemed to start and then turned to Jennings. A warm smile crossed her face and she rubbed her hands frenetically on her apron.

She was aged between forty-five and fifty, with a rosy face and laughter lines dancing each side of her eyes. Her hands showed all the signs of a hard life but still looked soft and caring. Her whole appearance was that of every child's memory of their mother. She finished her hand-rubbing, attempted a sort of curtsy and said awkwardly, "Mr Jennings, I am so glad to meet you. I am Ellen McDonald, your new housekeeper." The soft Edinburgh lilt made the words almost into a song.

"I'm delighted to meet you, Ellen, and I am sorry about being a little the worse for wear yesterday." Jennings felt uncomfortable not knowing whether she had seen him the previous afternoon.

"Och, don't you worry. After your troubles you deserve to let your hair down a bit, Mr Jennings."

"Thank you, Ellen, you're most understanding. By the way, if you are to be Ellen, my name is Allan."

"Oh no you don't, Mr Jennings." Her starched pinafore rustled in indignation. "I am your housekeeper Ellen – well, at least for a month – and you are the master of the house, Mr Jennings." She stressed *the master of the house* in such a way that Jennings immediately knew that, while he might pay the bills, Ellen would *run* the house. He found this notion strangely comforting.

"Would you like some breakfast, Mr Jennings? You must be fair starving without anything since yesterday lunchtime."

'Three square meals a day from now on,' thought Jennings to himself with satisfaction.

"I would love some please, Ellen. I could actually eat a horse."

"Well, I hope a good Scottish breakfast will do. You go and sit yourself down in the drawing room and read the paper, and I'll have your breakfast ready in a jiffy. The papers are already there – *The Daily Express* and the *Financial Times*." The 'sit yourself down' was not a suggestion but a pleasantly presented order. Jennings helped himself to a glass of orange juice, which he gulped down in one, and then obeyed his orders. At least now he did not have to obey at the double.

He threw the *Financial Times* on to the settee. 'Bloody Stuart Rittle trying to make me into a financier,' he thought. *The Daily Express* was started at the back for the sport.

"Would you like your breakfast in here, Mr Jennings?"

Jennings, who was deeply involved in the latest Surrey batting collapse, was a little perplexed at the interruption. "Sorry... eh, Ellen. I was miles away. Why don't we eat in the kitchen?" All his life the kitchen had been the place for breakfast.

On the kitchen table was a plate overflowing with eggs, bacon, sausage, grilled mushrooms and tomatoes, black pudding and, to Jennings's particular delight, sauté potatoes.

Jennings sat and devoured the mountain of food with undisguised relish. This was the sort of breakfast he could remember having as a boy.

He finished the meal, drained the coffee cup and refilled it again. He wanted to belch but thought better of it.

"Will you be wanting lunch today, Mr Jennings?"

The 'Mr Jennings' was beginning to grate a little but he said nothing because she was probably as nervous of him as he of her.

"No thanks, Ellen. I have a few things to sort out and will probably be out for lunch," Jennings lied, knowing only that he had to be outdoors after two years without the opportunity.

"Mr Rittle has hired a little car for you. It's in the garage. I believe that he has hired it for a month. In fact, he seems to have hired everything for a month." It was a statement rather than a comment.

"Ellen McDonald, if you still like me after a month, you stay here as long as you like, because after that breakfast I want you to stay for ever."

Ellen flushed and busied herself with clearing away the breakfast things.

Jennings went to the garage and pulled up the rolling door. Sitting there was a pale blue Ford Sierra. Jennings immediately thought of Stuart Rittle for the car was both sensible and bloody blue. He thought to himself, 'First job is order a new car.' He closed the garage door and wandered back through the kitchen to the drawing room, returning Ellen's smile as he passed. He picked up the paper and finished off the Surrey batting order, which took very little time. He threw the paper on the table and started to muse on his future. He was halfway between being a playboy and an international tycoon when the ring of the telephone interrupted his daydream.

"The Jennings residence," he heard Ellen say in her soft Edinburgh lilt. "Who is calling? Just one moment, I will see if he is here."

Her motherly features appeared around the door. "A Mr Cross is on the telephone. Do you want to speak to him?"

Jennings nodded and picked up the extension on the drawing-room table.

"Jim, how are you?"

"I'm fine and free. You told me to give you a ring when you were out, so I have." Cross's voice was bright and cheerful.

"Look, why don't you come down and stop for a few days and we can have a serious chat about what we want to do? There were a lot of ideas, but now we're not locked up we ought to do something about them. We can run through the various business interests I've got and make some definite plans."

They agreed that Cross would sort out one or two personal affairs and come to Woldingham in four days' time.

Jennings had hardly replaced the receiver when it rang again. He picked it up, gave his number and a familiar voice said, "How is the head this morning?"

"The head is fine and the inner man has just been feasted by Ellen. She's a real gem, Stuart."

"I thought you would be impressed," said Rittle. "However, you and I have got to get together and go through your business affairs and tidy up all the documentation. When would suit you?"

After making several efforts at a date and time, none of which fitted Rittle's diary, Jennings wondered who the time was supposed to suit. Eventually they agreed on one week's time. Jennings told Rittle about Cross and that he was to be involved.

"Bloody good thing that you and this chap will be taking up some interests. It'll stop you addling your brain in the pub every day. See you next week." With that the line clicked dead.

Jennings mooched about the house for another hour as if he were rediscovering all the nooks, crannies and secrets he had forgotten. Eventually he decided that he must do something. He went out to the garage, started the Sierra and drove. He went first towards Croydon, passing through Chelsham and Warlingham. At Sanderstead he turned towards Purley and followed the Brighton road. When he reached Redhill, he turned back towards home. Anyone who has never been incarcerated can never understand the unadulterated pleasure of just driving alone to wherever you want. He had driven all the roads many times before but today they seemed fresh and exciting.

He stopped the car in Bletchingly outside the Jaguar dealer. On a whim he went in and ordered a new XJ12, delivery in two months. When the salesman asked about colour, he was told, "Anything but bloody blue." For someone of his means the purchase was not a major item, but it gave him an absurd pleasure to indulge himself.

The next two days were spent pottering about both at home and around the surrounding countryside. Both evenings were spent checking the continuing quality of the Friary in The Haycutter. This particular pastime was excellent for the ongoing success of Jack Martin's taxi business. The only place in the area he did not go was Chalkpit Hill.

On the second evening Tony Hacker came in. He ordered two pints and sat down next to Jennings.

"How do you fancy a game of golf tomorrow? After two years without playing I might stand a chance of taking money off you."

"That sounds a fantastic idea. I can still beat you by talking you out of it," Jennings laughed. They arranged to meet at the golf club at nine in the morning.

The next morning Jennings arrived at Tandridge Golf Club sharp at eight-thirty. The clubhouse was almost as familiar as his own home.

As a boy he had cycled to the club every Saturday, Sunday and school holidays to earn his pocket money by caddying for the members and their guests. Whilst his father was a rich man he had believed firmly that every boy should earn his own way. The caddies had their own shack and had hacked out their own two-hole course on the rough ground behind it. The caddies were supposed to be at least twelve years old, but Alec the professional was not the best judge of age. If a lad was very small, Alec would insist that the member hired out a trolley for the boy to pull rather than carry the bag. For a fee of five shillings a round, or twelve shillings and sixpence a day, the boys would lug huge golf bags around the six and a half thousand yards of the course. If the golfer had a good round, the tip could be quite useful, but if the round was bad you might get a sixpence tip.

One of Jennings's happier memories was caddying for the captain of Walton Heath in a match against Tandridge. When asked about club selection, he had guessed correctly and his golfer had won six and five in the morning and five and four in the afternoon. The man was so pleased that not only had he given Jennings five pounds but he had also passed him a pint of shandy out of the changing room window.

Jennings went into the bar to have a cup of coffee. Rasher, the steward and another former caddy, was behind the bar preparing for the needs of the thirsty golfers who would descend on the place in about three hours' time.

"Morning, Rasher," Jennings said breezily.

Rasher turned from his chores and a huge smile spread across his craggy red face.

"Allan!" he exclaimed with evident pleasure. "Where have you been? I haven't seen you for years."

"Long story, Rasher. I'll tell you some time."

Just then Hacker came in. He greeted Jennings and Rasher in turn and equally, as all three were from the caddy school and could never act the roles of member and steward. They had coffee and went through to the changing rooms to change their shoes and argue over how many shots one or other should have.

The round of golf was sheer ecstasy for Jennings after two years of confinement.

He stood on the tee of the fourteenth hole, where the drive was down into a heavily wooded valley with the second shot uphill to a raised green surrounded on three sides by beautiful trees, and wished that he could stay there for ever. The rays of sun peeped through the trees and danced joyfully across his shoulders. The freedom and space were like a drug to Jennings. The clean fresh air caressed his lungs and his eyes were assaulted by the beauty which nature and man had combined to create. His golf was also serene, much to the displeasure of Hacker.

"How the hell can you not play for over two years and still thrash me five and four?"

They sat at the bar, with a pint in hand, replaying the morning round, as every golfer does, each remembering their good shots and forgetting those of their opponent. Rasher was behind the bar throwing in the occasional barbed comment designed to wind up one or other of the protagonists. The banter ran on through the roast beef sandwiches, which were rare with enough horseradish to complement the meat to perfection. The teasing was also accompanied by several more pints, which would be more good news for Jack Martin's profits.

Eventually Hacker said, "I want to be serious for a minute. About your problem. I think I may have a name that will help you. There's this bloke I have known for years. We were in the force together and he went out to join the police in Hong Kong. He now runs his own agency and has got connections all over the Far East. If anyone can find your Mr Lee Kim, then he can. This is his address."

Jennings took the proffered piece of paper and opened it. "Richard Sutcliffe, PO Box 1106, Hong Kong," he read aloud. "Thank you, Tony. Can I use your name with him?"

"Of course you bloody well can. That's why I have suggested him."

The conversation switched back to golf.

Chapter Six

Cross arrived in Jack Martin's taxi the next morning.

Jennings was having coffee in the drawing room, giving Ellen's huge breakfast a little time to digest while reading about the continuing traumas of Surrey County Cricket Club. When they weren't in a batting collapse, their bowlers were being dispatched to various parts of the Oval. He heard the taxi on the gravel drive and walked across to the window. Cross emerged from the passenger seat of the taxi and pulled a small valise from the back seat. He paid Jack, obviously giving him a good tip as Jack grabbed the valise and escorted him to the door and rang the bell.

"I'll get it, Ellen," Jennings shouted as he went into the hall. He opened the door to the only friendly face he had seen in his two years in Colchester.

"Jim, it's so good to see you again," Jennings exclaimed with genuine affection.

The two men embraced as brothers. Behind them Jack shuffled uncomfortably with the valise. This sort of display was, to him, a little bit unmanly. Jennings looked and realised that Jack was beginning to become a little embarrassed. He took the case from Jack and said, "Jack, this is Jim Cross. He and I have been through some very nasty times together."

Jack muttered a greeting and made for the safety of his taxi. The taxi spat gravel from the back wheels as Jack sped from the drive back to the commuters who showed no feelings but still tipped well. The two men roared with laughter at his hasty exit.

Inside, with coffee in their hands, they exchanged stories of their deeds since leaving Her Majesty's service. Whilst it was only a few days, their freedom was so precious that every detail had to be told and heard. After a while both realised that they were giving totally unimportant information in huge amounts of inconsequential detail.

"What the hell are we blathering on about?" Jennings laughed. "Do you really want to know whether the stone in the bunker was to the left or the right of the ball?"

"Well, you must have been incredibly interested in how many different types of cheap fares there are on British Rail," Cross retorted and both men roared with laughter.

Only someone who has been imprisoned could understand the need to detail every moment of freedom to another who would appreciate that need. They sat quietly for a moment, simply enjoying the other's company, knowing that they were no longer forced to stay in the same room as the other.

"To be serious for a moment." Jennings finally broke the silence both men were enjoying. "Stuart Rittle is coming down on Tuesday to go through all my affairs and interests with me, and you of course, partner. In the meantime I think that we should enjoy ourselves. Just for this weekend I intend to revert to the age of nineteen."

"Well damn it, I'll be nineteen and a half," said Cross, slapping his thigh in delight. "You need an older person to keep you out of trouble."

They went racing at Lingfield, where Cross won and Jennings lost. They went to the Orchid Ballroom in Purley and tried to pull some 'birds'. Jennings pulled and wished he hadn't; Cross didn't and wished he had! They also spent much time and money in The Haycutter and on Jack Martin's taxi.

Ellen McDonald fed the inner men with huge breakfasts, dinners and midnight suppers. She seemed to understand their need to re-enact their youth and savour the simple pleasures of a teenager. They would return after closing time and emerge from Jack's taxi singing rugby songs. The cocktail cabinet would be raided and Ellen would get out the frying pan and produce supper.

On Monday night they met Hacker for a few drinks in The Haycutter. Hacker's eyes flashed briefly with a hint of recognition when introduced to Cross. The three men yarned for several hours about their days past. The subjects ranged from school to the army and police. Cross had been to school at Whitgift in Croydon, and the two ex-John Fisher schoolboys deduced that they had probably met Cross as all had played football and cricket for their schools against each other. Hacker seemed to be greatly interested in Cross's background.

At one time Cross said jokingly, "I can tell you're a bloody copper. You never stop asking sodding questions."

Hacker rode the remark with a comment about the job doing it to everyone.

"I know him from somewhere," Hacker said to Jennings, while Cross was in the toilet returning the residue of the Friary. "I can't tell you where from but be careful."

"Bullshit! The guy's straight," Jennings snapped. "I spent six months in the same bloody cell as him and I know the bastard a damn sight better than you."

"Just be careful – please, Allan."

Cross returned and the conversation went back to sex, alcohol and the repercussions of both, in particular the detrimental effect of the latter on the former.

The next morning Rittle's BMW skimmed into the drive, showering the flowerbeds each side with gravel. He bustled through the door and straight into the study, where he assumed a position in the brigadier's old chair. He placed his camel-skin briefcase on the leather-topped desk and started removing papers from it. Jennings and Cross followed like dutiful schoolboys being ushered into the headmaster's study for a caning.

"Sit down and let's get on, my time is your money," Rittle muttered amiably. He looked up from the papers and realised that Jennings was not alone. He stood and offered his hand to Cross while introducing himself. The introductory process completed, he sat down and assumed a legal persona.

"There are a number of things to go through, Allan, but firstly I have to ask what the exact position is between you and Mr Cross. There are obviously some matters to be discussed which must be confidential between you and I as your father's legal representative, and others which are a matter of general business."

"Look, you pompous old sod," Jennings said with genuine affection, "Jim here and I are going to be working together to develop and expand some or all of the current interests and develop new ones where we think it will be profitable to do so."

"Good. I understand you two will be ongoing business partners. In that case I think that we should go through your holdings first." Rittle pulled a file from the pile of papers and passed each of them a copy of a document.

"This is a list of all the current shareholdings you have. There were more but some, unfortunately, had to be sold to meet the insatiable appetite of the revenue for capital transfer tax. The list is divided into quoted companies and private companies. If you wish to expand your interests, I presume that the private stakes will be of more value to your plans than the quoted companies." He pulled another bundle of documents from the heap and passed it to Jennings.

"I am afraid that I only have one spare copy of this," he mumbled. "It is a financial analysis of each of the investments. It has been prepared by Woolen & Reiss, who were your father's stockbrokers. I presume they will continue to be yours, but that is your decision. It shows the fields in which the companies operate, their current market value – in the case of the private companies it is obviously an estimated figure – and the immediate and long-term projections on their future development."

He then ran through the list of some sixty companies, giving a brief resumé of each. The outline he gave was very brief for the quoted companies and more detailed for the private companies. Both Jennings and Cross interjected with questions as the summary continued. Where possible Rittle answered their questions and where not he made a note to find out and advise them later.

There were seven private companies where Jennings had an interest of over twenty-five per cent with a huge variance in trades: a company manufacturing specialised electronics for the computer industry; two import companies; two car dealerships (one being the Jaguar dealership he had ordered his car from); a small department store; and an insurance broker in the City of London.

The synopsis of the holdings completed, Rittle opened another file and passed a document to Jennings. The paper was headed DIRECTORSHIPS. It appeared that Jennings or his nominee were entitled to be a director of all seven companies, and in the case of one of the import companies and the insurance broker either chairman or deputy chairman.

"The old man never had time to be a director of this lot and run half the bloody army at the same time. How did he manage it?"

Rittle handed him another sheaf of paper, the title of which read NOMINEES AS DIRECTORS. Each company was listed, and against them the name of the director nominated by his father. Only two names appeared. Stuart Rittle and Gene Reiss had been two of his father's oldest and obviously his most trusted friends, as they were the only two names appearing. Reiss had four directorships and Rittle the balance. Rittle, of course, had both the deputy chairman's positions, which was no surprise to Jennings.

"I suggest that you study the summaries of each company and decide on whether you wish to take up the directorships. Gene and I will continue as directors until such time as you have made a decision, provided that is okay with you, Allan."

Rittle then politely asked Cross to leave as the matters following were confidential.

Cross left and Rittle produced various bank statements and mandates to be signed. In all, there were liquid funds in excess of £400,000 in current and short-term deposits. The main bank was NatWest in Oxted, where there was a current and linked deposit account.

"I would suggest that you appoint an accountant as a matter of urgency." Rittle passed Jennings a card, saying, "This is the partnership your father dealt with, and I think you will find them totally satisfactory."

When all was added up, Jennings had total assets of over £3,500,000, plus the house, which added another £250,000.

Finally, Rittle went to the cabinet in the study and explained how all the documents were filed, and, putting on his best court voice, he told Jennings of the dire consequences of failing to keep proper books and records.

"Well, that's that. I presume you now want to buy me lunch." Rittle's tone changed from barrister to friend. "How does The Barley Mow sound?"

All three men jumped into Rittle's BMW and sped off in the direction of home-made steak and kidney pie.

Chapter Seven

Over the next few days Jennings and Cross went through Jennings's various holdings. Cross was particularly interested in the import–export side and the possible interconnection with the department store. Jennings, on the other hand, felt an affinity with the insurance broker. They decided that they would each spend some time with each of the major holdings and then discuss the possibilities each found. Cross would look at the two import companies – the car dealerships and the department store – and Jennings the electronics company and the insurance broker. They made appointments to see each of the companies over a two-week period and then went their own way.

Jennings first went to the electronics company, thinking that being on the edge of technology development must be highly interesting. He soon learnt lesson number one – that any subject, no matter how interesting, could be incredibly depressing when explained in the minutest detail by a boffin. The managing director of the company was a hands-on engineer with a passion for bits, bytes and microchips. He had the fervent passion of an evangelist trying to convert the universe to micro-electronics.

Jennings was sitting listlessly while his assailant droned on remorselessly about possibilities for the future. He pulled a cigarette packet from his pocket and a piece of paper fell to the floor. He picked it up and read the name of Richard Sutcliffe. He had forgotten that Hacker had given this to him. Closing his intellect to the offensive being launched by the engineer, he began, in his mind, to draft a letter to this man about Lee Kim.

That evening he wrote to Sutcliffe and enclosed a cheque for £500 as a retainer.

The following day Jennings went to his meeting with the chairman of the insurance brokers. He arrived at the offices of Corby, Lannin & Davies in Mark Lane just before noon. He was greeted by a receptionist with long legs and a short skirt. She showed him to the boardroom and offered coffee, which he declined.

He lit a cigarette and looked around the room. The centrepiece was a solid mahogany table about twelve feet in length. The table was surrounded by chairs of the same wood with ruby red upholstery. There were three large old prints on the walls depicting golfers of the last century, the largest being *The Society of Goffers at Blackheath* by Lemuel Francis Abbott. On the far wall stood a huge cocktail cabinet containing a plentiful selection of the alcohols of the world.

The door opened and a man, at least three inches taller than Jennings and slightly rotund, entered. He had silver-grey hair which clashed with his dark brown eyebrows. He offered his hand, saying, "Charlie Corby."

Jennings took his hand and introduced himself.

"Ex-army, aren't you?"

Jennings nodded in confirmation.

"What do you say that we go and have a beer before lunch?"

Without waiting for a reply Corby opened the door and made for the exit. Jennings thought that this was an odd way to impress a shareholder but followed him obediently. Corby turned into Hart Street and immediately into The Ship Inn.

"Theakstons." The word was delivered more as an order than an enquiry.

Again Jennings nodded and noticed that Corby's pint was being pulled even before he ordered it. They collected their drinks and sat on two high stools in the corner of the bar.

"I knew your father from my schooldays. We used to play cricket together when we were kids. He was one of the nicest men you could ever hope to meet and a good friend to me." Corby took a long pull at the beer and smacked his lips.

"When the others and I wanted to start this company in 1958, your old man helped to bankroll us. He knew sod all about the business but said that if I thought it was a good investment that was good enough for him. Fortunately we've made a few bob over the last ten years." He drained the glass, smacked his lips again and waved at the barman for two more pints.

Jennings thought that he could put beer away, but this man was a plus six handicap at it.

"What can I do for you, anyway?" Corby enquired.

"It's quite simple. I've got to do something with the rest of my life and would like to know what you do and how you do it and whether it would suit me. I'm looking at all the businesses I have investments in."

"Lucky young sod you are. One thing I can tell you is that this business is the best if you're good enough. Plenty of travel if you want it, and the potential to make a lot of money if you want to. It's the type of business where you work hard and play hard."

Both men finished their drinks and made off in the direction of lunch. They walked down Lime Street, past Lloyds of London, and downstairs to the Marine Club. It appeared that Corby was known to all the other patrons of the club. Drinks were ordered and menus left to be studied. Jennings ordered the ogen melon followed by fillet steak.

Corby toyed with the wine list for a short time and said, "I don't drink this stuff, but do you want some?"

Jennings declined, saying that he preferred beer, which seemed to please Corby enormously.

Over lunch Corby gave Jennings a brief run-down of the business of Corby, Lannin & Davies. Whilst the company was called an insurance broker, in fact they dealt only in reinsurance.

"It's basically insurance of insurance companies. Any company can only take a certain amount of risk. Over and above that they go out to someone else and reinsure the rest of it. It's a bit like a bookie laying off bets." Corby's explanation of the intricacies of reinsurance was somewhat basic but eminently understandable. "Why don't you come up here for a couple of weeks and get an idea of what we do? I can arrange for you to spend some time in Lloyds and with a couple of companies. That way you can get a feel of the business. I presume that you will take over as deputy chairman instead of that old fart Rittle, so even if you decide on something else it will help you understand what we are blathering about at board meetings."

Jennings was beginning to take a serious liking to Corby and readily agreed. They finished lunch and walked back to the office. Corby went to the bookcase and pulled out a book, which he passed to Jennings.

"That's Golding on reinsurance. It was written about forty years ago but is still the best introduction to the business. Have a read of it and I'll contact you once I've got an itinerary organised for you."

Jennings took the book, shook Corby by the hand and left.

A week later Jennings started on his introduction to the reinsurance industry. Studying Golding had been an immense help as he knew most of the basics now. He spent time with the brokers placing the business and the underwriters accepting the business. It soon became clear to him that a great deal of business revolved around personal relationships. He also learnt that the marketplace was constantly alive with rumours and stories. These were usually transmitted in various hostelries. He also learned that work and play had a great tendency to overlap. A large degree of business was transacted over lunch or dinner or in a nightclub following dinner. He learnt that there was an art to serious entertaining. The broker, in particular, had to ensure that the venue for entertainment suited the client or the underwriter rather than himself.

The people at Corby, Lannin & Davies made sure that Jennings was introduced to both their clients and the underwriters. The venue for the entertainment varied, with certain places recurring more often than others. The Bunch of Grapes in Lime Street was one of the most popular haunts with non-marine underwriters. If you wanted to know the latest market gossip, this was the place to go. The Chez When Club was a favourite venue for lunch. Jennings became partially addicted to their devilled crab. The Marine Club was another regular haunt. If a client was being looked after in the evening, dinner would normally be up west, followed by a nightclub. Miranda's seemed to be the reinsurers' place for leering drunkenly at young females removing their clothes.

After two weeks of working quite hard and playing very hard Jennings was becoming convinced that this was the business for him.

"Take a couple of weeks to think about it and let me know if you want to join us on a permanent basis." Corby had realised that Jennings was both very bright and had the personality to become a real asset to the company.

Jennings had virtually decided when he received a letter from Hong Kong.

Chapter Eight

Dear Mr Jennings,
                Subject: Lee Kim

I thank you for your letter regarding the above and set out below the information I have obtained to date.

Lee Kim was an area commander in the so-called People's Freedom Party. When the armistice was reached about two years ago, certain of the senior people in the PFP were to be given government jobs within the new Government of National Unity. This Government of National Unity came about as part of the cessation of military activity negotiated between the British Government and the PFP. The interim government was to be in power for two years, at which time elections were to be held and full independence granted by the British Government.

Lee Kim was given a position within the Ministry of Defence. He was responsible for the procurement of all military equipment. Lee Kim not only procured defence equipment but also a very substantial bank balance for himself, courtesy of certain major arms dealers. This came to light approximately one year ago. The local government did not want this scandal to become public knowledge, particularly as Lee Kim was a so-called hero of the PFP.

The result was that Lee Kim left the country about a year ago under orders not to return. He initially went to Singapore, where he renewed an existing connection he had with the Dragon Triad. This is a particularly nasty group who are effectively the mafia of the Chinese. The Dragon Triad has tentacles over all of

Asia and in many of the Chinese communities throughout the world.

Lee Kim threw himself enthusiastically into his new life and became particularly adept in matters of protection, prostitution and drugs. He climbed the ladder in the Dragon hierarchy very quickly. At the same time he became somewhat richer. He is known to have substantial funds located in Switzerland, Liechtenstein and Bermuda.

Three months ago the Singapore police were making Lee Kim's seat somewhat warm. It appears that they had an informer planted within Lee Kim's operation and were slowly developing a case for putting the man away for many years. Unfortunately Lee Kim also had his own informers and was warned of the possibility of prosecution. He absconded from Singapore two months ago.

He has now surfaced in Hong Kong and appears to be the number one Dragon Triad man on the Island of Kowloon. In his position he is, obviously, heavily protected, and it would be difficult to get to him. His headquarters are in a club named The Sunrise on Kowloon.

Should you wish to take this matter any further please advise me.

Yours sincerely,
Richard Sutcliffe

Jennings read and reread the letter, his forgotten anger now boiling inside him.

Just then Cross came in, waving some papers.

"I think I've got just the deal for the importers and the store. This small manufacturer—"

"Read this." Jennings cut him short and passed him Sutcliffe's letter.

Cross read the letter and rubbed his chin thoughtfully.

"Allan, why don't you just forget all this and get on with the rest of your life? If you keep chasing this, it'll eat you away to nothing."

"It wasn't your old man that got murdered. I have to try to find out what happened."

"Okay, okay," Cross said wearily. "If you have to do this, I'll come with you. We can kill two birds with one stone. This paper's all about a company in Hong Kong with just the right products to run in the store. Apart from that, I can keep you from getting your head blown off."

That afternoon Jennings telephoned Sutcliffe and arranged to meet him.

In The Haycutter that evening they both took stick from Hacker, who showed uncommon envy of their trip to Hong Kong. He knew that Jennings was not on a pleasure trip, but could not resist the opportunity of the friendly banter.

Before he left the pub Hacker leaned across to Jennings and whispered, "Be careful with Cross."

*

Three days later the two friends boarded a British Airways 747 for Hong Kong.

Landing at Hong Kong airport is not an experience for the faint-hearted. The aircraft swoops down between skyscrapers which tower on each side of the runway. It seems as if the wing-tips are almost touching the windows of the buildings. Cross decided that it was better to study the stewardesses' legs than look out of the window.

The immigration hall was unbelievably humid, despite the air-conditioning. The two men progressed through and collected their bags. The courtesy Mercedes from the Mandarin Hotel was waiting for them with the large boot open for their luggage. They checked into the hotel and were shown to their rooms on the fifth floor. Jennings had no sooner dropped his case on the bed than there was a knock at the door. The valet bought in a pot of steaming China tea and placed it on the table. He then proceeded to unpack the baggage and hang Jennings's clothes in the spacious fitted wardrobe. The Mandarin had the reputation of being one of the finest hotels in the world and was most certainly living up to it.

Jennings and Cross arranged to meet in the bar in the lobby. The bar was cool, set out with plush low seats and matching low tables. For the more traditional drinker there were tall stools at the bar.

There were about a dozen people in the bar; most of them appeared to be tired businessmen.

Jennings and Cross made their plans for the next day over very cold beers. Both men were suffering the wearing effect of the journey and the eight-hour time difference. They finished their drinks, crossed the lobby, and went up the palatial staircase to the Clipper Lounge. Neither wanted a full meal, so they ordered the Clipper Club sandwiches. The young Chinese waiter repeated their order, "Two Crippa Crubs."

Jennings studied the ceiling and Cross the floor, and neither dared look at the other for fear of collapsing into uncontrolled giggling.

At breakfast next morning Cross was talking animatedly about the possibilities of the deal he could make with the manufacturer he was seeing that morning. Jennings merely nodded absent-mindedly, hoping the signs of assent were in the right places. The previous night his dream had recurred.

Cross left for his appointment, promising to be back before three that afternoon, when Jennings was to see Sutcliffe. Jennings went out of the back entrance of the hotel. He could see the HongKong Shanghai Bank building dwarfing those around it. The streets were thronging with people all bustling about their business. He had never seen any other city that was so vibrant and alive. He noticed the shops and thought that this was not the place to bring a lady. Any woman worth her salt would think that she had died and gone to heaven. Every other shop was a jewellers.

He wandered the streets drinking in the atmosphere and the pure energy of the place. He watched the charades played out in the shops. The Chinese would never buy anything without some process of bargaining. The customer would sit on a stool one side of the counter while the salesman bestooled on the other. Glasses of Coca-Cola would be supplied and the bartering would begin. Both knew at the outset what the eventual agreed price would be, but the charade was necessary for both parties to retain face. It was a centuries-old tradition of the Chinese that neither party should lose face in a negotiation. The product was prodded and every minute defect was pointed out in great detail. The salesman would then show off the assets in even greater detail. All the time the offers and counter offers were moving towards the point at which they knew there would be agreement. When agreement was finally reached, there would be an excessive show of the warm feelings each party felt for the other.

Several hours flew by without Jennings realising it. He remembered the time he had spent as a boy in the colony and the affinity he had developed for the way of life here.

Hunger finally reminded him of the passing of time. He spied a dim sum restaurant, where people were bustling in and out. He found a seat and waited for the waiter to come with the trays of steamed dumplings. He overindulged but ate with immense relish, washing the food down with several bottles of Chinese beer. He listened to the conversations around him, particularly the one about the European eating on his own. The speaker looked very sheepish when Jennings wished him farewell in Cantonese.

The Rolex on his wrist told Jennings that it was time to go and meet with Sutcliffe. He wandered down the hill towards the Mandarin Hotel. It was only when the cool conditioned air enveloped him that he realised how hot and humid it was outside. He went into the bar, ordered a beer and took it to a table in the corner. The bar was virtually empty.

Cross came in and brought another drink across to the table. He started talking animatedly about the commercial possibilities he had discovered that morning.

A man no more than five foot eight tall entered the bar carrying a black attaché case. He looked around as though lost. He studied Jennings and Cross for a moment and came across the bar.

"Mr Jennings?"

Jennings nodded, and introductions followed.

Sutcliffe could only just have been tall enough to qualify for the Surrey Police, but was broad across the shoulders and thick in the chest. The three exchanged pleasantries, and Sutcliffe made the requisite enquiries after the health and welfare of Tony Hacker. Jennings confirmed both the fitness and well-being of their mutual friend. The formalities required by British culture were completed with the arrival of an orange juice for Sutcliffe. His still slightly yellow pallor showed a hint of the bout of hepatitis from which he had recently suffered.

"Well, Allan, you have had my report. What I would like to know is what your interest is in this man and how can I help further."

Jennings told him some facts behind his reason for wanting to trace Lee Kim and more particularly to talk to him. He did not mention his father's death.

"I am afraid that it will not be possible to talk to him." Sutcliffe was opening his briefcase. He pulled out a copy of the English-language *The China Times* and placed it on the table in front of Jennings.

NEW TRIAD WARS?

> At one o'clock this morning a car bomb exploded outside The Sunrise Club in Kowloon. The bomb is thought to have been aimed at the Dragon Triad, some of whose members are suspected of using the premises. Twelve people were killed in the explosion, including the owner Lee Kim.

Jennings felt his inner self crumbling as he screwed the newspaper into a tight ball. He was fighting to keep his self-composure and not crack in front of this stranger. His only link to the reasons for his father's death and his own incarceration was now broken. He would now never know why his life had been destroyed or who caused it to happen. He took a long pull at his beer while he regained enough composure to trust himself to speak.

Sutcliffe saw the pain in Jennings's eyes and said nothing.

"Well, thank Christ for that. You can now get on with your life and put the past behind you."

Was Cross just being cruel to be kind? What he said was true. Jennings could no longer look back so he must look forward. Jennings remembered Hacker's warning and said nothing.

"Would you like to join us for the evening, Richard? We could have dinner somewhere and then drown some frustration." Jennings had regained his poise, at least for the time being.

"Why don't you be my guests for dinner at the Jockey Club? I won't be able to join you for the drowning bit as my liver hasn't yet recovered from a bout of hepatitis," Sutcliffe replied. He could see that there was something more to Jennings's grief than simply being wrongly imprisoned. His eyes looked older than his body.

The Hong Kong Jockey Club is one of the most exclusive clubs in the world, let alone Hong Kong. To join the club one had not only to be extremely rich but, more importantly, very well-connected. The three men met in the bar and were fussed over by the stewards. The menu was a superb mixing of Chinese and European dishes. Both Jennings and Cross bowed to Sutcliffe's knowledge and suggested that he order for the three. He ordered a light fish mousse to start followed by khobi beef, which was specially imported. Caviar would have been a more economical choice.

During the meal Sutcliffe pumped Jennings for more facts about Lee Kim and the connection to Jennings. The pumping was subtle, as would be expected from a trained investigator. Jennings, whose own interrogation techniques had been learnt from the intelligence corps, recognised that he was being quietly interrogated but only allowed the information he wanted to be drawn out of him. Cross ate quietly, observing the performance.

As they were leaving, Sutcliffe said to Jennings, "If you want me to do any more digging on your behalf, I will. I'll see what I can find out about the rest of the PFP hierarchy or whether anything can be traced back through the triad."

"Thank you, but no. I think it's about time I started to look forward rather than backwards."

"Well, you've got my address if you change your mind." Sutcliffe was sure that he would hear again from this man. Anyone with that much pain in his eyes would have to relieve that torment some time.

Sutcliffe dropped them at the hotel, wishing them a safe journey home, and left. Jennings and Cross made for the bar to undertake the ritual drowning of some frustration.

There was no way Jennings could get drunk that night. The more he drank the clearer his mind became. He could not dull the thought of the bridge to the solution being blown right at the start of the journey. Cross, on the other hand, suffered no difficulties in achieving a state of sublime incapacity. Jennings eventually took him to his room and put him to bed, all the while being told that he was the best friend a man could ever have.

Jennings slept fitfully that night. The backs of his eyelids were alive with images. One by one he dreamt of abandoning his friends. He dreamt of Murph falling, crying, "Allan, help me." He was trying to get through a wall of fire but could not. His father's voice called, "Allan, help me," from the other side of the fire. He was part of a firing squad. Even with blindfolds he recognised Trooper Wilde and Captain Butcher. One by one, throughout the night he heard the unanswered cry for help from the dead.

Sunlight streamed through the chink in the curtains. Jennings mouth was dry, his hair wet with sweat and his eyes red. He rang for the room valet and ordered China tea. He stood under the shower and let the pinpricks of water wash away the horrors of the night. He shaved yesterday from his chin and dressed in today's clothes. He telephoned Cross, whose tongue and brain were still slightly out of tune, and arranged to meet him for breakfast. He had decided that the past and the future were not separate but were all one and the same. He could not be a person in two halves, discarding one and carrying on with the other.

Two days later they returned to England – Cross with his import contract and Jennings with nothing other than resolve.

Chapter Nine

CLASSIFIED

15th August 1971

Subject: Allan William Jennings

A private investigator, employed by the above, ascertained the whereabouts of the former terrorist Lee Kim. Before Jennings could make any contact with Lee Kim there was an explosion at a club in Hong Kong. One of the fatalities in the explosion was the said Lee Kim. *It is confirmed that Jennings had no contact with the gentleman in question before his demise.*

With the elimination of Lee Kim, Jennings no longer has any viable route to follow. Close surveillance is no longer needed. There will be no need to install the listening devices that were proposed. The current arrangements will be maintained for the time being.

This file should now be treated as PENDING – NO FURTHER ACTION, to be reviewed in twenty-four months.

CLASSIFIED

15th August 1971

To: Hong Kong Centre

Subject: Richard John Sutcliffe

Please institute, with immediate effect, grade 4 surveillance on the above subject.

Should he institute any enquiries relating to the PFP and/or any of their current or past personnel surveillance must immediately be upgraded to grade 1 and we must be informed at once.

Chapter Ten

Jennings telephoned Corby the day he returned to tell him that he wished to join Corby, Lannin & Davies as soon as possible. He did not intend to take up the position of deputy chairman at the outset, but to learn the business and then take up the position.

Corby was genuinely pleased Jennings was joining the company as he had seen that he had all the attributes needed for a first-class broker and producer. He made arrangements for a crash training course in the basics of the business. Jennings was to be sent on two introductory courses. He would then spend a month in the office learning the systems and procedures. From October to early January he would be in the market with the brokers who placed the business with underwriters. February and March would be spent in Zürich, with one of the largest reinsurance companies in the world, whose quality of training was second to none, according to Corby. Subsequently he would travel with some of the producers to get a feel of how they operated. After a year of intensive training he would, as Corby so eloquently put it, "Sink or bloody swim your way to the top."

Jennings started his new life on 1st September 1971. He learnt very quickly that the business was so varied that every type of personality could be accommodated. He met dull people who had an enormous wealth of knowledge. These were normally the technicians responsible for administering and accounting the business. He came across extroverts who overcame their lack of technical knowledge with the strength of their personalities. The most impressive of all was the extrovert who also had an abundance of technical know-how. These people carried a respect verging on godliness in the marketplace.

Jennings had no difficulties in settling into the workings of the place. He had an ebullient character and a fast, active and enquiring mind. His enthusiasm to learn was insatiable. He never stopped asking why and how things were done. Not even the smallest point was left alone until it was fully understood. The underwriters he met found Jennings to be the ideal recipient for the wisdom they felt was their duty to instil in all and sundry. Jennings just listened and learned.

After four months he had assimilated knowledge that a lesser man would have taken years to accumulate. His IQ was over 140 and he had a particular aptitude for mathematics and languages. This was an ideal combination for the business of reinsurance. In addition he was effusive in character and he carried the air of self-confidence which impressed all who came into contact with him.

In early February he took a Swissair flight to Zürich. In the taxi from the airport to the Schplugenschloss Hotel he remembered Corby's comment about the hotel.

"We always stop at the Schplugenschloss because it's the only Swiss name that you can still pronounce if you're pissed as a parrot. In fact everything you say sounds like bloody Schplugenschloss."

The hotel might have had the perfect name for a drunken Englishman but it was also superbly run and very comfortable. Jennings's room was large with plenty of light. There was a small but friendly bar and the food in the restaurant was truly magnificent. All the staff were efficient and friendly. The night porter, a man called Max, was famous for being the closest thing to Basil Fawlty other than Basil Fawlty himself. He would order the guests about in the most outrageous manner. The Anglo-Saxon guests would collapse laughing at his antics, whilst those of Germanic origin often failed to see the humour. As a result the clientele of the hotel was heavily weighted towards British, American, Canadian, South African and Australian. Owing to the proximity of the hotel to the offices of the Swiss reinsurer, a good proportion of the guests were in the reinsurance business.

The two months Jennings spent with the Swiss company were somewhat varied. He found out that the Swiss were both multicultural and multi-charactered. The French-speaking nationals were in the main suave and smooth as treacle slipping from a hot spoon. The German-speakers were solid and serious. If there were rules, these had to be obeyed. The Italian-speakers were usually expansive and excitable. Then there were those who had been sent to the various overseas subsidiaries of the group and subsequently returned. These people carried a personality combining the attributes of the country in which they had worked as well as those of their native land.

The most endearing character Jennings met was a man called Peter Huber. Peter was born and bred in Zürich and still carried the Zurcher-Deutsch view that there was only one correct way of achieving an end. He actually believed that Hitler had not invaded Switzerland because he was afraid of the Swiss Army. Peter had, however, spent three years in Sydney and had also assumed many traits typical of New South Wales. Normal conversation had to be carried on at a bellow, disagreements at a level of decibels that would carry the sound across the lake.

Jennings and Huber felt an immediate affinity with each other. Huber took Jennings out to dinner on his second night in Zürich, and it soon became clear that his drinking and socialising habits had been heavily influenced by the Australians. After dinner at a superb little restaurant in Bahnhoffstrasse they made for the old town and a tour, in Jennings's honour, of all the English pubs in Zürich. The finishing point was The Oliver Twist where a number of very expensive pints of Bass were consumed.

The second weekend Huber took Jennings to Flims.

"We will eat, drink and I will teach you how to ski." Huber's orders were delivered in an accent that was half German and half Australian.

Jennings did not bother to tell Huber that he had skied in the downhill for the British Army and had been a reserve for the British Olympic team.

Saturday was spent on the nursery slopes with Huber yelling instructions on snow-ploughing with the skis. On Saturday evening they feasted on *fondue bourgignon* washed down with large quantities of Hurliman beer. Sunday morning was to be Jennings's introduction to 'proper skiing'. They took the cable car to the top of the mountain. The views from the peak were breathtaking. The snow glinted in the bright sunlight. Jennings was reminded of his days in Finland with the SAS. He remembered Colin Crafts, who was a formidable slalom racer. They were both in the army team which had won the European Army title. His throat tightened at the memory but he cast it aside and followed Huber to the bar to take on board some warming fuel for the downhill descent to follow. They drank strong black coffee to wash down the schnapps.

Huber lectured Jennings on matters of safety and told him not to try too much. He demonstrated how he thought Jennings should negotiate the steeper slopes by slipping sideways rather than skiing them. They went out to the top of the run and donned their skis.

"Good luck, my friend," Huber pronounced as he pushed himself off towards the slope.

At first Huber did not recognise Jennings. It was just a flash of someone skiing past him very fast. He realised that it was Jennings's outfit when he was some thirty yards ahead. A teacher being passed by the student was not acceptable to Huber, and he drove his ski poles deep into the snow to catch and overtake this impudent Englishman. All his efforts were to no avail as Jennings became smaller and smaller in the distance. When Huber reached the bottom of the run, Jennings was stood there, leaning on his skis and roaring with barely controlled laughter.

"I believe you have skied before this weekend." Huber's voice carried some rancour because he felt that his dignity had been assaulted.

"Actually I was a reserve for the 1968 British Olympic team. I'm sorry I took the piss, Peter, but you were so bloody serious on the nursery slopes yesterday that I couldn't have told you."

"You bloody arrogant English bastard." The Australian in Huber took over as he recalled diligently teaching the snow-plough to a near-Olympian, albeit a British Olympian. The two men put their arms around each other and made for the nearest bar.

*

The two months in Zürich flew by. Day by day, Jennings was learning more about the business in which he had decided his future lay. He made many new friends, both in the Swiss company and outside.

The week before he was due to return, the company had their annual shooting competition. All the Swiss were or had been at some time in the Swiss Army, and the annual shooting contest was a long-standing tradition.

"I suppose you are an international shot." Huber still occasionally sulked about Jennings and the skiing embarrassment.

"I am, actually, quite a good shot," Jennings replied honestly.

"Should I have a bet on you in the visitors' shooting?" Huber's Australian side emerged.

"If you can get the odds, I'll have a go at the open pistol, provided you can get me a Browning 35mm. I was British Army champion."

Huber danced with delight. "That is my weapon! I have it at home! Tonight we will go to the range and practise to see if you are worth a bet."

It was the first time in the history of the company shoot that a visitor had won an open competition. Jennings set a new record score by dropping only two points to a maximum, both deliberate. He also came third in the open rifle and would have won this had he not, again deliberately, pulled two shots.

On his last night in Zürich Huber took Jennings out to the best restaurant in town on his winnings from the unofficial book. Both men drank too much and swore a lifetime of loyalty to each other.

Chapter Eleven

Jennings arrived at Heathrow in the middle of the afternoon. A couple of drinks on the plane had removed the last vestiges of the damage caused by Huber's farewell party.

During the drive back to Woldingham he noticed that the landscape was beginning to emerge from its winter slumber. There were hints of the emergence of blossom on the flowering cherry trees. These trees were always the first to welcome spring. Soon the blossom would decorate the Downs, and the wild orchids would awaken from their winter slumber and begin to bloom. Lambs would frolic in the fields. Everywhere new life would appear and old life was rejuvenated. Spring was a time for restoration, a time to look ahead to a balmy future. Jennings felt at peace with the world as he chatted amiably with Jack Martin about Zürich and the Swiss in general.

The house felt warm and secure. From the kitchen the aroma of gently roasting lamb wafted through the house. If there was a definition of contentment, this was it.

Ellen emerged from the kitchen, her ruddy face showing genuine pleasure at Jennings's return.

"It's lovely to have you home, Mr Jennings." She looked down at his suitcase and chuckled. "But I'm not so sure about your dirty washing."

Jennings reached inside his holdall and produced a bottle of Chanel No. 19 and a huge box of Frigor Swiss-made chocolates. Ellen had two major weaknesses, and Jennings had found both. She thanked him effusively while at the same time scolding him for the ridiculous waste of money. She then issued him with orders on where to put the washing and the dry cleaning, and at what time and with whom he was to eat that evening. Cross had arranged for Hacker to join them for an early dinner followed by a reintroduction to proper beer rather than the continental muck he had been drinking.

Over a dinner of roast shoulder of lamb, Scottish of course, roast potatoes, minted peas and broccoli, the two quizzed Jennings on his adventures while in Zürich. When coffee arrived, Cross became serious.

"Allan, I have been offered a very good job by a chap I know in the West End. I have been through all the holdings you have and after a bit of reorganisation they are all running as sweet as a nut. They should carry on making you a lot of money. You don't need me any more and this new job is consultancy work doing the same sort of thing with other companies. I like mending companies but get bored with them when they are repaired."

Jennings thought for a moment, wondering whether to make some sort of counter offer but he could see from Cross's eyes that he was determined to set a new course for his life.

"If you think it's the best thing for you, Jim, then go for it. You and I have been through some good and a bit of bad. We'll always be mates and that's the most important thing."

Jennings noticed that Hacker was apparently concentrating on the pattern of his coffee cup. Jennings had learned over the years that Hacker always turned his attention to an inanimate object when he knew he should say something but did not intend to. At school it had been his cap badge or his satchel. Jennings wondered what was on Hacker's mind.

The moment passed and the conversation returned to more normal topics. Jennings, being a lifelong supporter of Arsenal, proceeded to extol their current virtues, particularly when compared with the doldrums in which Spurs languished. Hacker and Cross, as Spurs men, were unimpressed.

The three finished their coffee, thanked Ellen profusely for a marvellous meal, and suggested that she should not wait up as they could be late back from The Haycutter. Jennings knew that she would be waiting up when they returned with sandwiches and drinks and he quietly thanked Stuart Rittle and God for finding such a gem.

Two weeks later Cross moved into his new flat in Chelsea.

Chapter Twelve

Jennings's enthusiasm for his new career grew in leaps and bounds as he became more involved in the company and the business. He had always felt that insurance would be serious and sombre. Reinsurance he found exciting and stimulating.

All the contracts he dealt with were made up of large risks, and consequently huge premiums. This was counterbalanced by the downside of monstrous claims. He found the claims fascinating - not just due to the size, but the complexities and legal ramifications. The claims running through his office ranged from huge natural catastrophes to people suffering calamitous injuries at work or on the roads. He felt an affinity with the claims managers. These men had to read about other human beings suffering all sorts of disasters to themselves, their families and their property, but then detach their minds from the human distress and view it as a cost to their employers. To an extent their attitude was similar to that of the professional soldier. The professional soldier never ambushed a human being but an inanimate object collectively known as the enemy. Jennings felt that these men dealing with claims had to be stronger mentally than soldiers because they had to close their minds to the most basic human compassion without the help of battlefield adrenaline.

The travelling was another part of the business Jennings cherished: the chance to revisit places he knew and to see new parts of the world. He could see the way different cultures pursued the same objective. He studied how different nationalities dealt with buying and selling. The Chinese would never accept the first price offered as negotiation was part of their basic concept of business. An Arab would bring gifts of friendship but expect something of equal or greater value in return. The Latin nations tended to want whatever was the cheapest, rather than the best. The Germans wanted the best. The French wanted the best, but only if it was cheap. The Scandinavians tended to negotiate with a glass in their hands. The Americans were a mix of so many cultures that it was impossible to define one style. The British, New Zealanders and, in part, the Australians wanted a good deal but preferably only with someone who was a gentleman. The Swiss, who were probably the best businessmen of all, were all things to all men.

Jennings found his knowledge developing in many diverse areas. There was economic forecasting and how inflation and currency exchange rates would be affected. Seismology and changes in weather patterns were vital in assessing probabilities of natural catastrophes. The different legal systems and how they would be interpreted around the world could affect the cost of claims. Medical development and practices would have an effect on the value of claims. One claims man had once said to Jennings, "The trouble with doctors is that they are getting too bloody efficient. They can't mend them but they can keep them alive. A dead body will cost less than a cripple. You don't have to nurse a dead body."

In June that year Corby asked Jennings to a private lunch in the boardroom at only an hour's notice. Jennings wondered whether the invitation was combined with a study of his expenses, but ignored the thought as he owned a third of the company.

Lunch was pure and traditional British: leek and potato soup followed by steak and kidney pudding, with jam roly-poly to finish.

Jennings was studying the menu, wondering how many miles he would have to run to remove the excess calories, when Corby bustled through the door. He poured himself a large gin and tonic and raised the glass to Jennings.

"Cheers Allan!" Corby was smiling and obviously in a wholesome mood. "That bastard Bryan has been in my office to try and bludgeon a bloody great rise out of me for him and his sidekick. He says he has been approached by Manning Steele, and if I don't give him a deal he and his bloody mate will fuck off and take the Far East account with them. I told him to stick his head up his bloody arse and blow as hard as he could. That means now he's resigned and is being turfed off the premises."

Jennings raised his eyebrows but said nothing for he knew that Corby had more to say.

"The reason I did that, Allan, was because I now know that you can do a much better job than that little fat shit. Will you take over the Far East and Australia and, by the way, also be deputy chairman? I'm getting fed up with the bullshit I get from Stuart Rittle every month while he's trying to show what a clever little frog he is."

Jennings suppressed a smile. Corby obviously did not know the difference between a frog and a toad, one of the problems of being born and bred in Chelsea.

"If you think I am ready for it, I'm delighted." Jennings tried to hide his inner exultation. The compliment to his ego was unexpected.

"Ready for it?" bellowed Corby, downing the gin. "You can do it standing on your bloody head. You speak the buggers' lingo and they bloody like you. What more do you want?"

Lunch became a celebration for both men – Jennings for the recognition he was getting, and Corby for getting out of a hole with his largest shareholder. Corby knew that the little fat man would take business away but that would now be Jennings's problem. If Jennings happened to keep any of the business, that would be a secondary bonus.

Jennings spent the next two months studying the portfolio of the business he had taken over. He went through all the contracts in fine detail, finding out every quirk of every agreement. He produced updated statistics and analysed the details of the market where each piece of business was placed so that any future problems would be foreseen and eliminated, if at all possible.

After all the analysis he could see that one particular market would be a problem as the underwriter was a great friend of 'the little fat shit' and would, almost certainly, be obstructive if Jennings kept the business. He spoke to a few other underwriters and arranged for the potential problem to be replaced.

All the arrangements were made for Jennings's first business trip as the account executive. He would attend the International Reinsurance Congress in Monte Carlo in the first week in September. There he could have preliminary meetings with a number of clients. The congress was attended by insurers and reinsurers from all over the world and made a good meeting place as it was part business and a lot of pleasure.

After the congress he would spend a week in the office updating all his files and then leave for Hong Kong, Singapore and Australia. On the way back he would stop off in Toronto and New York to do a bit of corporate flag-waving and possibly a lot of drinking.

While all the plans and itineraries were being put together Jennings felt a growing excitement in his stomach. He had the same feeling he had experienced when he commanded his first patrol in the jungle: the excitement of the challenge ahead combined with the gut-gnawing fear of failure.

Chapter Thirteen

Terminal One at Heathrow was as tattered as ever. Jennings wandered through passport control and made straight for the bar. He might as well have been in The Grapes in Lime Street. All the doyens from the London market were elbowing each other to try and get their drinks first. The two barmen were looking a little distracted trying to keep pace with the drinking needs of the swarm of underwriters and brokers that crowded the bar.

Jennings spied Corby, who had lodged himself at one end of the bar. Miraculously a pint was produced for Jennings, much to the consternation of the waiting hordes.

"Arrive early, drop the barman a fiver and you'll always get good service," Corby whispered as he passed the pint to Jennings.

"Here's to a successful week." Corby drained his glass and another two beers arrived.

The two men chatted generally about their plans for the week. Mostly they had separate appointments during the day, with dinners arranged with the most important clients at night. Corby briefed Jennings on the dos and don'ts relative to each client.

The flight was called and the hubbub left the bar and transferred itself to Gate 32, and from there to the British Airways 737 bound for Nice.

The stewardesses on the flight were run off their feet trying to keep up with the thirst of their passengers. Eighty per cent of the flight was business class so most passengers felt it their duty to obtain the maximum benefit from the extra cost of their tickets. As the only real benefit was free booze this had to be taken advantage of.

Nice Airport was hot and disordered. Bags eventually arrived and people dispersed in the direction of taxis, Avis Rental or the helicopter. Jennings and Corby jumped in a taxi. The drive along the Grande Corniche had some spectacular views. The hillsides were stark rather than lush, as Jennings had imagined. There were still obvious signs of the fires that had ravaged the area the previous year. Monte Carlo itself seemed to be a collection of buildings which did not match each other, all dumped in a hollow carved out of the mountainside.

They arrived at Leouws Hotel and checked in while the porters were unloading the luggage from the taxi. They were shown to their rooms, which were adjoining. Corby winked at Jennings and remarked, "See you in the Piano Bar."

Jennings phoned room service and ordered a club sandwich.

By the time he had unpacked there was a knock on the door and his food was delivered. He devoured the snack, washing it down with a bottle of Stella from the minibar. He showered, put on lightweight trousers and a white silk shirt. Now he felt ready for the fray.

As he wandered along the corridor to the lift he noted the blue and white geometric wallpaper which seemed to be used everywhere in the hotel. All the floors and all the rooms were the same, with the exception of some were facing the sea and some did not. It was always considered a coup to obtain a sea view, and many francs changed hands in pursuit of this.

The Piano Bar was a throng of brokers and underwriters from all parts of the world, with a few lawyers and accountants thrown in for good luck. Corby was holding court at one end of the bar and waved at Jennings to come over. He was introduced to a general manager from Bermuda, a vice-president from Chicago and an attorney from Boston. Polite discussion lasted for about five minutes and then Corby excused himself as he had another appointment. The four men remaining chatted amiably.

The general manager was in the middle of extolling the scuba-diving off Bermuda when Jennings was struck in the back by what felt like a large brick. The shock was followed by a greeting bellowed in a cross between a Swiss and Australian accent, "Allan, you flash shit, how are you?"

Jennings turned, trying to regain the breath that had been driven from his lungs, and was confronted by the grinning features of Peter Huber. The two men shook hands warmly. Jennings ordered a drink for Huber and the two made their excuses to the other three. They found a table away from the piano and sat down. Jennings noticed that the design of the cushion cover was exactly the same as that of the wallpaper.

The management from the Swiss head office always had suites in The Hermitage.

"I've been transferred to the subsidiary in Sydney, in case you don't know. That's why I'm here and not at The Hermitage," Huber answered Jennings's question before it could be asked.

The two exchanged stories of their accomplishments since they had last met. Huber had been in Sydney for two months as part of a two-year secondment. He also had responsibility for the underwriting in the contact offices in Hong Kong and Singapore.

"We've got a very bright and bloody gorgeous-looking girl in the Hong Kong office. If you are ever there, you must go and see her."

Jennings told Huber that he would be in Hong Kong in a couple of weeks and would make sure he looked her up.

"Pansie Lam is her name. Just mention me and she will make sure you are looked after."

Jennings winked at Huber, who reacted by cuffing him around the head and saying, "Not like that, you randy little bastard. She is head of underwriting there and knows the market inside out. If you want any information, she can help, and I'm sure she will take you out to dinner, with a chaperon of course."

On the Sunday Corby and Jennings played golf with the general manager from Bermuda. Mount Angel, which is the home of the Monte Carlo Golf Club, is aptly named. The golf course is on the top of a mountain and it would be a huge advantage to fly rather than walk the course.

"You need to be a mountain goat with breathing apparatus to play this bloody course," Corby muttered as he struggled up the hill from the fifteenth green to the sixteenth tee.

Corby's mood was not helped by the fact that his golf was not the best. Jennings, however, was only two over par gross and was winning quite a lot of francs from Corby. The Bermudan, who was a six handicap at Mid Ocean, was all square. Jennings finished par, birdie, birdie, to complete a very depressing afternoon for Corby and a disappointing finish for the other.

On the Monday morning Monte Carlo was awash with brokers and underwriters scampering up and down the hill from Casino Square to Leouws Hotel. The Café de Paris was seething with people peering at each other's name badges trying to find their next appointment. The bars in the Hôtel de Paris and Leouws were much the same. At lunchtime all three emptied as delegates disappeared to the restaurant of their choice. At about two-thirty they all reappeared and bustled about importantly. It was too early to make actual business decisions for the next year, but Monte Carlo was a useful place to put down markers and to put faces to names.

The rest of the week was a round of meetings, lunches, cocktail parties and dinners, the latter usually followed by a session either at the bar or on the tables in Leouws Casino. Jennings had a good week for both business and pleasure. He made a number of new contacts and won over five hundred pounds on the blackjack tables.

Nice Airport was even worse than Heathrow. Not only was it seething confusion but it was also very hot. The bars were crowded with the returning mass and the bar staff were as flustered as those on the outward journey. The conference delegates were somewhat more tetchy than on the outward journey. They had suffered a week of limited sleep combined with too much rich food and booze.

Jack Martin met Jennings at the airport.

As he alighted from the taxi at his home Jennings was greeted by the most wonderful aromas from the kitchen. Ellen McDonald had prepared home-made steak and kidney pie with mash and plenty of gravy. After a week of eating everything cooked in rich cream and wine sauces she knew that Jennings would be desperate for something simple and English. Jennings ate his meal in the kitchen with Ellen. They chatted about something and nothing. For the past week Jennings had been putting on a show for the clients and it was a delight just to chatter inconsequentially.

Jennings cleared his plate and mopped up the remains of the gravy with a crust of freshly baked bread.

"Mr Cross phoned while you were away" – Ellen was talking over her shoulder as she busied herself at the sink – "and I told him you would probably be in The Haycutter tonight as you've been a week without proper beer. He said he might see you there."

"Ellen McDonald, you can read me like a book."

Jennings went into the study and phoned for a taxi to pick him up. While he waited he opened the post waiting for him. Most were rubbishy circulars beseeching him to purchase something that was of little use. One, however, had been posted in Hong Kong. He opened it and read the contents.

Dear Allan,

I have come across something that may be of interest to you in your enquiries relating to your problems.

During the course of other investigations I have discovered that a former associate of Lee Kim is now resident in Hong Kong. It appears that this person has no connection with the triads, and I believe it is pure coincidence that he is now living here.

Should you wish, I will pursue this matter further and report back to you. I await your advice at your convenience.

Yours sincerely,
Richard Sutcliffe

Jennings reread the letter and felt all the old wounds reopen in his heart. He was being torn by indecision. Should he forget the past and look only to the future? The future looked excellent in his new calling. He relished his life in reinsurance, the personal relations, the challenge of competing for the business and the travel. Should he rake over the past and perhaps revive the torment he had suffered and repeat it? The conflicting thoughts sparring in his head were interrupted by Jack Martin honking his hooter outside. Jennings put the letter down, deciding to defer any decision until the morning. He shouted a goodbye to Ellen and made for the taxi.

Tony Hacker was sitting on his usual bar stool at the end of the bar. He turned and greeted Jennings then waved at the landlord for a pint. The two chatted about matters in general. Jennings related some of the more exotic tales from Monte Carlo. Hacker seemed suitably shocked when told that a bottle of beer was over four pounds in the hotel bars. He was even less impressed to find out that the cheapest drink in the bars was champagne. Hacker related stories of who and what was happening in the local community. Jennings's mind wandered back to the letter from Sutcliffe.

"Are you listening or am I talking to myself?" Hacker's voice interrupted his thoughts.

"I'm sorry, Tony, but I had a letter from that bloke Sutcliffe in Hong Kong. Apparently he has now found someone who was with that bastard Lee Kim in the PFP. He wants to know if he should make further enquiries. I'm buggered if I know what to do."

"It depends entirely on what you want. Do you want to let the past die or do you want to find out what happened?" Hacker's voice was conciliatory. "If you want to know what happened, go for it; if you don't, tear the bloody letter up."

"What would *you* do, Tony?"

"Well, I'm a bloody copper so I would want to know what happened, but when I found out I might wish I had never bothered."

"That's a great bloody help. I'm off to Hong Kong next week, so I think I might arrange to see Sutcliffe, just to see how far he can go."

"Are you going to buy me a pint or not?" Neither had seen Cross come in. He was standing behind them, smiling. "You look pretty good, Allan. Have you been somewhere hot and sunny?"

"No, I've just got back from a boring business conference in Monte Carlo."

"Monte Carlo! You flash bastard. How come *I* get conferences in Birmingham and *you* get to go to Monte Carlo?" Cross's voice was raised in mock indignation.

"You're in the wrong bloody business, that's why."

The three men settled down for a night of exchanging stories and solid beer drinking.

Jennings woke the next morning, the alarm clock dragging him away from a very pleasant encounter with a blonde film starlet whose one desire in life was to make Jennings happy. His mouth was slightly furred and there was nagging pain behind his eyes. He showered and shaved. He dressed in light slacks and a cream polo shirt. He remembered agreeing to play golf with Hacker and Cross and hoped that they would both recall the arrangement. By the time he had consumed the fry-up Ellen produced, his headache had disappeared.

Jennings loaded his golf clubs into the boot of the Jaguar, waved to Ellen and drove to Limpsfield Chart Golf Club.

Hacker was waiting in the car park when Jennings arrived. He was a member of the artisan section of the club, which meant that they had to be off the tee before nine o'clock. They were changing their shoes when Cross arrived in a taxi. Hacker had brought a spare set of clubs for Cross and he swished them very professionally before drawing his drive around the dog-leg to about sixty yards from the green. Jennings, who tended to hit the ball with a fade, found the middle of the fairway with a long iron. Hacker was about to have a day that matched his name. He topped the drive, which ended in deep rough seventy yards from the tee. He then proceeded to hack along the rough before finally surrendering after six attempts to find some grass that had been mown. The match ran much the same way for the remainder of the round. Jennings and Cross walked the fairways whilst Hacker hacked about in rough, bunkers and trees.

"Are you going to see Richard in Hong Kong?" Cross's question was an apparent social enquiry. "You were talking about it when I came in last night."

"I'll probably have a few beers with him," Jennings answered, a little defensively.

"Please make sure it is just for a beer. Don't go ruining your new life by trying to dig up the past. You're more relaxed than I have seen you since we met. Don't fuck it up now." The advice was offered in a friendly, paternal manner.

Jennings just nodded assent.

The game ended with Cross winning the money on the last green with a birdie. Both Jennings and Cross had won Hacker's stake by the fourteenth.

The three friends had a couple of drinks in the bar. They arranged to meet in The Haycutter that evening and went their own ways.

That afternoon Jennings telephoned Sutcliffe and arranged to meet him in the Mandarin Hotel.

Chapter Fourteen

CLASSIFIED

16th September 1972

To: Hong Kong Centre

Subject: Richard John Sutcliffe

    The above has been under grade 4 surveillance since last August. It is now required that full grade 1 surveillance be instituted and an immediate report made to us in the event that he has any dealings or meeting with any former member of the PFP. We also require details of any dealings or meetings the subject has with Allan William Jennings.

Chapter Fifteen

The next week Jennings spent most of his time with the administrative people in the office preparing the figures and other information for his forthcoming trip. He felt his excitement growing as the week progressed. The challenge of trying to retain the business the fat man wanted to take away gave Jennings the same buzz as stalking and taking an enemy in the jungle. His initial task was to stalk, but take he would.

The British Airways flight to Hong Kong was uneventful. The cabin service, as usual, was efficient and courteous. The food was better than normal airline fare, and the seats wide and comfortable. As the flight approached Bombay for a refuelling stop-over the cabin was sprayed with some form of disinfectant. Jennings smiled inwardly: the thought of Bombay being free of bugs and insects and travellers being sprayed to stop any infiltration struck him as being as useful as a coalman wearing a white tuxedo while delivering his wares.

Jennings shared the courtesy Mercedes with a banker from Manchester. He was in Hong Kong to raise more capital for a manufacturing company in the Midlands and seemed to want to bestow the fine detail of the business plan on Jennings. Jennings half ignored and half listened to the droning pouring into his left ear. It was not until he realised, too late, that he had accepted an invitation to a drink in the Clipper Lounge that he began to concentrate. The concentration lasted but a few minutes. Jennings lapsed back into the inner space called jet lag. His body told him it was time to sleep, but his watch told him he should be awake and alert. During the flight he had lost a night's sleep which was gone for ever.

The check-in at the hotel seemed convoluted. He eventually made it to his room with the Mancunian message of, "See you in the lounge in half an hour," still ringing in his ears. Thankfully the room valet soon arrived with a pot of green tea and began to unpack Jennings's case.

Half an hour later Jennings, showered and wearing fresh clothes, was sitting in the Clipper Lounge nursing an ice-cold glass of beer. He surveyed the bustle in the reception. The banker – Jennings smiled at the opportunities offered by rhyming slang – scampered across reception and made his way into the downstairs bar. Jennings finished his drink, ambled down the stairs, across the reception area and down into the bar.

"I thought you had buggered off to bed." Manchester was looking slightly indignant.

"I'm sorry," Jennings replied, as politely as he could. "I thought we were to meet in the Clipper Lounge."

Manchester looked a little sheepish and muttered, "Is there more than one bloody bar here then?"

They ordered drinks – Jennings a beer, and a large scotch for Manchester. The business plan was again run out in great detail and lack of sleep popped back into Jennings's brain.

"If that slitty-eyed prat had not got himself blown up, this deal would have been signed and sealed bloody months ago."

Jennings was jolted from his state of inertia.

"Who got blown up?" Jennings asked, a little bit too enthusiastically.

"Some Chinky called Lee Kim. He was going to put the money in as a sleeping partner. He was all lined up, and then some bloody fool planted a bomb outside his nightclub."

"How did you come to know this Lee Kim?"

"When he was buying for the Government of National Unity after the PFP and the government made friends. He used to run a lot of the orders through a company owned by him and the minister, Lin Chow. Obviously a bloody fiddle, but we all made money out of it." Manchester was becoming more enthusiastic and loud. "The kickbacks were pushed into the banks here and in Switzerland. Lee Kim was a very rich slitty eye when he caught it."

Jennings was now fully alert. He must find out more about Lee Kim's partner.

"If this Lee Kim is dead, who is going to invest now?" Jennings tried to make the enquiry sound casual.

"Lin Chow, of course. Now that Lee Kim is a bucket of ashes the boss slitty has left the government and moved to Hong Kong to pick up all the business interests Lee Kim used to run." Manchester's voice was patronising. It was obvious to anyone but an idiot that Lee Kim's partner would pick up all the pieces. "He flits between Hong Kong, Bermuda and Zürich. I've got to sell him the deal tomorrow morning 'cos he's off to Bermuda in the afternoon."

Jennings wanted to ask many more questions but it was not the right time to press too hard. They had a few more drinks, exchanged business cards. By that time Manchester was beginning to become a little incoherent. The combination of lack of sleep and several large Teacher's began to disconnect the link between his brain and his tongue. They took the lift to the fourth floor and Manchester eventually managed to open his door. Jennings wrote *Lin Chow* on the back of Manchester's business card and put it in his briefcase.

Jennings booked an early wake-up call, undressed and collapsed into his bed. He slept a dreamless sleep.

The telephone was ringing insistently and Jennings was jerked into wakefulness. He thanked the operator for the call and looked at his watch. He had slept for nine hours but he felt as though he had only just nodded off. He showered and shaved and began to feel a little more human. Room service delivered breakfast, which he ate with relish. He sat in the lounge and reread the notes he had prepared for the meetings he had arranged that day. The first meeting was with Pansie Lam, who had also invited him to dinner in the evening. Jennings wondered whether she would live up to the description given by Peter Huber.

Jennings arrived at the Swiss company's office just before ten. He gave the receptionist his name and took a seat as instructed. He picked up *The China Times* and browsed through it. Over the top of the paper he saw walking towards him the most shapely pair of ankles he had ever seen. The ankles were topped by a pair of beautifully formed legs which stopped at the hem of a skirt just above the knees. The woman's figure was sensational, with her curves accentuated by a beautifully cut Chanel suit. Her face was slightly rounded and topped with jet-black hair. Her eyes were hidden behind a large pair of tinted glasses. She offered him a beautifully manicured hand and said, "Mr Jennings, I am Pansie Lam. Welcome to Hong Kong." Her voice was soft and sensuous.

Jennings stood up somewhat clumsily and took the proffered palm, hoping he was effusing graciousness rather than lust in returning the greeting.

He followed her through reception and into a large office. All the furniture was mahogany and the seats were upholstered with a deep ruby red cloth. He thought of the boardroom at Corby, Lannin & Davies and wondered whether everyone in the business had the same tastes in furniture. She indicated a chair and Jennings sat down. Her movements had the grace of a tiger stalking its prey.

"Coffee, Mr Jennings?" She smiled, showing teeth that were pure white and perfectly formed.

"I would love some, milk no sugar, thank you, and please call me Allan."

She poured the coffee and passed it to Jennings.

"Peter has told me a lot about you, Allan. I understand you have spent some time in Zürich." She leaned back in her seat and removed her glasses.

The realisation struck Jennings like a thunderbolt. She had stunning dark hazel eyes. *The last time he had looked into those beautiful orbs he had had a* kukri *at her throat.* His mind was suddenly a jumble of different thoughts.

Before he could unscramble his mind she said quietly, "Why did you not kill me, Allan?"

"You are much too beautiful," was the only reply Jennings could make.

"Thank you," she smiled and returned her glasses to her face. "We can talk more of how our paths have crossed over dinner tonight. But for now what can I tell you about the Far East markets?"

For the next hour they discussed who was doing what in the business. Pansie's knowledge of the business and the competition was excellent. Her grasp of the commercial realities was even more impressive. The hour meeting flew by and Jennings wished that he had left more time for it. They arranged to meet at the Mandarin Hotel that evening, and Jennings left for his next appointment.

The appointments for the rest of the day ran smoothly. Names were put to faces and markers for the future were put down. Jennings did not know whether or not he would keep all the potentially departed business but felt much more confident that he would retain some of it, at least.

...tled into the bar just before six. He shook Jennings ... hand. His Martini arrived soon after the initial ... been exchanged. His liver had obviously recovered ... of hepatitis.

"What have you got to tell me, Richard?" Jennings enquired casually.

"Lee Kim's commanding officer in the PFP and his business partner in the backhander business has left the government and moved to Hong Kong. It seems that he is picking up all of Lee Kim's legal and illegal ventures. He is sure to know how they knew about your patrol. I have a few connections and I think I might be able to get him to talk to me."

"This is presumably Lin Chow you are talking about."

"It is, but how the bloody hell did you know that?" Sutcliffe was a little taken aback that his surprise was already known.

Jennings related the story of the Mancunian banker. "I just put two and two together and fortunately they made four. If you can find out any more about the ambush from this guy, I obviously want to know, but I want you to be very careful because to date there have been one or two deaths which may or may not be coincidental."

The two finished their drinks and parted company, with Sutcliffe promising to report back as soon as possible.

Pansie arrived on the dot at eight. She ordered a vodka and tonic and sat in the easy chair opposite Jennings. They chatted politely while the drinks were consumed. Both finished their drinks and took the lift to the gourmet Cantonese restaurant on the top floor of the hotel. They were given a table in a quiet corner. More drinks arrived as they studied the menu. Jennings eventually suggested that Pansie should order for the two of them. To the Chinese a meal is as much a social occasion as a need to consume food. All the food ordered is for the consumption of all at the table. There is not the English concept of 'yours and my meal' – everything on the table is *our* food.

Pansie ordered a selection of dishes. There was shredded beef in black bean sauce, lemon chicken, sweet and sour prawns, and sizzling lamb. These were complemented with fried rice and crisp stir-fried vegetables. They sat and enjoyed the food and the company. They talked mainly about each other and how the quirks of life had brought them to be in this restaurant and back in each other's company. Both were relaxed and at ease in the companionship of the other.

Pansie had been born of a poor family. At an early age someone had recognised that she had exceptional ability, particularly in mathematics and the sciences. She had been given a scholarship to Beijing University, where she had studied mathematics. She had also received the dubious benefit of constant tutelage in the glories of the communist Chinese system and the grinding cruelty of the capitalist regimes. It had been a natural step for her, when she left university, to be recruited by the PFP in their just war against the plundering capitalists. She had excelled as a jungle fighter, and only once had she been in any danger from the enemy. She winked at Jennings when she made the last statement. As time went by she had realised that the leaders, who quoted the highest communist morals, such as Lee Kim and Lin Chow, were actually feathering their own nests. With the cessation of the guerrilla action, she was so disillusioned that she went to Singapore and effectively became a capitalist. She had got a job as an actuary with the state insurance company and had soon become an underwriter. After a year she was offered a job in Hong Kong by Peter Huber's predecessor which she had accepted.

"A true communist to a money-grubbing capitalist in two years. That could be the title of a best selling book."

Even though the statement was made with ample irony, Jennings could see that she felt inner pain at her forced change from the purist view of all men being equal to that of all men having an absolute right to be unequal. Jennings thought, 'If you're not a communist at eighteen you do not have a heart, and if you're still a communist at thirty you don't have a brain.' He remembered well his father telling him this before he went up to Cambridge.

Jennings's life story was also unfolded and he saw the sympathy in her eyes when he spoke of his father's death while he was still in prison. Something about the obvious compassion showing in those dazzling eyes tempted Jennings to ask the question which had haunted him for nearly four years.

"How did your people know we were coming on that patrol?"

"It was arranged." Her answer was given in a matter-of-fact way, as though it was obvious to anyone with even a smidgen of basic intelligence.

"What do you mean – it was arranged? Who arranged it and why?"

"Allan, the PFP were losing the battle in the jungle. The British soldiers were getting better and better as fighters. We were losing good men and women and having to replace them with boys and girls. We had to look for peace, but a peace that left us with honour. We could not go to the negotiating table empty-handed. The Chinese Government, who financed us, would not have allowed this. So it was arranged that we would record a small but, in publicity value, a major victory. Your military command wanted the whole matter settled, so we were given, as a sacrifice, an SAS patrol. The problem was that *you* rather spoiled the concept." Her smile at this statement was almost an invitation to what Jennings hoped might happen later.

Jennings forced his thoughts away from the stirring in his groin and mused, "Why should *I* have spoiled the party?"

"After the ambush you killed our people. It was obvious that you would have realised the ambush was planned using the information we had about your movements. Neither your military command nor the PFP could afford to let that information out. You had to be found and either eliminated or discredited. If people believed you, the peace process would have collapsed."

"I don't understand why the bodies of my patrol were taken away while you buried your own men."

She smiled at him. The smile was both sympathetic and inviting.

"We did not know who was missing from your patrol. We took the bodies away so that the British liaison officer could identify the dead and tell us who escaped. If we had not known that, we could not have given your name in our freedom paper. We had to have your name in case you made it back to your own side. If you did, we could then denounce you as a traitor." She held her palms upwards. "One discredited witness and no one to believe him."

"Who was the liaison officer?" Jennings was beginning to feel the anger igniting inside him.

"Tomorrow morning I will tell you, while we have breakfast in your room. Let's live the present now and leave the past to another time." She touched his hand across the table and he felt his body shiver with expectation.

The champagne in the room remained untouched.

Pansie shivered as the zip slid softly down her back. Her skin was luxurious to the touch. He held her and felt her heart pumping against his chest. A craving grew inside him. In all his previous sexual encounters self-gratification had been his goal. She was different. He had to please her, make her want him for ever.

She had dreamed of this moment. When he had left her alive, she had known that one day their paths would cross. In her fantasies they had made love in that dank jungle. Her body was crying out for them to be one.

He took her in his arms and carried to the bedroom. Her body trembled as he gently placed her on the bed.

A human has five senses, all of which can be stimulated. Pansie Lam knew how to bring each of Jennings's senses to a new level of awareness. He saw her exquisite eyes above soft and yielding lips. Her breasts were firm above her flat stomach. Her legs were long and beautifully formed. When they touched, he felt her soft hands exploring his body. Her nipples were hard, like two small buttons being pressed into his chest. They kissed and he tasted her. He kissed her body and savoured the piquancy of a woman ready for love. He smelt the fragrance of Chanel No. 5, which only partly masked the musky aroma of sexual excitement. He heard her cry in the ecstasy of pain as he tried to press his manhood deeper into her. Then the gasp as her orgasm rose like a volcano erupting inside her. Finally there came quiet, broken only by the gentle breathing of two people holding each other after scaling the Everest of ecstasy.

The French call an orgasm *le petit mort*, 'the little death'. Jennings and this voluptuous beauty died several times that night.

Jennings awoke feeling refreshed and vital, even though he had only cat-napped. He looked at Pansie. She was lying on her back, her hair spread across the pillow like a jet-black halo surrounding her delicately formed features. He leaned over and kissed her. Without opening her eyes she enveloped him in her arms. They held each other, neither speaking but simply enjoying the feel of the other. After a few minutes the realities of life forced their way into his brain.

He kissed her and sighed, "I had better order some breakfast."

Pansie resisted his initial efforts to disentangle himself but eventually conceded defeat. Jennings picked up the telephone and dialled room service. He ordered scrambled eggs with smoked salmon and cinnamon toast for two.

Breakfast arrived while Pansie was showering. She appeared dressed in a huge towelling bathrobe. They ate breakfast voraciously, washed down with cups of steaming hot coffee. Jennings took his coffee to the easy chair in the corner and lit a John Player Special.

"You said you would tell me the name of the liaison officer who identified the dead." The words were delivered as a statement rather than a request.

"I do not know his name. He was not tall, was pale-faced and had a short pointed beard. He was wearing the insignia of a captain."

Jennings sat bolt upright in disbelief at what he was hearing. He asked her for more detail, which she gave. The more information Pansie offered the more the conclusion to which he did not want to come seemed to be the only logical one. The man she was describing was Captain Harris. The same Harris who had interrogated Jennings. The anger boiled inside. All the time he was questioning Jennings he had known the true story.

Chapter Sixteen

The sun's radiance made little dancing specks of light on the wave tops. They looked like a living painting of fireflies against the dazzling turquoise of the ocean. The cabin cruiser rose and fell gently on the swell.

Lin Chow donned the heavy aqualung and weight belt. He turned to the man at the helm and asked, "Is this the place?"

"The old wreck is down there, about forty metres. There will be all the fish you could ever wish for." He walked down to Lin Chow and checked the air bottle. "I'll have lunch ready for you in one hour, okay?"

Chow nodded his agreement, donned his flippers and mask and dropped over the side.

Scuba diving was like heroin to Lin Chow. From the first time he had dived with the fish as one of them he had been hooked. As he swam gently down to where an old ship lay wrecked he saw that the undersea creatures were slowly converting the hulk into a desirable residence. Men's follies often become the assets of other creatures. Coral was starting to decorate the rusty hull. There was a huge gash down the side of the dead ship. Along the gash flourished hundreds of sea anemones. As the water washed in and out of the wound, their tentacles undulated, capturing the plankton carried on the surges of water.

He swam down to the ship and entered through the cleft. As he moved past the anemones they seemed to clutch at the water he was pushing aside. Inside, the hull seemed jammed with every type of fish of which one could conceive. Colours unimaginable on land danced in front of his eyes. He stopped to let the elixir of the sea wash into his mind. With such beauty, colour and movement to see, the mind could only be crystal-clear. All his senses seemed enhanced.

Lin Chow floated, letting his eyes wander from side to side as his brain absorbed the spectacle nature had provided. It was as though he were detached from his earthly form and had become a soul living its eternity in the heaven of its imagination. The parade of colours, shapes and graceful movement flowed in a pageant around him. He was no longer a man in a clumsy aqualung but part of the graceful ballet that now surrounded him.

Without warning, his throat became constricted. Something strong and merciless had him in its grip. He struggled as his dream turned into a nightmare. He felt himself being dragged backwards, all the time feeling his head being held in a vice-like grip. Now he was not breathing oxygen but water. The mouthpiece that sustained him now attacked him with the bile of salt water, which flooded his lungs and tore at his chest. In a trance he saw his wife, his children and his home. He revisited all the places he had ever been. Then he was floating down to this place and knew that only blackness would follow.

Three hours later a diver from the Bermuda marine patrol found the bloated body of Lin Chow inside the wreck at the bottom of the calm blue sea. The hose from the aqualung had been torn apart on the jagged edge of the fatally wounded ship and he had been entangled in the debris of the ship's last calamitous struggle.

Chapter Seventeen

12th November 1972

To: Central Control

From: Hong Kong Centre

Subject: Richard John Sutcliffe

I have received advice from the sub-unit in Bermuda that the potential line of communication or enquiry raised by the above with Allan William Jennings no longer exists. Please advise if you still wish to continue grade 1 surveillance.

14th November 1972

To: Hong Kong Centre

From: Control

Subject: Richard John Sutcliffe

It is now considered that all known lines of communication have been eliminated. Surveillance may now be terminated.

Chapter Eighteen

Jennings's days in Hong Kong were both successful and rewarding. A good number of the clients promised to leave the business in his hands and each night was spent in the soft embrace of Pansie. They had become part of each other. In four nights they had spent a lifetime together. As their bodies entwined their minds also melded. Each knew what the other was thinking. Each knew when and how to please their partner and that was both their wish. The days apart were purgatory but at night they became one. Neither had ever experienced feelings as impassioned as those they now felt for each other.

Two days before he was due to leave for Singapore Jennings was called by Sutcliffe.

"I'm beginning to think that you or I are some sort of hex, Allan."

"What do you mean, hex?" Jennings's voice was relaxed and happy.

"If you read *The China Times*, on page seven, there is a report of a tragic diving accident in Bermuda."

"So what? They happen all the time."

"The thing is, Allan," Sutcliffe's voice betrayed his fear, "the person killed in this accident was none other than Lin Chow. It would seem that whenever I find someone who may have information about your patrol they end up dead before we can talk to them."

Jennings caught his breath. His mind started racing with other possibilities. Was Pansie in danger? Could he protect her?

"I need to think about this, Richard. Let's meet for lunch tomorrow and we can talk."

The next day they met in a small bar on Kowloon. The place was throbbing with Chinese. Jennings and Sutcliffe were the only Europeans in the place. They ran through the events of the past. Jennings's father had been about to make a lot of noise about the patrol and then had died in a hit-and-run accident. Lee Kim had been traced and then blown up before they could talk to him, and now a diving accident had blocked another line of enquiry.

"Someone is going to a lot of trouble to stop you asking awkward questions. The thing is, who is it?"

Jennings could offer no answer. He thought of telling Sutcliffe about Pansie's past but discarded the thought, as the fewer people who knew the better. There was no way that their pasts could be connected, he hoped.

"I think that now is the time to put an end to the whole bloody thing." Jennings's voice reflected the worries now chasing around in his mind. "If we carry on, it can only end in trouble for either you or me." Jennings knew, in his heart, that it was not the end but he wanted Sutcliffe out of jeopardy. In a short time he had grown to like and respect him.

"I think that it would be best for all." Sutcliffe nodded gravely in agreement.

The two shook hands and went their ways.

That night Jennings and Pansie made love fiercely. Jennings held her tenaciously, trying to drive away the nagging thought that she could be lost if the wrong people knew her past. Pansie responded, knowing that tonight was their last night together. She wanted him to fill her with enough love to last her until they could be together again. As her orgasm exploded she pulled him to her with all the strength she had left. She screamed, "I love you! I love you!" until there was no breath left.

They lay in each other's arms, neither wanting to let the other go. If there were a heaven, they were both there at that moment. They slept, both still in the embrace of lovemaking.

Jennings awoke to the sound of the shower in the bathroom. He saw the outline of Pansie's perfectly formed body swaying gently as the soothing projectiles of water massaged her soft skin. He opened the shower door and entered. They held each other while the warm water coursed down their bodies. They made love, gently at first, then becoming more and more frantic as the beautiful pain rose, slowly at first, and then quickening to a starburst of satisfaction. At that moment they both knew that their destiny was to be with each other for life.

Pansie wore the white towelling robe as they sat over breakfast. As she leaned forward to pour more coffee Jennings could see her firm, smooth breasts. He smiled and said, "Do you want me to miss my flight?"

"If you want to," she pouted. "I could suggest something better to do than watch a boring film on a plane."

"If only I could," he sighed.

The shrill ring of the telephone interrupted the moment. Jennings answered and was told his car was ready. He took her in his arms and they kissed long and sweetly.

As he waved from the Mercedes his heart sank. He knew they would see each other again but felt only the pain of separation. The drive to the airport was surprisingly quick. For some reason the permanent embolism of traffic which clogged the veins of Hong Kong was missing that day. As Jennings checked in his mood became more morose. Did he need to do this? He was rich. Why did he bother to work? He could turn about and spend the rest of his life making love with this exquisite lady with the eyes of a goddess.

He made his way to the club lounge and poured himself a beer. He was settled in a corner watching the smoke from his JPS spiral upwards when a voice behind him bellowed, "You look as though you wish you were somewhere else." The ample bulk of Peter Huber towered above Jennings. "I hear that you've been fucking my underwriter, you randy bastard." This statement was delivered with a huge smile and the customary blow to Jennings's back.

"Piss off, Peter! Some day I'm going to marry that woman." Jennings surprised himself with that declaration.

"Well, you had better come and live out here. I'm not losing my best underwriter to some bloody London broker. She's too honest to be one of you lot." The dig at brokers was expected and Huber always obliged.

The journey to Singapore was lively, and both Jennings and Huber had their share of pain-relieving alcohol. They arrived at Singapore Airport in what could be described as a jovial mood. Each had a car to meet them at the airport. Huber was staying at the Oriental, and Jennings at Raffles.

"The British always stop at Raffles. The trouble with you bloody Swiss is that your only history is about mountain goats and shooting apples off people's heads with a bow and arrow. We used to own most of the world and this bit we ruled from the long bar in Raffles." Jennings's brief history lecture was clearly hooch-based.

The two went their separate ways, having arranged to meet in the Long Bar later that evening.

The Somerset Maugham suite, which Jennings had reserved, was little changed from his last visit. The suite was one long room with party walls separating the lounge, bedroom and bathroom. The suite, from lounge to bathroom, was longer than a cricket pitch. The lounge was furnished with wicker furniture. Probably the only change since before the war was the introduction of air-conditioning and the minibar. The bedroom was simply furnished with a six-foot bed, two easy chairs, and small bedside cabinets on which porcelain lamps stood. In the bathroom was an old-fashioned cast-iron bath that was big enough for even a man of Jennings's six foot three inches to stretch out in comfort. As he looked at the huge bath the thought of sharing it with Pansie leaped into his mind.

Jennings showered and changed into a cool silk shirt. He picked up the telephone and dialled a Hong Kong number. Pansie answered before the second ring. It was only hours since they had been in each other's arms yet it seemed a lifetime. Jennings told her of meeting Huber and she told him of the teasing she had received when Huber knew of their feelings. They chatted for a while about something and nothing, just enjoying the sound of the other's voice.

Finally Jennings could not hold back his fears and asked, "Does anyone else know of your background with the PFP?"

"Only Lee Kim, and he is now dead. Why do you ask?"

"What you told me about the ambush is something I have been trying to find out myself. A man in Hong Kong has been making enquiries on my behalf. He found Lee Kim and later Lin Chow, but before I could speak to either they were both dead. I don't want the same to happen to you."

She knew from the edge in his voice that his fear was genuine. She had covered her past well before she arrived in Singapore. The past of Pansie Lam was documented in full. Lee Kim had made sure that her new identity would stand up to scrutiny. Her old self had disappeared completely, other than in her memory. She told Jennings that he should not worry.

"I *do* worry, because I love you." Again he surprised himself. He had often told women he loved them but never had he meant it. His heart ached for her.

"I will be careful, Allan. Now you go and get drunk with Peter, and I will go to bed and dream of your body."

Huber was already settled in the Long Bar underneath one of the ceiling fans. The installation of air-conditioning had not reached this area of the hotel. He was nursing a Singapore sling in his hand. Another stood on the table awaiting the arrival of Jennings.

The two talked and drank for some time before deciding that food should also be a part of the evening's entertainment. The restaurant was air-conditioned and served by a small bar which also had the cooling benefit of modern technology. The food was served in dainty translucent porcelain dishes. Each dish complemented the others. Huber let Jennings have the full benefit of his knowledge of the local market, both reinsurance and black. They finished their meal and sat contentedly sipping Courvoisier and smoking Havana cigars.

"How did you come to know Pansie?" The question was delivered as a conversation piece not a serious enquiry.

"Interesting girl – and bloody gorgeous, you randy sod." The smooth cognac had put Huber in a mood of calmed ease. "It was David Howie, who ran this territory before me, who found her. She was born in Chinatown here in Singapore."

Jennings's mind filled with a picture of Chinatown: hundreds of narrow streets with open sewers running down one side; each street jammed with stalls which all seemed to have been designed by Heath Robinson. You could buy a copy of virtually every consumer product made anywhere in the world there. The story was that the reason many companies were so vehement about trying to ban these copies was that the copies were better quality than the originals.

"She was lucky. She had a fantastic brain and got a scholarship out of that dump. She went to a British-run school and then to university in Kuala Lumpa, where she got an honours degree in maths. She then got a job with the state insurance company here, which is where David met her. He liked what he saw and persuaded her to join us."

"You say she went to university in Kuala Lumpa?"

"That's right, Allan. I've seen the degree, and very impressive it is. What's more important – is she a good fuck?"

Jennings ignored the jibe. What was more significant to him was that Pansie did seem to have a new life unconnected with the PFP.

The two men had a few more Courvoisiers and decided to retire hurt and sleep off a long day. Huber insisted on riding in a *tuk-tuk* back to his hotel. He mounted the small cabin at the back and nearly overturned the whole contraption when he involuntarily tried to exit from the opposite side to which he had made his entrance. He eventually collapsed back into the less than ample seat and roared, "Tally ho to the Oriental," to the driver. The rickety machine disappeared, oscillating from side to side as Huber lurched about yelling directions to the driver.

Jennings's schedule in Singapore was very full. Every day he had appointments from ten in the morning through to dinner in the evening. Even with such a tight programme, he still made time to telephone Pansie each day. As each day passed, his worries for her safety diminished. After three exhausting but successful days he found himself in the first-class cabin of the Qantas flight to Perth.

The Sheraton in Perth was much as would be expected. It was efficient, comfortable, and impersonal. The basic aim of most major hotel chains seemed, to Jennings, to be to process customers rather than accommodate guests.

Jennings telephoned his secretary in London to find out what had been happening on the home front. They chatted for half an hour about the trip and how successful or not it had been. As an afterthought Jennings asked her to find an enquiry agent. He gave her the basic details of Captain Harris and told her that he wanted to trace his current whereabouts. He gave her a story about Harris being an old friend with whom he had lost touch and now wanted to trace. Her tone of voice made it clear that she did not believe his story but as a good secretary she would do the job anyway.

After a fitful night's sleep Jennings was wakened by the insistent knocking on his door by the room service waiter. One of life's small luxuries is breakfast in bed. This is a fact well known to all hotel proprietors throughout the world. In order to ensure that such a luxury can only ever be enjoyed in your own or someone else's home, all hotels adopt the same methods. Firstly the room service waiter will bang the door loudly to ensure that the guest has to get out of bed and open the door. If the guest is very obdurate, then plan two is put into action. If the door is not answered by the time the breakfast has gone cold, the waiter will use his pass key to gain entrance. The guest will be waiting patiently in bed, relishing the thought of eating breakfast without moving. The waiter will eye the room and select a surface as far away from the bed as possible on which to place the breakfast tray, thus ensuring that the guest must leave the bed if he wishes to eat. This hotel was no different. Jennings opened the door and the tray was deposited in his room.

After food and a shower Jennings felt a little more human. He telephoned Pansie. They chatted for half an hour about something and nothing. When he replaced the receiver he felt lonelier than he had ever felt.

His first day in Perth was free until the evening when he was to have dinner with the general manager of the state insurance company. He walked into the centre of the city and spent a couple of hours browsing round the shops. On a whim he went into a large jewellers.

The Argyle mine in Western Australia is the only diamond mine in the world where pink diamonds are found. As such diamonds are very rare, they are also extremely expensive. If you want to purchase such a diamond, then the best place is Perth.

Jennings went through the jeweller's stock of pinks using an eyeglass to look for the tell-tale black spots of carbon. The colours of the pinks varied considerably, from nearly white with a hint of pink to a light ruby colour. The darker the diamond the more imperfections were apparent under the glass. These occlusions, which cannot be seen by the naked eye, affect the reflective power of the stone. The more small faults the less the light can travel through. A brilliant cut diamond will reflect the same light many times as it bounces off faces which are cut to complement each other. The purist will say, quite correctly, that the only perfect diamond is pure white. This is true since colour is a defect, but to see a pink with hardly a flaw is to see sunlight turn to fire.

Jennings spent two hours entranced by the beauty of the stones, which had been accentuated by the skill of the cutter. He would have liked to buy several, but Pansie, he hoped, would wear a diamond solitaire on her wedding finger. He eventually selected a beautiful salmon-pink stone which was just over half a carat. He gave the delighted jeweller a cheque for eleven thousand dollars.

The remainder of the trip was both busy and successful. Jennings had an affinity with the Australians and their country. They, in their turn, took to his easy manner and apparent and growing knowledge of the business and the market.

By the time he reached the Four Seasons Hotel in Toronto he had retained eighty per cent of the business which could have been lost to the fat man. He thought it fortuitous that he had outperformed their expectations, as his accumulated telephone bills were slightly excessive. He had called Hong Kong at least once a day and often more. His love for his Chinese Venus grew day by day.

Chapter Nineteen

A letter from Jennings's office was delivered by courier on his second day in Toronto. He had returned to the Four Seasons extremely tired and somewhat tetchy. He had just spent several hours in a client's office, which was both smoke- and alcohol-free. In his room he threw the unopened envelope on the table and poured a beer. He was savouring the drink and the flavour of his first JPS for some hours when he opened the missive from home.

> *Dear Allan,*
>   *As you requested I contacted Mr Bob Searle, who is a private detective the company has used several times in the past.*
>   *I enclose a copy of his report which has just been sent to me.*
>
>   *Yours sincerely*
>   *Mary Cantor*

Jennings thought of Mary Cantor, the secretary he had inherited from the fat man. She was aged somewhere between twenty-five and fifty, slim with mousy brown hair and very large spectacles. She was also incredibly efficient and organised both the office and her boss with equal vigour. He smiled at the thought of Mary desperately wanting to know the real reason why Jennings wanted the information requested but being much too professional to even consider asking.

Jennings tossed the covering letter on the table and read the brief report attached.

Dear Ms Cantor,

Re: Captain Harris

I thank you for your instructions relating to the above. I have been able to trace the above relatively easily through certain connections I have in the MoD.

Captain Harris was invalided out of the army just over a year ago on health grounds. He was found to be suffering from cancer of the prostate gland, which required surgical removal. Unfortunately for the captain, the removal of the prostate was too late to stop the spread of the disease. He underwent radiation treatment and it was thought that the cancer had gone into remission. It has, I am afraid, returned, and it is now thought that his illness is terminal. He is currently living in Faversham in Kent with his wife, and his address and telephone number are shown on the attached.

I have visited Faversham and kept observation of the subject for three days. He receives a visit from the district nurse twice daily. I learned from that nurse that he is incapacitated and has to be cleaned up and turned. He is not expected to survive more than another few months at most.

Yours sincerely

Bob Searle

Jennings's heart sank as he read the last sentence. Every time he opened a new door fate or someone else seemed to close it. How could he force the true story from a dying man? Was God now conspiring to stop him?

He threw the report on the table, picked up the telephone, dialled the travel agent and told him to organise a flight home the next day. He then telephoned both the clients he was due to see in New York and gave them a very plausible reason for being unable to see them. Then he packed his bags.

Dinner that evening was particularly difficult. The president of the non-smoking teetotal company who had tortured him that afternoon turned out to be someone who could represent Scotland in a scotch-drinking contest and who had a cigar permanently dangling from his mouth. His other main attributes were that he was both opinionated and boring. Jennings, with much fortitude, managed to survive the evening without pushing the scotch-soaked cigar down the man's throat.

Back in his room he telephoned Pansie. Sometimes a person does not need a conversational partner but simply an ear to listen. Pansie realised that Jennings wanted only to pour out all the pent-up emotions which had built up inside him. She listened for an hour, occasionally making suitable noises to show that she was still there. Finally she said, "Allan, you must do what you have to but be very careful because I love you too much to lose you."

Jennings was jolted out of his self-inflicted bout of melancholy. "I love you too. I want to spend the rest of my life with you."

Chapter Twenty

It was early on a crisp November day. The sky was clear blue and the marmalade sun was low and bright. Jennings turned the Jaguar off the A2 towards the town centre. Faversham was an old Kentish port. Even though the river was now heavily silted, there was still a boatyard where small vessels and sailing barges were repaired. Near the creek was the Shepherd Neame Brewery. They boasted of being the oldest independent brewers in the country.

Jennings stopped and asked directions to Harris's home. The house was on a small estate set on a hill to the north of the town. There were neat rows of detached and semi-detached houses and bungalows. All the gardens were neat and well-groomed, with the exception of one, which Jennings guessed, correctly, to be the Harris residence. The lawn was more moss and clover than grass and the plants in the borders, once so lovingly tended, had grown spindly and weak. Jennings thought this little house would have been the happy home for Harris at the end of his career. Now it was only a stopping-off point on his way to the terminal ward.

He sat in the Jaguar trying to plan what he would say when the glass-panelled door opened. Would it be Harris or his wife he would talk to? Would he call Harris a liar? Could he look at this man and keep the embers of his anger in check or would they burst into raging flame? He thought of starting the car and driving off, but he knew he could not. He got out of the car, slowly walked to the door and rang the bell.

Mrs Harris was a petite woman with auburn hair just starting to grey at the sides. She was dressed in a wrap-around kilt and mohair jumper. Her eyes were pale blue, almost grey, and lines of worry extended in a triangle from each eye towards her greying hair. In her youth she must have been beautiful, but recent anxiety had clearly taken its toll.

"Can I help you?" she asked politely. Her voice sounded irresolute, as though she expected bad news.

"Is Captain Harris in?" was all Jennings could manage.

"I'm afraid he is not. Can I give him a message?"

"It is important that I speak to him. My name is Jennings." He began reaching into his pocket for a business card.

Mrs Harris paled when Jennings gave his name. She looked from side to side, as though she were being watched, and whispered, "Are you the Sergeant Jennings that my husband knew?"

Jennings was puzzled by both her reaction and the question but answered, "I presume so, unless there was more than one Sergeant Jennings."

She grabbed his arm and pulled him into the house, slamming the door behind him. She motioned him to a door on the left of the hall. It was a small but comfortably furnished lounge. A log fire was flickering brightly and the air was filled with the sweet smell of burning cherry wood. She indicated a chair and Jennings sat.

"I'm sorry - I must have a few minutes to pull myself together. Let me make you some tea."

Without waiting for either assent or dissent she turned and what is best described as scampered to the kitchen. Jennings heard the sounds of a kettle being filled and crockery being prepared.

Five minutes later Mrs Harris reappeared with a tray of tea and biscuits. Most of her colour had now returned and the hands carrying the tray were steady. She asked his preferences on milk and sugar. The biscuits were offered and accepted with the tea, and finally she sat. For what seemed an age she stared at the steaming tea in her hand as though she were plucking up courage to do something. She sipped the steaming brew and looked up at Jennings.

"My husband must have done you a great disservice, Mr Jennings."

Jennings was taken aback by the bluntness and unexpectedness of the enquiry and simply nodded his head.

"I do not know what wrong my husband has done to you but I do know he wants to put it right."

"It can never be put right." Jennings was choosing his words carefully. "But it would ease my hurt if I knew why certain things happened."

"Mr Jennings, have you time to let me tell you what I know?"

Jennings nodded acquiescence.

"My husband is dying of cancer. We have known this definitely for some six months. When he was told that his condition was terminal, he began to get very agitated about you. He told me he had wronged you and wanted to put things right with you. He was becoming more and more upset about this, so I decided I had to do something about it. I contacted his former senior officer, Colonel Herne, to ask if he knew anything about you. His reaction was, to say the least, odd. He told me that my husband was suffering from some form of delusion and that I should ignore it. When I told him I could not forget as it was affecting my husband's health, he promised to make enquiries. Two days later I was visited by a rather nasty-looking young man who told me that I must not try to find you as you were some sort of homicidal maniac. He also told me that if I tried to contact you, both myself and my husband would be breaching the Official Secrets Act and that we would be prosecuted and punished. I have done nothing since as I was too frightened.

"My husband is now in the local hospice and will die soon. When he is coherent enough, through the pain and the painkillers, he is becoming more and more disturbed about setting matters right with you. I wish I knew what happened between you and my husband so that I could help him, but it seems that only you can do that. Mr Jennings, will you see my husband and help him die with his mind at peace?"

Jennings looked at this unhappy lonely soul and remembered his father, who had watched his young wife slowly die of leukaemia. He had only been six at the time but now he remembered the lost expression in the brigadier's eyes. He saw the same look across that small cosy lounge. Instinctively he crossed the room and took her hand, saying, "Of course I will, Mrs Harris."

She sobbed uncontrollably on his shoulder.

*

The room in the hospice had no windows. The only light came from a small bulb in the ceiling. The sides of the bed were raised to stop the patient falling as he tossed and turned, trying to escape the pain that racked his body and grew stronger every second. Painkillers were administered every four hours but their effect lasted a few minutes less each time. Harris was still in bed, numbed by the tablets of peace he had received less than an hour ago. His breathing was even but it was easy to hear the insidious invasion of his lungs by the fluids that would eventually kill him. His small pointed beard was now white and wispy. His face was gaunt and sallow. His arms were scrawny and his fingers like broken matchsticks.

Soon the drugs the nurses fed him every four hours would not be enough. A morphine pump would be attached to his chest then. Every hour the machine would exhale, like a lover blowing a kiss, and a shot of morphine would mix with his blood, rush to the centre of the pain and extinguish it. The pain would be gone and Harris would be in the limbo between life and death. He would float there while his lungs slowly filled with the bile of death. Just before his demise he would become lucid. His eyes would open and he would see the room which was his last domicile on this earth. He would look for his loved ones and touch them to wish them farewell. Then there would be nothing left for him in his earthly form and he would abandon it.

This would come soon, but for the moment Harris was still fighting the uneven battle he was bound to lose.

Mrs Harris sat by the bed, holding her husband's hand and quietly sobbing while Jennings stood uncomfortably just inside the door.

It seemed as if hours passed but it was only thirty minutes later when Harris slowly opened his eyes. He squeezed his wife's hand with whatever strength he could muster and forced a smile to his lips. He whispered something that Jennings could not hear. She smiled, turned towards Jennings and whispered back. Harris's body stiffened and he pressed his lips to her ear and said something. Mrs Harris stood, crossed the room to Jennings and said, "He wants to speak to you alone. I will go and get a cup of coffee."

Jennings sat by the bed and looked at the shell of the man he had hated but now for whom he felt only pity. He rummaged in his pocket and found the ON switch of his portable Dictaphone.

"Have you heard of COBRA?" Harris whispered. Jennings shook his head. "It is a group of people with influence in all fields, who say their aim is to make our country great again. They say politicians have dragged the country to the brink of humiliation and should be stopped. They have influence all over the world where Britain is represented."

Jennings wondered whether this was the ramblings of a drug-affected brain but nodded and waited for Harris to continue.

"I was recruited to COBRA several years ago by Colonel Herne. He was my link to the council. We were told that if your group were ambushed, there would be great political gain for a leading member of the council and the influence of COBRA would be increased enormously. It could be the first step to political control of the country, control for the benefit of the people not the politicians. I believed them and helped to deliver you into an ambush. When you escaped we had to discredit you, so we falsified the evidence with the help of the PFP. Oh God, please forgive me – I was so wrong. All they want is power for their own good. They threatened to kill my wife if I spoke out."

"Who is supposed to be on this council?" Jennings was still sceptical.

"I only know the council member who recruited me and that was Colonel Herne. There are twelve council members, each in control of a separate group who know only that council member. We were briefed on the activities of each group by our co-ordinating council member. It was better for security to organise that way."

"What do you know about the council members?" Jennings was beginning to feel that perhaps this was not as far-fetched as he had first thought.

"All I know is that they come from the military, the secret service, the diplomatic service and industry, and I believe there is also one politician. That politician's career benefited directly from the end to the war with the PFP."

Jennings's mind raced. This tied in with Pansie's comments about saving face before making peace. He looked Harris in the eye, saying, "This is just a story – I have to have proof."

"I cannot give you proof. You will have to find that yourself, but I can tell you that the accident to your father was not an accident – it was arranged by COBRA. Please stop them before their influence is too strong." Harris lay back in bed and started coughing as the pain returned to the attack.

Jennings pressed the CALL button for a nurse as the sick man's hacking became uncontrollable. The nurse bustled in and gently turned Harris on to his side. Slowly his breathing returned to normal, except for the wheezing in his lungs.

"Come tomorrow," Harris croaked. "I will tell you all I know."

Jennings nodded although it seemed as if he were nodding at unseeing eyes.

That night Jennings stopped in a small pub in the town. The place was friendly and comfortable. He played dominoes in the bar with some of the regulars, managing to hold his own and only losing a few pence.

That night the dream which had haunted him for years was back and even more vivid. All night his father and his comrades were crying out for help. No matter how Jennings tried he could not reach them. The smell of burning flesh and cordite invaded his senses. He felt his hands burning as he reached into the flames, but he could not reach them, he could not help.

He woke in the morning bathed in sweat. The bedclothes were dishevelled and damp and the pillows beaten shapeless by his frenzy.

A shower and breakfast helped him feel more human but a depression sat on his shoulders like a monkey on his back. He knew that from today he could no longer push the past back into the depths of his subconscious. He could not pretend that he had only suspicions: now he had confirmation of them.

He arrived at the hospice just before noon. Harris's wife was in reception attacking the coffee machine. The mind in turmoil will make the body take vengeance on any inanimate object that fails in its duty. This machine had failed to give a cup and the coffee had been lost. She beat the unfeeling panels of the machine, screaming, "Where's my coffee!"

Jennings took her by the shoulders and finally she lost the self-control she had shown to the world for so long. The distraught woman broke down and sobbed unrestrainedly on his chest. Her weeping eventually subsided into short gasps of pain.

She looked up at Jennings and burst out, "I'm sorry! He relapsed overnight! He's dead! He's dead!"

Jennings had never heard anyone scream in a whisper before. He comforted her until a nurse, obviously used to the tragedy of death, took her to see her husband's body.

Jennings sat in the small reception area, his thoughts spinning out of control. Once more an avenue of information had been blocked by fate. He looked up when Mrs Harris returned. She seemed to be in control of her emotions. It is often said that a few silent minutes with the deceased, touching the hands and the face of a loved one for the last time, are better therapy for the grieving than hours of counselling.

"Might I ask you one favour?" Her voice was controlled yet gentle.

Jennings nodded and said, "Of course, anything."

"Will you take me home and stay with me until my sister arrives? She should only be an hour or so."

Jennings parked the Jaguar on the drive and followed her into the neat semi-detached. He sat where Mrs Harris pointed and listened to her bustling in the kitchen with coffee-making equipment.

The coffee was brought in Royal Doulton porcelain mugs with a choice of biscuits to accompany it. Jennings mused on the British and how biscuits and a hot drink seemed to be the cure for all ailments of the soul.

"My husband wanted to tell you more. Last night he told me to make sure you were coming in the morning. He was quite lucid until the last injection."

The words 'last injection' slammed into Jennings's thoughts. Had Harris merely died or was this another unacceptable coincidence?

"The new doctor was very kind. He sat with me for an hour, and then John started to have convulsions. He passed away soon after that."

Jennings could not trust himself to speak. A new doctor, followed by convulsions, was an eventuality beyond his acceptance of chance. His mind raced trying to find the correct question to ask. He had to know more but could not inflict additional pain on someone already overburdened with anguish. As the thoughts scattered about his mind in no semblance of order, she came to his rescue without realising it.

"Thank God there will not have to be a post-mortem. I could not stand for him to be cut up. Dr Clarke said it was not needed and there was no necessity for me to suffer the pain of it. He told me that John's heart could not take the strain any more. He was very kind."

She sat quietly for a while stifling an occasional sob by drowning it in coffee. Jennings said nothing. He knew that all she wanted was to sit and think but not be alone. Then the red-eyed woman seemed to start from a daze and looked at Jennings.

"I don't know if I can tell you anything that will help you, but if you want to ask anything I will try to answer."

"This is not the time or place for me to trouble you," Jennings replied gently. "I would only ask for one thing – the address of Colonel Herne."

"Of course." Mrs Harris attempted a smile and reached into her handbag. She took out a gold-embossed address book, opened it and passed it to him.

Jennings copied the address and telephone number into his Lloyds diary and returned the book to her.

They sat for another hour, sometimes talking sometimes not, until a large middle-aged lady bustled in through the door and began to take charge. A hot water bottle was produced from nowhere and Mrs Harris was relocated to the bedroom complete with sleeping tablet and hot milk. Jennings was thanked and dispatched to his car and away. This lady knew that grief should be properly organised.

Chapter Twenty-One

CLASSIFIED

26th November 1972

To: Central Control

From: Colonel Herne

Subject: Allan William Jennings

    I was advised that on the 24th November Harris was visited in hospital by the above. As Harris was a potential information leak I put a plumbing operation into immediate effect. I have no information on the conversation between Harris and the above but took the decision to eliminate any risk.

    It is now a serious possibility that Jennings has a source of information unknown to us, and a full scrutiny should be made of all his connections.

    I would like a report on the investigations within the next two weeks.

Chapter Twenty-Two

Jennings's return to the office was met with the annual chaos which besets the reinsurance business. Nearly all the contracts placed expire on the 31st December each year. This means that a renewal of each have to be negotiated with the underwriters. The last two months of each year sees brokers frantically scampering around the market seeking quotations. These then have to be sold to the client, who always thinks that he is the only person in the world who should be offered better terms. The Far East accounts are even worse because of the insatiable desire of the Chinese to negotiate before acceptance. When agreement is reached, the client then expects immediate confirmation of cover even though only one or two of possibly forty underwriters have been seen.

There were three telex machines in Jennings's offices, which chattered away day and night transmitting offers and receiving counter offers and, hopefully, acceptances. Jennings had daily meetings at eight each morning with his team of brokers, who would update him on the progress and problems encountered. Following these meetings there would be a get-together of the directors, over coffee, to determine any needed changes in strategy. Often one particular underwriter would decide to become unpredictable and decisions had to be made to deal with his eccentricity. Sometime the chairman or deputy chairman would be dispatched into the fray to use his perceived importance to lean on the recalcitrant underwriter.

By ten o'clock Jennings was normally back in his own office to scan the *Lloyds List*, *The Times*, and other periodicals which rained into his in-tray. He was paging through *The Times* when an item in the obituary column caught his eye. Harris was to be buried the next Monday at St Catherine's Church in Faversham at eleven o'clock. Jennings knew that he had to be there and see who attended the funeral. The renewal season would have to do without him for one morning.

St Catherine's Church was a sturdy, flint-faced building with the statutory bell tower pointing skywards. The church and graveyard were between the railway and a small cul-de-sac of detached and semi-detached houses. The houses faced a small orchard.

Jennings had borrowed Ellen's Mini since he needed to be inconspicuous and the Jaguar did not fit that classification. His Nikon lay on the passenger seat beside him. Jennings parked where he had a clear view of the entrance to the church and churchyard and waited.

The first mourners to arrive were Mrs Harris and Colonel Herne. The chauffeur-driven Rolls glided to the entrance and stopped. As they alighted, Jennings could see them clearly through the long lens of the Nikon. As more people arrived the camera whirred, recording the faces of each. He noticed that certain of the attendees seemed more interested in the surroundings than the church. These had to be security. To the untrained these men seemed to be a part of the general proceedings, but Jennings could see their alertness. They were big men but light of foot and quick of mind. Jennings counted five such men. The mourners started to file into the small church. Jennings had what he had come for in the two rolls of film now lying in the glove compartment of the Mini. He started the car and drove quietly away.

That night he developed and printed enlargements of his morning's work. Some faces seemed familiar but the only name he could put to anyone was Colonel Herne. He put the photographs and negatives in a large brown manila envelope. He opened his father's safe and placed the envelope inside.

As he was closing the door he noticed a metallic glint at the back of the safe. He reached in and felt his hand close around the butt of his father's Luger. It was a souvenir taken from a Panzer officer who had surrendered his squadron to his father in Normandy in 1944. The weapon was still in perfect condition. The brigadier had cleaned it every week of his life. Next to where the pistol had lain was a box of 35mm ammunition.

It was illegal for Sir Charles Jennings to keep the unlicensed weapon, but every time he had stripped and oiled this beautifully made engine of destruction he remembered how just two Churchill tanks had completely outmanoeuvred a Panzer squadron, leaving them trapped directly under the guns of the Churchills. Jennings smiled affectionately as he remembered his father recounting the story while he polished the Luger with a soft cloth. The story had always finished with the same line: "You don't have to outnumber them, just out-think the bastards." Jennings knew he was outnumbered, so out-thinking would have to be performed. He put his father's memories back in the safe, turned the key and spun the combination dial.

He poured two fingers of Glenfiddich, sat in the leather chair at his father's desk and closed his eyes. His mind meandered but kept returning to the soft alluring goddess who was so far away in Hong Kong. Eventually he picked up the phone and dialled. The sound of her voice was like balm to an aching limb. He closed his eyes and could see her lips pouting as she reproached him for not phoning for three days. They talked for half an hour, each enjoying the sound of the other's voice.

"I will be in London at the end of January. Do you know a good hotel?" Her voice was laughing at him.

"I know a first-class place in Surrey, but you will have to share your room with a retired soldier."

"As long as he doesn't have a large knife and tie me up" – Pansie was now giggling like a teenager embarking on her first date – "or, at least, leave me tied up and disappear into the urban jungle."

Jennings replaced the receiver feeling better. His mind was clearer and he knew that in January she would be his for ever.

The human mind has an extraordinary ability to refocus on a subject which has been relegated, temporarily, to the filing system at the outer perimeters of thought. A name or a solution to a problem will suddenly appear. Just such a thought leaped into Jennings's consciousness. He picked up his father's address book and thumbed through the names. He dialled a London number.

"Pinter speaking."

"Uncle George, it's Allan here. How are you? Haven't seen you for ages."

"That's because you haven't phoned me. I presume you either want a favour or you're in some sort of trouble. What can I do for you, Allan?"

"Don't be such a suspicious old fart. I just thought I would like to buy you some lunch as I'm now working in the City."

They arranged to meet in El Vino, in Fleet Street, two days later. Pinter's parting shot was to remind Jennings that he particularly favoured one hundred year old Courvoisier with his coffee.

After consuming one of Ellen McDonald's superb dinners Jennings could not settle down. He tried reading some papers from the office but could not raise the required concentration. The television seemed to offer only soap operas and repeats of not very funny comedy shows. He eventually gave up the unequal fight with his restlessness and telephoned Jack Martin. He would alleviate this problem by exchanging inconsequential stories in The Haycutter.

The usual crowd was sitting at the usual stations around the U-shaped bar. The banter between the originals and the newcomers had already started. Tony Hacker was sitting in the neutral area nursing a pint. He was genuinely pleased to see Jennings, clasping his hand and slapping him across the shoulder.

"Penny gone out then?" Jennings enquired.

"Another charity meeting," replied Hacker. "Women are funny creatures. She was going out to find ways to pay for holidays for deprived kids but had to wear all her best gear. I bet their meetings are like a bloody fashion show."

"The committee is all women, I suppose," said Jennings. Hacker nodded. "What else do you expect then?"

They both laughed. They had seen the amount of clothes required by the lady members at the golf club. One outfit to travel to the club, another to play in and a third in which to have afternoon tea.

They sat and chatted happily for an hour. They had not seen each other for two months, and Jennings bored Hacker with every minute detail of Hong Kong in general and Pansie Lam in particular. His eyes shone with pleasure as he described her in detail, even down to the small beauty spot on her shoulder.

"I can see you are smitten, but it's a bloody mole not a beauty spot," Hacker laughed and ordered some more beer.

"By the way, have you seen Jim Cross lately?"

"Not since we saw him in here," replied Jennings. "Why?"

"He phoned me and said he would be in here tonight. I wondered if he had phoned you."

Cross arrived soon after nine. He appeared full of himself. He had that morning completed a deal which, so he said, would make him thirty thousand pounds.

The three of them sat and swapped stories. Hacker chided Jennings when he repeated his fulsome description of Pansie for the benefit of Cross.

"If this lovesick prat goes on about her any more, I'm going to go into a bloody trance," Hacker announced, as the mole became a beauty spot for the second time.

"Go on! He's in love, so he's allowed to bore us bloody silly for one night," Cross rejoined.

The evening flew by. Since they last met, Hacker had transferred to the Metropolitan Police Special Branch and Cross had set up two new companies. The three talked easily about themselves and listened, with genuine pleasure, to the successes of the others.

At closing time Hacker said good night and tottered in the direction of his home, and Cross went back for a nightcap with Jennings. They chatted until two in the morning, by which time it had been decided that it would be more sensible for Cross to stay the night.

Conversation over breakfast was stilted. Both men's brains were still trying to re-establish a viable connection with the outside world. Cross asked whether Jennings had seen Sutcliffe and Jennings related the story of Lin Chow.

"So you've given up on that bloody stupid idea of being the new Hercules Poirot?" Cross said absently.

"I haven't really got any choice. There is no bugger left to ask," Jennings hoped his matter-of-fact answer would end the conversation.

"Bloody good job. I don't like the idea of a friend of mine leaving a trail of dead bodies around the world."

Chapter Twenty-Three

George Pinter was sitting at his usual table in the corner of El Vino. He was a striking-looking man of six foot, with shaggy white hair and a neat white waxed moustache. In between and in contrast to these were bushy brown eyebrows. The waxed moustache was his particular eccentricity. During the war he had spent most of his time in Yugoslavia organising the Resistance. He would explain that only the British waxed their moustaches and after having had to look like a bloody Slav for four years he was most certainly going to look British for the rest of his life. He wore a tweed jacket and cavalry twills. The jacket and trousers were bespoke, made by Gieves & Hawkes. On the table was an ice bucket which was gently chilling a bottle of 1968 Puligny Montrachet. A Sobranie black Russian cigarette burned in the ashtray.

George Pinter had loved the life of operating underground in the war. When it ended, much to his disgust as he was enjoying himself, he had attempted several alternative careers. He had tried the intelligence services but found them to be riddled with intellectuals and 'poofters'. A foray into the City was an abysmal failure. "I haven't got a plum in my mouth and I have got a bloody chin, so I'm wrong on both counts" was his dismissal of City expertise. Finally journalism had discovered him.

He was working on a local paper when an old friend from Special Operations had told him of a potentially juicy little scandal in MI5. Pinter had followed up the tale and ended up with a nice story, which had elements of both sex and spying. As he was skint at the time he had sold the story to the national newspaper which had offered him the most money and a permanent job. He had been *The Record*'s specialist in security matters ever since. He probably knew more about the operation of the security services than either the heads of MI5 or MI6. He certainly knew substantially more than any prime minister. Many of his stories had been stopped by D-notices, but

Pinter had them stored away for the future. The book he was planning would explode a few dearly cherished myths.

As people entered the bar most nodded a greeting to Pinter. The younger ones were in awe of this legend of Fleet Street.

"Good afternoon, Mr Pinter," they said effusively, hoping that some of Pinter's Midas touch would transfer itself to them.

The ones of Pinter's generation offered a simple, "Afternoon, George."

Pinter's thoughts were miles away, remembering his young days with Charles Jennings and the times the two of them and their wives had enjoyed together. He was suddenly dragged back to the present when the chair opposite him was pulled out and an empty wine glass deposited on the table.

"Must be a bloody good story if it's worth a bottle of that stuff."

David Sacher had been with Pinter in the Special Operations Executive. He had been called to the Bar after the war and was now the head of a large chambers in Essex Court. He had the well-earned reputation of being one of the finest civil law advocates in the world. It had been said that his mind was sharp enough to cut diamonds. He was trim and not very tall. His gold-rimmed spectacles glinted in the dimly lit bar. His hair had thinned rapidly, probably due to his being bewigged for most of his working life.

During the war Sacher had been the controller for all the operatives in Yugoslavia. He had been responsible for Pinter meeting his wife. Special Operations insisted that each operative should make radio contact with the same radio operator in England. By insisting on this the radio operator could often spot if the operative had been taken and the messages being received were not his own. They were so skilled that they could hear the difference if the Morse key were used by another person. After the war Pinter insisted that he meet the hand which had operated the Morse key at the other end of his transmissions. Sacher had arranged the meeting.

Gwen was a pert, bouncy, Welsh redhead. In Pinter's eyes she had the body of a Greek goddess and the face of a film star. He had fallen in love five minutes after meeting her. They had now been married for twenty-six years.

Pinter poured Sacher a glass of wine and replied, "No story. I'm meeting Charles's son here for lunch. He's paying and he must be as rich as you are so he can afford it."

"Oh, you poor old downtrodden hack, how is the Bentley running?"

"Piss off. You know that is my only extravagance." Pinter smiled as his old friend savoured the oak flavour of the Montrachet.

"You two are not still at each other's throats, are you?" Jennings had arrived without either of the two old friends noticing.

"Allan, good to see you." Pinter was genuinely pleased to see Jennings even though the young sod had started to beat him at tennis when he was thirteen.

The three shook hands and exchanged pleasantries. Sacher made as if to leave, but Jennings stopped him.

"I do have something serious to discuss with Uncle George, but I would like your thoughts as well if you have the time."

'To have free access to an intellect such as Sacher is an opportunity not to be missed,' thought Jennings.

"Well, if you keep buying the 1968 Montrachet—"

"Don't forget the 1865 Courvoisier with the coffee," interjected Pinter.

"And the 1865 Courvoisier", Sacher repeated, "you have my undivided attention for the afternoon."

While Sacher telephoned his chambers to cancel the afternoon's appointments, Jennings and Pinter caught up with each other's news.

Sacher returned and the three ordered lunch and another bottle. Jennings stuck to beer as he knew that both his guests were legendary in their ability to consume a good wine.

The three had all ordered game pie with game chips and salad, which arrived in plentiful portions, with a basket of freshly-made French bread. Over lunch they chatted about what each was doing and how they were doing it. Most of the time Jennings listened, delighting at both the humour and wisdom of his companions.

"Better off acting for the insurance companies, not against them. If you act for them, they never query your fees, win or lose. If you are against them and win, they will have the tax office on your neck before you even ask for the bloody costs." Sacher's views on the moral fibre of Jennings's chosen profession were slightly biased.

"What else do you expect from a load of chinless prats in ill-fitting three-piece suits?" was Pinter's contribution.

The coffee and Courvoisier arrived just as the third bottle of Montrachet had given its last. El Vino had emptied. There were a few hardened drinkers left. In one corner two columnists, having finished their weekly contribution to the well-being of the nation, were discussing an inconsequential topic in great detail. At the other end of the bar a couple of barristers, presumably with no briefs on which to exercise their expensive time, were ordering another bottle of the house claret. The bar staff were collecting the remains of the food and the dregs of drink left at the tables.

"Well, you haven't spent a fortune on food and drink to find out about my social life. What's your problem?" Pinter, although a journalist, was not a verbose man.

"What do you know about COBRA?"

"They are bloody great snakes with big heads that can do you a very nasty damage." Pinter decided to be obtuse until he knew the facts.

"Not snakes, you old fart! It is supposed to be some sort of secret organisation, possibly connected with MI5 or MI6."

"That's a blast from the past, don't you think, David?"

Sacher nodded his head in agreement. He was no longer relaxed, now alert. "What is *your* interest, Allan?" Sacher's voice had taken on a gravity totally in contrast with the jollity of a minute earlier.

"You tell me what you know and then I'll tell you a story if I need to," Jennings answered cautiously.

"The first time I came across that name was during the Atlee Government after the war." Pinter spoke quietly as though he had no wish to be overheard. "It was said that this group within the security services had their own agenda, which did not coincide with much of the Labour Government's policies. It was rumoured that if certain members of the Labour Party ever became cabinet ministers, they would take action. They were supposed to be trenchantly anti-communist but, if the stories I heard were right, they were vehemently pro their own interests.

"After the Churchill Government was elected in '51 the rumours disappeared. The stories did start again quite soon after Wilson became prime minister. It was rumoured that certain ministers were actually under surveillance, although if they were it would have been a private operation rather than official. At the time it was thought that the whole thing was just gossip trying to revive an old dead story."

"I am not so sure it *was* just gossip," Sacher interrupted. "It was said, in the Temple, that not only were the security services involved but there were, allegedly at least, sympathisers among the senior judiciary and the Bar. It was the Wilson Government, not Atlee's, when I first heard it."

"Well, we've told you about an old rumour, now you had better tell us where you got the name from and why you want to know more." Pinter's journalist's nose was beginning to smell a story.

Jennings ordered more coffee and brandy and started to relate the tale from the beginning. He was reminded of his meeting with Stuart Rittle by the interruptions and probing questions he received from both men. He told the whole story, the exception being that he made no reference to Pansie or her involvement. He said that he looked for Harris simply on a hunch.

Sacher chided him, "Absolute bollocks, old boy. You had a better reason than that, but if you prefer not to tell us it is of no matter."

Jennings recounted his meeting with Mrs Harris and the subsequent encounter with Harris. He took out the pocket Dictaphone he had concealed in his pocket when he spoke to Harris, placed it on the table and clicked the PLAY button.

"*Have you heard of COBRA? It is a group of people with influence in all fields who say their aim is to make our country great again. They say politicians have dragged the country to the brink of humiliation and should be stopped. They have influence all over the world where Britain is represented.*"

Harris's voice sounded metallic and unreal.

"*I was recruited to COBRA several years ago by Colonel Herne. He was my link to the council. We were told that if your group were ambushed there would be great political gain for a leading member of the council and the influence of COBRA would be increased enormously. It could be the first step to political control of the country, control for the benefit of the people not the politicians. I believed them and helped to deliver you into an ambush. When you escaped we had to discredit you, so we falsified the evidence with the help of the PFP. Oh God, please forgive me – I was so wrong. All they want is power for their own good. They threatened to kill my wife if I spoke out.*"

"Who is supposed to be on the council?" Jennings hardly recognised his own voice.

"*I only know the council member who recruited me, and that was Colonel Herne. There are twelve council members, each in control of a separate group who know only that council member. We were briefed on the activities of each group by our co-ordinating council member. It was better for security to organise that way."*

"What do you know about the council members?"

"All I know is that they come from the military, the secret service, the diplomatic service and industry, and I believe there is also one politician. That politician's career benefited directly from the end to the war with the PFP."

"This is just a story – I have to have proof."

"I cannot give you proof. You will have to find that yourself, but I can tell you that the accident to your father was not an accident – it was arranged by COBRA."

Pinter pressed the REWIND button and replayed the last sentence, muttering, "Bastards."

Harris's wheezing voice continued, *"Please stop them before their influence is too strong... Come tomorrow. I will tell you all I know."*

They replayed the tape several times. Pinter became more angry each time there was a reference to Charles Jennings's death. Sacher just listened with his head cocked to one side. Jennings wondered why barristers always seemed to do this. He concluded that as they only wanted to hear one side of the story they would only offer one ear to listen.

"I have spent many years listening to evidence and then cross-examining witnesses to find flaws in that evidence. After all these years I pride myself on being able to tell whether I am being told the truth or a lie from the tone of the voice and the manner of speaking. That man was not lying," Sacher stated resolutely.

"I went back the next day to see Harris," Jennings continued, "but overnight Harris had been seen by a doctor not known to Mrs Harris. Soon after that, Harris suffered a seizure and died."

"Is this the only hard evidence you have?" Pinter was holding the tape and beginning to sound like a barrister.

"Yes, with the exception of these." Jennings produced an envelope holding a set of prints taken at the funeral. "In there are pictures of all the people attending Harris's funeral."

Pinter took the enlarged photographs from the envelope and began to thumb through them. He passed each in turn to Sacher. As he studied them, Pinter occasionally clicked his teeth and frowned.

Sacher, as would be expected of a barrister of his standing, remained totally inscrutable.

They studied the likenesses captured by the Nikon for fifteen minutes. Pinter then collected them into a neat bundle and returned them to the envelope.

"Well, David, I see two from MI5, one from MI6, a deputy commissioner of the Met Police, and the head of Army Intelligence."

It appeared as though Jennings would be an observer in this conversation rather than a participant.

"I recognise a vice-president of the Law Society, chairman of the Bar Association, the chief executive of a major bank, and, to top it all, a senior appeal court judge." Sacher was nodding his head gravely, reminding Jennings of Badger being informed of the latest escapade of Mr Toad. "This seems to be a rather high-powered group of people. Why should they be at the funeral of a lowly retired army captain?"

"I honestly think that Allan has stumbled on to something very sinister here." Pinter spoke quietly. "The ones I know make Genghis Khan look like a moderate."

"I would put the others in the same bracket," Sacher said in reply.

Pinter turned to Jennings and asked, "Is this the only set of these you have?"

"They're for you, Uncle George, and the tape. I have the negatives and the original tape at home."

"Make another set of both and deposit them somewhere safe. If Harris was telling the truth and these people know these things exist, they will want them, probably at any cost."

Pinter warmed his brandy in the palm of his hand, watching the amber liquid cling to the bowl of the glass.

"David, I think that you and I should make up a little dossier on each of the people we know in those photographs. Let's see what connections we can find between them, if any."

He dropped the tape into the envelope, sealed it and put it into the worn leather briefcase that sat by his chair like a well-trained dog.

The three had one more coffee and accompaniments and chatted some more about old times. The conversation was a little stilted because all had the contents of Pinter's briefcase foremost in their thoughts. When they finally parted, both Pinter and Sacher told Jennings that he would be in touch, soon.

Chapter Twenty-Four

CLASSIFIED

12th December 1972

From: Central Control

To: Colonel Herne

Subject: Allan William Jennings

It has been brought to our attention that the above met with George Pinter and another (now ascertained to be David Sacher QC) two days ago. A bundle of papers which looked to be photographs and a cassette tape were given by the above to Pinter.

It is known that the three above are long-time acquaintances and this meeting may be purely coincidental, but in view of current investigations we felt you should be kept informed.

Please also find attached a communication received from Hong Kong Centre.

CLASSIFIED

10th December 1972

To: Central Control

From: Hong Kong Centre

Subject: Allan William Jennings

We have examined the background of all connections in our territory. We believe that the source of information may be a Pansie Lam. We have investigated her background. The records at Kuala Lumpa University show certain inconsistencies which indicate that they may be created rather than actual.

In 1969 Lee Kim had a female lieutenant operating in the same sector as Jennings's patrol. This female appears to have disappeared from the face of the earth. We have obtained a detailed description of this female. This description fits Pansie Lam. It is our belief that both females are, in fact, one person.

We await your instructions on further action.

CLASSIFIED

14th December 1972

To: Central Control

From: Colonel Herne

Subject: Allan William Jennings and associates

Please institute the following procedures:

Allan William Jennings	– maintain current operational status
George Pinter	– continue current surveillance
David Sacher	– institute Grade 4 surveillance
Pansie Lam	– advise London immediately of all movements

If it is felt that any further action is required it should be instituted immediately. *Prior approval by myself is not a necessity.*

Chapter Twenty-Five

The next three weeks were a confusion of reinsurance renewals and parties. During the day Jennings and his team were chasing around the market trying to complete all the business before the year's end. Most evenings and many lunchtimes there were cocktail parties to attend. Christmas was coming and had to celebrated for at least three weeks prior to the actual day. It seemed, to Jennings, that the reinsurance business was designed to create the maximum stress by arranging that the busiest time of the year also coincided with the occurrence of the most social events.

The week before Christmas Jennings attended yet another cocktail party in the Captain's Room in Lloyds. As usual, several bars had been set up around the room. Jennings took a beer and scanned the room to see if there was someone who had not been at the previous seven parties in the last week. He saw all the same familiar faces around the room. Corby was talking to a tall man with fair hair. Jennings did not recognise the shock of blond hair and decided to join them in the hope of hearing some new conversation.

"Hello, Allan." Corby looked up as Jennings crossed the room. "Let me introduce you. Allan Jennings – Cameron Carter." Corby waved his hand between them. "Cameron is one of the deputy chairmen of Lloyds. In fact, he is the youngest ever to be elected."

"Should I genuflect or curtsy?" Jennings smiled.

"A subservient bow will do," Carter laughed as the market-style banter was exchanged. "I've heard quite a lot about you."

Jennings was unable to see whether the last comment was repartee or not. He studied Carter. Somewhere in the recesses of his mind a memory was stored and this face was trying to nudge it out. They chatted for a few minutes and then parted to go and have the same conversation with someone else. As Carter turned, Jennings suddenly knew where he had seen that face.

Ellen was sitting in the drawing room nursing her nightly cup of cocoa when Jennings arrived. She chastised him for being late and ruining his meal. He knew that supper was always something which would not spoil and smiled.

"I still have some papers to go through, so I'll have my supper in the study. See you in the morning." He smiled at Ellen and made for the kitchen to collect the sustenance. Jennings took the tray through to the study and placed it on the leather-topped desk. The Luger glinted as the safe door swung open. He touched it lightly and then removed the manila envelope and placed it on the table beside the tray. He took a swig of beer and opened the envelope. Slowly he thumbed through the photographs. The blond mane appeared in several. One, in particular, caused Jennings to clench his fists in anger. Carter, his arms around Herne, was greeting the butcher like a long-lost friend. Jennings stared at the picture, his anger growing and his hate of these people gnawing at his insides like a malignant cancer.

He picked up the phone and dialled.

"Pinter speaking."

"Uncle George, it's Allan. I've managed to identify another of the bastards at Harris's funeral. His name's Cameron Carter. He's deputy chairman of Lloyds and chairman of one of the biggest broking firms."

"That's interesting. It seems that we have a nice selection from the security services, the judiciary and the Bar, military intelligence and commerce. The only professions missing seem to be politics and industry. David and I have got all but four of the players, and with your man that leaves three." Pinter knew that whatever information they had was not enough to expose the real intentions of the players. "Look, Allan, forget about all this for now and enjoy the festivities. We're still invited to your place for Christmas Day, I presume?"

"Of course you are. It wouldn't be Christmas without you." Jennings replaced the receiver. The photographs were returned to the envelope and locked in the safe.

That night Jennings dreamt. It was not the dream which usually tortured him, but a dream of vengeance. Herne was crying for help through the yellow flames that licked around him and Jennings could only laugh.

Chapter Twenty-Six

Christmas is a time for rest, recuperation and enjoyment. It was a brief two-day respite from the lunacies of reinsurance renewals for Jennings. He left his last pre-Christmas party about four in the afternoon on Christmas Eve. London Bridge was awash with the remains of parties and the people attending them. This was a good evening to own a taxi company. There was a great deal of money to be made returning commuters from the station where they woke up to the station where they should have alighted.

Jim Cross had arrived about an hour before Jennings got home. Ellen had made him comfortable with supplies of mince pies and other Christmas goodies.

Jennings was looking forward to the break. He had no immediate family and neither had Cross. Ellen McDonald would mother them and ensure they ate too much, and they would each ensure that the other drank too much. For the previous two months Ellen had gently questioned Jennings to find out about any particular family rituals. She had found that home-made pickles were a vital necessity, as was the consumption of honey roast ham, with eggs, on Christmas morning. Fortunately they were not attending midnight mass. When Jennings had told her that midnight mass was always followed by sherry and Christmas pudding, Ellen had considered this to be a ritual punishment.

The house smelled of Christmas. The pork and turkey had been part-roasted ready to be completed the next morning. The aroma of freshly baked mince pies wafted through the lounge. The cherry logs glowed in the grate, occasionally spitting as a knot surrendered to the flames. The bouquet of cherry wood burning is, to some, superior to that of a fine wine. The Christmas tree lights sparkled and the small glass ornaments on the tree reflected dancing patterns on the wall as they tinkled together in the movement of air. Under the tree was a pile of presents all wrapped in brightly coloured paper and decorated with bows and ribbons.

The two friends sat in easy chairs and chatted amiably about matters of no consequence to anyone but themselves. They talked about Colchester Prison. The memory has the ability to forget the worst of things past, or, if not to forget, to make the memory amusing not painful. They laughed about Sergeant-Major Bonner when the true memory should have made them cry. Jennings told anecdotes about solitary and the so-called exercise he had taken. The pain of the punishment had gone but the futility remained. The absurdity of a grown man running around a small yard with a sandbag held above his head had the two of them crying with laughter.

Ellen came in to offer more sustenance, and Jennings insisted that she join them.

"I'm not a drinker but a wee Glenfiddich won't do any harm," she said coyly.

They chatted about Scottish Christmases, Irish Christmases and Christmas anywhere in the world one or other had been. Ellen made it clear that Christmas came a poor second to Hogmanay but she would try extra hard for the poor Sassenachs. The poor Sassenachs expressed their thanks with another wee Glenfiddich. The doorbell rang.

"Go on now, that's Jack to take you down the pub."

The Haycutter was already buzzing with festive spirit when they arrived. Hacker was sitting at one of the tables in the corner with two pints opposite the empty seats he had saved for Jennings and Cross. Streamers were beginning to fly across the bar and the decorations were starting to sag under their weight as they hung like coloured icicles. Occasionally there was a small outbreak of fire as a dangling streamer made contact with one of the candles decorating each table. Such events seemed to make the celebrating throng more cheerful.

"I've arranged for Jim and myself to go riding on Boxing Day morning. Why don't you come with us, Tony?" Jennings asked the question with a wink, knowing that Hacker's last attempt at equestrianism had been less than comfortable.

Cross expressed surprise at this news. Whilst he could ride, he had not done so for some years.

"Don't worry, they will find you an old plodder. A good gallop across the bridleway through to Old Oxted and back will blow all the cobwebs away."

Cross still appeared dubious and his confidence was further dented by Hacker.

"You go and enjoy yourself, Jim. Last time he put me on his definition of an old plodder the bastard ran away with me and dumped me in the old pound."

"Best place for you," Jennings chuckled. "You ride like a medieval serf. That pound was probably built to impound your ancestors' cattle for bad debts."

"Jim, just make sure you walk in front of him if he's riding Sheba. She'll kick anything in sight if she gets half the chance." Hacker was now enjoying Cross's obvious discomfort.

The subject changed, leaving Cross to ponder his destiny.

Penny, Hacker's wife, arrived. She had completed all the last-minute tasks, with the exception of depositing Christmas stockings in the children's room while they were asleep.

This was Hacker's job, as Father Christmas had to be of the male gender. This particular tradition must have resulted, over the years, in many children growing up thinking that Father Christmas stinks of alcohol and always stubs his toe on the bed.

Jennings put his arm around Penny and kissed her on the cheek. As always, she blushed deeply. She still remembered that, whilst it was Hacker she married, it was to Jennings that she had surrendered her virginity.

Hacker knew this and always pretended not to notice her embarrassment. He went to the bar and returned with a glass of Irish Mist, which he set in front of Penny.

The subject moved to who was doing what for the holidays. Penny seemed proud of how her husband had made his way in life. He had been born on a council estate but was now an inspector in the Metropolitan Police and one of the youngest ever. She told them, her voice showing obvious delight, that they had been invited to cocktails at the home of the deputy commissioner on New Year's Day.

"Leonard King is one of the nicest people you could ever meet," she told them with discernible pride. "I know he takes a special interest in Tony's career."

Hacker was beginning to feel abashed at the demonstration of wifely pride. He knew that Jennings was the cause of the demonstration of endearment. He decided that it was time for Father Christmas to trip over the bed, shout, "Fuck it" and deliver the Christmas stockings.

As the Hackers left, the picture of Leonard King, taken at Harris's funeral, was clear in Jennings's mind.

Chapter Twenty-Seven

Christmas is a time to revert to childhood, a time to indulge the whims of that part of the mind which stopped developing at about the age of ten. The brightly-coloured wrapping paper has to be ripped from the presents, and the assortment of socks, shirts and other uninteresting objects has to be met with a whoop of delight followed by a lengthy speech of humble gratitude.

In order to fully enter into the world of the pre-teens an adult needs some assistance.

Two bottles of Bollinger nestled in ice buckets awaiting the coming of George Pinter. It was another family tradition of the Jennings household to await the appearance of Uncle George, at which time the presents could be assaulted. As a child the time between wakefulness and Uncle George's arrival seemed an eternity. In fact it was no more than two or three hours.

Pinter and his diminutive wife Gwen appeared, as usual, on the dot of nine o'clock. There was a great exchange of greetings and much hand-shaking and kissing; the latter was aimed only at the tiny figure of Gwen.

More presents were piled under the festive tree ready for the ritual assault on their decorative exteriors. The champagne was opened and Merry Christmases were fulsomely exchanged. Ellen joined them from the kitchen where breakfast was now ready, apart from the final touches. Cross was put in charge of the distribution of the goodies and had to make sure that all received a present so there could be a simultaneous opening, followed by simultaneous whoops and thanks.

The ritual of gift unwrapping was immediately followed by the ceremonial opening of the second bottle of Bollinger. This had to be opened and consumed before breakfast could be taken. Christmas breakfast was always identical. The honey roast ham was complemented by warm boiled eggs and home-made tomato chutney. Outsiders who had been with the Jenningses at Christmas for the first time often expressed surprise at this mixture so early but then always proceeded to ask for second helpings.

The rest of the morning was spent playing with presents which could be played with, looking at presents which should be looked at and attempting to avoid trying on the socks and shirts no one ever wears but always buys as presents.

Just after noon it was time to cajole Gwen into taking the male members of the party to The Haycutter where more festive greetings could be exchanged. Ellen put up some small resistance but eventually agreed to join the party at play.

The Haycutter was buzzing with people, some showing off new products and others skulking in corners, having to wear some dreadful piece of apparel given to them by one of their guests. "You must wear it down the pub, it looks lovely on you" is one of the most distressing statements to be confronted with over the Christmas holiday.

On their return to the house Ellen made for the kitchen to start cooking the vegetables, closely followed by Gwen. Jennings, Cross and Pinter decided to test out the stack of Shepherd Neame bitter sitting in the utility room.

After a sumptuous lunch everyone settled down in the lounge and the board games were produced. Cross played Monopoly in the style of a Rachmanesque landlord, his acquisition of houses and hotels finally forcing all the other players into ignominious insolvency. Scrabble was the perfect game for Pinter as the written word was his living. There were a few skirmishes in the direction of the dictionary, particularly when he produced the word '*Swadeshi*'. He won the game by as many points as Surrey usually lose by runs.

Finally, everyone but Ellen and Gwen ran out of steam and gently nodded off. The two ladies made for the kitchen and the kettle.

In the evening Pinter went out to his car and returned with a large manila folder. He passed it to Jennings, saying, "This is what Stuart and I know about the guests at your Captain Harris's funeral. There's a separate sheet for each of the ones we know, with as much information as we have. I have a copy, as does David. I suggest that you read it and also let us have what you know about your Lloyds man. We can talk in the New Year."

Cross saw and listened to the exchange but made no comment.

Boxing Day morning was crisp and clear. The sun shone brightly in the sky and the trees glistened with the overnight frost. Jennings and Cross were up early. Jennings had lent Cross his father's jodhpurs and riding boots. The spare hat needed a little padding but it was now a snug fit. They drove down past Oxted Manor to the stables. Two horses were standing in the yard, a hint of steam rising from their necks. Sheba was a beautiful strawberry roan of just over sixteen hands. The other horse was dappled brown and at least a hand taller. He was a cross and undoubtedly had some Welsh cob in his ancestry. His neck was short and thickset. His shoulders were wide and powerful.

"Good morning, Allan." The stable girl was attractive, with dark brown hair. The jodhpurs showed off her long shapely legs.

"Hello, Mary," Jennings smiled. "Are these for us?" he asked, pointing at the two horses.

She nodded. "I think you had better ride the Major, Allan." She pointed at the big part-cob. "We've got him here to school, so he could be a bit lively for your friend, but you can handle him."

Jennings agreed, a little disappointed as he would have preferred Sheba.

The two friends mounted and walked along the road towards the bridle path. It was only about half a mile to the entrance to the park but Cross had dropped back some thirty yards. Sheba was always lazy walking, but Cross would be in for a surprise on the gallop. In her younger days Sheba had competed at Badminton.

The gallop across the park and back was pure ecstasy. To feel the power of a fit animal slowly accelerating through the trot to the canter and then the full gallop can only be described as unadulterated stimulation. The rider and the horse become one, moving in unison with each other, the rider's hands and legs urging the animal forward.

Cross, who had been somewhat apprehensive, was grinning like a two year old with a bag of toffees. He had forgotten the buzz he used to feel as a child when he had his own pony. His eyes were streaming from the air-buffeting they received as Sheba cut a swathe through the cold still air.

They left the park and turned along Barrow Green Road towards the riding stables.

Jennings saw the Range Rover in the distance before it dipped behind the hedgerow. He took little notice as it seemed to be travelling slowly. He was some thirty yards ahead of Cross when it appeared around the corner. The headlamps were blazing and the hooter was blaring at the animals. The Major reared at this strange animal with huge shining eyes bearing down on him. Jennings managed to keep his seat as the big horse turned to try and escape this apparition. Jennings was fighting the horse, trying to keep its head down and stop it from bolting. He could see down the road to Cross, who had fared less well.

Sheba had leapt to the side, losing Cross out of the side door. He now lay on the road, his legs stretching into the middle. It seemed to Jennings as if the world had suddenly switched into slow motion. He saw Cross lying in the road, and the Range Rover, instead of trying to avoid him, changed direction, aiming directly at Cross.

Jennings heard himself screaming, "Jim, move! For fuck's sake move!"

Cross seemed not to react until the car was upon him. At the last minute he threw himself to one side. Jennings heard the sickening sound of the heavy grill smashing into some or all of Cross's body, throwing him into the grass verge. The Range Rover sped on. Jennings saw that the number plate was masked. A face looked backwards, a familiar face to Jennings.

The Major had calmed down but Jennings could still feel his huge body shivering with fear. He kicked the horse on and cantered to where Cross lay. Sheba had decided that discretion was the better part of valour and bolted in the direction of the stables.

Jennings dismounted. The Major was still skittish. There was a gate a few feet away from Cross and Jennings opened it. He put the horse inside and tied the reins to the gatepost.

Cross was lying, half in a ditch and half in the hedgerow. His left leg had been smashed by the impact of the car's grill. Jennings gently laid him on the grass verge. Cross's face was white with the agony of his shattered leg.

A Land Rover arrived and Mary from the stables tumbled out.

"Go and phone for an ambulance and then get me some towels and bandages." Jennings's tone was calm but authoritative.

Another car arrived and the occupants were disgorged. They began to mill about asking stupid questions and getting in the way.

"Look, go and warn any traffic that there has been an accident. We don't want another car ploughing into us."

The car's occupants scampered off in opposite directions to do his bidding.

Mary returned with bandages and towels. Jennings used one of the towels to immobilise Cross's neck. He used the other towels and the bandages to strap the fractured limb to the good one. Cross winced with pain as the broken bone was straightened and held firmly in place.

The ambulance arrived after what seemed like a lifetime.

"Not much for me to do here," the paramedic muttered as he replaced the towel with a neck brace. "Where did you learn this?" he said, indicating the broken limb but not really requiring an answer.

Cross was lifted gently on to a stretcher and loaded into the ambulance. The siren wailed, as if it were sharing Cross's pain, and disappeared along the road.

Jennings took the Land Rover back to the stables. The Jaguar sat in the yard. Jennings gunned the 4.2 litre engine and followed the ambulance to East Surrey Hospital.

After half an hour a doctor told him that Cross was to be taken to the operating theatre as extensive repairs were needed on both the tibia and fibula. He suggested that Jennings return in the morning because Cross was unlikely to be conscious before then.

Chapter Twenty-Eight

Jennings paced the study. He had telephoned the hospital twice but Cross was still in surgery. His mind was in a turmoil. *He* should have been riding Sheba. Had he been the intended target of the Range Rover? The face he had glimpsed so briefly haunted his brain. He knew the face, but where from? Suddenly it clicked – he had seen that face at Harris's funeral. He opened the safe and pulled out the manila envelope with the photographs inside. He thumbed through the pile of images and suddenly stopped. The face in the car which had tried to kill either him or Cross was staring at him from the photograph. Jennings clenched his fists when he realised that the man was alighting from the same car as Colonel Herne.

Jennings opened the file left by Pinter and thumbed through. Inside was a copy of the photograph now staring at him from his desk. The face was ringed and the number six was written across the face. He found report number six and read it.

Name:	Colin Marden (Wing Commander)
DoB:	14th July 1943
Occupation:	Head of Air Force Intelligence since October 1968. Educated Harrow and Oxford, degree in mathematics. Said to be a high-flyer with ambitions for the very top. Known to be ruthless in pursuit of his own objectives.
Associates:	Has no real close friends with the exception of Colonel Alec Herne, who has the equivalent post in the army.

Jennings closed the file deep in thought. Herne and Marden seemed to be linked. At some time in the future this man would have to be confronted.

Jennings was jolted out of his thoughts by the shrill ring of the telephone. He picked it up and absently gave his number.

"Allan, is that you? Are you all right?" Hacker's voice sounded genuinely concerned. "The local police told me there was an accident and you were involved."

Jennings told him the story, omitting any reference to Wing Commander Marden.

"You mean it was deliberate, not an accident?"

"I know it was," replied Jennings, "and I think that *I* was the target not Cross. I would normally be riding Sheba."

"Do you want to talk about it? I can come up if you want."

"Thanks, Tony, but not tonight. I'll see you in The Haycutter tomorrow night, if that's okay with you."

Hacker confirmed and the conversation ended.

Jennings returned to the notes left by Pinter. He browsed through the potted details of each without really absorbing the information until a name sprang from the pages at him. The document read:

Name:	Lord Justice William Appleby
DoB:	14th July 1907
Occupation:	Master of the Rolls – Court of Appeal
Associates:	Stuart Rittle (his most successful pupil)

Jennings's brain did not want to accept what his eyes were telling him. Stuart Rittle was his father's oldest friend. Was he one of these so-called COBRAS? Had Rittle arranged his father's death?

He stared numbly at the paper in front of him. What web of intrigue was he becoming enmeshed in? He wondered whom he could trust. Would he have to confront Rittle at some time hoping that his suspicions were unfounded?

He closed the file and returned it and the photographs to the safe.

Jennings was feeling desperately alone and needed a friendly voice to speak with. He dialled the well-remembered number in Hong Kong. Just the sound of her voice was enough to bring him out of his melancholy mood. They spoke for an hour about nothing in particular. He wanted to hold Pansie in his arms. He wished he could swim in the deep greeny-brown pools that were her eyes. His whole being ached with love. It was still three weeks before she came to London – an eternity to wait.

He went into the utility room and poured himself a beer. His mind was trying to analyse what was happening and why. Some bits of the puzzle fitted but not many. He picked up the telephone and dialled Pinter's number.

"Uncle George, it's Allan. We must have a talk."

"What's the problem, my boy? Has something happened?"

Jennings related the details of Cross's injury and the involvement of Marden, his uneasiness about Rittle's connection with one of the players and how he might be connected with his father's death. There was a short silence from the handset when he finished. He could almost hear Pinter analysing the information he had been given.

"David and I may have made some progress. We may have found a connection between the suspects at the funeral. We will come down on Saturday for a round table. In the meantime don't do anything. okay?" Pinter's tone was concerned.

The next morning Jennings went to the hospital and found Cross in a surprisingly jovial mood. His colour had returned and he peered over the hump in the bed where his shattered leg lay.

"Well, I survived the horse but had a bit of trouble with the car."

"I don't know what you find so funny. That bastard was trying to kill you," Jennings reproached him.

"I think that he was probably trying to kill *you* not me, actually. He just got the wrong one."

Jennings nodded. "I think you may be right. I know who one of them was, and it's connected with my past not yours."

"Well, tell the bloody police and get the bastard put away!" Cross snapped.

Jennings wondered whether the angry reaction was real. He was beginning not to trust anyone. His own response angered him.

"There is a lot more to this than you realise, Jim." Jennings was trying to keep his voice unruffled and to control the anger that now constantly simmered just below the surface. "I have to find out a lot more before I can do anything. Just trust me."

Cross nodded, somewhat unconvinced.

*

Hacker was perched on a stool at the end of the bar. He smiled when Jennings joined him and ordered another round.

"How is Jim?"

Jennings told him about plates and screws and other repairs which had been made.

"How did it happen?" Hacker enquired.

Jennings stated the facts as he had seen them. How the Land Rover, its lights blazing and the horn blaring, had seemed to aim itself at Cross; also the fact that the number plate was masked.

"I presume you have told the local police all this." Inspector Hacker was now in 'plod mode'.

"No, I haven't. I've told them it was a hit and run, and that's all. This has got something to do with my father's death, and I am going to find out what."

Hacker recognised the stubbornness in Jennings's voice which had been there since they were children. He knew there was no point in arguing. He had known Jennings long enough to know that he was not getting the whole story, but in time he would.

Chapter Twenty-Nine

Pinter and Sacher arrived just before lunchtime on Saturday. Conversation over lunch was stilted, as though all knew what should be discussed, but the meal table was not the place. Ellen had excelled herself. The pheasant was roasted slightly crisp on the outside but tender and juicy inside. The game chips were home-made and the broccoli perfectly cooked. The Chardonnay complemented the game perfectly. After lunch Ellen took the coffee into the lounge. The crystal brandy bowls were set out on the cabinet along with the liqueurs. Pinter poured the coffee while Jennings attended to the production of one cognac and two Armagnacs. The three settled into the easy chairs and sat quietly savouring the ambience of being well fed and at ease with life.

Eventually Pinter stood and retrieved his briefcase from the corner of the room. He produced a file of papers and placed it on his lap. He glanced at Sacher and said, "Stop me if you think I am going wrong please, David.

"Allan, both David and I think that we may have stumbled on to something much bigger than we could have imagined. We have now identified most of the major people in those photographs, and I can tell you that it is a very impressive list of luminaries. I suggest you read this." He handed Jennings a single sheet of paper.

ATTENDEES AT FUNERAL OF CPT HARRIS

A) Security and Law Enforcement:
    i)   Controller of MI5
    ii)   Controller (Eastern Europe) of MI5
    iii) Controller of MI6
    iv) Commander of Army Intelligence
    v)   Commander of Air Force Intelligence

       vi)   Deputy Commissioner of the Metropolitan Police
- B) Law and Judiciary:
  - i) Master of the Rolls
  - ii) Chairman of the Bar Association
  - iii) Vice-President of the Law Society
- C) Commerce and Industry:
  - i) Chief Executive of Martin's Bank
  - ii) Deputy Chairman of Lloyds of London
  - iii) MD of Inter Electric
  - iv) Chairman of Porterfield Industries

"That is an awful lot of high-powered people to be attending the funeral of a mere captain in Army Intelligence. It looks more like a list of mourners for a cabinet minister."

Jennings nodded in agreement.

"Both David and I", continued Pinter, "are convinced that there is something in this story of COBRA. If past rumours of this organisation are true, these are the type of people who could carry out whatever aims they have. They cover law enforcement, security, espionage and counterespionage, the law and its operation, supply of money, industry and commerce. The only obvious area missing is politics, but it is very possible that whoever is involved in politics for COBRA did not attend the funeral."

"That's all very well, but what in hell are the objectives of these people? What do they need that they don't have already?" Jennings probably knew the answer to his own question, but wanted to hear it from someone else.

"That's simple, Allan – they have power but they all want more," Sacher interjected. "What worries me is in what way they will exercise that power."

Pinter continued. "David and I have been trying to find some connection between all of these people. Having tried the obvious, to no avail, we started looking at the more cryptic possibilities. We now think that we have found the connection and that it also links into the political end." Pinter indicated to Sacher to carry on the narration.

"As you would guess," Sacher began, "we started looking at political views, common associates and acquaintances, schools and the like. This came up with a dead end. We then tried to see if there was any similarity in locations, where they were born, where they lived or their family had lived. That search came up with nothing. In desperation we tried clubs or associations and got a connection. First, all of them are members of the Combined Universities' Club. That gives us a connection with Oxford and Cambridge. When we looked further, we found out that all, apart from one, are members of the Honourable Artillery Company in City Road."

"But that's a TA unit who fire twenty-five pounders in ceremonies. They can't all be in the TA!" Jennings found it a little hard to envisage the Master of the Rolls breech-loading a twenty-five pounder.

"They have, in their time, been members of the HAC and are all now social members. The HAC, my dear boy, is as much a club as a military unit. We also checked the people, now dead, who were strongly rumoured to have COBRA or similar connections in the past and found that the HAC was common to all."

"You are not trying to tell me that the HAC is a hotbed of revolution and intrigue, are you?" Jennings was incredulous.

Sacher smiled at him as he would a small child.

"Not at all. I believe the HAC *is* the recruiting point. In order to become a simple gunner, you must be proposed and seconded. This means that there is automatic selection of a certain type of person. It is highly unlikely that *I* could join such a unit. I do not have the pedigree. On the other hand, *you* would probably have been welcomed with open arms." Sacher was proud of his poor Jewish upbringing. He considered inherited wealth and power to be anathema. This would not, of course, apply to his own offspring, who would receive the full benefit of Sacher's tax-avoiding skills.

"How does this take us forward, if it's true?" Jennings could not see how this information aided their search for the reason his father had been killed and by who.

"The impatience of youth." Sacher smiled at Pinter. "This boy would never make it at the Bar, George."

Pinter gestured his agreement and continued the tale.

"We believe that what this gives us is the *political* connection. It gives us a good chance to guess what the actual intentions of this group are. We believe that they intend to take power in this country."

"That's preposterous! This is a democratic country. You can only obtain power through the ballot box." Jennings was wondering whether senility had set into the pair of them.

"If you let me carry on, without constant interruptions, you can judge for yourself whether it is preposterous or not," Pinter said gruffly. "The political connection is Marcus Banton."

Jennings whistled through his teeth. Marcus Banton was the youngest member of the cabinet. His rise to the political heights had been spectacular. He had been the former prime minister's *protégé*, first as a whip and then progressing through junior posts at the Foreign Office, finally becoming foreign secretary at the age of forty-six. The new prime minister was less enamoured of young Banton, particularly because of his views on the European Union, and had instantly demoted him to the Welsh Office. It was generally felt that he was only clinging to a Cabinet post by his fingertips and that once the mourning for the deceased prime minister ended so would Banton's career.

"All the men on that list are known to be, in principle, against integration with the other Europeans. So is Banton," Pinter continued. "The prime minister, on the other hand, is pro integration. There is a substantial minority of the party that agree with Banton. He could command a lot of support in a leadership contest. To do that, he must first bring down the PM."

"This is all speculation. How do you connect Banton with COBRA?"

"I'm sorry, Allan, I should have explained. First, Banton is a member of both the Universities' Club and, more importantly, the HAC. He was the junior minister who dealt with the undeclared war in which you were involved. He was the one who got huge political kudos for ending the conflict. He got his promotion on the back of the cessation of hostilities. He was the politician who gained advancement as a result of your patrol being destroyed. The Chinese had to have a victory to take to the table before they would negotiate, and you were it. Do you want any more?"

Jennings shook his head.

"Who is the one who *isn't* a member of the HAC?" Jennings was trying to find a fault in the logic being presented to him.

"I would have thought that it would be obvious, even to you, Allan," Pinter said as a teacher to an errant pupil. "A wing commander in the Royal Air Force is not going to be in the artillery, is he?"

"Allan," interrupted Sacher, "we have identified thirteen people, but we were told by Harris that there are twelve on the so-called council of this organisation. We think that Banton *must* be on the council, which means that we have fourteen. Some of the bodies we have identified may not be the top tier. We have to leave our minds open."

"How the hell do we find out who's who?"

"We observe, we listen, and discreetly we enquire." Pinter, the investigative journalist, had his professional hat firmly on his head.

"I don't have time for that crap!" Jennings snapped. "These people killed my father and I will find out who and why."

They talked for another two hours, with Pinter and Sacher urging Jennings to restrain his emotions. The anger within Jennings grew. He knew in his heart that some or all of these people had murdered, or conspired to murder, the man he had revered. His father had been the rock upon which he had built his life. That rock had been shattered because it was expedient for someone. He knew what had to be done.

Chapter Thirty

4th January 1973

Jennings had left the Jaguar in a car park in the town. Herne's house was two miles from the town, set back from the road in an acre of land. It had not been difficult for a man with Jennings's training to enter the grounds unnoticed. He waited, hidden behind the Helderas vine that cloaked the garage. The Luger sat comfortably in the holster under his arm. His mind was clear and focused.

Herne left the house and walked towards the garage. The control on his key ring was activated and the seven-foot door began to rise. The electric motor whirred like a giant bee in search of nectar. Jennings slipped under the rising door and squatted on the passenger side of the Mercedes. Herne opened the driver's door and eased his ample bulk into the driving seat. Without warning he felt something hard and pointed being pushed into his ribs. He saw the bluey glint of the Luger's barrel.

"Just start the car, reverse out, close the garage door and then go where I tell you."

Even without the reinforcement of the Luger the voice held such menace that Herne would have obeyed anyway. After the initial shock he might have thought of protesting, but Jennings's eyes suppressed the notion. He started the car, the 3.5 litre engine whispering into life, and reversed. He closed the door with his electronic toy, wishing that he had an excuse to leave the car. He was told where to drive and followed the orders to the letter. The Luger still pressed into his ribs. Herne tried to look sideways, but fear determined that he did not. He drove for about a mile and was instructed to turn into a small country lane. The road ran alongside the railway.

Another half a mile and the voice beside him said, "Pull into that lay-by and stop and turn off the lights."

A train rattled by in the cutting some fifty feet below the road. Sparks were thrown out as it drew power from the live rail.

"Switch off the engine and give me the keys." Something hard and thin nudged Herne's ribs.

"Now turn on the inside light and let me look at you, you bastard."

Herne had spent all his post-university life in the army. He should have been a man of moral fortitude. He wasn't. His military career had been spent manipulating, assessing risks and directing other people to take those acceptable risks. He had never faced personal injury or worse. Jennings knew this.

"Colonel Herne, we meet again. Only this time I have orders for *you* to obey."

At first Herne did not recognise Jennings and blustered, "I don't know what the hell you are playing at, but you are in big trouble!"

"Balls!" was Jennings succinct reply.

Slowly recognition dawned in Herne's eyes. As he recalled Jennings's face his subconscious threw in the memories of the doomed patrol and then Brigadier Charles Jennings. Without realising, his eyes registered fear, a fear which not all could see. Jennings had seen this dread in other eyes and other places. Jennings took the car keys and placed them on the dashboard.

"Now, Colonel Herne, I *know* that you sent me into an ambush and I believe that you arranged my father's death. If you want to prove me wrong, please do so."

"I have no idea what you are talking about," said Herne, desperately trying to put up an assured front.

"Colonel Herne, I and my patrol obeyed your specific orders - we were ambushed and should have all been dead. I, unfortunately, did not die. If I had died your strategy would have been perfect, but I didn't. I survived, and to protect your position I had to be disgraced. My father tried to help me and he was killed. Is that a fair summary of the situation?"

"You don't understand. To gain a cessation of the terrorists' activities your patrol had to be sacrificed. It had to be Special Forces to give the Chinese something to gloat about." Herne's mouth was now running ahead of his brain.

"Why was my father killed?"

"He had an accident – it was nothing to do with me."

Jennings's anger was now turning into rage.

"Tell me about COBRA."

For a second, panic registered in Herne's eyes. "What are you talking about? A cobra is a snake," he blustered.

Jennings, for the instant, lost control of his feelings. He swung his arm and the barrel of the Luger smashed into Herne's face. His head jerked backwards and was stopped by the restraint on the seat. Herne clutched at his face and felt the warm blood dripping across his hands. He searched for something to stem the flow. He looked at Jennings's cold eyes and knew real dread for the first time. He knew that this man could kill him. His intestines were knotted as panic invaded his brain. His heart pounded, as if trying to make up for its imminent failure. He felt hysteria invading his logical mind.

Jennings looked at this man, who had been a man to respect, and only saw a pitiful, pusillanimous being. Pity was not on Jennings's agenda.

"Colonel Herne, you will tell me all you know about COBRA now. If you don't, you will never tell anybody anything."

Herne made one last effort at pretending ignorance. "I don't know what you are talking about."

Jennings's hand rose again. Before he could strike, Herne broke.

"Don't, don't..." His voice was now a whimper. "What do you want to know? Just tell me."

"Who killed my father?"

"I don't know - it was left to Marden to arrange."

"Why was my father killed?"

"He knew about COBRA and was threatening to go to the press. Ten years ago we approached him about joining us. Your father was a fool - he could have been one of us, he could have had real power and influence." Herne immediately regretted his bravado as pain shot through his leg from his now shattered patella. "No more - please, no more," he pleaded.

"Stick to the facts and keep your fucking comments to yourself then. Who approached him?"

"I don't know. I think it was someone from the Bar, maybe Appleby."

Jennings could see in his mind's eye the reference to Rittle on Appleby's summary.

"Give me the names of the Council of COBRA."

"I can't do that – they would kill me!" snivelled Herne. He looked into Jennings's cold eyes and knew that he would die if he didn't tell.

He tried to offer some wrong names in the hope that this animal would be satisfied. Pain racked him as the Luger smashed his cheekbone.

"Don't lie to me, Colonel – I just want you to confirm what I already know."

The names tumbled from his swollen lips. Two were new to Jennings, one totally unexpected. These were stored in his memory.

"Thank you, Colonel Herne. That is all I wanted to know."

Herne became bolder. "That information will do you no good. You will be history very soon. We will have the means and the power, then I will repay you with interest. What happened to your pompous overbearing old fool of a father will be nothing compared to what you will suffer."

"What do you mean, you will soon have the means and the power?"

"Within six months COBRA will be making the decisions in this country, and the first one will be to finish you like we did your arrogant father."

Jennings's anger was now erupting and out of control. "You won't be here to see it, you bastard!" He spoke through clenched teeth.

He grabbed Herne by the back of his neck and smashed his face on to the dashboard. Herne flopped, unconscious, over the broken steering wheel.

Jennings calmly assessed the situation. This possibility had been planned for. He removed his tie and then that of Herne, took the keys of the car and walked round to the driver's door. He switched on the ignition and started the car. The engine hummed gently. He pressed the controls and lowered the front and rear windows. The neckties were tied together and looped over the gearshift, the ends over the back seat like silken bell ropes. The gear lever was pulled to neutral. He placed Herne's heel hard on the accelerator and slammed the door. The engine roared as it turned at five thousand revs. Jennings leaned in through the back window, took the ends of the neckties and jerked. The gearshift jumped to drive. The big car accelerated along the verge. The ties sprang through the window into Jennings's hand like a snake striking at a mouse.

Jennings watched impassively as the Mercedes crashed through a fence. Momentarily it seemed to slow. Halfway down the slope it started to roll. The car seemed to increase speed until it crashed, roof first, on to the railway line. Showers of sparks leapt into the air, like a burst from a Catherine wheel, as the car earthed the live rail. There was the initial hint of fire and then an explosion.

Jennings smiled grimly. It was poetic justice that Herne should die in a blazing inferno, as had his father. He wiped the blood from the Luger with Herne's tie and walked away.

He heard the wailing of sirens in the distance as he eased the Jaguar on to the main road. He felt no elation. His father had not been avenged. Now he knew, the game had only just begun.

Chapter Thirty-One

CLASSIFIED

8th January 1973

To: Central Control

From: Hong Kong Centre

Subject: Pansie Lam

I refer to our previous report on this subject. We have now ascertained beyond any doubt that the above is the former associate of Lee Kim. The records shown in both the school and university files are known to be forgeries.

Please advise whether you wish us to take any further action.

10th January 1973

To: All Council Members

From: Central Control

Subject: Wing Commander Colin Marden

At the next meeting of the council, the chairman will formally propose that Wing Commander Marden be elected to the council to replace Colonel Herne and take responsibility for all security matters.

Wing Commander Marden has been immediate deputy to Colonel Herne for the last three years and is clearly in the best position to fill the gap left following Herne's death.

10th January 1973

To: Central Control

From: Colin Marden

Subject: Colonel Herne (deceased)

I have completed my initial investigations into the death of the above. It appears that the inquest will record that the death was accidental and that there were no other parties involved.

It is my opinion that this may not be the true state of affairs. Certain of the injuries suffered by the deceased are not consistent with the accident. Both the nose and the cheekbone suffered fractures. It appears from the angle of the injuries that Herne suffered two blows to the head. To be consistent with the accident, damage would have occurred to the right cheekbone, whereas the actual damage was to the left.

There was also a fracture of the left patella which is incompatible with the angle of fracture of the femur.

Further, it has been ascertained from the remains that the deceased was wearing a suit but no tie. This is inconsistent with his habits.

It is my opinion that there is a probability Herne's death was not accidental. The evidence suggests that he may have been assaulted from the passenger's side of the car before the accident.

I have studied the security files directly under the control of Herne. All people under surveillance could have reason to remove Herne, but there are three who currently seem to be active against the interests of COBRA. These are Jennings, Pinter and Sacher. A summary of their details are attached.

Of these three, Jennings would be the most obvious possibility. He is the only one whose whereabouts was not known at the time of the incident. If he was responsible for the demise of Herne, it may be that has obtained information which may be detrimental to the objectives of COBRA.

I propose that we adopt a safe rather than sorry attitude and terminate the potential leak forthwith.

12th January 1973

To: Colin Marden

From: Central Control

Subject: Allan William Jennings

Your proposal of the 10th January will be put to the council at the next meeting.

Chapter Thirty-Two

The arrivals hall at Heathrow was crowded with people. There were relatives waiting excitedly for the overseas branch of their family to arrive. Chauffeurs stood holding name boards, looking bored beyond redemption. Husbands waited for wives, boyfriends for girlfriends and *vice versa*. Cleaners muttered darkly as litter was scattered. It never appeared in places which had to be cleaned but only where they had already done their chores.

Jennings sat in the coffee bar watching the spiral of smoke from his JPS gently wend its way to the roof. Pansie's flight was delayed for two hours and he was on his fifth cup of dreadful coffee and his second packet of cigarettes.

At last the board showed her flight 'Landed 0732'. Jennings lit another cigarette. It would be another half an hour before passengers were reacquainted with their luggage. Eventually the board flashed 'In Customs Hall' against the British Airways flight from Hong Kong. Jennings walked across the hall to where the passengers would arrive.

Pansie appeared through the automatic doors pushing a trolley loaded with luggage. Jennings's heartbeat quickened as his eyes caressed her from a distance. She was wearing pale green slacks which accentuated her long shapely limbs, finished with a beige top decorated with *diamanté* humming birds. Her eyes showed the weariness of thirteen hours' travelling, but sparkled into life when she saw him. Her face broke into a smile which could have launched a million ships. Jennings held her, drinking deeply of her lips, not wanting to let go. She in turn embraced him with a strength that belied her slender body. The warmth of his face, his hands and his body blew on the slumbering embers of her passion. To them the arrivals hall was empty. The other milling bodies faded into nothing. They were alone with their love.

"Excuse me, please," a voice said gruffly and the moment was gone. They were back among the jet-lagged, the tired and the ill-tempered.

Jennings took the trolley and they made for the car park. The baggage was loaded and Pansie nuzzled into the soft leather seat of the Jaguar. They drove in silence, Pansie trying to keep drowsiness from controlling her eyes.

Ellen, at Jennings's request, had prepared a breakfast of scrambled eggs with smoked salmon to be followed by cinnamon toast.

Pansie smiled when the plate was put in front of her, mischief in those huge hazel eyes. "You remembered."

"Will I ever forget!" Jennings could see the room in the Mandarin and Pansie curled up on the bed like a kitten even now. He remembered that first night of lovemaking, when they had both found true bliss in giving pleasure to the other.

After breakfast they made love. They took each other to the heights of indulgence. Their delight in each other's bodies was like that of a collector finding an undiscovered masterpiece. Afterwards they held each other, each enraptured by the feel of the other.

Pansie soon fell into a deep sleep. The rigours of the journey and the eight-hour time-gain finally overcame her passion. Jennings gently pulled the duckdown quilt over her exquisite body and left her to dream.

At five that afternoon he heard her stirring. He took her green tea, which she drank with appreciation. They sat holding hands. At that moment the world was at peace.

Jennings sat in the lounge while Pansie showered and dressed. He was jolted into alertness by the shrill ring of the telephone.

"Allan, my boy, I don't know if you are aware but your Colonel Herne has been involved in a motor accident and got himself killed." Pinter's voice was both tentative and inquisitive, perhaps not wanting to know the truth.

"I had heard that, Uncle George – it would seem most unfortunate. By the way, I do have some additional information that may help us with our snake problem." Jennings knew that with George Pinter some things needed no small talk.

"When can we talk then?"

"Why don't you and Gwen come down for the weekend? I have got someone here for you to meet."

"If it is that girl you have been dewy-eyed about for the last six weeks, we will be delighted."

"It is and I haven't, you old sod."

"You have been like a badger on heat since Christmas. I am dying to see this vision who could get you that excited. We will be down about eleven on Saturday. See you then."

Jennings replaced the receiver, smiling to himself.

Pansie appeared in the doorway, her black hair shining like finely polished ebony. She wore a silk *négligé*, with the fine line of her body just discernible through the slightly translucent material. Jennings wanted to carry her whence she had just come and make love again.

"What should I wear?" she enquired pertly.

"Perfume, under a silk sheet," Jennings replied, not totally in fun.

She smiled and pouted her lips. "I meant *before* that. Are we going out tonight?"

"Tonight, my darling, I am going to show you off. But first sit down – I have something for you." Jennings went into the study and twirled the mechanism of the safe. He removed a small box and returned. He sat beside her and placed the box in her hand.

"What is it?"

"Before you open it I must tell you that I bought it for you to wear on your left hand." Jennings had never proposed before and he felt both awkward and apprehensive.

Pansie opened the box and gasped with delight. The pink diamond flashed as it gathered in and then expelled the light, having first enhanced it. It was surrounded by pure white teardrop-shaped diamonds. The whiteness of the surrounding stones accentuated the colour, and the fire danced from stone to stone as she moved her hand. The shank was hand-made and decorated. Without hesitating she put it on the third finger of her left hand.

"Does that mean you will be my wife?"

"Just try and stop me." Her eyes shone with tears of happiness.

Jennings lifted her into his arms and swung her around. He wanted to dance down the road telling the world how lucky he was. Instead he went into the kitchen and collected a bottle of Bollinger from the refrigerator in one hand and Ellen McDonald in the other. He had to have an audience. Ellen looked a little bewildered but followed him meekly. Jennings opened the champagne and poured three glasses.

"Ellen McDonald, I want you to meet the future Mrs Jennings."

That night the celebrations were exuberant. Jennings ordered free drinks for anyone who crossed the threshold of The Haycutter. All the males were jealous of the man who had not only found this vision of loveliness but had persuaded her to be his wife. All the wives were both irate at their husbands' open flirting and totally enchanted by Pansie's obvious happiness.

"I know why you hid her in Hong Kong – she's gorgeous enough to die for." Hacker's opinion was partly influenced by fine malt whisky. "I hope you will both be very happy. Make sure you enjoy every moment you have together." Hacker was beginning to become slightly melancholic.

That night Jennings and his oriental goddess made love as though it were both their first and last night together. They awoke at ten next morning still in each other's arms.

They visited Cross in the hospital that afternoon. He was now getting about on crutches and soon to be released. Despite Cross's protests, Jennings and Pansie insisted that he recuperate at the house in Woldingham. Several more bottles of Bollinger were consumed as not only Cross but the whole ward celebrated the engagement. Jennings wanted the ecstasy he was feeling to stretch unbroken for ever. He had known pain but now he knew a joy that could not be imagined.

Only one thing is certain in life. At both ends of the spectrum are the extremes. Extremes of happiness and extremes of desolation. To live a life all humans must enjoy the one and suffer the other.

Chapter Thirty-Three

George and Gwen Pinter arrived just before noon. Gwen carried a bouquet for Pansie and box of Swiss chocolates for Ellen. She fussed around Pansie like a mother hen. She had no daughters of her own and firmly intended to fill the role of the bride's mother. Pinter restricted himself to ogling surreptitiously and trying to hide his lust-driven envy of Jennings.

Ellen, knowing Pinter's love of game and root vegetables, had prepared venison casserole and mashed parsnips with a hint of Bramley apples. They chatted over the meal, Gwen already talking about the wedding arrangements. "There will be a lot to do and you cannot start soon enough." She ignored Pansie's pleas that she would have to go back to Hong Kong and sort everything out, including her job. "There is no point in putting things off. What is left to tomorrow will not get done." Gwen had her own home-spun proverbs.

They took coffee in the lounge. After his second cognac Pinter rose and said, "We have something to talk about, Allan." Jennings wished that Pansie was involved, but Gwen had no interest in men's silly games and could not really be left alone. For the moment Pansie would have to be left to be mothered.

Jennings opened the safe and took out his file. He placed a single typewritten sheet in front of Pinter.

COUNCIL OF COBRA

CAMERON CARTER
Chairman of Manning Steele International
Deputy Chairman of Lloyds of London

MARCUS BANTON
Minister of State for Welsh Affairs

LORD JUSTICE WILLIAM APPLEBY
Master of the Rolls

GORDON CARRITT
Leader of the Liberal Party
MP for Arran

COLONEL JAMES HERNE (*deceased*)
Head of Army Security

LEONARD KING
Deputy Commissioner of Metropolitan Police
(Commissioner from 1.4.73)

GEOFFREY PIPER
Head of MI5

MARTIN LEACH
Head of MI6

HAMISH McHENRY
Chief Executive of Martins Bank

ROBERT WEBSTER
Chairman of Porterfield Industries

PHILIP MYERS
MD of Inter Electric Limited

VICTOR BARRETT
Chairman of 1922 Committee
MP for Thanet East

Pinter studied the document. His eyes revealed nothing.
"Vic Barrett is a surprise though not totally unexpected, but I am perplexed that you have Gordon Carritt in there. How confident are you that this information is correct?"

Jennings was unsure how much should be told. " I *know* that I am right. Don't ask me how because I won't tell you. *That* is the Council of COBRA."

Pinter knew that sometimes a source could not be revealed. He also had an inkling that it had been obtained without the application of accepted legal rules.

"If that is what you tell me, Allan, it is a fact. Let's look at the implications. If Carritt is a party to this, the Tory party has an ongoing majority. If the socialists get a majority, they will still need the Liberals, but if one of the two major parties chose to manipulate the votes by withdrawing candidates from seats they could not win they would increase the chances of their partner winning. If either the Conservatives or Labour had such a pact with the Liberals, there would be a virtual certainty of a working majority."

"But why should they?" Jennings could not, or did not, want to envisage the possibilities.

"Power, my dear boy. Carritt will never make it with his own party. If he allies himself with one of the others, he will have power. All politicians want to leave a monument. He can't leave his own monument, but he can have a stone in someone else's. That should bolster his ego." Pinter had spent many years dealing with politicians and his opinion was tainted. "Can't you see what we have actually got here?" Pinter was beginning to get a little tetchy with the innocence of youth, which Jennings was displaying with great determination.

Jennings shook his head as much from dutiful respect rather than ignorance.

"There are all the trappings of total power. McHenry is the chairman of the biggest bank in the country. He is also tipped to be the next governor of the Bank of England. He has probably recruited a lot of other like-minded bankers to the cause. He gives COBRA the control of the money supply.

"The next big financial arm is the insurers. Carter and whoever he has tied up are the other main money suppliers. Most normal people save in banks, building societies and insurance companies.

"Porterfield Industries gives you the biggest manufacturer of consumables and, more importantly, chemicals. Inter Electric is the biggest company in defence and weapons.

"Next you have the police, MI5 and MI6. This sets you up nicely with control of the civilian population and all security matters.

"They also have the Master of the Rolls, who has probably recruited all the other geriatric old bastards who sit in judgement on us. Apart from them, he probably has a good sprinkling of heads of chambers in the Inns of Court who all think they know better than the rest of us.

"With that lot behind you, all you need is to get political power once and you will never lose it. What this lot do not have is leadership of the Conservatives. If they got that, there would be no way of stopping them."

"But they haven't, and don't look likely to." Jennings, having had the small boy lecture, was trying not to sound smug as he destroyed Pinter's theory.

"For Christ's sake, Allan, think like a bloody politician not some poxy insurance salesman." The edge in Pinter's voice showed that his concerns were real. "Marcus Banton is the star of the right wing of the Conservatives. If the present prime minister were not here and Banton had Vic Barrett to kick the backbenchers into shape, he would walk straight into the party leadership. If that happened now, he would be PM before you know it."

"But it just can't happen! We have a prime minister, and Banton would not dare to challenge him."

"If I was part of this lot," Pinter waved the sheet at Jennings, "I would arrange for the Right Honourable PM to have a nasty accident or illness. Even better, I would get my misinformation specialists to knock him off and blame the commies. Then I would have an election and increase my majority to make sure I kept Carritt in his place."

Herne's last words leapt into Jennings's mind: '*Within six months* COBRA *will be making the decisions in this country and the first one will be to finish you just like we did your father.*'

"If I told you my information is that COBRA will be making the decisions within six months, what would you say?" Jennings chose his words carefully.

"If that is what you have been told then we have to do something— and bloody fast. If they are talking about a timescale like that they are going to knock the old bastard off soon." Pinter's mind was racing. Up to that moment he had been thinking of an academic problem and how to put spokes in wheels. Now he had a time limit to work to and very little information to work with.

"How good is your information? I am going to have to shake a lot of trees and upset a lot of important people if it is true." Pinter needed to be sure.

Jennings took a small cassette from the file and placed it in the pocket Dictaphone. Pinter listened with his eyes closed. He heard the conversation, the muffled sounds and the whimpers of pain from Herne. In his mind's eye he saw exactly what had transpired and knew that Jennings had had to do what had been done. During the war he had found it necessary to kill men in cold blood. He had always told himself that the end justified the means.

"I am going to have to call in a lot of favours on this, Allan." Pinter was already planning a strategy. "Do not do anything until I have had a chance to sort out a few allies."

Jennings nodded.

Both Pansie and Gwen noticed that the two were more sombre when they returned to the living room. Gwen had seen these changes in Pinter many times and knew that she would know what troubled him when the time was right. Pansie would ask later and be told. She would then worry about her beloved Englishman, not knowing that she would also be a player as the story unfolded.

Chapter Thirty-Four

Gatefield Manor, Caversham, 16th January 1973

"It is proposed that Wing Commander Colin Marden, who is known to you gentlemen, be elected to the council as replacement for James Herne. His function will be to control the Military Security section of COBRA. Those in favour please show."

Lord Justice William Appleby looked around the table and noted that all had raised their hands. "Would someone please ask Marden to join us now?"

Appleby was in his late sixties. His pate shone through a thin layer of hair. The rest had failed to survive the attentions of a horsehair wig over forty years. His face was ruddy and his nose clearly showed his love of port wine. He sat at the head of the large oval mahogany table.

He had been recruited to COBRA soon after the war when it had seemed as though the whole world wanted to become communists. The values of his youth were being attacked and they had to be defended. The aims of COBRA were a reflection of his own values. Power should only be in the hands of those who were born and bred to use it. Wealth and power were synonymous. Central redistribution of wealth was an abomination to him. Governments only exercise power at the behest of the true ruling classes.

Around the table were people who shared his view and would take action to protect their positions. Their backgrounds were similar and their desire to maintain their positions burned like a furnace in their hearts. They did not see themselves as malicious power-hungry bigots. They were patriots who would do anything for their country, provided their positions of wealth and power remained intact.

Appleby nodded to Marden as he joined the table.

"The first item to discuss is Wing Commander Marden's report on the demise of Colonel Herne. Would you like to make any further comments on your report, Wing Commander?"

Marden referred to the bulky file in front of him. He outlined the history of the episode from the ambush to the present. He gave details of Sir Charles Jennings's threats to involve the press and the action which had been deemed necessary.

"The situation, as I see it, is that there is a possibility that Herne's death was not accidental, and Jennings may have been involved. Colonel Herne may have been attacked and then murdered. We must consider this and whether our own security has been impaired. With Operation Bell approaching we cannot afford any breach of security." Marden's presentation was brisk and efficient.

"Do we actually have any proof of this Jennings person's involvement or are we just guessing without any real evidence?" Philip Myers had made it to the peak at Inter Electric by deviousness rather than ability. He was in COBRA entirely for his own benefit. He had no deeply held values other than self-enhancement. He had no qualms about destroying another man's career, but did not have the stomach for some of the violent necessities of COBRA.

"My dear Philip, we are not in a court of law." Geoffrey Piper's tone was condescending. "Operation Bell is the culmination of over twenty years' work. It will give COBRA the real power it should have. If we perceive anything to be a risk to its success, then we must eliminate that risk irrespective of how great or how low that risk is."

The head of MI5 had no misgivings about levels of probability when assessing a risk. If a risk of any sort existed, it had to be eliminated.

The discussion continued for some time. The members of the security services were insistent that any leak, actual or notional, must be plugged. The politicians agreed with anything that would not be against their personal interests. The men from commerce and industry were a little more squeamish but followed the majority. Eventually it was agreed unanimously that the leak should be closed.

"Do you need any assistance from the council?" Appleby enquired. He hoped that his involvement would not be needed as he felt himself above the dirty part of any operation. It is easy to approve an action as a third party but demeaning to be the one who carries it out.

"No, sir, the basic operation is planned. All I am now waiting for is the details of the movements of his Chinese sleeping partner to put the whole thing in motion."

"I can tell you where she will be next Wednesday, if that helps." Carter had been quiet up to this point.

"That would be very helpful, Cameron," Marden answered.

"She is having lunch in our boardroom and then spending the afternoon with a couple of my directors. In the evening I am hosting a dinner for her."

"It would be most helpful if you arrange dinner at a venue that is secluded and quiet. I don't want hordes of passers-by." Marden had already sketched out an overall plan in his mind.

"Her company is extremely important to us so I would suggest La Gavroche, if that suits you."

Marden nodded his approval. Upper Brook Street would be very quiet late at night and offered several alternative ways in and out.

"I will talk to you about timing et cetera later."

Again Marden nodded his head.

"If that is all we have on Jennings, I suggest we have an update on the progress of Operation Bell." Appleby was thankful to change the subject. He disliked detailed discussion on what he considered to be unpleasant subjects. "Would you like to give us the latest situation, Martin?"

Martin Leach was a big-boned man with huge hands. His little finger was thicker than most people's thumbs. He had pale green eyes which never showed a trace of emotion. He had been with MI6 for twenty-five years and had reached his exalted position without the patronage of any politician. He had spent many years working in the field and was adept at most of the associated unsavoury skills.

"Operation Bell", he began, "is on course and on time. The means of entry to and exit from the Commercial Union building are being arranged and are on time. Leonard is in charge of security for the visit and will organise that to suit us."

Leonard King motioned his agreement. As deputy commissioner of the Met he would automatically control security. He knew the plan and could leave virtually unnoticeable gaps in the police's security procedures to ensure its success.

"We have now finalised a full contingency plan with Vic and Marcus just in case the soundings on voting intentions change," continued Leach. "Equipment and personnel have all been organised, none of which can be traced to us in the unlikely event of a cock-up. It is now just a matter of waiting until June."

"Thank you, Mr King. Does anybody else have any points?" Appleby peered under his bushy eyebrows, using the look that frightened Queen's Counsel into silence in his court. "Good. Then I suggest we adjourn for port."

Chapter Thirty-Five

One of the advantages of working for the biggest company in the world in its field is that when you travel you are viewed as important enough for the hosts to select and pay for the finest food and drink.

Pansie sat in a deep plush armchair, sipping a Kir royale while the head waiter explained the intricacies of each mouth-watering dish on the menu. La Gavroche fully merited its Michelin stars. Cameron Carter was at his most charming and the other two directors fussed to ensure that nothing could spoil the evening.

The meal was a trip to a culinary wonderland. The Gruyère cheese soufflé floating on a bed of cream was the most wonderful start to a gastronomic extravaganza. The tournedos melted in the mouth, the crust of cheese and crushed peppercorns complimenting the beef perfectly. The sauce was both rich and light and the vegetables were cooked to perfection. These delights were washed down with a fine Montrachet and a rich full-bodied Fleurie. The dessert was the crowning glory: a *soufflé framboise*, with a soufflé so light it could float to heaven, and a raspberry sauce, the sharpness of which perfectly balanced the sweetness of the soufflé, served with raspberries that melted on the taste buds and electrified them.

The four sat in the lounge with coffee and their choice of Armagnac or port. Pansie had never felt so content. She had just eaten a meal which could only have been cooked by a god, and soon she would be in the arms of the man she loved. If heaven existed, she was now in residence.

The waiter spoke to Carter, who nodded.

"Your car has arrived, Pansie; ours will be about ten minutes. There's no need to wait. I know you want to get home to that fiancé of yours."

Pansie smiled and thanked him for a superb evening.

"That's all right, I'm glad you enjoyed it." He turned to one of the others and said, "Can you take Pansie to her car?"

Pansie collected her coat. The Daimler was parked on the other side of the road. She reached the bottom of the steps and caught a sudden movement out of the corner of her eye. Her escort shot forward and crashed on to the pavement in a heap. The knife glinted in the lamplight. Out of instinct she moved towards the figure to try and parry the thrust she knew must come. The blade struck upwards. Her step forward might well have saved her life. The steel drove into her abdomen rather than just below her ribs and into her heart where it had been aimed. She heard a scream as if from a distance and then nothing.

The scream from upstairs surprised Carter and he spilled his coffee. A waiter ran down into the restaurant and spoke to one of the diners. The man rose and left with the waiter.

Norman Buckell had been in the operating theatre at St Mary's all morning. He had seen three patients in Harley Street that afternoon. He had finished early because he had a very special anniversary to celebrate that evening.

On the pavement outside the restaurant he saw a stunning young woman clasping her stomach, blood oozing from between her fingers. He tore her dress apart. The wound was obviously deep and blood pumped from it. All he could do was to apply pressure and try and stop the loss of the life-giving fluid. The ambulance arrived. The paramedics took over his attempts to stem the flow of blood. A drip was inserted to replace the fluid.

A voice behind Buckell said, "You must go, Norman – they will probably need you."

Veronica had married Norman Buckell twenty years ago that day. She knew that the sick would always come first. He was the surgical consultant at St Mary's Hospital, Paddington, and that was where this frail young body must go.

Jennings was half watching an old movie on the television when the telephone jangled. The clock told him it was eleven-twenty when he picked up the receiver.

"Is that Mr Allan Jennings?"

Jennings answered in the affirmative.

"Mr Jennings, do you know a Miss Pansie Lam?"

"Of course I do, she is my fiancée. Who is this?" Jennings's voice showed his agitation.

"I'm sorry, sir, I am Sergeant Collins of Paddington Police."

"What's happened?" Jennings felt his stomach knotting with fear.

"I am afraid she has been injured in a attempted theft. She is at St Mary's Hospital in Paddington, sir."

"I'm on my way!" Jennings shouted and slammed down the receiver. He threw on his jacket and shouted, "Ellen, Ellen!"

Ellen McDonald had been busy knitting for the new bairn her niece was expecting. She jumped at the sudden rumpus in the lounge.

"Pansie's been hurt! I have to go! Can I use your car? Mine is in the garage." To Jennings, in his panic, the extra minute needed to move his own car from the garage could not be spared. He did not wait for an answer. He took the spare key and left, shouting, "Use the Jag if you need to go anywhere."

Everything seemed to be laughing at him. The traffic lights winked to red at his approach. The street lamps flickered as though saying, 'Her sparkle is ebbing away.' The traffic moved only in slow motion. The more he shouted and swore the slower his progress became. Fear gnawed at his stomach and panic filled his mind.

"She is in theatre now. She received a deep stab wound to the abdomen and we had to operate to repair the damage." The nurse's voice was calm and reassuring. "Fortunately our surgical consultant was eating in the same restaurant and came with her in the ambulance so she could not be in better hands. Can I get you a cup of tea?"

'Empires were built and saved on those eight words,' thought Jennings.

Three hours took three weeks to pass. The kindly nurse had Jennings awash with tea. He was pacing the small room, feeling the frustration of being unable to influence anything or anyone.

"Mr Jennings?"

Jennings started at the interruption to his own world.

The words had been spoken by a tall, distinguished man wearing the statutory white coat.

"The operation went extremely well and I do not think that there will be any after-effects. The young lady is very strong and should heal quickly. We have her in intensive care, as a precaution, but, with luck, that will only be for a few hours."

Jennings only heard the words 'with luck'.

"We should be able to transfer her to a ward tomorrow morning," the gentle voice continued.

"Will she be all right?" The words croaked from Jennings's throat as fear knotted his larynx.

"There is absolutely no reason why she should not be." The voice was reassuring.

Relief flooded into Jennings's heart. He wanted to kiss the purveyor of the news. He wanted to say something but his brain refused to suggest anything other than whoops of delight or cartwheels, which seemed inappropriate.

"When can I see her?" he mumbled, trying to bring his elation under some form of control.

"You can see her now, but only for a couple of minutes. She is still be under sedation but she will be all right."

The loss of blood and the yellowish artificial light combined to give Pansie a complexion similar to an old parchment. Her skin seemed transparent yet opaque. Her effervescence seemed to have drained away. The machines to which she was attached appeared to live a life independent of her.

Jennings sat and held her limp hand. He spoke to her unheeding ear telling her of his love. He caressed her unfeeling hair begging her to live. The comforting words of the surgeon were now in the distant past. His future lay in this bed, pale and unconscious. He willed her to fight. To fight for herself and for him.

"I am afraid that you will have to go now, Mr Jennings. Go home and get some rest. We will call you if there is any change." The nurse's voice was soft but insistent.

Jennings grasped Pansie's hand. He did not want to leave. He looked at the nurse and shook his head. The nurse took him gently but insistently by the arm and led him from the room. He was fed the obligatory tea and sent on his way.

He sat in the Mini, his mind seeing Pansie's pale beautiful face. He kept telling himself that she would be all right. He tried hard to believe it. Finally he started the small engine and headed towards Park Lane.

Out of the corner of his eye he saw Paddington Police Station. He signalled and pulled in. He did not actually know what had happened and now he had to find out.

"Sergeant Collins, please." Jennings's enquiry was met with a quizzical look. "Could I please see Sergeant Collins?" His tone was now more insistent.

"I am sorry, sir, there is no Sergeant Collins at this station," the young constable behind the desk replied.

"There must be – he telephoned me earlier tonight."

"Can you tell me what this is in connection with, sir?" The officer was pleasant but uninterested.

"Earlier this evening a Sergeant Collins telephoned me from here to tell me that my fiancée had been assaulted and was in St Mary's Hospital. I have just come from there and now I would like to know what happened."

The authority in Jennings's voice prodded the young man into some action.

"Where did this take place?"

"I don't know what happened or where it happened. I only know that I have just left my fiancée in intensive care with a bloody great stab wound in her stomach, and I want to know what happened."

"I am sorry, sir. Please take a seat, and I will make some enquiries." He picked up the telephone and dialled. "Hello, Bill, do you know anything about a stabbing tonight?" He nodded his head. "Yes, it was a woman." He listened again.

"Is the lady Chinese, sir?" He addressed this to Jennings, who nodded. "Yes, Bill, she is."

The voice on the telephone spoke again. He replaced the receiver and turned to Jennings. "Detective Sergeant Munroe will see you in just a minute, sir."

The police definition of one minute coincided exactly with that of an airline pilot. If the pilot tells you that there will be a delay of ten minutes, an absolute minimum of thirty can be expected. They either learned from or trained the police. After some twenty minutes a fair-haired man with a broad Glasgow accent asked Jennings to follow him.

The interview room made Jennings's stomach turn. It could have been a replica of the interrogation room at Pai Ling Camp. Jennings was invited to sit and offered more tea.

"I am sorry, sir, but I was not given your name." It was both a statement and a question.

"Allan Jennings. I am Pansie Lam's fiancé. You must know that – your Sergeant Collins telephoned me last evening."

"I am afraid that there is no Sergeant Collins at this station. I also know that no one here has contacted you, sir." DS Munroe's tone was non-committal. "I do know that since Miss Lam was attacked we have been trying to trace someone who knew her. All we know is that she was stabbed in Upper Brook Street just after eleven last night. She was not robbed, although this may have been because someone raised the alarm. Can you think of any reason why someone should attack Miss Lam other than for theft?"

Jennings could not take in the information he was being given. He had received a call from Sergeant Collins who knew that Pansie was at St Mary's. Who had contacted him and why? He knew the answer but did not want to accept it. He shook his head to indicate a negative answer.

"Mr Jennings, could you have been mistaken? Could it have been the hospital or perhaps someone else who telephoned you?" Munroe did not like facts which did not fit together. His simple mugging had now, possibly, become more complicated.

"I was telephoned by a man who called himself Sergeant Collins who said that he was from this station. That is all I can tell you."

"I would be most obliged if you would make a short statement for our records. It may help to find the person who attacked Miss Lam."

Resigned, Jennings agreed.

Chapter Thirty-Six

Hyde Park Corner was flooded with the morning rush-hour traffic as Jennings made for home. Once over Vauxhall Bridge, his run was clear. On the other side of the road commuters edged towards their places of employment at a snail's pace.

It was about ten-thirty when he climbed the hill past Woldingham Station towards home. Before he reached the turn into his drive he saw lights flashing through the trees which screened his house from the road. He turned into his drive to be confronted by all the paraphernalia of the emergency services. Firemen and policemen were standing around, apparently doing little.

Jennings stopped the car and jumped out. A large policeman spotted him and came in his direction, saying, "I am sorry but you cannot come in here."

Jennings's thoughts were in a turmoil and the blunt denial of access to his own home irked him.

"What are you talking about? I bloody well live here!"

The policeman motioned him to stay and spoke into the radio pinned to his lapel. Jennings looked beyond the fire appliance and his stomach churned. Parked in front of his house was a three-ton army lorry emblazoned with ROYAL ENGINEERS: BOMB DISPOSAL.

"What has happened?"

The policeman ignored the question and continued talking to his lapel. "I'll keep him here until you arrive."

He turned to Jennings and stated as importantly as he could, "A senior officer will be with you in a minute, sir. Please wait here." The last statement was an order rather than a request.

Jennings paced about trying to make some sense of the events.

"Allan! Thank Christ you are okay!"

Jennings immediately recognised Hacker's voice and turned to greet him.

"I thought that you were in that lot," Hacker continued.

Jennings stopped him in mid-flow. "You thought *I* was in what lot, Tony?"

Hacker looked surprised. "Has *nobody* told you what happened?" He did not wait for confirmation or denial but continued, "Someone planted a bomb. It was in the garage, probably in your car. It went off about an hour ago. The bomb squad are checking the area to make sure there are no more surprises waiting. They should be finished soon, but until then we have to wait here."

A radio crackled and Jennings heard a tinny voice say, "All clear. The only damaged body was in the car. You can bring your clean-up boys in now."

The words 'damaged body' struck Jennings like a bolt of lightning. "Where's Ellen, Tony?"

He grabbed Hacker by the arm. "Where the fuck is Ellen?" he shouted.

Hacker looked away. "There *was* someone in the car. We cannot identify who as yet. Let's go in the house and we can talk."

Jennings's first sight of the damage shook him to his core. The garage was completely demolished. Most of the windows in the house were shattered and debris lay everywhere. The front door was locked and his heart sank.

In the kitchen a note was stuck to the refrigerator door. He recognised Ellen's spidery writing.

> *Gone to Oxted to get something for dinner. Be back soon. Have to use your car but don't worry, I'll be careful!*

Jennings screwed up the paper and closed his eyes, trying to stop the tears that wanted to flow. He sat at the kitchen table, the table at which he had shared so many meals with Ellen McDonald, and wept. What had he done? Why were the Fates selecting him for their cruel japes?

Hacker produced a large brandy and gave it to him.

"I am so sorry, Allan." His voice was sympathetic. "Why was Ellen using your car?"

Jennings told him of the attack on Pansie, the panic in his mind and how he had taken the first available car. Hacker just listened. He knew that talking would be a balm to Jennings's anguish.

A disembodied voice from Hacker's radio said, "The army want to talk to you, Chief Inspector."

Hacker acknowledged, asked Jennings if he would be all right and went out of the kitchen door.

Jennings closed his eyes. He could see Ellen clearly. She was sitting at the scrubbed pine table, her knitting needles clicking like a racing commentator with loose false teeth. Her round, ruddy face was wreathed in smiles while she talked of her brother's bairns. She regularly supplied them with enough woollens to clothe a regiment in the Arctic. She had told Jennings about her brother being the most photographed man in Inverness. Each night he would pipe the sunset at the Culloden House Hotel, surrounded by American and Japanese tourists and their cameras. Jennings remembered the piper from the time he had stayed at the hotel on a golfing tour. He shivered, but it was not the draught from the shattered windows which caused it. Was he to be a danger to all his friends and loved ones? Could he rid himself of the curse COBRA had put on him?

"I have just spoken to the officer in charge of the Royal Engineers."

Jennings had not heard Hacker return.

"He thinks that the explosive used was Semtex. The only people who are known to use this are Her Majesty's forces and the IRA. This was probably some sort of revenge attack from your times in Northern Ireland."

Hacker was now a chief inspector in Special Branch and had a job to do. "I am going to have to get a statement from you, Allan, but not now."

Jennings was grateful, as he needed time to sort his thoughts into some semblance of order. First, he must make sure that Pansie was safe and well.

The nurse on the Lindo Wing of St Mary's was both efficient and sympathetic. Pansie was out of intensive care and breathing unaided. She was no longer in a critical condition and would recover fully with rest. As Jennings thanked the nurse a weight lifted from his heart.

That evening Pansie was sitting propped up with pillows. Some colour had returned to her face. She smiled when Jennings appeared from behind an enormous bouquet. He kissed her gently on the cheek. She held him as if never wanting to let go. The television, in the corner of the room, played the familiar music for the evening news.

"A bomb, believed to be the work of the Provisional IRA, has exploded at a house in Woldingham, Surrey." Pansie loosened her hold on Jennings and looked towards the flickering screen. "One person was killed and extensive damage caused." Jennings felt Pansie stiffen as pictures of his home appeared. "The bomb is believed to have been planted in the owner's car. The man, a former member of the Special Services, was not at home. The device exploded when his housekeeper started the car early this morning. No one has yet claimed responsibility for the explosion."

Pansie pushed Jennings back and said, "Ellen!"

Jennings nodded. "It was meant for me but I used Ellen's car to come here last night."

The lump in his throat stopped Jennings from saying any more.

Pansie wept on his shoulder. She had known Ellen only a few days, but had liked her instantly. Ellen could have been the mother she never really knew. Her tears ran freely. The shock of the attack and now this was too much to hide inside. Jennings held her until the sobbing subsided. He was grateful that he could be the strong one. They could take their strength from each other.

They talked. Both were subdued. Both avoided the subject they most wished to discuss. They knew that the events of the past days were connected but not how. This would have to wait until Pansie was stronger. She showed him a telex from Peter Huber ordering her to get better. She showed him the flowers from Tony Hacker which had arrived just before Jennings.

The surgeon arrived for his evening round. "This is the young lady who ruined my anniversary dinner." The nurse smiled at the joke. "How are you feeling tonight?"

He asked Jennings to leave while he examined his work.

"I think we should keep you here for a week or so, but there should not be any after-effects. It was a nice clean wound and tidied up nicely." He squeezed Pansie's hand reassuringly.

As he left he told Jennings that Pansie would be fine and that she now only needed to heal and regain her strength to be as good as new.

"The police will have to see her, of course, but I suggest that that be left until tomorrow. I think it might be better for her if you are here when she sees the police, just as a bit of support. Shock can be a funny thing." The words were delivered professionally but with the interests of his patient uppermost.

Jennings thanked him.

"Good, I will tell the inspector to come back tomorrow at this time."

"The police are coming to interview you tomorrow night. I will be here." Pansie squeezed his hand and nodded. "What happened? Do you know who attacked you?"

She shook her head. "It was all a blur, it was so quick. I do know he wanted to kill me. He struck for my heart but we ex-terrorists know a thing or two."

"Do you remember anything?" Jennings asked.

She told him that she had been leaving the restaurant and that she was about to cross the road to the car, which was on the other side of the street, when suddenly she had been attacked. She did not know who raised the alarm but assumed it was the driver. She could remember nothing else.

They sat for another hour studiously avoiding the subject of the past.

When Jennings left, he saw the policeman sitting at the end of the corridor. He glanced at him and nodded a greeting. The policeman returned the salute.

The training Jennings had received was aimed at heightening both conscious and sub-conscious awareness. He was halfway down the stairs when he realised that the uniform he had just seen was *not* that of the Metropolitan Police. *The buttons were wrong.*

He turned and ran up the stairs. The seat at the end of the corridor was empty. His heart was pounding as he ran along the corridor and burst into Pansie's room. He saw the knife held behind the man's back. Instinctively he drove his clenched fist into the side of the figure's neck. The man fell, the knife still clasped in his hand. Jennings stepped forward and drove his heel on to the clenched fist. He felt the carpals and metacarpi smashing as his fourteen stone was concentrated in the blow. The man screamed in anguish as the intricate bone structure of his hand disintegrated. Jennings dropped on to the prone body and, using the collar of the assailant's tunic for torque, drove his knuckles into the figure's windpipe. The struggle was brief. The front stranglehold cut off the man's supply of life-giving oxygen and a blue tinge appeared around the lips and eyes. He ceased to struggle and Jennings released his grip.

Pansie sat rigid with fear, initially for herself and then for Jennings. She had screamed at him to stop when the man went blue. Without realising, she had grabbed the CALL button and had it squeezed in her hand. A nurse rushed in and stopped dead in her tracks. She was totally unable to comprehend what her eyes were telling her.

"Call the police please, nurse." The voice came from a man who was standing over a prostrate policeman.

She hesitated.

"Call the police, NOW!"

This was an order not a request. She ran from the room. Two minutes later two security men burst into the room. They saw the prone body in uniform and Jennings standing above him.

Before they could decide on any action Jennings said, "He is not a policeman and he is not dead. I suggest that in addition to the police you also call a doctor as he has a very bruised windpipe and the hand holding the knife is in a bit of a state."

Jennings held Pansie in his arms. Her whole body was shaking with fear and shock. Her hands trembled and her eyes shed tears of both fear and relief. Slowly she began to control herself. A nurse and doctor were fussing over the unconscious would-be assassin. The two security men stood in the door puffed up with their importance. This was proper security work.

The police arrived. One was allocated to escort the injured man to casualty. Another policeman was placed outside Pansie's room, and a third at the end of the corridor. Detective-Sergeant Munroe arrived and took up residence in the night sister's office.

"That was very efficient, Mr Jennings. You obviously know how to look after yourself." Munroe made the comment casually.

"I did learn a few things of value in the army, Sergeant," Jennings replied non-committally.

"How did you know that something was wrong? I understand that you were leaving."

"It was the uniform – it wasn't Metropolitan Police," Jennings answered. "The buttons were wrong. I did not realise until I was halfway down the stairs."

"Mr Jennings, do you know why anyone should attempt to kill your fiancée?"

Jennings had a very good idea who and why all this had happened. He also did not know who could or could not be trusted. He shook his head, saying, "No."

"Do you know the man in Miss Lam's room?"

Again Jennings shook his head.

"Well, I'll find out eventually. That's if I can get the bastard to speak after the damage you did to him."

"I'm sorry, what do you mean?" Jennings asked.

"He had to have an emergency tracheotomy so that he could breathe, and his hand is smashed beyond repair. He'll never carry a knife in that hand again.

"I would like you to come in tomorrow and make a full statement. In the meantime I will station a man outside Miss Lam's room."

Chapter Thirty-Seven

Jennings arrived home just after eleven that evening. Glaziers had repaired all the windows and the house had been secured. The garage had been cordoned off by the police. The house was cold and silent. The inglenook fireplace contained only ashes. Jennings poured a long drink and wandered to the kitchen to burrow in the refrigerator. He found some cold beef and made a sandwich. He turned the television on, to be confronted by a soap opera. He switched off. He heard the gravel in the drive crunching under the wheels of a car. Pulling back the curtain, he saw George Pinter alighting from his Bentley. He went to the door and greeted his old friend.

"I heard about the bomb this morning. I've been trying to ring you all day. Are you all right?" Pinter's tone was scolding. He viewed Jennings as the son he had never had.

"Come in and have a drink, Uncle George," invited Jennings. "I'll tell you what's happened."

Pinter sat silently while Jennings related the events of the last few days. His only intervention was to throw in the occasional expletive. While Jennings spoke, Pinter made occasional notes, underlining some.

"Are you certain that this is all connected with COBRA, Allan?"

"I cannot see any other possibility. If it wasn't, that would mean that Pansie was actually mugged and the mugger decided to have a second try in the hospital. Also, by coincidence, the Provisionals chose to try to blow me up at the same time. To my mind, that is beyond the realms of probability." Jennings knew it had to be COBRA but he did not quite know why.

They spent the next hour going over all the information they had but could find no acceptable reason for what had happened. Their only conclusion was that COBRA must have something planned, and soon. What it was could only be surmised. Finally the two men ran out of ideas and sat in a mood of prevailing depression.

"What is happening to Ellen's stuff?" Pinter asked, more to break the silence than to obtain information.

Jennings knew that in two days Ellen's sister would arrive from Inverness to collect her belongings. He would have to sort out her room, but had no stomach for the job. To see and touch her belongings would fuel both his grief and anger.

"I have to sort it out. Her sister is coming down the day after tomorrow."

Pinter could see that it was a task not relished by Jennings and said, "Come on, son, we'll go and do it together now."

Ellen's room was neat and tidy. Everything was in its right place and folded to the same size. Jennings wondered if she had ever been in the army for her room looked as though it was ready for inspection by the provost marshal. He took down the two large suitcases which were stacked symmetrically on top of one of the wardrobes. Inside one was a cassette recorder. Jennings held the machine, surprised, as he had never heard it being used. Out of curiosity, he rewound the tape to hear what type of music Ellen had listened to in the privacy of her own room.

"*Report for Central Control for the seven days ended 23rd January 1973.*" Ellen's Scottish brogue was unmistakable. Pinter dropped the bundle of sweaters he was holding. "*The Chinese woman Pansie Lam is stopping at the house. She has not, to my knowledge, made any references to* COBRA. *Her visit to England seems to be purely business. I am, however, unable to monitor all conversations with the subject.*

"*On Sunday the subject was visited by Pinter. Following lunch the subject and Pinter spent two hours in the study having a private conversation. Without proper equipment I am unable to monitor such conversations and do not know whether either has any knowledge of Operation Bell. I suggest that full surveillance equipment be installed. This can easily be arranged while the subject is not in the house. I would also recommend that we bring in an expert to open the safe as there are documents in there which may be of interest to us.*"

The recorder became silent.

Jennings stood looking blankly at the small machine, refusing to believe what he had just heard. Pinter was just as perplexed. Neither wanted to accept that this plump jovial woman, who had become a friend rather than an employee, was an infiltrator. Pinter was the first to break the stunned silence.

"It looks like you have had a Judas in the camp all along."

Jennings shook his head. He still could not believe the evidence of his ears.

Pinter started to pace up and down the room. His mind was sorting information into a logical order. He realised that what they had just heard could be the edge they needed.

"Look, Allan, it is obvious that since you came out of Colchester this COBRA operation has had you under surveillance. They must have feared that you would try to do something contrary to their interests. How did Ellen come to be working for you?"

"Stuart Rittle chose her. She was here when I was released."

Pinter whistled in surprise. "Do you think that old Frogface is one of these people?"

Jennings held his hands up in a gesture of total confusion.

"Either he is or someone has used him, that's for certain." Pinter was beginning to organise the files in his head. "If he is not one of them, he was probably used by Appleby. They are great mates, are they not?"

Jennings agreed.

"What they don't know is that we now know about Ellen. If you leave it that way, they will try to put in another plant. If they do that, we can then feed them what we want and maybe find out what the blazes Operation Bell is."

Jennings was now becoming interested. If COBRA could be lured into the open, they could self-destruct.

"First things first, Allan. We have to go through everything here with a fine-tooth comb." The investigative journalist in Pinter could now smell a very big story fermenting.

During the next two hours they went through every item in Ellen's room. They searched through every pocket, looked for secret compartments and studied every item of clothing. It was not until they reached the last drawer that they found the address book. They scrutinised every entry looking for some form of code. Some seemed obvious. They were names, addresses and telephone numbers of relatives and friends. Others meant nothing to either Pinter or Jennings. After studying the book for over an hour they decided to leave further examination till the morning.

Pinter elected to stop the night and telephoned Gwen to tell her.

Pinter was sitting in the lounge, nursing a large cognac, when it struck him. He sat up suddenly, nearly spilling his drink, and said, "Allan, give me that address book."

Even though his conscious mind was not addressing the problem the subconscious was still active. Pinter was a crossword fanatic. He opened the book and exclaimed, "There it is! Lorron Cobact! I thought it was a strange name!"

"What are you muttering about?" Jennings was mildly annoyed at Pinter's antics.

"My dear boy, Lorron Cobact is not a name – it's an anagram."

"An anagram of what?"

"Use that tiny brain of yours. Lorron Cobact is an anagram of COBRA Control. I'll have twenty pounds with you that the address here is the location of their headquarters. Gatefield Manor, Caversham – that rings a bell, but I don't know why. I'll have a dig round tomorrow and see what I can find out." Pinter could feel the adrenaline rising. He loved the chase – the kill mattered less than the hunt and its success.

Pansie looked more like herself the next afternoon. Most of her colour had returned and the brightness was back in her eyes. The doctor had told her that she would be kept in hospital for another five days and then she must convalesce for about three weeks to regain her strength. Jennings told her of Ellen's dual personality. Pansie was both surprised and saddened as she had felt a great affection for the motherly Scot. It had been the same with Lee Kim. He had been both her lover and her role model until she realised that he had no morals and all his actions were simply in the pursuit of self-interest. She could see the hurt in Jennings's eyes at the betrayal by someone he had trusted and liked.

Jennings left the hospital just before six and drove to Paddington Police Station. Sergeant Munroe's desk reminded him of his own in the middle of the renewal season. It could best be described as a controlled jumble.

"I am afraid that this matter has become somewhat more serious, Mr Jennings." Munroe was looking at a file rather than into Jennings's eyes. "The man who attacked your fiancée in hospital died in the early hours of the morning." He took a piece of paper and read, "Cause of death: severe crushing injury to the oesophagus."

One of the more useful skills of being a broker in Lloyds was the ability to read upside down. Jennings could see the signature on the death certificate. The doctor's name was Clarke. Was it the same Doctor Clarke who had been the last man to see Harris alive?

"I am afraid that I will have to take a full statement from you. I will have to send all the documentation to the Director of Public Prosecutions. It is unlikely that any action will be taken but I have to go through the formal procedures."

"Wait a minute, Sergeant!" Jennings rejoined. "There is no way that I killed the bastard. I simply disabled him."

"That, I am afraid, is not what the doctor says. I have to go through the due process."

Chapter Thirty-Eight

"The first security operation under your direct control has been a complete cock-up, Wing Commander." Appleby peered over his half-moon glasses at Marden, who shuffled uncomfortably in his chair. "Not only did your people fail to remove either target, but you also managed to blow up our own operative and lose one of our enforcers. If the whole thing weren't so serious it would be bloody laughable!"

The others sitting around the table deliberately avoided looking at Marden. They had all, in their time, suffered a tongue-lashing from the Judge and knew how his verbal barbs could sting.

"I am preparing a remedial plan, which will be instigated as soon as possible. *I* will take personal charge to ensure that there are no mistakes." Marden was trying to sound efficient.

"You will do no such thing. This man Jennings seems to have more lives than a bloody cat. So far we have tried three times and failed three times. I think that we should now approach IT from another angle. What we need is Jennings out of circulation until after Operation Bell is completed. Arrangements are in hand to achieve this." Appleby had decided that the rapier might be more effective than the bludgeon.

"It was fortunate that we had a man at St Mary's, who tidied up for us. There is also a side benefit. I am now arranging for Jennings to be formally charged with murder. It does not matter whether he is found guilty or not. What matters is that he will be held on remand until the trial, which will be well after our objectives are achieved." Appleby did not bother to look for agreement or disagreement. The decision was made as far as he was concerned.

"What about Pinter and the Chinese woman?" King, being a policeman, wanted everything neat and tidy.

"I don't think the woman is a danger. She was simply an initial source of information. As for Pinter, we have him under close surveillance," Marden interjected, thankful that the previous calamity now seemed to be a closed book.

"Good," said Appleby. "Now can we have a progress report on Operation Bell. You first, Mr Carter."

"The invitations have all been accepted for 2nd June," started the insurance broker. "The equipment will be delivered the previous day to the Commercial Union building. It will be installed on 1st June. All the services are on the top two floors and that is where the equipment will be stored."

"Good," nodded Appleby. "Now Mr King."

"The security will be very tight. All surrounding buildings will be searched either the previous night or in the morning. As the Commercial Union is the largest building in the area it will be the first to be screened. I expect the building to be cleared before 11 p.m. All searches will be completed before noon. Armed officers will be placed strategically. I will ensure, however, that the inside of the Commercial Union building will be free from unwanted scrutiny. All security arrangements will be finalised one week before. Any changes will be notified to Piper."

"Thank you, now Mr Piper."

The head of MI5 was a tall, narrow-shouldered man with a shock of grey hair. His eyes were light blue and as cold as ice.

"The training is running perfectly to schedule. We have four possibilities, all expert and well-trained. Should there be any unforeseen problems any one of them can survive for seven days in the container. This will give us ample time to cover all our tracks."

"Excellent. Now, let's see – what about the following few weeks? I believe this is for you, Hamish."

Nobody knew why but Appleby always used surnames with the exception of Hamish McHenry.

"Well, William," McHenry's accent was definitely Glaswegian but with the softness of Edinburgh, "you will have seen over the last few weeks that the markets have been a little skittish. The reason for that is we have been testing our ability to move prices and values both up and down. I am pleased to say that there are a lot of young hot-blooded people in the markets and I don't think there will be any problem in changing the mood of the markets from day to day. Last week we aimed to depress the market by thirty points and achieved it without difficulty. The week before we moved it up twenty points.

Also both Robert's and Philip's companies are of such a size that they can put either negative or positive vibrations into the market. I am confident that we can exert the influence if we need to."

Appleby expressed his approval and turned to Barrett. "Finally, what is the situation on your front, Mr Barrett?"

"The soundings have not changed from my last report. We are better than even money to achieve our aim. All we need to do now is to add a touch of theatre and we will be virtually there."

Appleby raised his eyebrows and glanced obliquely over the top of his spectacles. "A touch of theatre?"

"Shall we call it public relations?" Barrett regretted his use of the vernacular. "There are one or two matters in which Marcus, in particular, and Gordon, to a lesser extent, can obtain real benefits on 2nd June. I have a few ideas which I will discuss with them."

"Provided we are all kept informed." Appleby sounded like a Victorian chief clerk ordering the junior to fetch more coal for the fire. "If nobody has any further matters to raise, I suggest that we adjourn till next month."

The statement was made as an order rather than a request. All these men were at the top of their professions but none would stand between Lord Justice Appleby and his port.

Chapter Thirty-Nine

The next two weeks were frenzied for Jennings. He had to visit both New York and Los Angeles at short notice and at the same time arrange for a nurse to look after Pansie when she was released from St Mary's. Cross was also discharged and clumped around the house in a plaster from thigh to ankle. Pansie was regaining her strength, and Cross became more agitated at his lack of mobility.

Jennings escaped one evening to The Haycutter following an invitation from Hacker. He was halfway through his first pint when Hacker arrived, bought a round and motioned Jennings to the corner of the bar.

"Someone with a lot of power has got it in for you, Allan," Hacker started. "I had lunch yesterday with an old friend of mine who works for the DPP."

"The who?" Jennings interrupted.

"The Director of Public Prosecution," Hacker sighed.

Jennings nodded, motioning Hacker to continue.

"He has had papers from Paddington police about the attack on Pansie. He tells me that, even though there is hardly a case against you, he is being pressured to bring a charge of murder."

"What are you talking about? I just disabled the bastard."

"I know, Allan, but this guy is getting pressure from on high to proceed against you. Can you think of any reason why?"

Jennings was, by now, unsure whether he could trust anyone. Hacker was one of his oldest friends, but so was Rittle. He decided to let slip as little as possible. "I think that there was more to my father's death than appeared. I believe that there are people who want me out of the way but I don't know who nor do I know why. I do know that Jim Cross's accident was not an accident and I think that I was the target. I am also sure that I was the target for the bomb. For what reason, I have not the faintest idea."

Hacker stared into his drink. Jennings had made powerful enemies. "Tell me exactly what happened from the time you saw the man in Pansie's room."

For the next hour Jennings recounted the events. Hacker interrupted with questions as the tale progressed. He was making notes and seemed to cross-reference different parts of the story. Jennings went to the bar to get another round. He watched Hacker while he stood at the bar waiting for the beers to arrive. Suddenly Hacker smiled and slapped the table.

When Jennings sat down with the replenishments Hacker said, "They can't do you."

"What makes you think that, Tony?"

"You told me that the copper Munroe said that your attacker had an emergency tracheotomy." Jennings nodded. "Right, then how the blazes did this bastard die from the injuries caused by your stranglehold when he was actually breathing through a hole in his bloody throat *below* the injury you inflicted? If he died of strangulation, he would have had to have been strangled *below* the tracheotomy not *above* it. That means that someone else killed him and is setting you up to take the blame."

"I'm with you Tony, but, how do I prove it?" Jennings knew, from his own experience, that justice was not done, only seen. "If someone has the muscle to lean on the DPP, they've certainly got the muscle to lean on me."

"Allan," Hacker's tone was now indulgent, "the post-mortem has to show that there are injuries both above and below the tracheotomy. As a consequence you could not have killed the bastard."

The two chatted for another hour before Jennings called the ever-reliant Jack Martin to take him home.

Pansie was asleep, her soft and lovely face enhanced by the Belgian lace pillow that surrounded it. Jennings kissed her gently on the forehead. His heart ached with the desire to hold her close. She was a victim of something he did not yet understand, but if a COBRA was the enemy he would be the mongoose.

Cross was sitting in the lounge, his plastered leg propped on a stool, looking like a storm-ravaged silver birch. He twirled the empty glass in his hand, obviously wanting a refill but lacking the enthusiasm to haul himself to his feet and lumber across the room to pour it. He smiled when Jennings entered and said, "Thank God, a serving person has arrived."

Jennings replenished the glass with Willems, noting that the pear in the bottle was near to being exposed to the air. He made a mental note to buy another bottle so that the sanctity of the pear could be maintained. Jennings poured himself a Glenfiddich and sank into the rocking chair opposite Cross. He was tired, confused and mostly angry.

"I wish you the best of health, Allan, even though you look like shit. Why don't you get a good night's sleep, and bugger the rest of the world?"

Cross's incapacity caused him to find solace in a bottle, thought Jennings.

"If only it was that easy, I would," was the reply.

"It could be. I don't know what is bugging you, but if I were you I would forget it. If it's your father, it's in the past. What happened then has got no connection to today. Just remember that."

"You don't know what the fuck you are talking about!" Jennings's temper had finally snapped. "Every fucking thing that has happened recently is connected. There are some arrogant bastards out there who want something, and for some reason me and mine seem to be in their way. You don't really think that what happened to you was an accident, and you know it wasn't you that they were after."

Cross sipped the Willems. He watched the thick pear liqueur gently slide from the rim of the crystal. He knew that his next statement could make or break his friendship with Jennings. He had consumed half a bottle of the fiery pear liqueur, but now his mind was as sharp as a rapier's point.

"Allan, I was put into Colchester to keep an eye on you. I am a freelance who was employed by Special Forces Command to find out why you had caused so many waves in the security services." Jennings started to speak, but Cross held up his hand and said, "Let me finish and then you can have your say."

Jennings subsided into sullen silence.

"Following your return from the patrol, Special Forces Command were given orders that they were not to have any involvement with you. They were refused access to you for debriefing. They were not advised of the charges brought against you nor were they advised of or given any details about your court martial. The first information they received about you thereafter was notice of your sentence and dishonourable discharge, and that was from their own man, Starkey."

"But that is against all the regulations," interrupted Jennings. "They have to formally advise your own unit."

"Just shut up and listen!" Cross snapped. "Both you and I know that Special Forces are both close-knit and overly loyal to their own. When Command found out that you had been put in the general population in Colchester – again contrary to regulations – they became even more suspicious. When they subsequently heard about your father's death and some of the traumas you were going through, they decided to take action. I was signed up to be put into Colchester, firstly to back you up and secondly to find out anything I could from you about the ambush, your trial or your father's death. I learnt very little but at least got the bastards off your back."

Jennings sat in stunned silence, his mind racing. This man whom he had taken for his friend was just another bloody spy, albeit on his side. That was, if Jennings could believe him.

"How did you manage to get yourself into Colchester and allocated to the same cell as me?" Jennings was determined to verify the story he was being given.

"That was quite simple," Cross smiled. "The court martial was paperwork. As for the second, Major Parker spent several years with the Special Operations Executive on secondment from the military police. SOE wanted a favour and he did it."

"Tell me exactly what you know, Jim." Jennings wanted to trust him.

"We know very little. We know that the pressure to have you court-martialled came from the very top of Army Intelligence. We do not know why. We also know that for a reason which is not apparent all the patrols searching for you were commanded by officers from the intelligence corps. We do not know how they knew that they had to look for you. Nobody, apart from Intelligence possibly, had seen or even knew of the underground newspaper that implicated you until after you had been captured. Lastly, your father's death was clearly suspicious and Command do not like coincidences."

Jennings was unsure. "Are you still spying on me, Jim?"

"My job was finished when we came back from Hong Kong. I sent them a final report and got paid."

"Who the fuck do you work for now?"

"I've been a man of leisure for the past three months. Prior to that it was the CIA," Cross answered matter-of-factly. "I learned my business with MI5 for seven years and then became freelance. I work for whoever pays the money, provided they are legitimate."

Jennings knew that at some time he would have to trust someone. This man had become a friend. He seemed to have been honest about his past and the reasons for what he had done. If he had to take a chance on anyone, it would be Cross.

"You say you were with MI5?"

Cross nodded.

"What made you leave them?"

"To be honest, there was too much internal politics and too many people with their own hidden agendas. Most of the top people were tied in with one or other politicians or pressure groups. The security services run on the basis that action is only taken when there is a benefit to one or more people in the higher echelons of the service. I started with the asinine idea that I was acting for the overall good of the country. I soon found out that I was actually risking my bloody life to massage some bloody fool's ego. I realised that if I was massaging egos, I could do the same in the private sector and make more money."

"Would you work for me?"

The question took Cross by surprise. He could see from Jennings eyes that he was deadly serious.

"The general answer is yes, but it would depend on what you wanted me for," Cross answered non-committally.

"Firstly," Jennings started, "have you ever heard of an organisation called COBRA?"

"It is questionable whether it actually exists. If it does, it is alleged to be a group consisting mainly of security operatives and right-wing politicians. The stories go that their objective is to try and get their people into positions of power so that their ideas on how the country should be run can be adopted. The best description I can give is a sort of secret lobbying group. The masons of politics is also a good description."

"Suppose I tell you that they do exist and that their methods are a lot more drastic than lobbying? Suppose I tell you that they were responsible for yours and Pansie's injuries and the bomb that killed Ellen. Would you believe me?"

"I would have difficulty in believing it, but go on."

Jennings went into the study and opened the safe. The manila folder was now bulging. He picked up the cassette recorder with his spare hand and returned to the lounge.

"I'll tell you a story," Jennings said.

It was two in the morning before Jennings finished and Cross said, "It looks like I've got a new job."

Chapter Forty

12th February 1973

"I knew that I had heard of the bloody place, it just took me time to find it." Pinter was pulling a battered file of papers from his briefcase.

Jennings, Cross and Pinter were sitting at the corner table in the Chez When. When Jennings had told Pinter how and why he had confided in Cross, Pinter had been extremely suspicious. He had made his own enquiries of his own sources and Cross's story stood the examination.

"There you are – Gatefield Manor," Pinter continued. "The headquarters of the Association for Democratic Conservatism."

"What the hell does that mean?" Jennings queried.

"The aims and objectives are..." Pinter shuffled through the file. "Er, to promote the development of parliamentary democracy and the market economy in the developed and the developing world. I investigated this operation a few years ago. It seems to support some, shall we say, right-wing governments and political parties. It was also rumoured to finance some extremist terrorist groups in both South America and Africa. I could not find anything about its source of funds other than the fact that it is not short of money."

"What did you find out?" Cross asked.

"Absolutely bugger all," Pinter replied with his usual subtlety. "The whole thing seemed as pure as driven snow, which usually means that it stinks. Nothing can be as clean as that."

"What's the connection with COBRA, other than the address in Ellen's book?"

"Just have a look at the trustees." He showed them a list of names. "There are five of them – Carter, McHenry, Webster, Myers and, to top them all, Vic Barrett. That is a list of the COBRA Council members who can be named without embarrassment. You could not have a minister, a judge, a copper or the heads of MI5 or 6 actually named as trustees. Equally, the leader of the Liberal Party could not put his name to it."

Cross shuffled uncomfortably in the low seat. He was now out of plaster but his movements were still restricted and he was in a lot of discomfort. As he looked at the paper Pinter had passed them something nagged at the back of his mind.

"What should our next step be?" asked Jennings.

"I know that place!" Cross interrupted. The niggle had leapt from the inactive to the active side of his brain. "An old friend of mine was working there about two years ago. His speciality was undercover work. I don't know who he was working for but he was there for about a year."

"Can we trust him and would he work for us?" Jennings and Pinter both had the same thought.

Cross nodded. "You can most certainly trust him if he works for you. Nobody could operate as a freelance in this business for long if they tried to play both sides."

"Let's fix it up to meet, as soon as possible."

The house seemed empty and without soul when the two returned that evening. Pansie had returned to Hong Kong to make arrangements for her move to England. Jennings had not wanted her to go as he still thought her too weak to undertake such an trip. She had told him that she was as strong as an ox, and just because he had been lucky in the jungle he could not treat her like a porcelain doll. Jennings had been a little taken aback by her fiery independence.

Cross went into the study and made several telephone calls. Jennings busied himself in the kitchen exercising the frying pan. The need for a new housekeeper was now becoming a matter of urgency.

They sat in the kitchen, each attacking a plate piled high with anything that had been in the refrigerator and was capable of being fried. Cross explained, between mouthfuls of bubble and squeak, that he had left several coded messages for his associate and would now be contacted through his private mailbox. The system used was secure even if the phone was being monitored.

"It will be a couple of days," Cross declared as half an egg disappeared into his mouth.

Three days later the four men were lunching in the Marine Club opposite Lloyds. John Hubbard had a swarthy complexion.

Somewhere in his past he had Hispanic ancestors. His hair was thick, wavy and jet-black. He peered out from underneath dark bushy eyebrows. His neck seemed to be non-existent, with his head apparently directly supported by two massive shoulders. Here was a man perfectly designed as a tighthead prop for the All Blacks. His hands were like shovels with the backs covered in fine black hair.

"Jim has told me that you have an interest in the so-called charity. I have spent some time digging about there, so how can I help you?" Hubbard was obviously not a man to beat about the bush.

"We think that there is a lot more than just charitable works going on at Gatefield Manor," Pinter replied. "We would like to know what you know and why you were working there."

"The second point is easy," Hubbard retorted through a mouthful of devilled crab. "A South American government was a little disturbed about the amount of charity and assistance being offered to certain elements in their country. They employed me to dig around and find out whatever I could about the ADC. I got a job there as a but basically I found out bugger all."

"What were you doing there?" Jennings interjected.

"I was employed by the security company they use. I have never seen such tight security in a bloody commercial company, let alone a charity."

"Surely that must have allowed you to do a fair amount of digging about. As a security guard you would have had full access." Jennings was asking a question rather than making a statement.

"Afraid not," Hubbard replied through another mouthful of crab. "We were only looking after the grounds and the public areas. The west wing was where all the private stuff was kept and we were not allowed near there. They had their own people for that. The only thing I can tell you is that about every three or four weeks everything was tightened up for a so-called founders' meeting. All our people were doubled up and the west wing was tied up as tight as a fish's arsehole. Normally about a dozen turned up, all in big chauffeur-driven motors, and they went straight in through the back entrance of the west wing. They normally started about five in the evening and, I presume, they had dinner afterwards as the caterers arrived at about six. They certainly had a taste for the good things. One of the caterers told me that only Taylor's 1926 or 1929 port was acceptable."

"Appleby," Pinter said quietly. "He is notorious for being pernickety, to say the least, about port."

"Lord Appleby – that was one of them," said Hubbard.

"Do you know who the others were?" Cross asked.

"Most of them," Hubbard nodded.

"Try these then," said Jennings, passing over a list of the COBRA Council members.

Hubbard was forced to stop eating and accept the proffered paper.

"There are a couple of names here that I don't know, but the rest were all there. Mind you, I couldn't identify two of the bastards, so it could be them." He passed the paper back to Jennings and resumed shovelling food.

Pinter leaned across to Jennings and whispered, "I think we are going to have to look inside this place."

Jennings nodded in agreement.

"We need your assistance, John. We have to get inside the west wing and see what we can find. Will you be able to help us?"

Hubbard wiped away the remnants of crab which had missed his mouth while he thought about Pinter's question. He studied the cut and quality of Jennings's suit as he pondered his answer. After some quick mental arithmetic he replied, "The price is five hundred a week with no guarantees. If you want anything further, like a bit of violence, that's an extra."

Jennings did not bother to canvass Pinter or Cross. He knew that he needed what Hubbard had to offer. "You're on," he said simply. "I need you immediately and I want you ensconced at my house by tomorrow night."

Hubbard took the card tendered by Jennings and dropped it into his breast pocket. "Tomorrow night it is," he said and proceeded to attack the T-bone steak that had just been placed in front of him.

Chapter Forty-One

Gatefield Manor,
18th February 1973

William Appleby was not in the best of tempers as the meeting convened. That morning he had been told that the House of Lords had reversed his judgement in the appeal court. It incensed him that all five of the geriatric old fools had disagreed with his view. He imagined them sitting in the Carlton Club, drinking malt whisky and gloating over how they had put that young upstart in his place. Once COBRA had the political muscle, the first thing to go would be the Law Lords. The case had set certain precedents which would have been of value in the future and he had expended a lot of energy persuading his colleagues in the appeal court to concur with his opinion. Having obtained a unanimous judgement from the appeal court, the last thing he had expected was that those Alzheimer-ridden old bastards in the Lords would overturn it.

He turned to Marden and peered over his glasses. He did not like the man, and as a result had decided that he must be incompetent. He said nothing but simply nodded in Marden's direction.

"Firstly the situation relating to Jennings." Marden started hesitantly; he knew that his news would be met by a withering rejoinder from Appleby. "It was, unfortunately, not possible to proceed with the proposal to have Jennings held on a charge of murder."

Marden had struck the detonator and Appleby exploded.

"What the hell do you mean it was *not* possible? It was arranged with the DPP that charges would be pressed! I want to know who fucked up and why." The judge seldom resorted to expletives other than when approaching a purple rage.

Marden shuffled his papers, desperately trying to think of a way of sugaring the pill or passing the buck along the line. Fortunately, Leonard King came to his aid.

"I am afraid that the evidence clearly showed it could not have been Jennings who inflicted the fatal injuries. Unfortunately we did not know that, subsequent to Jennings stopping our man, the hospital had to carry out an emergency tracheotomy. The injuries that killed him were below the operation area and consequently could not have been inflicted by Jennings. This point was made by the investigating officer in his report and the DPP had no option other than to drop any thought of charges. The case remains open, but with Jennings, unfortunately, in the clear."

Appleby was now apoplectic with rage and decided to vent it on the deputy commissioner.

"What is the point in having people in your position on the council if you are totally incapable of managing your own people and produce for us half-baked and incorrect information?" He then turned his attention to Marden. "As for you, Mr Marden" – the name was spoken as an insult – "do you employ people with brains? Your man must have seen a bloody great tube sticking out and decided to ignore it! Are your people's brains in their heads or do they sit on them?"

Hamish McHenry came to the rescue of the recipients of Appleby's anger.

"It is unfortunate, I know, William" – his soft lilt seemed to act as oil on troubled water – "but there is no point in looking backwards. What has happened is a fact of the past – now we have to decide how we go forward, don't you agree?"

Appleby knew that his reaction was not based on logic but his need to take someone to task. Marden and King were merely substitutes for the real targets of his anger. He nodded at McHenry and turned to Marden.

"Please carry on, Mr Marden," he said stiffly.

"It appears that Jennings has now recruited further help," Marden continued nervously. "He now has working for him a man, who is possibly a bodyguard, by the name of Hubbard. I have given the details I have to Mr Piper to see if he has any information on this Hubbard."

"I actually received a report on him this morning," Piper broke in. He produced a set of papers which he started to pass around the table.

"Hubbard was formerly a member of the Special Boat Service. Since leaving the services, he has been operating as a freelance for whoever wants to hire him. He is an excellent undercover operative and both MI5 and MI6 have utilised his services in the past. His main employers, however, are South American, African and Asian governments, particularly those with communist leanings. I would also add that Cross, Jennings's other cohort, is a similar operative. He has a more traditional clientele including ourselves, the CIA and Mossad. I would guess that Cross, or possibly Pinter, has brought Hubbard in. It's all in the report I have just passed around."

Appleby scanned the paper in front of him. After years at the Bar and then many more on the bench he could scan a document in seconds and extract all the relevant information he needed.

"It is now obvious to me that this Jennings and his associates could represent a risk to our objectives. We do not know what information they have obtained but they must, I feel, be treated as an unacceptable risk, against which action has to be taken. Would anyone disagree with my summary?" Appleby addressed his comments to the meeting.

"What sort of action would you envisage?" Philip Myers was not enthusiastic about the so-called necessary violence which had occurred in the recent past.

"I do not think that this is a matter for you to concern yourself with, Mr Myers," replied Appleby. "I believe that matters of security are best left to the experts rather than the squeamish." The last comment had the desired effect of silencing any other potential objectors. "Do you have any proposals, gentlemen?"

King spoke on behalf of the forces of law and order. "We discussed this prior to the meeting and have concluded that firstly we have to eliminate both Jennings and Pinter. These are the main dangers. We have several possibilities and I suggest that we set up and execute our plans and report back at the next meeting, hopefully with acceptable news."

"I do not like the word 'hopefully'. We expect to hear a positive result at the next meeting." Appleby turned to Piper. "Operation Bell: what do you have to report?"

"The operative has now been finally selected. He is currently undergoing final specific training. The progress is excellent." Piper was delighted to be able to offer some positive material. "We have retained one standby to cover any eventualities. The other two may be of assistance with the Jennings problem."

"Are there any other matters to be discussed?" enquired Appleby. He did not bother to await a reply. "Next meeting 10th March. Shall we adjourn for dinner?" As usual, the last remark was not intended as a question but given as an instruction.

*

Hubbard's body was stiff and aching. The cold gnawed at his hands as he fumbled to load the camera with infra-red film. He was hidden in a small thicket to the west of the manor about fifty yards from the entrance to the west wing. He had been there since four that afternoon, noting and photographing the arrivals. He made careful notes on the movement of the security guards. He had been doing this for the previous week. Tonight he noticed that the external security had been doubled and he knew that there was to be a founders' meeting. As the shiny Daimlers and Bentleys arrived, his camera buzzed like a bumblebee trapped in a net curtain. His pocket bulged with seven rolls of used film. The chauffeurs leaned on their cars exchanging opinions, probably about the merits or otherwise of the occupants of the plush rear seats of their respective vehicles. Only one seemed to stay aloof. Even standing beside the Rolls-Royce Silver Shadow he looked big. He moved with both grace and menace. The other drivers showed him great deference when he deigned to move in their direction. This man was not a simple chauffeur. He had other duties.

Hubbard heard the tinny sound of a two-way radio to his right.

"Positions for departure," the disembodied voice barked.

Hubbard knew that this meant that the 'founders' would soon be leaving. He had done this many times before as a security guard at the manor. He watched as the guards moved to predetermined positions and scanned the area. He knew that most of the guards would only be taking a cursory look because nothing ever happened. He noted which guards went to which stations and the enthusiasm with which they undertook their task. The camera whirred as the founders spilled from the building and made their farewells to each other. He saw that all, with the exception of Appleby, shook hands before climbing into their transportation. Appleby was met at the door by the big man and ushered to the waiting Rolls. The big man's eyes darted from side to side until his charge was safely in the car.

As the cars left in a long procession along the meandering driveway several of the security men ambled across to the stables. Hubbard heard the dogs barking as they approached. The dogs were always released into the grounds at dusk except on the nights when a founders' meeting was to be held. On those nights they were contained until after the luminaries had departed. It was now time to leave. Hubbard eased backwards from his hiding place and moved silently, but a little stiffly, to the boundary wall. He started the Cortina, turned the heater to maximum and started the two-hour journey back to Surrey.

His bones had thawed sufficiently to be tingling by the time he reached Staines. He was soon on the A22. At the Caterham roundabout he turned toward Woldingham. The Cortina climbed steadily up the hill, past the station, towards a warm bed. The golf club was in darkness as he passed. Hubbard was slowing to turn into Jennings's house when, out of the corner of his eye, he glimpsed a car parked in the trees. He did not know why but he drove past the house and on around the lazy bend in the road until he was out of sight. He parked the car in a small lay-by and sat. The car could contain a courting couple, although there were better and more private knocking spots along the same road. Instinct made him feel uneasy about the parked car and he elected to investigate.

He moved silently through the trees, occasionally cursing a bramble that tore at his face or hands. He approached the car from the rear and stopped a few feet away. He heard two voices, both male, and hoped they were not a courting couple. His eyes were now attuned to the dim light scattered by the watery moon. He caught a few words from the partially open window of the car.

"I'm bloody freezing. Sod all has happened for the last three hours. Can't we just bugger off?"

"Just shut up! Orders are to observe until morning and that's what we're going to do, so just stop bleating," a gruff voice replied.

Hubbard saw one of the occupants raise binoculars to his face and scan Jennings's house and grounds. He watched them for another hour. Saliva ran in his mouth when the aroma of coffee wafted through the open window.

Having seen enough, he circled away from the car and around the grounds of the house. He approached the house from the rear, unseen by the occupants of the car, and went in through the back door. The house was in darkness and he left it that way. Silently he climbed the stairs, avoiding the window, and went into his room. He watched them for another three hours through the infra-red binoculars. The two men observed and made notes. When the dawn chorus began to stir, the car eased back on to the road and left. Hubbard was exhausted and, fully clothed, collapsed on to the bed into a deep dreamless sleep.

It seemed as if only five minutes had passed when he was woken by a cheery voice and the smell of fresh coffee. The morning sun was already dispersing the previous night's frost. The steaming coffee scalded the back of his throat and brought his eyes into some sort of focus.

"You must have been knackered last night. You haven't even changed. What time did you get in?" Jennings's voice was distressingly jovial.

"The bloody founders turned up last night so I was there till nearly eleven. I then got back here and there were two blokes keeping the house under observation. I decided that I had better see if I could find out what they were up to."

"Who were they?"

Hubbard turned his palms upwards in an expression of ignorance.

"Let me have a shower and I will fill you in over breakfast."

Hubbard felt better after scrubbing away the residue of the previous night. The kitchen was full of the smells of the traditional English breakfast. Cross was duty cook, so the aroma of burning toast was added to that of bacon and eggs. Hubbard poured a cup of strong black Kenyan coffee and downed half the cup in one mouthful. Jennings sat at the table engrossed in an airmail letter Hubbard assumed to be from Pansie. Jennings, whom he had come to like, was besotted by this woman, and Hubbard could not wait to meet her. If she was just half as attractive as Jennings expounded, she should be a goddess.

Three breakfasts were transferred from the frying pan to the plates on the table. The three sat and Hubbard attacked his. He was ravenously hungry, having not eaten since the previous afternoon.

They finished and Jennings poured more coffee. He lit a JPS, blew a smoke ring and turned to Hubbard.

"What's all this about the house being watched?"

Hubbard told them of the events of the previous night and the snatches of conversation he had heard.

"They were definitely watching this house?" Cross enquired.

Hubbard nodded. "The car was a bronze Capri. The number was PFN 56L, if that's any help."

"Let's see if they turn up tonight. If they do, we'll have to have a little talk to them." Jennings addressed his comment to neither man in particular. "How did it go at Gatefield Manor yesterday, John?"

"As I told you, the founders arrived last night. The security arrangements were exactly the same as when I was there. Manual security was doubled and the dogs were kept in until they all left. The chauffeurs all stayed outside, but one of them wasn't just a driver. He looked too sharp to be a door-opener and hat-doffer."

"Which car?"

"Appleby's. He certainly isn't the same dickhead who used to drive the old bastard. Also, judging from the founders' behaviour when they left, Appleby is the main man. He kept himself aloof from the rest."

"Have you got enough information about Gatefield for our purposes now, John?"

Hubbard nodded to Jennings. "More than enough."

"Can you develop the film today and we'll all have a talk tonight? I'll get George down as well."

Cross and Jennings left, Jennings to his city brokers and Cross for another appointment with a very pretty physiotherapist at Oxted Hospital.

*

The four sat around the large coffee table poring over the photographs taken by Hubbard over the previous week. Pinter was still complaining bitterly about the indignity of having to travel on the floor in the back of the car. He did not care who knew he was there and made certain the others were aware of his views.

Several images on the table showed the grounds and access routes to the manor, others the arrival and departure of the founders. There were also diagrams showing the disposition and patrols of the security men. The routes were marked in different colours denoting the alertness or not of a particular guard. Each man had a different idea of how the building should be approached. Eventually they reached common ground. By the time all their ideas had gelled and merged, it was nearly midnight.

"Let's have a look and see if we still have visitors." Jennings spoke while he stood and stretched his long limbs.

They went upstairs to Hubbard's bedroom, their eyes adjusting to the darkness.

The Capri was nestling among the trees in exactly the same place as the previous night. Jennings took the camera and studied them through the infra-red lens. The car's occupants were obviously getting bored with their task. One was trying to hide a lighted cigarette in his cupped hand. The other idly scanned the house and garden with his binoculars. The first man looked familiar to Jennings but he knew not why.

"It's time to go and see who our visitors are and find out what they want," said Jennings, looking at his Rolex. "I think we had better leave the old man and the broken leg here, don't you, John?" Jennings smiled as he was given two single-digit salutes simultaneously.

The two men changed into dark sweaters and slacks. Jennings took the Luger from the drawer in the desk and pushed it into his waistband. They left by the back of the house, Jennings following Hubbard. They stopped ten feet behind the Capri and listened. As on the previous night one occupant was complaining about the cold and the other was telling him to shut up. Jennings and Hubbard moved silently along opposite sides of the car. In unison they wrenched open the doors, pulled the occupants sideways and their fists struck flesh with one accord. Surprise was total and resistance non-existent.

"Well, well, Corporal Hyde. I haven't seen you since Colchester." Cross was looking into the frightened eyes of the first man as he opened the door to Jennings, Hubbard and their two captives. The second's eyes showed evident terror. His neck was in the iron grasp of a huge hairy hand, while his arm was being driven through his shoulder blades.

"Get them down the basement and tie them up," Jennings passed the Luger to Cross. "George, come with me and we'll get rid of the car."

Cross pushed Hyde towards the basement door, followed by Hubbard dragging the other man. Both Hyde and his consort were shoved down the narrow steps into the cellar where they crashed on to the stone floor. They were picked up bodily, tossed into chairs and bound hand and foot.

"You stay with them, John, and I'll make sure everything upstairs is okay." Cross climbed the stairs, leaving Hubbard with the two captives.

Jennings drove the Capri down Chalkpit Lane and into Oxted. He left it in the free car park. Pinter followed in the Jaguar.

Corporal Hyde and his sidekick were trussed like turkeys ready for Christmas. Their faces looked ashen in the glare of the single 150-watt light bulb. The huge hairy man who stood over them looked dangerous in the extreme. A simple observation job had turned into a nightmare.

"Well, Corporal Hyde, my friend tells me that you were not very pleasant to Mr Jennings in Colchester. Perhaps a little retribution is due." Hubbard's voice was soft but ominous. "I think it might be in your best interest to tell us why you and your friend have been spying on us."

Both men stayed silent. Hubbard stepped forward, his hands bunching into fists the size of a mace. The second man's eyes showed abject dread.

"We're just obeying orders! We don't know why they wanted you watched!" he blurted out.

"Shut up!" snapped Hyde.

He immediately regretted his intervention as one of Hubbard's huge fists connected with the side of his head.

"And who might *they* be? Who do you work for?" Hubbard spoke to the first man.

"Military intelligence." The reply was unconvincing.

Jennings and Pinter clumped down the steps and saw immediately that Hubbard's temper was near to boiling.

"Leave it for now, John." Jennings's tone indicated that this was not a request. "I think that these two could do with a night down here in the cold. They will probably be ready to discuss matters in the morning, provided the cold hasn't killed them."

"You can fuck off," Hyde muttered defiantly, and the other fist left a matching bruise on the opposite side of his face.

Jennings checked the bindings of both men and indicated to the other two to go upstairs. He turned to Hyde, the anger that he thought he had left in Colchester churning at his insides.

"If I were you, I would think carefully about what you can tell us tomorrow. My friend John can actually be most unpleasant." He climbed the stairs, switched off the light, locked the door and wedged a chair under the handle.

He went into the lounge, where the others were sitting, and poured himself a drink. He was regretting taking the two spies as now he was not sure what to do with them. Hubbard produced the solution.

"It's quite simple. Tomorrow morning they will give me all the information we need."

"Just a minute," interrupted Pinter. "Just because we are dealing with vicious bastards doesn't mean that we have to be the same."

"George, you underestimate me," Hubbard continued sanctimoniously. "Whilst I would actually get enormous pleasure out of beating the crap out of Mr Hyde, Pentathol, which I happen to have, is much more effective. I can find out all we need to know within a couple of hours. After that, I have connections and can arrange for the two of them to go on a long trip. I can put them out of circulation for six months."

Pinter looked more than relieved.

Chapter Forty-Two

Hyde opened his eyes, expecting a harsh light to assault his mind. Nothing happened. He turned his head to try and see a source of light. He saw none. Gradually his eyes became accustomed to the darkness and he could make out the shape of someone slumped opposite him. He could feel that there was movement underneath the floor but he did not know why. The room's darkness became lighter as his iris expanded to absorb what little illumination there was. The place was cold and the floor hard. It was a huge room, with no lights and no doors. His head hurt, his body hurt and he could not remember where he was or why.

His companion stirred. Perhaps he could ease the growing panic that was now attacking him. The walls of the room were not walls. They were dark, hard and unforgiving. Where was he and why?

His companion sat up and mumbled, "Where the fuck am I?"

Hyde confirmed that he had no idea where they were or why. There was a constant movement and dull reverberation in the room. There was a smell of the countryside mixed with diesel oil. The feeling of movement became more acute. Hyde tried to massage his eyes and found that he could not move his hands, as they were secured behind his back. He then realised that his feet were also secured, both together and to something else. The realisation made him struggle to free himself of the bonds that held him, to no avail. The room was hot and humid and sweat poured from him. His companion was now going through the same slow comprehension of his plight.

"Where am I?" he pleaded.

"Just shut up and let me think," snapped Hyde. His memory was slowly returning, at least in part. They were sitting in the Capri, observing Jennings's house. Their job was to plan how to eliminate Jennings and his cohorts. The next memory to surface was being in a cellar with one bright light assaulting a growing headache. There was a huge man, with fists to match, which were matted with thick black hair. He remembered an enormous black fist as it struck him.

There were four men, but this one was dangerous. The memory of the second blow sprang into his mind. They had slept and then the hairy man and another had returned. He remembered nothing else. Everything was blank.

There was a scraping sound above his head and a square shaft of light leaped downwards. The light changed shape as the outline of a head, wearing a peaked cap, appeared as a silhouette in the square of light.

"I think they're back in the land of the living now, Skipper." The voice was detached and not really in the same world as Hyde.

Another silhouette appeared.

"Good morning, gentlemen," a voice said. "We are currently three hours out of Sheerness. You are going on a nice trip to Brazil and we hope you are going to enjoy it. My friend Hubbard has paid me extremely well to ensure that you are both unavailable for the next six months. Enjoy your trip."

The shaft of light disappeared.

Chapter Forty-Three

"Your erstwhile friends are now enjoying the pleasures of a cruise on one of the most grubby grain carriers in the northern hemisphere." Hubbard was pouring a beer as he spoke. "I suggest that you get yourself a drink and I'll tell you a story about a snake."

Jennings threw his jacket on the back of a chair, closely followed by his tie. He enjoyed the life of a reinsurance broker but not the dress requirements. He poured himself a drink and sat in his father's old rocking chair. The winged back seemed to cocoon him from the world. As a child, this chair had been his haven from strife. He took a long pull at the glass and savoured the flavour of hops and malt. He nodded at Hubbard to show that he was now in the mood for snake stories.

Pinter poured a large whisky and nestled into the soft leather of the settee.

"Our COBRA is planning a strike," Hubbard began. "We had a little chat with your former prison comrade and he has been doing some very unusual training, as has his friend."

Jennings raised his eyebrows as Hubbard continued.

"For the past month our two little spies have been undergoing specific training at a disused army range in Essex. The training has been quite specific. They have had to become accustomed to spending considerable periods of time in a small enclosed space. The space is about ten foot long, and four feet in diameter – rather like a large oil drum. The drum is fitted with battery lights and they were having to remain inside, absolutely silent, for up to forty-eight hours."

"What the hell for?" Jennings asked.

"That, I am afraid, they did not know. At the present I can only guess that the training was for some sort of concealment. What is even more interesting is the second part of the training. They have been doing target practice, but of a very specific nature. They have been practising using two different weapons. First a .762 FN self-loading rifle, and secondly a Lee Enfield .303."

Jennings's mind was racing. The Lee Enfield was still the finest sniper's weapon in the world. It had a bolt action, which limited its value for rapid fire, but as a single-shot gun it could not be bettered. The FN was the second choice of the sniper. It had the advantage of being self-loading and several targets could be engaged in rapid succession.

"I think you are ahead of me," continued Hubbard. "The two weapons being used are probably the two best sniper firearms you can get. What seems obvious is that our snake is planning to do someone in. What is even more intriguing is the type of shot or shots they were being trained for. It is quite specific. The distance is about two hundred yards, but the target is something like two hundred feet below the sniper. The other factor is that the last hundred yards of the trajectory are sheltered with no wind, but the first hundred are not. Just to add a little twist, there is no wind from the rear."

"On that basis, I would guess that the shot is to be made from inside a fairly tall building. I would also surmise that the target will be between buildings, probably in a street. It's likely that the shot is being made across a road into a street that runs at right angles to it."

Cross had been drawing sketches showing possibilities since that morning. He had heard of but never seen Pentathol in use and was astonished at how effective it had been.

"Why the two different guns?" Jennings could see no reason for any indecision. He had operated as a sniper and had always had his favourite weapon. There was never any need for choice. He had always used a Lee Enfield while others preferred the FN and one always insisted on a Bren.

"I wondered that until they told me they were practising two different shots. It looks as though there are going to be either one or two targets. They have been practising both a single shot at one target and two rapid at two targets up to ten feet apart. The Lee Enfield would not be much good for the latter. First the bolt action would slow you down, and, second, the round is a much lower velocity. With the FN the second shot would be on its way before the sound of the first had even reached the target."

"Okay," said Jennings. "COBRA are planning a strike and are going to a lot of trouble. Now they have a problem – their hit men are now on their way to distant places."

"Afraid not." Hubbard was enjoying feeding the tale piece by piece to Jennings. It was like playing a salmon – feed some line then draw him in again. He knew that Jennings was his intellectual superior and he was relishing keeping him dangling on the hook. "It seems that our playmates at COBRA are a little bit more astute than that. The two we took last night were the failures. There were four under training and what we got were the two discards. Apparently, of the two left one will get the job, with the other as the understudy. The two failures we got had been given a new task."

Jennings decided not to interrupt as he knew that Hubbard was now playing games.

"Their new task", Hubbard continued, "was to plan and carry out the removal of both you and George. I got the distinct impression that the removal was to be permanent rather than temporary. It seems that there is a nice man called Wing Commander Marden who doesn't really like you."

"I'm not really very keen on him," snorted Jennings. "I don't think that Jim is ragingly enthusiastic either after having his leg smashed up by the bastard."

"Well, the thing is, these two guys are supposed to observe your movements for a few weeks and then come up with a foolproof plan to knock you off. They have a free hand, but before taking any action they must obtain approval from Marden. What is quite handy is that both of them can put their heads down at Gatefield Manor."

"How long before they are missed?" queried Jennings.

"I would say that we've got a week to ten days before anyone even thinks about enquiring, would you not think, Jim?"

Cross agreed.

"Did you find anything out about the manor?" Jennings knew that Hubbard did, otherwise he would not have introduced the subject.

"We actually know quite a lot. Their quarters are in the west wing, which is where the outside security people are not allowed. It's a big rambling wing with twenty rooms. They even drew us a map." He laid a sheet of paper on the coffee table. "Access to the wing is limited and controlled by digital locks. The code is changed every morning. The actual number is a six-digit number made up of the number of letters in each of the first six words in the third column of page seven of *The Times*."

"It's lucky they don't use *The Record* – there would be a lot of threes and fours. I think that George is the only one there who knows a word longer than four letters, and that's Pinter." Jennings ducked as a well-worn Hush Puppy flew by his head.

"Stop the pissing about, children," Hubbard chided them. "Apart from telling us how to get into the manor, our friends also told us about the security arrangements." He pulled a thin steel tube from his pocket and held it up. "Dog whistle. Two short, one long, one short tells all the nice Dobermanns that you are a friend. Inside, two guards permanently on duty from sunset to dawn. Other times the exterior is patrolled. The internal guards have to key in at set security points around the building every hour. These are shown on the map." There were eight rings on the plan each marked with an 'S'. "These guys have been doing this for two or three years and have never seen or heard a bloody thing. Apparently, they punch their keys but walk about with tunnel vision. Our Mr Hyde was going to report the lax security next time he saw the brave Wing Commander. Crawling little git," he spat. It was clear that Hubbard had no love for Hyde and would have preferred to use old-fashioned methods of interrogation rather than Pentathol.

"Do you think that we could get into the manor?" Jennings knew that somewhere inside that Victorian edifice lay the answers to many questions.

"As I see it," Cross answered before Hubbard, "it should be quite easy. We go in, using the Capri, during the day. The outside security know the car and will take little notice of us. We know how to gain access to the west wing and there won't be any security in the building, leaving us free to do what we want."

"I know it sounds feasible, but it's too risky," interrupted Hubbard. "I used to work with those people and the tightest area is gate security. They will not just accept the Capri. They will have a good look at the occupants. The only time to go in would be just before dusk. The light will be poor and the guard will be wanting to go home to his supper. That's the time when they will be lax."

"What about the inside men?" queried Pinter.

"They go straight into their first circuit of the building as soon as they arrive. We wait and follow them in. They will be on their rounds and we can make straight for Hyde's quarters, which are not on the guards' circuit. We then follow them, two rooms behind and plant listening devices. We won't have time to search thoroughly."

The four talked about the alternatives well into the early hours. Finally it was Hubbard's plan which was accepted. The next Friday was chosen as the time to execute the plan. It had the advantage that the guard on the main entrance would not just be getting away to his supper but also for the weekend. Cross and Jennings, who most closely matched the looks of Hyde and his sidekick, were selected as the two to go in. Hubbard and Pinter would wait in the Jaguar by the west wall of the grounds to provide the transport home.

The evening was typical February. Dark clouds totally obscured the rising moon. A persistent drizzle caused small rivulets of water to distort the images seen through the tinted windows of the Capri. The tarmac of the road looked like a river of oil meandering through the dormant countryside.

Jennings parked the Capri on a patch of wasteland and turned off the lights. A pair of lights appeared in the mirror and rushed towards them. There were two men in the Range Rover that passed, its tyres hissing on the wet surface. It turned into the grounds of the manor and slowed momentarily. The gate guard waved it on and the car accelerated. They watched as it wended its way along the drive and around the building. They waited a few minutes and then started the Ford. As they turned into the manor the security man walked into the road. He recognised the Capri and waved them past. Gravel crunched under the wheels as though trying to warn the occupants of the manor. As they turned behind the building Jennings switched off the lights. The drive was visible from the west wing and they did not want to announce their arrival.

The words *'The parties commenced litigation following the...'* flashed into Jennings's mind as he punched the numbers 3-7-9-0-9-3 into the keypad. *The Times* had carried a story of a dispute between two neighbours over the right of ownership of a stray cat which they had both been feeding. There was a faint click as the lock released. The hallway was dimly lit. An oblong of bright light shone from under the door of the guards' quarters. They went past and turned towards the room occupied by Hyde and Co.

It was sparsely furnished with two beds, two chairs and a television. The door to the bathroom was in one corner. They switched on the lights and the television. Cross sat by the door waiting for the guards to return. Jennings opened the holdall. Inside was a selection of listening apparatus of different shapes and sizes, a selection of equipment designed to gain access to anything from a house to a desk drawer, and an explosive device, small enough to hide and large enough to destroy a small bungalow. He tested the remote control unit on the detonator and reattached it to the bomb.

Footsteps came along the hallway and a loud voice said, "It sounds like the fucking KGB are back. I wonder what oh-so-important things the wankers have been up to for the last few days." The voice was deliberately loud and derisory.

"Sticking their noses into someone else's business, probably," came the reply.

Cross winked at Jennings. The brief conversation and its tone confirmed that Hyde was not popular and not to be socialised with.

It was an hour before the footsteps returned, accompanied by the first voice saying, "Let's go and punch those fucking keys again. You could go barmy in this job." The reply was grunted and inaudible.

Ten minutes passed before Cross eased open the door. The two watchmen were now into their rounds. Cross and Jennings followed in their footsteps.

The first three rooms were used as storerooms. Stationery and circulars were neatly stacked on shelving attached to the walls. The circulars were the usual moral blackmail for which most charities are famous. They are designed to play on the conscience of the recipients and then make them dive into their wallets. Cross placed a small bug in each room, even though it seemed unnecessary.

The next room contained four desks, each equipped with a typewriter and telephone. A small microphone was inserted into each telephone earpiece. They went through a door to the adjoining office. This was more sumptuous with a large mahogany desk, the latest IBM typewriter and an intercom/telephone. There were three metal filing cabinets, all locked, against one wall and a Xerox photocopier on the other.

Cross indicated to Jennings to tap the telephone and set about opening the cabinets. Many companies relied on these cabinets to store confidential information. It took Cross less than a minute to unlock all three. Most of the contents related to fund-raising and spending. There were staff files and accounts. As Jennings flicked through the last cabinet he found a file marked FOUNDERS' MEETINGS. Listed inside were the dates of past and future meetings with details of attendees at previous meetings. Jennings knew that the security men would be on the other side of the building by now and he switched on the Xerox. He photocopied the last three lists of attendees and the roster of meetings. Whilst the machine whirred he jammed a small screwdriver into the copy counter. He replaced the file and Cross relocked the cabinet.

Along the corridor they found a massive office. It was dominated by a enormous leather-topped kneehole desk. The edges around the leather were ornately carved. Two telephones – one black and the other maroon – sat on opposite corners as though they had fought with each other. 'The occupier of this room is left-handed,' thought Jennings. Both telephones were set to be picked up with the right hand, leaving the left free to write. In one corner of the room was a coffee table with seating for eight people.

Cross picked the locks in the drawers while Jennings bugged the two phones. There was only one file in the desk and it was marked OPERATION BELL. There were a number of what appeared to be incoherent notes. The writer had his own version of shorthand. The only legible sheet was typewritten and headed *Timetable*. Various dates were listed with cryptic comments such as selection and training. The last three entries showed:

1st June 1973   Installation of operative
2nd June 1973   Execution
4th June 1973   Removal of operative

The word 'execution' was highlighted in fluorescent yellow. Jennings noted down the contents of the sheet, hoping that someone would be able to make sense of the jottings later.

Next to the lavish office was a conference room. The walnut table was about twenty feet long with an ornate carver dining chair at each end. There were six matching chairs along each side. A false ceiling had been installed, with the lights set into the polystyrene. Jennings stood on one of the chairs and pushed a tile away from the framework. He eased the bomb into the space between the real and false ceilings and replaced the tile. Cross placed a listening device in the space at each end of the table.

Jennings checked his watch and indicated to Cross that the guards would be returning in a few minutes. They went back to Hyde's room to wait.

They followed the guards' route on their next patrol, planting the microphones where needed. By midnight their task was done and they waited for the guards to disappear on their rounds. The drizzle had stopped by the time they left. The moon struggled to be seen through the damp, thin clouds. Cross pulled out the dog whistle and identified them as friends to the prowling dogs. There was a large oak by the west wall where the Jaguar would be waiting.

Jennings was the first to hear the dog approaching, its teeth bared. He stepped towards the animal, extending his left arm towards it. He had had training on how to deal with dogs, but it had never been put to use. The brute was black and ominous. It launched itself at the target presented. Jennings felt the fangs driving into his sleeve as he smashed the side of his hand between the beast's eyes. The jaws released their grip as their owner flopped to the ground. Both turned and ran for the wall.

"Trust you to find a deaf dog," was Cross's only comment as the Jaguar eased away from the manor.

Chapter Forty-Four

Passengers trudged wearily into the arrivals hall at Gatwick, clutching their duty-free bags and pushing trolleyloads of luggage. Flying may be the most efficient form of transport, but it is also uncomfortable and tedious. Some passengers had drunk their way through the boredom. Others had tried to sleep and now had aches in joints that had been locked in alien positions for many hours. Pansie's eyes wanted to rest as she scanned the throng waiting to meet and greet returning passengers. She saw Jennings, and the tiredness lifted from her. It seemed a year not a month since she had last held him. His strong arms enveloped her and she smelled the desire within him. It was minutes before she realised that George and Gwen Pinter were also part of the welcoming party. Gwen issued orders to the men to take baggage and parcels. Pansie was definitely going to be the daughter that Gwen had longed for but never had.

It was six the next morning when Pansie awoke. It was a crisp winter morning, the sky clear blue and the sun a bright orange globe creeping above the horizon. The robins in the garden trilled to each other as though saying, 'Nice morning'. As she showered she closed her eyes and imagined the soft touch of Jennings's hands on her body. She wanted him there and then. The night before, they had made love, gently at first, then, as their desire rose to a crescendo, they had become one.

She donned Jennings's dressing gown. He was asleep, sprawled across the bed. The release of his pent-up emotion the previous night had left him exhausted and he slept like a baby. She wanted him again but let him sleep.

Hubbard was in the kitchen, a steaming mug of black coffee in his hand. He had been making new friends the previous night in The Haycutter. It was his turn for the morning shift monitoring the goings-on at Gatefield Manor. When Pansie entered, he looked up and smiled.

"You must be Pansie. I'm John." He proffered his hand to her. "Allan has told me a lot about you, but you're even more gorgeous than he told me."

She bowed graciously.

"I understand that you are helping Allan and Jim." It was more a question than a statement.

They chatted over coffee about everything and nothing. Hubbard had spent some time in Singapore and they found, surprisingly, that they had several acquaintances in common. Hubbard laughed as he told her that his job had been to root out potential communist agitators.

"It's not long ago that we were on opposite sides."

"Ah, I was too good. You would never have caught me," she retorted.

"Well, Lee Kim got out before I could nail him. Was he a good teacher?" Hubbard's accentuated male ego did not like to admit that he could fail.

"He was one of the best guerrilla fighters ever, but he was weak and easily manipulated in the real world." She thought, wistfully, of the man who turned from being a tiger in the jungle to a rat in the sewers of life.

A pair of strong hands rested gently on her shoulders. She turned to Jennings. His hair resembled a demented mop and dark-blue bristles covered his jaw. Small lines of tiredness spread, like a delta, from the corners of his eyes. She touched his hands and immediately wanted him.

Hubbard left to spend the day looking and listening at the manor. It was three days since the bugging operation but no material of value had yet been gleaned. Cross looked weary when Hubbard arrived. The night shift was the worst as nothing ever seemed to happen. The only excitement was when one of the guards telephoned his girlfriend and went into the visceral detail of their sex lives. Hubbard had bought some bacon rolls which they ate together before Cross took the car and left.

The van was a dirty green colour, which blended in with the scrubby woodland where it was parked. The day security arrived at eight each morning so the van had to be moved to a different position each day. Hubbard started the engine and drove to the next location. He climbed from the driving seat into the back and donned the headphones. He checked the recording equipment and adjusted the antenna for the new site. He could hear the guards inside finishing their last tour of the west wing. A telephone jingled and one of the tapes began to whirr.

"Gatefield Manor, Barnes speaking." The voice had a heavy Birmingham accent.

"It's Marden here, Brummie. Can you get Hyde? I need to speak to him."

The line went silent. Hubbard could hear footsteps leaving the office. The indicator showed that the telephone being used was in the guards' quarters. The footsteps returned and a voice said, "He's not in his room; neither is his mate, sir."

"Do you know where he is?"

"No, sir. They came back three nights ago but we have not seen them. The Capri is still here but they aren't."

"They can't have gone anywhere without the car." Marden's voice was showing a hint of anger. "Hyde is supposed to report to me weekly and hasn't. Have you actually seen them?"

"You know him, sir - arrogant bastard. He was much too important to talk to us. We never saw them, we just heard them."

"Stay there, I'm coming down. I'll be with you in about an hour."

"Yes, sir." The accent did not hide the frustration in the guard's voice. Hubbard had listened to the recording of the conversation with his girlfriend and knew what had been planned before breakfast.

The equipment bleeped as a car broke the beam they had hidden in the driveway. Hubbard picked up the camera and slid back the window. It was the sixth time that morning he had been through this process, but no one had come to the west wing. Five cars were parked on the east side of the building. Hubbard recognised the staff of the charity as they arrived to work in the main offices. A Granada with military plates swung around the corner and parked next to the Capri. Two men alighted from it. Hubbard's camera clicked and whirred as he photographed both men and car. There was another bleep when they entered the door. Hubbard sat back and listened.

"Brummie, where the fuck are you?" a disembodied voice yelled.

Hubbard heard the sound of footsteps and a voice shouting, "Coming!"

"Where is his room?" It was not a request.

The footsteps disappeared. 'Why the hell didn't they tap the living quarters?' thought Hubbard as the voices went out of range. The voices returned. Marden was telling Brummie that if Hyde reappeared he must report. He heard the bleep as Brummie gratefully made his way out to go and savour the pleasures of his girlfriend's voice on the phone.

The earphones transmitted a door opening. The equipment signalled that it was the large office which had been entered. A telephone was picked up. A light flashed on to show it was the red handset. There were several clicks on the line; 'Probably a scrambler,' thought Hubbard. There was the sound of dialling and then a ringing tone.

"King speaking."

"It's Colin Marden. Can you talk?"

"Give me five minutes and I'll ring you back. Are you at the manor or in your office?"

Marden confirmed the manor and then hung up.

"I don't know what has happened to those two you sent me, Geoff, but I think we should brief Leonard's man in case we have to use him." Marden's voice seemed to be suppressing anger.

Hubbard thought for a moment. The only Geoff that could be was Piper.

"Is the guy any good?" a second voice asked.

"All I know is that he took care of the old general when the Jennings situation started to get embarrassing. He is supposed to be totally reliable."

The telephone burst into life.

"Okay. Colin, what do you want?" It seemed as if Marden were not the most popular man in the council.

"The position is that the two so-called expert operatives for the Jennings job may have done a runner. If they have, we are going to have to use your man, whether he likes it or not. I suggest that you brief him and have him on standby. We only have two weeks before the next meeting and we have to have a plan of action by then, at the latest."

"What makes you think that your people have gone walkabout?"

"They arrived back at the manor four nights ago. Their car is still here but they have not been seen or heard since that night. Also, that night one of the dogs patrolling the grounds was killed and there were signs of someone climbing over the west wall of the grounds. I know it isn't conclusive but we ought to have a back-up plan, in case. Otherwise the judge is going to take us, or me in particular, apart."

"All right, I'll have a definite plan from my man within a week and brief you before the meeting. Can you be at the Waterside Inn for lunch the day of the meeting?"

Marden confirmed that he would be there and that Piper would be with him. The phone went dead.

Hubbard watched as the Granada drove away, and settled down to listen to nothing for the rest of the day.

Later Jennings listened to the recording, his fists clenched and his anger burning. He had heard what he needed to hear. He would know who had killed his father and could seek retribution. He had started on this road to find out why Brigadier-General Jennings had been roasted alive in that lonely dark lane and who had killed him. He was getting closer to the who, but the why still eluded him.

Cross and Hubbard had created a diagram with all the facts they had learned and tried to see where one part of the puzzle could be linked with another. The data was shown in chronological order with different colours connecting items that seemed to be related. The connections were drawn both backward in time and forward. The threat to Jennings was linked to the attacks on Cross and Pansie. The link went back to the brigadier's death, Jennings's conviction and the patrol. There was also a possible link with the deaths of Lee Kim and Lin Chow. COBRA seemed to be involved in all these actions, but why? Jennings was sure that the answer had to be connected with his father. He knew that COBRA had approached his father but not how much his father knew of them. As time went by more pieces would be added to the puzzle, and perhaps a picture would emerge before it was too late. When the cobra was ready to strike, the mongoose must be prepared.

Over the next week further pieces of the conundrum were gleaned from the manor. The two who were training for the strike were moved to the Parachute Regiment Battle School in the Brecon Beacons. The cover was that they were part of Special Forces training for a mission.

Jennings remembered his time at the school. At six every morning each syndicate would be sent doubling up and down the hills around the camp in full battle order. The colour sergeant in charge would run beside them, armed with a heavy toggle rope which was used to assault anyone deemed to be flagging. This would be followed by a short breakfast and then either an hour on the assault course or a log race over the hills. The log race was especially character-building in military perception, punitive in human terms. Eight men were affixed to each telegraph pole and the teams would race each other over a hilly course of two miles. The last team to finish would be selected for the night's guard duty. The desire to avoid this was such that if one man fell during the race he would be dragged, along with the log, by the other seven until he regained his feet. The tallest had the choice of either running stooped, like Quasimodo, or erect. The former gave them backache but the latter meant that they would carry the whole weight of the log, lifting it from their shorter compatriots. Most chose to impersonate Quasimodo. Any spare time was spent in weapons and fieldcraft training. After two weeks of basic torture they were sent in twos on the Brecon course. Each was given a map, compass and twenty-four hours' rations. They were supplied with map references to report to over seven days and dropped off in the Beacons. It was supposed to be a test of orienteering and fieldcraft, but in Jennings's belief it was actually attempted murder. If it had not been for Murph he would not have made it to the end. The stocky smiling Irishman had cajoled and bullied him through the last three days.

There was a call from Porterfield confirming a delivery of equipment on 1st June at six in the morning. The call did not designate what equipment and to where it was going.

One particular day Appleby was in residence at the manor. He spoke to Marcus Banton ordering him to send drafts of six future speeches for vetting. Banton complied with a degree of subservience. This was followed by a terse warning to Marden to ensure that a full plan for ending the Jennings situation was presented at the next founders' meeting. Victor Barrett reported that the canvassing was progressing better than expected. What was being canvassed, and why, was not revealed to the listeners.

All the material was recorded on the chart, which still made little sense. Jennings, Cross or Hubbard, and Pansie spent fruitless evenings trying to make sense of the clues they had, but to little avail. Even the most imaginative lateral thinking produced no feasible answers. They knew that Operation Bell was the key to unlock the mystery, but the key was uncut.

Jennings left for a business trip to Singapore and Australia on 4th March. He had wanted Pansie to go with him but Gwen had other ideas. Weddings had to be planned. The date had been arranged for 30th June at St Mary's Church. Gwen was determined that the bride would be the most beautiful ever seen and the reception would be the talk of the chattering classes for years.

It was late morning and the sun was a fireball in the sky. The humidity hit Jennings as he left the terminal at Singapore, obediently following the chauffeur from the Shangri La Hotel. The air-conditioning in the Rolls revived him, so that instead of being hot and tired he was only tired. His bags were taken into the hotel and he went to register. A pretty Chinese girl with soft green eyes gave him his key and a message in a sealed envelope which has been waiting. He followed the bellboy to the room and gave him a ludicrously large tip as the travel agents had again forgotten to supply some small notes for such purposes. Jennings wondered whether the agents ever actually tipped, as they never seemed to consider supplying the wherewithal for tipping. Perhaps they had a commission arrangement with the bellhops.

He sat in one of the easy chairs savouring the cooled air which radiated around the room. The beer was ice-cold and slipped down easily. He opened the message and smiled.

> *Hope your flight was all right and you are not too pissed, you old bastard. Have a sleep and then meet me in the Long Bar at Raffles at 7 p.m.*

Jennings had not made any appointments before lunch the following day, knowing that Peter Huber was entertaining him that evening. He showered, fell on top of the bed and sank into a deep sleep. He was dreaming of being chased by an old-fashioned police car, its bell getting louder and louder as it approached. The dream ended when he woke with a start. The police bell was now the insistent ringing of the telephone.

"I hope you were not asleep. If you were, you shouldn't have been. It's six o'clock and you should be getting ready!" a familiar voice yelled.

"Mr Huber, how are you. Thank you for ruining a bloody fine dream."

They chatted for a while, confirming the night's arrangements. Huber informed him that a night to remember had been arranged. Jennings knew that Huber's idea of a night to remember would consist of consuming an improvident number of gin slings followed by enough food for three people. If eating were an Olympic sport, the Swiss would win gold, silver and bronze medals. Following the meal, as sure as a dog follows a bitch on heat, they would end up in a club or bar where nubile young ladies would remove their clothing for the benefit of the customers who were still sober enough to appreciate their efforts. Huber and Jennings would not fall into this classification. Huber's insatiable desire to see naked or semi-naked ladies was conditioned by being born in Zürich. A stripper in that town would be perceived to be debauched if her bra was removed. In order to calm the customers, the strippers' acts were interspersed with magicians and jugglers. As a result the customers were bored away from any possible exciting notions. Jennings often wondered how the nation, as a whole, actually reproduced. It had to be related to the cold weather in winter.

The Long Bar was, as usual, hot, sticky and very British. The early scrimmage to sit under one of the ceiling fans had been won and lost. The two barmen were demonstrating their ability to prepare an unending supply of gin slings to the wide-eyed tourists. Huber waved and attracted the attention of both Jennings and a waiter, which was his intention. He had, obviously, used his great bulk to advantage since he sat directly beneath a fan. The drinks arrived and a long night began. Knowing Huber's voracious appetite for alcohol, Jennings switched to beer after the first gin.

It was in the strip bar that Jennings first noticed him. The bar was on the outskirts of Chinatown and virtually all the customers were oriental. There was a group of American sailors in one corner. They were obviously American because they made the strange whooping noise, like a castrated chimpanzee, Americans seem to make at any event ranging from a baseball match to a presidential election. This man sat on the table next to the whoopers. He was Eurasian with frizzy grey hair. He had been nursing one drink for over an hour and whenever Jennings glanced in his direction he turned his head away.

Huber became tired of the parade of breasts and buttocks. The service was very slow, which also affected his opinion of the bar.

The two grabbed a bicycle rickshaw and headed for the Shangri La. The bar was cool. When their first drinks arrived, Jennings noticed the frizzy grey head. He was sitting in the reception area where he could see the bar. Jennings pointed him out to Huber, who immediately wanted to go and fight the intruder invading his privacy. Jennings restrained him and decided that much more to drink would lead the large Swiss into a state of unconsciousness. He had no desire to have to carry the hundred kilograms which made up Peter Huber and feigned a serious case of jet lag. He put Huber into a *tuk-tuk*, which careered up the road with Huber bellowing instructions from the rear.

The air was still heavy as Jennings walked along the street. He heard the soft footsteps a distance behind him. He turned a corner and slipped into a shop doorway. The soft steps approached and stopped.

"I wondered whether you had noticed me, Mr Jennings. May I introduce myself? My name is Inspector Lo Chow."

Jennings stepped from the doorway. Chow had stopped ten feet short of the door. Close enough to act but far enough away to react.

"Would you mind telling me why you have been following me?"

"Mr Jennings," he said, bowing, "your fiancée is an old friend of mine. She told me that you might be in danger and asked if I could allocate an officer to ensure your safe arrival and departure. When you were my enemy, Pansie saved my life in the jungle. I could not delegate such a task to anyone else so I carry out her wishes myself." He bowed again.

"Perhaps I should buy you a drink and you can watch over me from close quarters."

Chow bowed and followed Jennings back into the hotel.

Chow had been converted to the cause of communism later in life than most. He had been born of a peasant family and spent many years working in the paddy fields. He had seen the great riches of the plantation owners and the miserable poverty of the workers. Initially he had accepted that this was the way things were. When his mother had become ill from old age and years of deprivation, the doctor had suggested to the owner of the plantation that she should be hospitalised. The suggestion was dismissed, as it was cheaper to find a new worker than pay for hospital treatment. Within a month his mother had died. Chow had slit the throat of the owner and made for the jungle. He was found by a PFP patrol and had joined them. He was quick to learn, and had the presence necessary to command. He had been head of intelligence at the ceasefire and taken up a senior position in the new police force created by the Government of Unity. Unlike many of his former PFP colleagues, he still retained his values, and, whilst he was comfortable, he lived modestly.

Jennings asked him about the ceasefire and the part the massacre of his patrol played. The outline of the ceasefire had been agreed many weeks before Jennings's patrol had been despatched. Unknown to the government, the PFP had been on the point of collapse. Terms for a cessation were offered which were acceptable to the PFP. The only demand the PFP made was the sacrificing of a British patrol to allow them to be seen to come to the table undefeated. This was agreed with Colonel Herne of Military Security and a man called Leach, who, Chow thought, was MI6. The requirement of the British was that the ending of hostilities had to be agreed only after a week of tripartite meetings between the government, the PFP and Marcus Banton, who was a junior minister at the Foreign Office. Jennings's patrol was offered as the sacrifice.

"You nearly fucked up the whole arrangement, you know." Chow chuckled and dug Jennings in the ribs.

Jennings asked him about the negotiations and Banton in particular.

"That pompous bag of wind did nothing other than make rehearsed speeches to the press. The whole thing was a charade. Everything had been agreed weeks before without a puffed-up Banton or the British Government. The negotiations were a play put on for the benefit of the media. The fee was the aid that the new government received from Britain. The aid went into the pockets of the greedy ones," he said sadly. "I left and came to Singapore. The poor still starve in my country and the rich still let them."

"Did you ever hear of an organisation called COBRA?" Jennings had to ask the question.

Chow shook his head.

Jennings did not sleep well that night. All these seemingly unconnected facts bounced around in his mind. Marcus Banton was the key but it fitted only one lock and this was missing.

He rang Pansie the next morning and chided her about her arrangements for a guardian angel. She told him that anyone being entertained by Peter Huber needed a good Samaritan to follow them. They talked about Chow, and Jennings told her to pass all the information to Cross to solve. She told him that McHenry had told Appleby to watch the FT100 Index over the next week. He said, as a practice run, that it would increase by 15 points by the middle of the week and fall back 30 by the end. Jennings was utterly confused. Practice for what? Were they intending to manipulate the index for personal gain, or for a more sinister reason?

Jennings travelled on from Singapore to Perth and then Adelaide. On these trips he always tried to be in Adelaide for the weekend. He could then fly over to Kangaroo Island, where there was some magnificent scuba diving. He stopped at Adventureland Diving in Pennyshaw. The owner was an ex-para who had emigrated to Australia in the Sixties. He had bought a bulk cement carrier and taken up scuba diving as a sport. He had obtained all the instructors' qualifications and decided that lorry driving was not for him. He sold the small business he had built up and bought the place on the island. Since that time his hobby had also been his living.

The small Cessna swooped over Pennyshaw Airport. The airport consisted of a field with a shed in one corner. The light aircraft buzzed the field to frighten away the sheep, circled and landed. The pilot had learned his trade in the bush and could land his machine on a sixpence. Whilst the pilots were the best, Jennings worried about the business acumen of the flyers who owned Emu Airlines. It had always struck Jennings as a poor business decision to name an airline after a bird that could not fly.

The Cessna bumped to a halt and the three passengers unwound themselves through the tiny door. The Adventureland Diving Land Cruiser was parked by the shed, the owner, John, leaning on the bonnet. He was just under six feet, stocky, with a weather-beaten deep brown skin. His accent was somewhere between London and Sydney. In Australia it designated him as a Pom and in England as an Aussie. He was an easy-going man with the exception of when he was diving. Then the rules were there and they were rigorously enforced. Most diving injuries are received by instructors while trying to extricate pupils from their own idiocy. John did not intend to join the statistics.

That evening they sat outside, listening to the ocean. The crayfish and abalone were cooking on the barbecue. The beer was cold, the evening sun was warm and the company was congenial. It was not often that John had the company of people from the land of his birth. He enjoyed the irony of English humour. He had found his paradise, but a part of him still yearned for the wind, rain and snow. By midnight the world was definitely a better place.

Early the next morning the Land Cruiser bumped along the dirt road which was the expressway across the island. They were making towards the Remarkable Rocks. These were a landmark on the island. The sea and the wind had shaped these huge rocks into wondrous configurations. Looked at from different angles, they became diverse things. One person could see an eagle soaring, another would see a vulture gorging on its prey. Whoever had discovered them had named them accurately, for they were truly remarkable.

John reversed the Land Cruiser towards the sea, and his son unhitched and launched the boat. They donned their wetsuits and pushed out to sea. The rubber dinghy rounded a small headland and headed into a cove. Sea lions were basking in the sun. As the small craft came into view they lifted their heads. Jennings saw that as they came closer the sea lions slipped off the rocks into the sea. They knew that divers would soon be in the water and it was as though they had come out to play. The vessel anchored and Jennings and his instructor slipped off the side.

On land sea lions are ungainly. Underwater they are the epitome of grace. They flowed through the water like smoke wisping on a wind. They made the divers look clumsy. One sea lion was intrigued by the air bubbles emitted from Jennings's mask. It flew to the surface and returned to blow air into his face. They showed off, each competing with the others for the best trick. One was swimming with Jennings when suddenly there seemed to be a huge explosion in his head. The animal seemed to scream and then writhed in apparent agony. Blood filled Jennings's vision. His immediate thought was that a shark had appeared. The white pointer bred in these waters. As his head cleared, his first reaction was to swim clear of the red water. If it was a shark, the smell of the blood would call it back. He saw John signalling to him to go down. They swam to the bottom and sat. There was no sign of a shark or anything else. The sea lions had gone and so had the fish. The only sign of life were the antennae of a crayfish protruding from behind a rock. He saw that blood was oozing from John's leg through a tear in his suit.

John signalled to him to look up and locate the boat. He then pointed up with both hands and made a heart shape. The signal meant 'Up and in the boat'. As they rose they could see signs of frantic movement inside the rubber hull. They surfaced on opposite sides to see John's son frantically pulling on a wetsuit. When he saw them, the look of relief on his face was as though they had risen from the dead. Something touched Jennings's elbow and he started. It was a piece of sea lion flesh; side of the sea lion had been torn to pieces. It looked as though it had been attacked with a chainsaw. They climbed into the rubber boat. Jennings, without knowing why, pulled the lifeless body of the animal behind him. John started the outboard motor and turned the boat back towards the headland. One section of the port side had deflated, which slowed their progress.

They sat bemused, unable to comprehend what had happened. The small craft had been pulled right out of the water. John's son was bandaging a deep cut on his father's leg.

"What happened?" John was the first to speak.

"A motor launch came round the head," his son answered. "I warned them that you were diving and they made straight for where you were. The passenger dropped something overboard and then there was an explosion."

"Did you know them?" Jennings asked.

The reply was negative.

Jennings looked at the once-beautiful creature. He had seen that sort of damage before. It had been inflicted by a high-explosive grenade. If the animal had not been in a playful mood, Jennings would have been the lifeless body now lying on the shore.

The local police had never had so much excitement. There were statements to be taken and a scene of crime to study. The divers made their statements in the bar of the hotel in Kingscote and then drove wearily, the length of the island, back to Pennyshaw. John's wife fussed over Jennings but even more over her wounded husband. It might have been only three stitches but it deserved maximum attention. She had received a message for Jennings to telephone Cross. He used the office.

"Allan, thank God I've caught you in time! Unless you are careful you are about to have a diving accident."

"It's already happened, Jim. How did you know?" Jennings replied.

"Marden told King about it. He said that it would be unlikely his man would be needed. What happened?"

Jennings told Cross the tale of the afternoon. His anger rose as he recounted the story.

"Did you get anything else?"

"Sorry, I'm afraid that was about all. I just hope that we can get something out of the founders' meeting scheduled for next Monday. I'm putting in a second monitoring unit for that in case anything goes wrong with the existing one."

Jennings then spoke to Pansie, which was a mistake, since he felt even more alone.

The police returned late that evening. The motor launch had been traced. It had been found in Adelaide harbour, the owner shot dead inside.

Chapter Forty-Five

The taxi pulled up outside the Pinters' home. Gwen Pinter was still in giggling mode. Bollinger always had that effect on her. It was twenty-eight years since the spring morning she had vowed to love, honour and obey George Pinter. Each year had been happier than the previous one. They had been to the Grosvenor for dinner. They had spent one night there, which was their honeymoon in 1946. Every year since they had returned to celebrate their anniversary. Some years they had not been able to afford to eat for the next week but the anniversary had to celebrated there by tradition. It was a tradition of George's making but she happily concurred. This year they had been to the gourmet restaurant known as 90 Park Lane. The fare had been exquisite, the service exemplary and the ambience beyond comparison.

They had been disappointed that Jennings could not be there, as both looked upon him as almost a son. Pansie was, however, a more than adequate substitute. Tony Hacker, Jennings's oldest friend, had escorted her. Stories of good days gone by had been exchanged and wishes for the future made. Gwen looked at her man as he paid the taxi and knew that one decision made many years ago had been right.

There was not the normal welcome of warm air when they entered the house. Pinter muttered about the bloody central heating being on the blink again. She opened the kitchen door and was greeted by a blast of icy air. She switched on the light and saw the back door was open, its glass panel smashed. Before she could call out, something struck her.

The pale light of dawn was filtering through the drawn curtains. She shivered with the cold. Her head ached and the bed felt hard and uncomfortable. It wasn't the bed. She was lying on the kitchen floor. The cold air blasting through the broken panel seemed aimed directly at her. She felt the back of her head. It was sticky and her hair was matted with something. She looked at her hand. In the half-light it looked as though it were covered in treacle. Slowly she remembered seeing the broken glass and then nothing.

Gwen struggled to her feet, her stomach beginning to knot in panic. "George! George!" she shouted. No reply came. She half staggered, half ran from room to room, calling his name. The house was empty. She fought the panic now trying to take her in its grip. The telephone, where was the telephone? She did not know what room she was in. She sat down, closed her eyes and took a number of deep breaths. Slowly her hand stopped shaking and her befuddled brain began to clear. She saw the telephone. An efficient voice asked her which service she required. She could feel her collar wet with the warm blood that was dripping from her head. "Police," she cried. The strain was too much and she collapsed into insensibility.

She felt warm but her head throbbed as though some demon was using a piledriver to escape from inside. She heard a voice say, "I think she is coming round."

The room was white and a single light hung from the ceiling. Her head was propped on several pillows and the sides of the bed were barred. She panicked and tried to sit up but she felt a hand gently holding her and heard a voice say, "It's all right, Gwen, lie still." The voice had an accent.

Her vision began to clear. The voice belonged to a plump brunette with dark green eyes. The nurse's cap came into focus and then the uniform.

"Where am I?" She tried to keep the fear from her voice.

"You're in hospital – there's been an accident." The soft Irish lilt calmed some of her fears.

A man in a white coat appeared. He shone a light in her eyes. He whispered to others who were not in focus. Her eyes closed.

"She has had a severe blow to the head and is badly concussed. I am afraid that you will not be able to speak to her until, at the earliest, tomorrow morning, Constable."

The policeman thanked the doctor and settled down in his chair. This type of job was as boring as watching a chess tournament. The person under observation never moved. He pulled the Harold Robbins paperback from his pocket and eased back into his fantasy.

They pulled into the hospital car park. Hubbard had driven the Jaguar hard. Pansie was trying to suppress the terrible thoughts that had plagued her since the telephone had rung two hours before. All she knew was that Gwen had been in an accident and had asked for Jennings. She and Hubbard had left immediately, leaving Cross to contact Jennings.

The policeman was relieved to have something to alleviate his boredom and insisted on cross-examining them before he would permit them to enter. Even when he was satisfied, he insisted that he must clear it with his superiors. He was the classic jobsworth officer who would retire as a constable.

Once he had satisfied himself that everything was in order, he allowed them into the room where Gwen lay. Her head was swathed with white bandages. Her face was pale and drawn. Pansie sat beside the bed and held her hand. She felt Gwen's grip tighten. Her eyes slowly opened and tears welled up. Her dream had been about George but he was not there. She slipped back into the world between dream and reality. She wanted to dream: reality might be too forbidding to contemplate.

Hacker arrived late in the afternoon. *The Daily Record* had received a package by hand that lunchtime. Inside was a statement from a previously unknown South American subversive group calling themselves Freedom From Oppression. They said that Pinter was being held as a hostage and would be killed unless their government released all political prisoners. A photograph of Pinter, his face bruised, was in the parcel.

The whole case had been taken over by Special Branch, and Hacker was the officer in charge. The deputy commissioner was taking a direct interest. Hacker told Pansie and Hubbard as much as he was able.

Cross arrived in the early evening. His eyes were heavy from lack of sleep. He had left a message at the Sheraton in Sydney to await Jennings's arrival. He gave Hubbard the keys to the car he had hired and the keys to the van they knew as the Listener. He had catnapped during the day, the earphones on his head. For the next few days neither he nor Hubbard would get much sleep.

The newspapers in Australia are quite parochial. The story of the kidnapping of a British journalist only warranted three column inches on page seven. Jennings was thumbing through the paper simply to pass the time. The extra day he had spent in Adelaide answering interminable questions about the attack on Kangaroo Island had been exasperating enough. Then the Ansett flight from Adelaide had been delayed for two hours and he was, by now, more than fatigued. The steward had just brought another beer when Jennings sat bolt upright, nearly spilling the drink. He read the tiny report.

> George Pinter, a journalist with the British newspaper *The Daily Record*, has been kidnapped by a South American terrorist group. The group, known as Freedom From Oppression, have sent a statement to the paper demanding the release of all political prisoners.

The short article gave a brief description of Pinter and his past. As an afterthought it mentioned that his wife had been injured during the kidnapping and was now in hospital with head injuries.

Jennings reread the article, his mind in a turmoil. Frustration welled up inside him. He could do nothing. Why was he stuck in a huge tube flying over the Outback?

At the Sheraton, Cross's message awaited. The dialling tone rang, like a persistent wasp, but there was no reply. He guessed that Hubbard or Cross would be at the Listener, the other at the hospital with Pansie. He telephoned his office and spoke to Corby. His only appointment the next day could be rescheduled and Corby would fly out immediately to take over the remainder of the trip. The travel agent was unusually efficient, and two hours later he was on a British Airways flight to London.

'Don't leave Gwen alone.' He willed the thought to be in the mind of Cross and Hubbard.

The lights were burning when he arrived back at Woldingham. The flight had been abominable. He had not sleep nor had he felt like food. Alcohol could not dull the fear that taunted him.

Cross was sitting in the lounge nursing a drink. The side of his face was swollen and his eye partially closed. He looked up as Jennings came in and shouted, "Pansie, it's all right, the cavalry has arrived!"

She came from the kitchen and saw him. He took her in his arms and she wept uncontrollably. Slowly the story emerged through the sobs. That afternoon a strange doctor had arrived to examine Gwen. He had been about to give her an injection when Cross challenged him.

"I suddenly thought, Doctor Clarke!" interpolated Cross.

He had lashed out at Cross and escaped, but had dropped the syringe.

"I have only seen and smelt it once before, but I would bet my life that it was curare in that syringe," Cross stated simply.

"Who is with Gwen now?" Jennings remembered the second attempt to murder Pansie.

"It's all right, John is with her. We've had to rely on the automatic devices at the Listener. It was either that or drop dead from exhaustion. Also, following the good doctor's efforts, there are two coppers, neither of whom are now allowed to read about blow jobs in Harold Robbins' books." Cross remembered the constable with his head stuck in *The Betsy* while some stranger tried to knock off his charge.

Jennings slept fitfully that night. He finally gave up the attempt at getting further sleep at six the next morning. Pansie lay next to him, her firm round breasts rising and falling with her breathing. It had been the first night that they had been together and not made love. It was not simply fatigue, but with Pinter missing and Gwen fighting for life in the hospital it seemed wrong. They had said nothing but understood all.

Cross was in the kitchen drinking his third black coffee. There was much to be done that day and night. Tonight was the founders' meeting and both listening posts would have to be manned. Someone would have to be with Gwen and somehow they would have to find Pinter. To actually achieve all these tasks they would need eight people not four. His mind had churned over every possibility but there was no solution. He and Jennings talked through all the options but none was totally satisfactory. After an hour in which the devil's advocate won every argument, they decided that they could plan the next twenty-four hours in the hope that the goddess of luck would smile on them.

Cross left for the manor.

"I am afraid that she is slipping deeper into a coma. She seems to be losing the will to fight." The plump Irish nurse fluffed up the pillows around Gwen's head as she spoke. "Each time she has come back to us she has then slipped deeper into coma."

Jennings asked the usual stupid questions about drugs or any other treatment. He knew, however, that for Gwen to come round she must want to. He sat by her bed the whole day. He talked about the past, the present and the future. Sometimes she seemed to respond but he could not tell whether this was wishful thinking. He willed her to open her eyes, trying to transfer his desire for her to live to her. The policemen changed, the nurses changed, but there was no change in Gwen.

There was just time to shower and change before leaving for the manor. He did not know why but Jennings went to the safe, removed the Luger and put it in his waistband. They drove in the second van. This had directional listening devices as well as the same equipment contained in the first. The pulled up behind the other van just after six in the evening. Since he had spent the night at the hospital, they had expected Hubbard to look as tired as they felt. They were wrong. His eyes were clear and his step jaunty.

"We've *got* the bastards!" The delight in his voice was easy to hear. "Come and listen to this. Marden was here this morning and he had a call." He switched on the tape recorder.

"*We have him nicely under wraps. Any time you want to come and interrogate him, he's yours. We have already softened him up a bit so he should be easy.*"

Marden's voice replied. "*Don't you be too sure of that. He was one of the top men on Special Operations. The Nazis had him for five days before he escaped, and got fuck all out of him.*"

"*I'm sure that your people can do better than that,*" the first voice replied.

"*I expect we will,*" Marden responded. "*I will see you at the Dower House tomorrow. Keep a close eye on him.*" The line clicked dead.

"What does this tell us?" Jennings already knew COBRA had taken Pinter. This conversation only confirmed it.

"I know where he is," Hubbard smiled. "When I was undercover here, we occasionally had to put a guard on another premises about ten miles away in the middle of the country. It is called the Dower House. That's where George is."

This had to be the piece of luck Cross and Jennings had prayed for. They had until the next morning.

The three talked over the possibilities. It would have to look to COBRA as though Pinter had escaped without outside assistance. They could not risk revealing their hand. It was also vital to monitor the founders' meeting in case any more light could be shed on their plans. Cross was still not as mobile as he could be and would be left with Listener Two. Listener One could work automatically, they hoped. Hubbard and Jennings would go to the Dower House.

There was no moonlight and the ground was covered in a hazy mist. The weather had reverted to its early February mood. The two men had left the car a mile away from the house and approached on foot. The ground underfoot was soft. They stopped thirty yards short of the house. A patch of early potatoes offered excellent cover. There was a light on in one room at the rear of the building. No other lights were showing.

Hubbard circled the house to the front, Jennings to the rear. He could see into the lighted room. Pinter was trussed up on a chair on the wall facing the window. His face was puffy and he appeared to have taken quite a beating. Two men sat playing cards between Pinter and the window. Each had a Uzi sub-machine carbine resting against his chair. Jennings smiled to himself and patted the Luger. Both fired 35mm ammunition. Hubbard slid silently beside him. He signalled that there did not seem to any other occupants. Jennings whispered his strategy to him and he gave a thumbs-up sign.

"I don't think that you've got anything better than an ace high."

They had grown tired of beating up on this old fool, who would not say a thing.

"I told you so," the thug exclaimed delightedly as he pulled the money towards him. He turned to Pinter and sneered, "Do you want to see the news again? Your old tart might be dead by now. We've got friends at the London Hospital."

Pinter tore at the bindings, feeling them cut into his wrists.

"What's that?" said the other.

There was a scratching at the front of the house. They listened again. The noise got louder. Both men picked up their Uzis. One crept silently towards the sound. It seemed to come from outside the front door. Again it got louder. He cocked the carbine and checked it was set to automatic fire. The other man did the same. The noise became louder and more persistent. Holding the weapon in his right hand, the first man slid back the bolt. The noise stopped and he heard footsteps moving away from the door. He pulled the catch and swung the door open. A hairy fist, with the centre knuckle pointing like a spear, drove into his thorax. His voice box and windpipe shattered and he flew backwards. The gun clattered metallically on the floor.

Jennings knelt, his right hand extended, his left hand steadying his right wrist. It had to be a throat shot. The round must exit cleanly. The Luger kicked in his hand and the other man jumped backwards, his throat now a gaping hole.

Hubbard was already in the room untying Pinter. Jennings ran in and went to the wall where his projectile had finally come to rest. He dug it from the wall and put it in his pocket. The body lay by the window. Jennings replaced the Uzi in the dead man's hand and pressed the trigger. He sprayed the wall as though he had been falling. Hubbard dragged the other body back into the room and threw it backwards against the wall. They propped the second in front of the window and told Pinter to fire half a magazine into it. The lifeless torso hit the wall, its head smashing the window, and slumped forward.

"We have not got much time," Jennings's voice was urgent. "The story is that you freed your hands and took the first one out. You grabbed the Uzi and blew the other away before he could do it to you. You take their car and make for the nearest police station."

"I'm sorry, Allan, but I am going straight to the London Hospital." Pinter's voice was determined. He rummaged in the pocket of his former captor and took the car keys. Pinter went, leaving Jennings and Hubbard to make a short search. They found nothing to identify the dead men or their masters. They found two Browning machine pistols, which they took.

*

She was in a corridor. At one end there were steps going upwards. There was a woman at the top of the stairs dressed in white. She beckoned. Gwen moved towards her. A voice from behind called her name. She turned but the corridor was dark. She went back towards the voice but he was not there. The woman motioned for her to climb the stairs. She went closer. Now she recognised the woman: it was her mother. The voice from behind called again. She went back but still there was no one. She turned and went closer to the stairs. Now she was cold. Her mother held up a cardigan. It was the pink one she always wore to parties. Now she was shivering. She would go up those stairs and get her cardigan. The voice behind called again. It was persistent. It said it would take her to Mauritius. He was going to take her there for their thirtieth anniversary. A pearl in the ocean for a pearl anniversary. Her mother extended the cardigan to her. The voice was insistent. She turned and went towards the voice. Someone passed her and ran up the stairs. She could feel the air getting warmer. There was a light. She ran towards it. They were his eyes. Kind and gentle eyes. She did not see the bruises that surrounded, just his eyes. Why were they crying?

"Thank God you're all right," sobbed Pinter as he held her. She touched his face and smiled.

*

Sheraton Hotel, Sydney

Corby was exhausted. He had never flown directly to Australia. He had catnapped on the flight but not really slept. He was forcing his eyes to stay open, trying to concentrate on the trip notes Jennings had left for him. He knew the clients he was seeing but did not have an intimate knowledge of the business the company placed on their behalf. The first appointment was with the Government Insurance Office of New South Wales. They were, far and away, the most valuable client in the continent. He made notes of how the programme fitted together and tried to think of ways it could be streamlined. That would be the best method of pulling more business his way. Corby was losing the battle with his eyelids and decided that a cold shower would redress the balance in his favour.

The cold water startled his metabolism and lightened the heaviness over his eyes. He let the water cascade over him, tingling the nerve ends back to life. He did not hear the click as the door opened. The silenced Browning spat three times and he was thrown against the wall of the shower. His lifeless body collapsed and the shower washed away the blood that drained from his insensate torso.

*

Cross saw the lights of their car in his mirror and waved at them to stop.

"Marden has just reported that you have been taken care of, Allan," he blurted out. "Your body will soon be found in the Sheraton in Sydney."

Jennings was perplexed. Suddenly it stuck him. He had not checked out of the hotel and had left the room for Corby.

"The bastards have got Charlie Corby!" he spat.

"Just a minute," Cross pressed the earphones to his head. "King's just taken a call to tell him that George has escaped. Appleby is going apeshit."

They listened for a while, imagining Marden squirming in his chair. Appleby could cut through cast iron with his tongue. It seemed that the only saving grace was the demise of Jennings. 'Poor Marden,' thought Cross. 'He'll be chewed up and spat out when they know the truth.'

True to his nature as a newshound, Pinter had phoned through his story to *The Record*. It was the only paper to carry the story of his escape in the early editions. The headlines screamed RECORD'S HERO. The story told how Pinter, single-handed, had killed the two armed terrorists and escaped. The police team at the scene saw the evidence to support the veracity of his tale.

Hacker took several statements from Pinter. The police were baffled as to why Pinter had been the target. They could not identify either of the kidnappers nor had they ever heard of the organisation they were supposed to represent.

Corby's death only warranted a brief mention in the national papers. There was a full page obituary in *Lloyds List* and substantial coverage in the other trade papers. There was no connection made between the two stories.

Chapter Forty-Six

They were both appalling patients. Neither Pinter nor Gwen relished being fussed over by strangers. They had spent twenty-eight years fussing over each other and did not require outside help. The hospital decided to expel both as soon as possible. Jennings's offer of home comforts and nursing was accepted gratefully and both were discharged into his care. Pinter's ribs were still strapped and the bruising on his face made him look like a Post Impressionist portrait. Gwen had insisted that all the silly bandages had to be removed as they were ruining her hair. She did give in and agree to wear the surgical collar for an undefined period, which ended up as the day after she left hospital.

Jennings's life was temporarily taken over by the office. Charlie Corby's death had left an extensive hole in the company's management. Jennings was involved in meetings with the other shareholders deciding how to structure the operation. When the person who had laid the foundations and built the castle disappears, he is not easy to replace.

Cross and Hubbard went back to monitoring the comings and goings at the manor. Hubbard had the pleasure of listening in on the conversation, albeit one-sided, between Marden and Appleby when it was ascertained that it had not been Jennings in the hotel room in Sydney.

Gwen had decided that it was not possible to be ill when a wedding has to be planned. She took Pansie in hand and they started preparing agenda for the run-up to and the wedding itself. Pansie, who had never really known what it was to have a mother, succumbed, and in fact enjoyed the machinations of her self-appointed foster mother.

Pinter, whose ribs took an interminable time to heal, confined his activities to transcribing the tapes that arrived from the Listener. He developed Cross's chart, looking for links in the titbits of information gleaned.

Hacker was a regular visitor both officially and unofficially. The police had been unable to identify either of Pinter's captors. Their inquiries into Freedom From Oppression had produced nothing. The group was unknown, even to the security forces in their own country.

The weapons the two men had used were traced back to a theft at an army base in Wales two years previously. The Dower House had been rented for a three-week period through an agent. The agent had been paid in cash. The tenant's name and address were both fictional. Pinter had enquired who actually owned the Dower House, and Hacker told him it was a charitable trust called the Association for Democratic Conservatism. The trust used the premises for visiting notables, but rented it out when it was not needed.

It was the end of March when a snippet of information was picked up in the Listener which confirmed Pinter's own theories. Appleby had been at the manor with Marcus Banton and Hamish McHenry. As he typed up the conversation on the brigadier's rickety machine his worst fears were, in his mind, confirmed.

Appleby: *I have made several changes to the transcripts. There are some areas where I think that you should be a little more forceful. I have numbered the speeches from one to six to show the order in which they should be delivered. The last three will be given in the two weeks preceding Operation Bell.*

I want your name in all the daily papers. There is enough in these first three to get you on to the radio and television. Once you have their attention, the next three will keep it. There must be maximum media coverage.

What dates have you arranged?

Banton: *I have already definitely arranged for two of the final three. One at the Welsh Conservative Trades Unionists' Conference and the other at the Guild of Insurers. For the third, Vic Barrett is arranging a dinner for all members of the 1922 Committee the day before Operation Bell. I will be the speaker. This should be confirmed in the next week.*

Appleby: *What about the dates for the first three?*

Banton: *My ideas are that my constituency dinner on 14th April will be number one. I am opening an international legal convention on 26th April, where I will present the second, and the* coup de grâce *is the Confederation of British Industries Conference on 10th May. Again, I will be opening the conference.*

Appleby: *Good. Now, Hamish, is your side organised?*

McHenry: *After Operation Bell the markets will become jittery. We will ensure that situation remains until contenders for the leadership are declared. When Marcus declares himself, the markets will steady and spurt upwards. The media will have a field day playing with polls and the like. Any poll that seems detrimental to Marcus's position will result in a fall in the markets. By the time of the first ballot it will be clear to anyone but an idiot that the financial community is behind only one candidate. The support from industry will come from Robert Webster and Philip Myers.*

Appleby: *That only leaves the problem of Pinter and Jennings. It is highly likely that they know nothing of any substance. Our security has been tight, but we cannot take the chance of their guessing our intentions. I have given up on Marden and told Leonard King to put his man on to it. Thus far he has never let us down, although this bastard Jennings seems to have more lives than a cat."*

Pinter reread the brief conversation. He looked at the chart of facts and knew, in his heart, that this confirmed the theory he had been hoping would be dismissed by events.

That evening Pansie and Gwen were due to visit a dressmaker to look at designs for wedding gowns. Pinter suggested that the four men should go out for a quiet drink.

Jack Martin's taxi was a little small for the three younger men, who squashed in the back. Pinter was in a sombre mood and this transferred to the other three. Hubbard and Cross were sharing the burden of the Listeners. It had been decided that night-time surveillance was not needed unless there was a founders' meeting, so their load had eased slightly. Jennings had taken over as chairman of Corby, Lannin & Davies and was in the middle of reorganising the company.

The Haycutter was always quiet on Tuesdays and the four sat in their usual corner. Pinter did not have any subtle way to tell them of his fears.

"I've been listening to yesterday's tapes. I am afraid that the only logical conclusion is that COBRA intends to assassinate the prime minister on 2nd June and that he will be replaced by Marcus Banton."

"That's my gut feeling as well," said Cross quietly. "I heard that conversation, and that is all it can mean."

"Tell us how you got to that," said Hubbard.

"The conversation today was about putting Banton into the forefront with the media. That particular activity increases as Operation Bell gets closer. McHenry has plans to manipulate the Stock Exchange up and down to counteract any ups and downs in Banton's popularity. Banton will get maximum media exposure prior to 2nd June and, when he declares as a candidate, the markets will go up. If it looks as if someone else will be elected, the markets will go down. Conservative MPs are not going to buck the financial markets. They need them buoyant as an election is only eighteen months away. Add this information to the fact that we know two men are training for what can only be a hit on someone and you can only conclude that the target is the PM."

"So, we know the target and we know the date – what we *don't* know is where," Jennings concluded. "You can presumably get hold of the PM's schedule for that day."

Pinter shook his head. "Not always. Only certain movements are given. It used to be easy but the IRA has fucked all that up. Also we are only likely to get any information two days in advance. Security seems to be more important than publicity."

"Bloody hell, you look like the Four Horsemen of the Apocalypse!" None of them had heard Hacker come into the bar. "If you need cheering up, I can buy you a drink and tell you a story."

Hacker brought the round of drinks on a tray and placed it in the middle of the table. "George," he addressed Pinter, "you will be pleased to know that we have identified one of your abductors. It was a result of diligent police work and a bloody great chunk of good luck. As a last desperate act we tried immigration at all the major airports. By pure chance, a guy at Gatwick remembered the one you shot. The reason he knew him was that he had been particularly bolshy when he came in so the officer had given him a hard time to get his own back. He came in a week before you were taken, on a flight from Belize."

"Well, who was he?" Pinter asked.

"His name was Manuel Mendoza, or that's what his passport said. The immigration bloke said he spoke like a cockney not an Hispanic. We are currently making enquiries through the embassy in Belize and also through the intelligence people at the British Army garrison there."

"Is this official or off the record?" The instinct of the journalist smelt a scoop.

"We will be announcing it tomorrow, but if you want a little exclusive it's yours."

Pinter put his drink down and made for the telephone on the other side of the bar.

The conversation changed to the topic of Pinter's kidnapping. All three wanted to hear and discuss the theory put forward by Pinter but could not with Hacker present. Jennings felt a degree of shame at excluding his oldest and best friend, but Hacker was, first and foremost, a police officer. A lot of their actions were not exactly within the framework of Her Majesty's law. Also, whilst Jennings tried to dismiss the thought, COBRA did have tentacles in many unexpected places. His heart told him to trust Hacker but his reason told him to wait and see.

"Another interesting point is that the man who rented the house from the agent was not one of the bodies we have." Hacker continued the tale. "This is off the record." He looked at Pinter, who had returned from capturing a headline on yet another front page. "We have a description which could actually fit about one million people. In fact, if you were a few inches shorter, John, it could be you." He looked at Hubbard and smiled. "The only distinctive feature was that he had hands like buckets."

He turned again to Pinter. "By the way, I must congratulate you, George. You knocked over the second bloke with your first shot. The post-mortem shows that you hit him in the throat, which killed him instantly, and the rest of the magazine was unnecessary."

"It's like riding a bike, Tony – once you know how to do it you never forget." Pinter winked.

The conversation for the next hour meandered around the usual subjects discussed in public houses by the male of the species. Just before ten all five left – Hacker to walk to his home and the others to be chauffeured in a taxi.

Pansie and Gwen were in the kitchen poring over dress designs. Gwen shooed Jennings out, giving him a lecture about bad luck and the groom's seeing the bride's dress. The four men made for the cocktail cabinet in the study.

"I think that we have to assume that the target *is* the PM and that the date will be 2nd June. What else do we know that may help us?" Pinter had racked his own brains but got nowhere.

They discussed what information they had. They knew that the hit men were training specifically for a shot which would be taken from about two hundred feet above the target and that the distance was about two hundred yards. They surmised that the shot would be from a building along a street opposite. The need to sleep in metal drums was argued backwards and forwards but no reasonable explanation could be found.

The training allowed for the possibility of one or two shots being required. If there were to be two shots, *who* or *what* was the second target? There was no obvious answer.

They then considered their own security, particularly Jennings and Pinter. What was clear from the tapes was that COBRA was not deterred by their past failures. Cross and Hubbard wanted Jennings to go to ground until more was known. Jennings was adamant that he would not. The man coming after him was the same bastard who had murdered his father. He would make him play his hand and then strike back. Whoever he was, he would pay for his father's death.

That night Jennings made love with Pansie as though it were his last time. The woman in his arms was so crucial to him that he had to show her so. They lay together, her soft skin caressing his body. He talked of his fears and she of hers. She did not want him to risk his life but knew that he must. She felt him inside her deeper and deeper until her orgasm exploded with a fury she had never known. They clung to each other as the tidal wave of delectation swept them into a sea of peace. Their bodies had become one. Each sensation felt by one was mirrored by the other. The wonderful pain each felt as they reached a climax of ecstasy ebbed and flowed until they were both spent.

Hubbard's eyes were heavy that night. He had been hunched up in the back of the Listener since the early morning. The voices at the founders' meeting droned on. Operation Bell was still running smoothly. The logistics were all falling into place. They seemed, to him, to be speaking in code. They all knew where, when and how Operation Bell would progress. He knew when and part of the how, but was still completely in the dark on where. The debate he was hearing was clearly meaningful to the Council of COBRA, but to him it meant nothing.

"Under Any Other Business, I believe that Mr Barrett has some information for us." It was Appleby's voice.

"*Thank you, Mr Chairman,*" came Barrett's voice. "*The prime minister has decided that he will reshuffle the Cabinet before the Easter recess. This is very good news for us. I have been in discussion with the PM about various posts in the government where the current ministers are looked upon as weak by the party. One of these is the post of home secretary. We are not doing well in the polls in the matter of law and order. I have pointed out that this should always be one of the party's main strengths. We have traditionally been seen as the party who gives a strong lead in this field.*

"*The PM agrees with me that the present home secretary is seen to be weak. We both agree that it would boost the party if a stronger and more right-of-centre man were appointed. As you know, the PM does not have a great liking for Marcus, but I have persuaded him that it would be best for both the general perception of the government and for the party as a whole to appoint Marcus to the post.*

"*This will, of course, put Marcus in a much stronger position for the leadership election.*"

Hubbard heard murmurs of approval from the gathering.

"*The other matter we have to deal with is a report on Jennings and Pinter.*" Appleby spat the names rather than spoke them. Marden started to speak and was cut short by Appleby. "*You have been given ample opportunity, Marden, this is now out of your hands. Mr King, will you please report.*"

"*The problems we have had in removing these particular cancers have been mainly caused because of the failure to properly identify the targets.*" King spoke with new authority since his appointment as commissioner of the Metropolitan Police. "*Both are well known to my operative and he will not make the mistake of taking the wrong target. As he is known by both Jennings and Pinter, it will be difficult for him to act as the front line agent. I have had a second operative working with him for the last few weeks who knows the faces of both. Jennings will be playing golf on Saturday at Tandridge Golf Club. He will have a fatal accident on the fourteenth hole. Pinter is presently still recovering from injuries incurred at the Dower House. He will be dealt with subsequent to Jennings's demise.*"

Hubbard rubbed his hands. This was the edge they needed. COBRA was coming for Jennings but did not know they would be ready for the attempt.

*

"There are two possibilities on the fourteenth." Cross was brainstorming. "The first is some sort of fall. The walk down to the fairway is about a one-in-four gradient. It's feasible that you could trip and break your neck. The second has got to be the machinery sheds. All the equipment is stored there, leaving plenty of chances for an accident to happen."

"I would have to make a diabolical shot to go anywhere near the sheds," Jennings laughed.

"You don't have to hit your ball there. They don't want your ball to have an accident, they want *you* to."

*

Rasher pulled a pint and placed the frothing glass in front of Jennings. "Are you going to retain the cup, Allan?" he enquired.

Jennings joked with him about the last year when Jennings had only won the Spring Cup because the real winner had forgotten to sign his card and was subsequently disqualified. He picked up his drink and wandered across to the starting list. He was last to tee off at 12.32 with Colonel Harkness. The colonel was captain of the veterans and seventy years old. He carried a pencil bag with a half set of clubs and walked with a stick yet still played to a handicap of 16. He had used to use the boy caddies but had a reputation for extreme frugality. As a result, all the caddies disappeared when his Rolls arrived at the club.

Cross followed Jennings and commented that it was unlikely the colonel would be the hit man.

"Don't take anything for granted," Jennings observed.

The colonel was on the tee waiting when Jennings arrived. They greeted each other and discussed the weather in true British tradition. The colonel insisted on setting a suitable wager before they started. Cross wandered back across the tenth towards the fourteenth.

The machinery sheds were forward of and about thirty yards to the left of the tee. Hubbard approached them from the rear. There were no windows in the building. It was constructed of prefabricated concrete bolted together in sections. The roof was heavy asbestos sheeting. He moved around the building stopping and listening.

There was no sound. The door was ajar. Inside, he could see the small generator that powered the lights. There was no sound from inside. He slipped inside the door and stood in the semi-darkness letting his eyes adjust.

There were tractors, gang mowers and all the equipment needed to maintain the course. He scanned the walls, the ceiling and the floor and saw nothing. His eyes were becoming used to the half-light and began to probe the interior. The generator did not look exactly as it should. Hubbard knelt to look closer. Petrol dripped from the sump on to the concrete floor. A small plastic box lay on the part from where the fuel escaped. He picked it up and examined it. It was a crude but effective ignition attached to a minute radio receiver. He replaced it.

Hubbard studied the walls more closely. In the corners most of the restraining bolts holding the prefabricated structure had been loosened. Some were finger-tight, just enough to hold the structure together but weak enough that any shock would collapse the whole edifice. The petrol would be ignited by remote control causing the generator to explode. The force would bring down the outside walls. He examined the corners again. He was not an engineer, but, judging by the looseness of some compared with others, he guessed that the building would collapse forward bringing the roof with it. It would fall on anyone within fifteen feet of the door. Hubbard picked up the small radio-controlled ignition and put it in his pocket.

By the time he had reached the thirteenth tee Jennings had amassed twenty-eight points. The colonel, to the contrary, was not having the best of days. He seemed nervous and was chipping and putting like a beginner. This was usually the best part of his game.

"Could be in for the booby prize," he muttered as he teed up on the par three thirteenth.

Jennings had rolled off the green to the right, down a steep slope and into the edge of the woods. The colonel, for a change, hit a superb tee shot which ran round the contours of the green to within ten feet of the pin.

Jennings took his wedge and climbed down the slope towards where he thought his ball had ended up. It sat beside a clump of blackberry bushes. As he studied the shot, Cross's voice from within the bushes whispered, "They've rigged the machinery sheds to collapse. If he asks you to go near them, take your time."

Jennings nodded and played a marvellous recovery that caught the edge of the green and rolled to within two feet of the hole.

They putted out and walked to the fourteenth tee. The colonel thinned his drive, which failed to carry to the fairway some seventy feet below them. Jennings struck his from the middle of the club and the ball soared down the centre, catching the down slope and running to within an easy shot of the green.

"Did you see that?" the colonel spoke as Jennings watched his drive finishing. "There is someone over there in the shed. Bloody vandals! We've had about a thousand pounds' worth of damage recently. Would you go over and have a look, dear boy? My legs aren't up to the ground."

Jennings kept his driver in his hand and climbed down from the tee towards the storeroom. He picked his way through the undergrowth not looking back.

The colonel unzipped the side pocket of his bag and took out a small transmitter. He pulled the aerial out to its full extension and pointed it towards the door. Suddenly he felt a vice-like grip on his wrist and then his arm was twisted up behind his back.

A voice said, "I'll take that, thank you," and the transmitter was ripped from his hand. The voice shouted, "It's all right, Allan, I've got the bastard!" and Jennings turned. The voice whispered, "Well, Colonel, I think that we will finish the round, then we will have a drink, and then you will have some talking to do." The colonel was spun round and found himself looking down the 35mm barrel of a Browning machine pistol.

Jennings's golf for the remainder of the round reflected his mood. He hit every green in regulation and putted like top professional. The colonel's performance was the opposite. Their group had gained two spectators. One had a wicked-looking machine pistol and the second was as wide as he was tall and covered with black hair. His hands looked powerful enough to crush a man's neck with his forefinger and thumb.

The colonel's bowels were cramped by fear of what would happen when he left the sanctuary of the golf club. He picked up on four of the last five holes, praying to make it to the crowded clubhouse as early as possible. He was one of the few who had escaped from the Japanese in the war and now prayed for another similar miracle.

The Hackers were in the group by the eighteenth green when they finished. On hearing that Jennings had amassed forty-two points John commented, "El Bandito rides again."

Penny kissed Jennings on the cheek and whispered, "Well done."

Harkness's score was greeted with hoots of friendly derision. The only sympathy he received was from Penny, who said gently, "Everyone can have an off day, can't they, Colonel?"

While the colonel showered, he looked for an escape route. None materialised. In the bar dozens of members milled around. He was casting around looking for an exit route when Hubbard appeared in front of him.

"It is polite to buy your partner a drink and settle your debts, don't you think," he said, without menace but implying it. A mammoth hairy hand took his elbow and projected him to the bar. The colonel ordered the drinks and was propelled to a table in the corner where Jennings and Cross sat. The three chatted about golf, and Jennings gave a shot-by-shot account of his round. The colonel was struck dumb by gnawing fear.

The prize presentation came and went. Jennings became the first person in thirty years to retain the Spring Cup. They called the colonel's name for the prize for the player who had put in most effort.

As he walked towards the club captain the old man's eyes searched desperately for his accomplice. He knew that his back-up was in the room, but where? Morbid fear invaded his senses. It was supposed to be a simple job. The man Jennings was a danger to the aims and objectives of COBRA. He had been proud that a frail old man could help to achieve a better balanced world in which to live. Harkness had jumped at the chance to help.

Then he saw the face for which he had been searching and relief partially eased his knotted guts. His eyes implored the other to help him. The face indicated that help would be given. Harkness collected his prize, a fluffy rabbit, and returned to his tormentors.

Another drink awaited and he was ordered to consume it. Several more followed, which he forced down. By now he was becoming even more unsteady than normal. Other members and their wives came and offered congratulations to Jennings and commiserations to the colonel.

Jennings and Cross made a show of offering to drive the old man home. He protested to the gathering but they seemed to agree that he should be escorted. As he left he looked for his confederate. He looked in vain.

The figure stood behind the caddy shed, the .22mm match rifle held softly against the right shoulder. The silencer slightly unbalanced the weapon. The cross-hairs in the sight wavered in the centre of Harkness's forehead.

The colonel gave Cross the keys to the Rolls without argument. His golf bag was carried in one of Hubbard's hands. As he reached the car he broke out in a cold sweat and his stomach churned. He staggered to one side and was sick. As he retched he felt his chest collapsing. Pain leapt across his shoulders and his breast felt as though it were about to implode. A red haze blurred his vision.

"Call an ambulance!" Cross shouted as the colonel sank to the floor. He pumped at his breastbone, trying to revive the failing heart.

Hubbard cleared the vomit from the colonel's lifeless mouth and gave him the kiss of life. The ambulance men pushed them aside and carried on with the desperate first aid. Eventually they sank on their haunches and gave up the fight.

The figure behind the caddy shed melted into the background and disappeared. No one had seen it appear and no one saw it disappear.

A crowd had appeared from the bar and were morbidly observing the attempts to bring the life back to the colonel's frail body.

Jennings cursed silently. Every step forward became a step to nowhere.

"Did anyone see if the old bastard contacted anyone?" Jennings asked his comrades. The elation they had felt at capturing the colonel had dissipated and been replaced by melancholy. "We get a link to my old man's killer and he dies on us! Whose bloody side are you on anyway?" He looked heavenward.

"For Christ's sake, you three!" Pinter snapped. "In two and a bit months those animals are going to try to take over the government of this country! Are you going to sit and wallow in a temporary failure or get off your arses and do something?"

Chapter Forty-Seven

Gatefield Manor,
26th March 1973

"*I am sure that we all join together in congratulating Banton on his appointment as home secretary.*" Appleby addressed the other members of the founders' meeting. "*In his new post he is protected by high-level security, and consequently it would be unwise for him to attend these meetings for the time being. Mr King is arranging for the officers delegated as Banton's personal security officers to be reviewed. The current officers will be replaced by members of our group in the next few weeks and normal arrangements will be resumed. In the meantime Mr Barrett will keep Banton informed of our deliberations.*"

"*I will keep him fully apprised,*" confirmed Barrett.

"*Thank you,*" intoned Appleby. "*Now, to the matter of Messrs Jennings and Pinter. We left the last meeting with assurances that these particular thorns would be blunted. They have not, so perhaps you could tell us why not, Mr King.*"

"*I am afraid that I can only come to one conclusion.*" King's voice was calm and authoritative. "*Somewhere in our organisation there is a leak. The situation was perfectly set up for the removal of Jennings. However, before he had even come close to the target area Hubbard was seen searching for something. He was subsequently joined by Cross. Our operative was unaware of this and was taken in the act, or failure to act. It was obvious that they knew of the attempt and exactly where it was to take place.*"

"*Who else would have known that information?*" Both Leach and Piper asked the question.

"*That is simple,*" King replied. "*The members of this council, my two operatives and the four alternates for membership of the council.*"

There was a hubbub around the table. None had ever considered the possibility that one of their own could betray them.

Cross sat in the Listener. He knew that small seeds of doubt had now been planted in all their minds. These seeds would grow and perhaps he could supply some fertiliser.

"*I think, perhaps we should break for a short period.*" Appleby's voice cut through the murmuring. "*Could we have a word in the office, Mr King?*"

Cross checked his equipment. It was now likely that he would have to monitor more than one location. He switched his earphones to the office.

"*Are you sure that this is the only possible explanation?*" Appleby's voice now came from the office bug.

"*I am afraid so,*" King responded. "*The only occasion the time and place was given out was at the last meeting. It was also in the minutes shown to the alternates.*"

"*What about your two – are they sound?*"

"*One of them is dead. Old Colonel Harkness had a heart attack as he was leaving with Jennings and company. It was rather fortunate, as it saved my other operative the job of silencing him. The second has been with* COBRA *well over five years and has carried out several terminations for us including, of course, that old fool Jennings.*"

Cross bit his lip. He knew that the last comment would send Jennings into a flaming rage of both annoyance and frustration.

"*Harkness would have been totally trustworthy. He joined us after his wife died at the hands of some incompetent immigrant doctor,*" Appleby mused. "*And you say the other is totally in accordance with our aims and the means of achieving them?*"

"*I have no doubts on that,*" King responded.

"*What would you propose to solve this problem, Mr King?*" Appleby asked.

"*As we are presently organised, none of our members, other than the council, knows who is on the council apart from their controller. I regret having to propose this, but we will have to put every member and alternate under observation. If we wish to precipitate the situation, we plant a dummy proposal with the council and see who makes the contact with Jennings. Once we know the traitor, we can eliminate him.*"

"*What would you suggest?*"

"*I understand that Jennings is attending an insurance dinner on the thirtieth of this month in the Great Room at the Grosvenor Hotel. Following that, it is usual for the party to go off to a strip club called Miranda's. I suggest that I inform the council there will be a mugging when he leaves the club. If I am right, our renegade will find a way of telling Jennings. When he does, we have him.*"

"*Are you sure that your information is correct?*" Appleby had to trust someone, but was King the right one?

Cross assumed that King confirmed as no audible reply came. He saw that the equipment indicated it was recording both in the boardroom and the secretary's office. These would have to wait. He heard the door opening and closing and shifted his attention to the boardroom.

"*I find it difficult to accept that there is a Judas among our group.*" Appleby's voice was conciliatory. "*I am, however, aware that the evidence given by Mr King can be seen to be fairly conclusive. I have total trust in the people around this table but am less familiar with the alternates. I propose, for the time being, that details of these meetings are not passed to the alternates. I also propose that Messrs Piper and Leach arrange that a full investigation is carried out to verify the authenticity and commitment of these four. Does anybody have any comments?*"

McHenry, Webster, Myers and Carter all expressed their confidence in the person they had nominated as alternates. Appleby smoothed their egos. "*I am sure you are right, but people can change and we have to be certain. Operation Bell is so vital to ours and the country's future that it must not be jeopardised. Now, Mr King, do you have a further proposal on the Jennings front?*"

King gave the story he had agreed with Appleby.

*

"I think that they are beginning to get a little rattled." Cross spoke as the tape finished playing the conversation recorded in the Listener. "Perhaps we should shake them up a little more."

The others were still musing over the recording they had just heard. The Council of COBRA were now opening the door of misgiving. If it were possible to fuel that distrust, they could become vulnerable.

"I think Jim is the man for this," Pinter spoke. "We select one of the bastards and then make sure he is seen with Jim some time in the next couple of weeks. We then make sure that you are mob handed when you come out of Miranda's and they've got their turncoat."

*

"Oh, I'm terribly sorry! It's so crowded in here. Please let me get you another one." Cross flashed his most engaging smile and mopped up the spilled wine with his handkerchief.

She was in her early thirties with sparkling blue eyes and golden hair. She was dressed immaculately in a designer navy blue suit with a white silk blouse. Her skirt nestled just above her knee. She gave off an aura of confidence and efficiency.

"No, it's all right," she smiled. Her teeth were white and perfectly matched.

"I insist," replied Cross. "Was it dry or medium?"

She indicated it was medium and he returned with the replacement.

Cross could charm a tortoise from its shell and today he was at his most eloquent. At first she was restrained, as it was not her style to be picked up in wine bars. After half an hour Cross's wit and charm had broken through her reserve and they were laughing with each other.

She looked at her watch and said she would have to leave. She did not wish to but her boss was a stickler for punctuality and, even though she was his personal assistant, she complied with the rules as laid down by the managing director of Inter Electric. Cross suggested that they meet later for a drink, to which she readily agreed.

Cross was sitting at a table in the corner that evening when he saw her long, shapely legs coming down the steps into the wine bar. She saw him and smiled.

"I'm sorry I'm late but I had to reorganise some of my boss's travel arrangements." Her boss, Philip Myers, was extremely pernickety and everything had to be correct down to the smallest detail.

She and Cross chatted about everything and nothing for the next two hours.

When the idea of getting to know Myers's secretary had first been mooted, Cross had been less than enthusiastic. That was before he had met Jane Salisbury. She was one of the most attractive women he had known, and her personality was enchanting.

He suggested that they go for dinner and she replied, "I thought that you would never ask. If I don't eat soon, I will fall over."

They ate in a small Italian restaurant in Covent Garden. Over the meal she talked about her work. Myers was fastidious in his ways. He always had to sit in a certain seat when flying and insisted on using the same room in hotels where he stayed regularly.

Every Friday morning he would catch the seven-ten train from Paddington to Swindon. He would spend the day at the company's research centre, returning on the four-twenty in the afternoon. She joked that she had a standing arrangement with British Rail that seat 2F in carriage H was always booked. Apparently, Myers became very tetchy if his routine was disrupted.

The next Friday Cross boarded the morning train for Swindon. He made his way to seat 3F in coach H, sat down, and opened *The Times*. Myers arrived five minutes before the train departed. Cross offered a polite greeting, which Myers returned. Nothing was said for the first twenty minutes of the journey. Cross studied the other passengers, hoping to spot the tail. He decided that it was a choice of two. Both were innocuous, one apparently buried in *The Daily Express* and the other *The Daily Record*. Occasionally, both looked over their papers to where Cross and Myers were seated.

Cross noticed that Myers was reading an article about a company he had been involved with. This gave him the opportunity to open a conversation. Myers was pleasant enough, and the journey passed quickly. At Swindon both the *Daily Express* and *Daily Record* followed Myers and Cross off the train. Cross offered goodbyes to Myers and made off in the direction of the taxi rank. The *Daily Record* followed him.

Cross made for a café he used to know and was delighted to find it unchanged. The owner recognised him immediately and said, "Long time, no see. I presume the order is anything that can be fried, with a mug of tea?"

Cross smiled.

As he ate the monster breakfast which appeared after ten minutes, he noticed that the *Daily Record* was engrossed in a shop window opposite. Cross finished the spread and downed the remains of his tea.

He left and walked slowly in the direction of the main shopping centre, followed at a discreet distance by his tail. He went to a payphone and rang an old army friend and arranged to meet him for lunch in a small pub on the outskirts of the town. He wandered around the shops for a couple of hours and then took a taxi.

The Wagon and Horses was an old-fashioned English pub. To the left was the public bar, with the saloon bar to the right. His friend was sitting at the end of the bar, a pint already lined up for Cross. It had been several years since they had seen each other and the time flew past as they exchanged anecdotes.

The *Daily Record* sat in the saloon bar by the door. Cross thought that by the end of the day he would know the paper by heart. Eventually Cross looked at his watch and said he had to go.

Myers was standing on the platform when Cross arrived. Cross joined him, commenting on the coincidence of their being on the same train again. The journey back was uneventful. Both the *Record* and the *Express* kept discreet observation. Cross ensured that both the Grosvenor Hotel and Miranda's were mentioned loud enough for them to hear. At Paddington, Cross and Myers parted company, as did the two followers.

The Lloyds Brokers' Dinner had been up to its usual standard. The after-dinner speeches, with the exception of that of the Recorder of London, had been overly long, self-satisfied and boring. The two tables of motor underwriters had over-imbibed and were somewhat boisterous. The Recorder of London silenced the disorderly mob with a brilliant and amusing dissertation on the ups and downs of being the senior criminal judge in London. He was particularly cutting about the 'geriatrics' in the Court of Appeal, who would automatically reduce his sentences to prove they were more important than he.

Miranda's was awash with inebriated brokers and underwriters ogling the girls on stage and pawing the hostesses. One of Jennings's party had succumbed and was sleeping peacefully propped against the bar. At three in the morning Jennings told one of his co-directors to settle the bill and made his farewells to the throng.

As arranged, Hubbard and Cross were waiting outside the club. Cross noticed the *Daily Record* standing in a shop door opposite. The three left together, unsure whether the notional mugging would be attempted. It wasn't.

"Are you sure? I didn't think the squeamish little sod would have the guts." Appleby's voice dripped disdain.

"He and Cross travelled together to and from Swindon. My people were not close enough to hear all the conversation but both the Grosvenor Hotel and Miranda's were spoken of." King had been surprised that Myers was the turncoat.

Hubbard smiled to himself while he listened to Philip Myers's fate being sealed.

"You know what to do, Mr King. I do insist, however, that Myers's untimely death will be an accident. I don't need any details." The tone of Appleby's voice told that King the conversation was at an end.

The light flashed on the listening equipment when Appleby picked up the telephone. Hubbard switched his earphones from the room mike to the telephone bug.

"McHenry," a voice replied.

"Hamish, how important is Myers in your jiggery-pokery with the markets?" Appleby asked.

"Not at all. He has the influence with the CBI but his company is not a market player. The market movements will be created by ourselves and the other bank. Why do you ask?"

"I am afraid that Myers appears to have been our leaking vessel. He is about to have an unfortunate accident," Appleby answered.

McHenry whistled through his teeth. "Are you sure? I wouldn't have thought he had the guts to cross us."

"There is no doubt. I set a little trap and he walked straight into it. We will have to replace him on the council and I am calling a meeting for next Wednesday."

"I'll be there," replied McHenry and the line went dead.

Horse-riding is an extremely dangerous hobby. Nobody knew what actually happened. Myers had taken his hunter out for a hack around the estate. The animal had returned alone. Myers's body was found, after a search, by a small hedge with his neck broken.

The obituaries were followed by the announcement that Paul Carver, the finance director, was being appointed to the position of managing director of Inter Electric. What was not announced was that he also became a member of the Council of COBRA rather than an alternate.

"Who is the new man on the block?" asked Jennings while he studied the photographs from the founders' meeting the evening before the next meeting.

"That is Paul Carver. He has taken over at Inter Electric following the demise of Myers." Pinter was reading from a notebook. "He is quite a high flyer, only thirty-six, chartered accountant and a bachelor of law. He is involved in several government quangos including those on inner cities and race relations. He gives the impression of being a liberal, but obviously that is a front."

"Anything of interest happen at the meeting?" Jennings addressed Hubbard.

"The only thing was the report given by Marden on Operation Bell." Hubbard pressed a button on the recorder and Marden's voice started to drone.

"*We have now decided on the agent who will be used for the operation. Both are marksmen of the highest quality so this area was not part of the consideration. The prime reason for choosing this particular man was his ability to deal with the mode of transport. We will be putting the operative in on the morning of the first and not pulling him out until the fourth, possibly the fifth. During that time he has to remain concealed in the transport. There was a small question mark over the second man in this field.*"

"*What back-up plans are there?*" This was Appleby's voice.

"*Our second operative will be in the vicinity when the party arrives. If the plan goes awry, he will have to use his initiative to take the target out. I have now changed his training to a hand gun with much more flexible use.*"

"*Are they still training together?*" King interrupted.

"*No. As there had been considerable rivalry between the two I felt that it was best to separate them once the decision had been made. The back-up is now training at the army live ranges at Fingringhoe in Essex. He is billeted at a pub in the village.*"

"That brings back memories." Jennings spoke after the machine was switched off. "They've got a training area in the woods. You start off with a sub machine-gun, and as you go through targets appear which you are supposed to shoot. I had a Sten with a full magazine of thirty-two when up pops the first target. Bloody trigger stuck and I have to let off the whole magazine. The only thing I remember is the instructor behind me saying, 'Don't turn round'."

"I know the pub – had a few nights there myself when we were training," Cross commented.

"Following his past success as our undercover agent, perhaps Jim should see if he can identify this bloke," suggested Pinter.

"Can't do, I am afraid. These people know our faces and if they clock Jim we could blow the whole thing." All three knew that Jennings was right.

"They would not take any notice of two ladies on a touring holiday." Gwen had been sitting quietly listening to them. "I could be taking a friend's daughter on a short holiday. That part of Essex gives easy access to lots of places for little tours. I am sure Pansie and I could play the innocent holiday-makers."

Pinter immediately started to raise objections. Gwen looked at him and told him not to be so stupid. Jennings thought of arguing, but the look in Pansie's eyes dismissed the thought from his mind.

*

The low oak-beamed ceiling gave the bar and restaurant a feeling of homeliness. The rooms were adequate, with a comfortable bed and shower. It was not quite equipped with all the comforts of home but it was not far off. The logs in the inglenook fireplace spat occasionally, and the sweet smell of burning apple wood wafted through the bar.

Both women were tired, having been to Southend to do all the things that tourists do. There were a few locals in the bar, but not as yet the only other resident. Gwen was pleasantly surprised as she sipped her Kir. In most places the cassis was used to hide the fact that the white wine was more akin to vinegar than wine. This was different, as the wine would have been very palatable without the addition of the cassis.

Pansie indicated with her eyes that the bar had a new occupant. He ordered a drink and sat at the bar. He was not tall but was heavily built. His hands completely enveloped the pint mug as he took a pull at the drink. He chatted to one of the locals and then asked for the menu.

The meal was excellent: good simple fare served with fresh vegetables that had not been cooked until all the flavour was dissipated. Gwen and Pansie talked animatedly about their day. Anyone listening would have taken them for enthusiastic tourists. It was obvious that the elder of the two was trying to show the young oriental the real England. They elected to have coffee in the bar, accompanied by a Drambuie on the rocks.

Gwen sat Pansie on the bar side of the fireplace and extracted her camera from its case. She looked through the lens and set the automatic focus on the man at the bar. The camera flashed. She asked one of the locals to photograph them both and stood so that the man would be in the background. During the evening she took several more photos, apparently of Pansie, but actually of the stocky man.

*

"Jesus Christ, do you recognise him, Jim?" Jennings passed the photographs to Cross.

"Your favourite sergeant-major! So Mr Bonner *was* a plant at Colchester!" Cross replied.

Jennings told them of his experiences at the hands of Bonner whilst he had been incarcerated in the military prison. It was now obvious that he had, even at that time, been seen as a potential embarrassment. Now Bonner was to be back-up for Operation Bell.

*

Bob Searle looked around the bar of the Chez When Club. He saw Jennings and another man sitting at a table in the corner. He joined them and was introduced to Pinter. Searle had long been an admirer of Pinter's investigative work as a journalist. Over lunch Jennings explained the job he wanted Searle to do.

"What I need is a daily report on everywhere he goes and everything he does for the next two months."

"This is going to be bloody expensive," commented Searle. "Just for simple surveillance I am going to have to charge you £250 a day."

"That doesn't matter. I have to know all his movements."

"It's your money, I suppose. What is the name of the woman?" Searle's reaction to this type of job was that it had to involve some infidelity.

"There is no woman in this," laughed Jennings. "I just want to know whom he sees and where he goes. There is something going on which I have to know about before it happens."

Searle assumed that the whole thing had to do with Corby, Lannin & Davies. He had read of the death of Corby and surmised that political manoeuvring in the company was behind the request.

Observation was the most boring part of his job. This one was particularly so. He and his colleagues had now been keeping tabs on Bonner for two weeks. In that time he had only gravitated between the Old Oak Inn and the military ranges at Fingringhoe. Twice he had managed to get into the ranges. Bonner spent his whole time practising on the pistol range, mostly with pop-up rather than fixed targets. In the evenings he sat in the bar, had dinner, sat in the bar, and then went to bed. His only contact with anyone was casual conversations with the landlord and one or two of the customers. Each day Searle produced a report for Jennings saying exactly the same as the day before.

This evening Bonner was seated on his usual bar stool. He normally had a couple of drinks after dinner and then retired. This night he stayed later. There was a darts match taking place. The members of both teams were a little the worse for wear and each double or treble was followed by a roar of approval from half of the participants.

Bonner seemed to take little interest in them but kept checking his watch and looking at the door. Just before ten a well-dressed man came in and walked towards Bonner. They shook hands as though they had just been introduced. They ordered drinks and came to the table adjoining Searle. Searle tried to appear intent on the outcome of the darts but strained his ears to listen to the conversation on the adjoining table. He reached in his pocket and retrieved what looked like a Dunhill lighter but was actually a camera. He placed it on the table and focused. The tiny camera clicked and he repeated the process.

"Next Tuesday, I suggest," said Bonner's companion. "I can show you round the whole area. Shall we say ten o'clock?" With that he finished his drink, shook hands and left.

The following afternoon Jennings received the daily report from Searle. He expected the usual pub, ranges, pub story as he slit open the envelope. Instead, an enlarged photograph fell out. He picked it up and looked. What was Cameron Carter doing drinking with Bonner? He pulled the report from the envelope and read it. What area was Carter going to show Bonner and why?

The following Tuesday Searle detrained at Liverpool Street Station. He followed Bonner up Bishopsgate and across Leadenhall Street. Bonner went into a coffee shop in Leadenhall Market. Searle checked his watch. It was five to ten. He saw Carter and another man bustling across the market and into the coffee shop.

There was a telephone box on the corner and he rang Jennings. Five minutes later Jennings joined him. The three men were still drinking coffee and talking. Carter rose to leave, shaking hands with Bonner and talking to the other.

"What do I do now?" Searle asked. "Follow the one going or stick with the two that are staying?"

"We stick with these two," Jennings muttered. "The guy with Bonner is one of the other directors of Carter's company. If they go into Lloyds, you'll need me to get you in. Only members and alternates are allowed in the room." Jennings knew he risked being recognised by Bonner but the chance had to be taken.

The two finished their coffee and left. The first hour was spent wandering in and out of the buildings in Lime Street and Fenchurch Avenue. Virtually all the premises were occupied by insurers and reinsurers. It would seem to any casual observer that Bonner and his guide were a broker and his guest being shown around the market.

All the time Bonner made notes. They spent considerable time in 40 Lime Street. The building had eight floors and faced the new Lloyds building. It was known as the new building not because it was new but because it was newer than the old Lloyds across Lime Street. There were plans to demolish the old Lloyds building and construct a new high-tech building in its place. When that happened, the new building would become the old and the old the new.

At about eleven-thirty they went into Lloyds. Jennings followed, waving his pass at the waiter on the door and indicating that Searle was a guest. They did not bother with the ground floor where the marine and motor underwriters sat. Bonner was led up the stairs to the Non-Marine Gallery. They did not stop at any of the boxes but wandered around the outside of the gallery.

After an hour they went down to the marine floor and out through the other exit, turned left and up Lime Street. They went into The

Grapes and ordered a pint each. After half an hour Carter's sidekick left, as did Jennings. Bonner sat quietly reading whatever notes he had made. He stayed in the bar for the next hour and then left and wandered, apparently aimlessly, around the area. For a reason unknown to Searle he spent a considerable time studying the P&O and Commercial Union buildings. At about four Searle followed him to Liverpool Street and back to the Old Oak Inn.

The headline in the morning paper on 15th April was followed by a report on a speech given by Banton the night before at his constituency dinner.

NEW HOME SECRETARY GETS TOUGH

Marcus Banton said last night that it was his duty to cut out the growing cancer of crime that is pervading our society. He is proposing new measures to strengthen the hands of the police and all law enforcement agencies and to tighten the rules on immigration.

He firmly put part of the blame on the dependence culture which had developed with the benefit system. "We must cut out the cancer of dependence," he stated. He said that the country could no longer afford to support people who have no desire to contribute to the welfare of the country. He cited immigration as one of the major problems. He said, "People come to this country and receive handouts that are beyond their wildest dreams in their country of birth. We cannot afford to let more people into our overcrowded country unless they come here with a contribution to make."

The article went on to report much support from the grassroots for Banton's controversial views. It also reported the reaction of immigrant groups.

Jennings read the article with growing foreboding. He knew that the process had begun. The timetable had been set in motion and had to be stopped. They knew the plan but were powerless to stop it. They knew what was being planned but not where it would happen.

"I think that we had better all sit down tonight and get our thinking caps on." Pinter had been reading a report of Banton's speech in *The*

Record. "If a cancer needs cutting out, it's the bastards he is tied in with. We have to do something to stop this."

"There is not much in the post this morning." Mary Cantor was her usual buoyant self. "Except, well, you must be going up in the world." Jennings looked at her quizzically. "You have a letter from the chairman of Lloyds. He offers sympathy for Mr Corby and asks if you could attend the Coronation Anniversary Lunch in Lloyds as his replacement. I know it's a Saturday but I am sure you would like to go

Jennings thought this was typical of a market which deals only with the results of small and large disasters. Sorry he is dead, but it rather fucks up our table plan.

"Not only are you invited to the lunch," she continued, "but you are also asked to the private reception for the guest speaker."

"Who is that, then?" Jennings knew that the speaker had to be important, as Mary had delivered the last statement in a tone of near-reverence.

"It's the prime minister!" she announced triumphantly.

Jennings almost snatched the letter she was holding.

Dear Allan,

I must express my deepest regret at the tragic death of Charlie Corby. I knew Charlie from when we both started in this market. He was a young broker and I an enthusiastic and incompetent underwriter when we first met. Over the years he and I became close friends and he will be sorely missed in the market.

Each year Charlie would attend our lunch to remember the anniversary of the coronation. He was always the life and soul of the gathering and will be missed.

I am asking if you would kindly replace Charlie at this annual function and possibly say a few words in his memory. We are extraordinarily fortunate in that the Right Honourable James Dowie has kindly accepted our invitation to be guest speaker.

The reception for the guest of honour will be 12.30 for 1.15 in my suite at Lloyds, on 2nd June, to be followed by the formal lunch in the Captain's Room.

Yours sincerely

Jennings reread the letter while Mary stood by smiling. She knew that he would be delighted at the invitation not just to the lunch but the private reception. She was tempted to ask Jennings to get the prime minister's autograph.

Jennings had two reactions. The first was what a pompous ass the chairman was. He and Corby had never been on anything but nodding terms. Corby had thought the man an utter buffoon and the chairman had thought Corby an over-loud *nouveau riche* spiv. His second reaction was half relief and half renewed anxiety. Now he was sure of the venue but still not the how and precise when. He now understood why it was named Operation Bell. The Lutine Bell was the symbol of Lloyds and was always rung to mark major disasters and thus losses for Lloyds.

Jennings spent most of the day in the market. He did not do much reinsurance work while he surveyed the area surrounding Lloyds' main entrance to second-guess where the hit would come from.

The shot should come from a tall building and along a street with buildings on each side. At one end of Lime Street stood the Commercial Union building in St Helen's Place. If the information given by Hyde was totally correct, this was the only structure tall enough. If Hyde's estimate of height were awry the P&O building would also be a possibility. At the other end the possibilities would be 40 Lime Street, certain parts of 37/39 and the two adjoining buildings. As he studied the possibilities Jennings could still see no reason for the assassin's confinement in cramped quarters.

COBRA were saying that the operative would be installed on 1st June and taken out two or three days later. In that case there had to be somewhere to conceal him. The security services would know from where the shot emanated and would search the premises thoroughly.

Jennings went into each of the buildings to see if there were places where an assassin could hide himself both before and after the hit. The Commercial Union and P&O were both air-conditioned and he considered the ducting a likely place of concealment. He dismissed the idea as, whilst a small man could get into the space, the ducting would then be blocked and the fault investigated. There were nooks and crannies in all the buildings, but none with sufficient security to guarantee avoidance from detection.

He went around the Lloyds' building trying to think as an assassin would. It was then he realised that he had missed a risk. There was a third entrance in Fenchurch Avenue. If the prime minister were to use this rear entrance, five more buildings came into consideration.

Chapter Forty-Eight

"From what we have here there are ten, maybe more places from where the hit could be made." Cross was looking at the rough plan Jennings had drawn of the area. "There is no way we alone can cover them all."

"I think that we have to go to the police or security services and tell them what we know." Pinter was flicking through the transcripts from the Listener.

"In general, George, I would agree with you, but who the hell do we go to? King is head of the Met and the bosses of MI5 and MI6 are swimming with COBRA. We know that under each of them is a network of sympathisers. How do we know whom to trust?" Jennings's voice mirrored his frustration. "We have got to find a way of narrowing down the possibilities, and, if we can, stopping it."

"Why don't we knock off all the bloody council? That's the way a mongoose kills cobras – it bites their heads off." Hubbard always had a practical and invariably violent solution to all problems.

"That may be what we will have to do." Jennings's voice was sombre. "First let's try to reduce the options." He pulled three cards from his wallet and passed one to each. "These are Lloyds passes. They will get you past the security in any of the places we need to look. See if any of you can work out whether I've missed anything."

They sat over dinner two weeks later. Hubbard and Cross had spent every day trying to plan what COBRA had already done. Working out the shot was easy, the concealment impossible. They began to doubt both the location and the target of COBRA.

Three days previously Marcus Banton had delivered a presentation to the American Attorneys' Association at the Hilton Hotel. He had reinvented the wheel as presented by Enoch Powell and added his own garnishes. He combined his own thoughts on the dependence culture with the implication that the majority of the problem arose from uncontrolled immigration. He threw taxation into the casserole and let it simmer.

The speech was blatantly divisive to certain factions of his own party, but had been saluted by much of the tabloid press. Pinter's own paper had referred to him as a true patriot. He was riding on the sails of law and order and immigration, with which many of the electorate felt sympathy. The press, radio, and television seemed enamoured of this young, thrusting politician who spoke his mind and damn the consequences. He used statements such as, "We must do what is right for the country not what is politically pragmatic" and "The people have the right to spend their own money".

To the independent observer he was destroying his career. James Dowie had been prime minister for four years and was as politically astute as any post-war premier. He would let Banton have his day in the sun and then reap the benefits of the positive publicity himself. In the Cabinet Room he would stamp on any excesses, and when the tide of opinion turned he would bow to the will of the electorate and plunge Banton into obscurity.

Vic Barrett was also playing the same game, only with more political acumen. Within the 1922 Committee he supported many of Banton's perceived convictions but without the rhetoric. As chief whip he calmed the party members who were becoming restless by pointing out the positive surge in the opinion polls. He became even more of a regular on both radio and television, commenting on the underlying support for Banton's views. He was astute enough to be seen to both support the prime minister and have sympathy with Banton's views. His disciplinary hold on the parliamentary party strengthened.

"Look at this crap," said Pinter, holding one of the broadsheets. "*The party needs a strong home secretary, and Marcus Banton is the man for the job,*" he read. "*He is a politician with convictions and the will to see them through.*" Pinter threw the paper on the table. "These people are putting that windbag up on a pedestal! We know that he didn't even write those bloody speeches. They're all jumping up on the Banton bandwagon thinking it will eventually crash and they can jump off before it happens. What they don't know is that it won't crash and they will still be aboard when he becomes premier. Bloody editors – they've got one eye on the circulation and the other up the proprietor's arse!"

"The only thing we can do is to stop him," Jennings said placatingly. He raised his hand when Pinter tried to interrupt and continued, "At least we now know that Dowie is arriving at the main entrance of Lloyds." Jennings had received a letter from Lloyds telling him that the main entrance would be closed on 2nd June. "That means that COBRA's hit will come from St Helen's Place or Lime Street. We have all looked at the possibilities and can discount the P&O and anything further down Lime Street than number 40." Cross and Hubbard nodded agreement. "What we need now is his means of getting in and out, and we've got the bastard."

*

"*I think that you will all agree that things are running better than expected,*" Appleby addressed the founders' meeting. "*Not only has Mr Banton received publicity in excess of our anticipation, but Victor has also strengthened both his and our position.*"

Cross sat up. He had never heard Appleby use any Christian names apart from McHenry's.

"*Mr Banton*", continued Appleby, "*has presented the perfect front as required currently. Victor has been seen to be less aggressive but still shows that his ideology and his heart lean in the right direction.*" He laughed, again something Cross had not heard before. "*I do apologise – the pun was not intended.*" The microphone picked up the sound of polite laughter.

"*Mr Banton's next four speeches*" – Appleby's tone was now as if he were back on the bench lecturing a miscreant – "*will be progressively more moderate. It was vital that we had the early attention of the press and we all know how they love a bit of extremism.*" The chuckle around the table was muffled as no one knew whether a joke was intended. Cross heard papers being passed around as Appleby advised the gathering that they were the transcripts of speeches to come.

"Now, gentlemen, to Operation Bell. Can we have a full update? I think you should start, Mr Webster."

Webster reported that the equipment was virtually finished. The basic manufacture was completed and the testing was now underway at the company's specialist quality control operation. All would be ready for delivery on the required date.

Marden told the gathering that the training had gone better than expected. The back-up had studied the area and was happy that he could pick up in the event of the main plan's failing. He was followed by King, who detailed the security arrangements. All the surrounding buildings would be searched over the Friday night. Once each had been cleared, there would be police officers placed at all the entrances until after the departure of the PM. The cars would arrive via Leadenhall Street, which would be closed to all other traffic, as would St Mary Axe, Undershaft and Lime Street. He said, *"We are not expecting many sightseers,"* when asked about crowd control.

Appleby thanked him. McHenry followed, giving details of how the markets would be manipulated.

"Finally, Mr King has a report on the Jennings/Pinter situation."

King thanked Appleby. *"It is my opinion that they no longer pose a real threat to Operation Bell. One of our worries was the fact that these gentlemen seemed very active and were always one jump ahead. Following the unfortunate demise of Mr Myers we have neither seen nor heard much of either Jennings or Pinter. As we all knew, Myers had a somewhat squeamish streak, and it is my belief that he leaked our plans for Jennings to the man himself. Two meetings ago I gave details of the proposed mugging of Jennings to the council. Following that, Myers travelled to and from Swindon with one of Jennings's cohorts. Both of Jennings's associates arrived at the site of the proposed attack prior to Jennings. According to my observer, both appeared to be armed. The only feasible conclusion is that Jennings was warned by Myers. His accident was a timely intervention."*

"How do you know that Myers told him?" Carter asked.

"I am afraid that we had to put the whole of the council under observation, which was an insult to all but one member, but necessary. Myers was the only one who had any contact with Jennings's associates."

There was a general hubbub around the table, most of which was unintelligible to Cross. He smiled to himself, knowing that their bait had been swallowed hook, line and sinker.

The commotion was silenced by Appleby's voice. *"We will, of course, continue to keep these people under observation, and should they appear to be any threat they will be dealt with. This time, however, they will not receive any warning."*

*

"Allan, my dear boy, we haven't got together for months!" Jennings recognised Rittle's voice on the phone. "I've received the wedding invitation, and I would love to buy you both dinner and meet the woman who tamed you."

Jennings had tried to avoid Rittle for a long time. He knew of his friendship with Appleby but did not want to believe that he was part of the conspiracy. Rittle had been one of his father's oldest and dearest friends. It was only when he had joined the army that Rittle insisted Jennings stopped calling him Uncle Stuart.

"I spoke to Gene Reiss and he would like to meet your young lady as well," Rittle continued.

Reiss had been a close friend of the brigadier's and had handled his investments for many years. Jennings knew him less well but had invited him to the wedding as an old family friend. Dinner was arranged for the next week.

*

The piano player was caressing soft melodies from his instrument when they arrived at Chez Solange. Rittle was sitting in the small bar talking animatedly to a stunning blonde. Since his divorce he had been seen with a procession of young, extremely attractive and mostly dim young women. Jennings often wondered what could attract them to him. There was no way that the term 'macho' could be used to describe Rittle. Her name, Jane Salisbury, rang a bell, but Jennings could not remember from where. As they chatted over drinks it was clear that this woman was not one of Rittle's usual dumb bimbos. She was articulate and well-informed.

Reiss arrived with his wife. Polly was a mousy woman who made up for her plainness by hanging extremely expensive but loud jewellery from every part of her body to which it could be attached. She was American, as was Reiss, who had been born and brought up in the Midwest Bible belt. Reiss was immaculately dressed, the perfect advert for Gieves & Hawkes of Savile Row, where all his clothes were tailored. He was a New Yorker with the brashness to prove it.

The three ladies sat together, and Polly started to talk weddings. The other two listened politely but could not raise any real enthusiasm for the blow-by-blow account of a typical Kansas City wedding.

It took Reiss a little while to tell Jennings that his investments were being handled in an exemplary fashion. Jennings eventually stopped the sales pitch. "Gene, I know you are making a fortune in commissions on my money, but if I was not happy I would have sacked you long ago."

Reiss smiled and commented that he preferred Jennings when he had been a simple soldier rather than a captain of commerce. "You used to believe my bullshit in the good old days."

All three laughed.

Reiss knew of the changes at Corby, Lannin & Davies and would have liked a piece of their investment action. Before he could switch his line of attack Jennings stopped him.

"I am reviewing the company's portfolio at the moment. I may talk to you about it but not tonight. Tonight is for the ladies."

Jennings had seen that both Pansie and Jane were becoming a little glazed in the eyes and Polly was only halfway through describing the wedding ceremony. By the time she arrived at the cake-cutting both her companions would be comatose.

They were called to their table and Jennings sat at the head of the table with Pansie to his left, thus ensuring that table was not broken into male and female sections.

Over dinner the topic of Marcus Banton's latest speech was raised by Reiss. The reaction to Banton had been extreme, in both senses, at the American Attorneys' Association Conference. Some delegates had given him a standing ovation while others had offered little other than polite applause.

"I think that this guy has got guts," Reiss averred. "What he recognises is that democracy is inefficient and costly. The majority of the voters will vote for what is best for themselves, and bugger the rest. In simple statistical terms there are more people earning below the national average and they are inherently jealous of the ones who earn above it. What happens is that the majority vote to make themselves better off, and as a corollary the well-off get poorer. The people who make the wealth sod off to somewhere they are appreciated and then you end up with a country full of mediocrities."

"That is absolute rubbish." Surprisingly, it was Jane Salisbury who interrupted Reiss's flow. "If what you say is true, all the democracies would be in a state of permanent decline. The countries that are in decline are mainly the left-wing dictatorships. The communist countries can arm themselves but they cannot feed their people."

Reiss retorted that the Eastern Bloc were oppressive dictators not benevolent, and that the comparison did not stand up to scrutiny. Rittle joined the fray and brought immigration into the equation, which was a red rag to both bulls. Jennings decided that unless he intervened chaos would follow. "As host, I am banning the subject of politics, otherwise I will get indigestion." The anger that he saw growing subsided.

Jennings was surprised at the vehement reaction of Jane and also by the fact that Rittle simply stirred the pot rather than offering an opinion. Rittle seldom took a back seat in any discussion. As a barrister he was a wordmaster and usually took every opportunity to show off his skills.

The conversation reverted to a more social level. Pansie and Jane were required to give their life histories. It was then that Jennings realised where he had heard of Jane Salisbury. She had been married but her husband died. She did secretarial work while carrying on her education at night school. She had obtained an honours degree in economics while working for Inter Electric. She became PA to the managing director, who, sadly, had recently been killed in a riding accident. The new managing director kept his own PA, and so Jane was surplus to requirements. She had known Stuart Rittle for some time and he had suggested that she apply for the job as head of administration at his chambers. She had been interviewed by Appleby, as head of chambers, and got the job.

When the party broke up following dinner, Jane took Jennings to one side. "I have to speak to you, Allan. Will you ring me?" She slipped a piece of paper into his hand.

Jennings showed the note to Pansie as their car wound its way through Brixton towards home. It gave a telephone number and underneath a note said, *Do you know anything about COBRA?*

Pansie indicated the chauffeur with her eyes and put her finger to her lips.

Cross and Hubbard were having a late-night drink when Jennings and Pansie arrived.

"It must be some sort of trap." Pansie held the note in her hand. "She was close to Myers and now works with Appleby."

Jennings said, "My distinct impression was that she was not part of COBRA, but I only had dinner with her."

"I don't think that you have any choice. If it is a trap, they have to come into the open and that gives us a chance to nab them. If it isn't, she may have something that we don't know." Hubbard never approached anything from a direction other than head-on.

*

The Lime Club had only one entrance. Hubbard stood at one end of the bar, his eyes on the entrance. Jennings and Jane sat at a table which was out of sight of the entrance. There were only seven others there, all brokers or underwriters known to Jennings. He peered into the glass and, without looking up, said, "You wanted to meet me. What do you want to tell me?"

"Firstly, Salisbury is my maiden name. My married name was Butcher, Mrs Simon Butcher."

Jennings's eyes widened.

"That's right, Allan, my husband was Captain Simon Butcher, the officer commanding that patrol."

"I did not give any information to the enemy. I was stitched up." The revelation of her true identity had shocked Jennings, and his first reaction was defensive.

"I know that," she continued. "When it first happened, I was visited by a Colonel Herne. He told me that you had betrayed Simon and the others. I hated you. I hated the army. Simon would not have been on that patrol if Joe Starkey had not been ill. When you were finally charged with only lack of moral fibre, I hated you even more. I was alone, the man I loved had been murdered and the killer had not been properly punished. A year after your court martial an old friend of my husband visited me. Graeme Lawrence and Simon had served together in the Intelligence Corps. I poured out my heart to him. He told me that he was one of the interrogating officers and that he thought you were innocent. He said the evidence was too pat and suspected that what had happened was a set-up, probably by the security services.

"At the time of your interrogation he was convinced that you were guilty. After your conviction he became less sure. He went through all the evidence and found small parts that did not fit. More importantly, he found evidence which had been suppressed. When the bodies of the patrol were found, they had not deteriorated as they should have done. The initial medical reports stated that either they had been kept refrigerated or the time of death was two days later than reported. The reports also expressed surprise that there was no evidence of damage by scavengers." Her eyes began to well up with tears. "I'm sorry," she said and dried her eyes. "That report did not appear in the official papers forwarded to the prosecuting office. A second report was sent with the misgivings excised."

Jennings put his hand on hers. "Let me get you another drink. You can have a moment to yourself."

She smiled and thanked him.

"Do you mind if I fetch my friend over?" he asked.

"Of course not," she replied. "I wondered if you would bring a bodyguard."

When Jennings and Hubbard returned, Jane was in control of herself and continued. "Graeme told me that he questioned Captain Harris about the discrepancies between the file and the evidence forwarded and was referred to Colonel Herne. He was ordered to keep quiet about what he had seen, and reminded, in no uncertain terms, of his responsibilities under the Official Secrets Act. A month later he was sent on attachment to an infantry unit which was on its way to Belfast. He was killed in an IRA attack."

"You mentioned COBRA in your note. What do you know about them?"

"I'm coming to that," she replied. "I was not happy about what I had heard and decided that I had to speak to Harris. He had been discharged from the army and it took me over a year to find him. By the time I traced his whereabouts he was dead. I met his widow, who told me that you had visited him. She told me that her husband had left her a sealed note with the will and showed it to me. The note said that Harris had been involved with a secret group called COBRA and that she was in great danger from them. It stated that COBRA had arranged the ambush of the patrol and the conviction of Jennings. He told her to sell the house and disappear. She was in the middle of this when I met her.

"She also told me that Colonel Herne and three others had been through all of her husband's papers and taken many away. When she protested, they had told her that the papers were classified and consequently military property."

"Is that all?" queried Jennings.

Jane took a sip of her vodka and tonic. "Yes, until I started to work for Philip Myers. He always kept his own diary for personal appointments. He would tell me when he was unavailable and I would keep the business diary. He normally carried the personal diary with him when he travelled and I would contact him to check all appointments daily. One time he forgot it and I checked a date in it myself. There was an appointment the same evening which said, 'COBRA, Gatefield Manor'. I looked through and found that the same entry appeared about every four weeks. I knew of Gatefield Manor as Myers and the company supported a charity located there."

"The Association for Democratic Conservatism," Jennings offered.

She nodded. "What I did not see was why he referred to COBRA. I know now that one is a cover for the other. I went through his private files. The only thing I found was a hand-written note in his drawer which was headed *COBRA Council*. I copied the paper and put the original back. It was just a list of names, with the exception that by Appleby's name he had written *chairman*. When I heard of the job at the chambers from Stuart, I jumped at it."

"Have you found out anything since you've been there?" This time Hubbard intervened.

"Not much, I am afraid. I know that Appleby visits Gatefield Manor often. I see that from the chauffeur's bills. Also, his chauffeur is a little more qualified than usual. He is an ex-marine and used to run his own security company. He seems a little too high-powered to be a driver. The only other thing is that he lunches with McHenry and Barrett every Friday."

"What about Stuart Rittle?" It was a question Jennings had to ask but didn't really want to have answered. "Is he connected with them?"

"I don't know, but in my opinion he is not. I have heard him and Appleby having some fairly heated discussions on politics, and unless he is a very good actor Stuart's views are somewhat opposite to Appleby's. They do have a bet on whether Appleby will sit on the Woolsack. Apparently Appleby has wagered £5,000 that he will be lord chancellor before the end of 1974. My only reservation is the stories in chambers about Appleby and Stuart."

"What stories?" Jennings asked.

"Everybody knows that Appleby has unusual sexual leanings. As he and Stuart are so close some say that they are a couple," she replied.

"Hold on," Jennings interrupted. "Stuart was married for years."

"I believe that some people are what's known as AC/DC – is that the term?"

Jennings was unsure whether he was being fed a story or the truth. Jane seemed honest, but he had seen too many surprises to accept anything at face value. "Will you come and talk to some other friends of mine about this?" he asked. He trusted Pinter's judgement.

She agreed without hesitating.

*

"So, I was part of the intrigue." Jane Salisbury smiled at Jim Cross. "It wasn't me you wanted to meet but Myers's assistant."

"At the outset yes, but after I had met you it was a labour of love." Cross's voice oozed charm.

Jennings brought her down to his house to meet the others. They sat in the lounge and Jane recounted everything she knew. She narrated the tale without any emotion. All three men asked her questions, which she answered if she was able. Eventually Cross volunteered to take her home.

"She's either a bloody good actress or she's telling the truth," Pinter expounded after she'd left.

"Just to be safe, I asked Bob Searle to verify what he can of her story. He has confirmed that she was Butcher's wife and the rest of her history."

In his heart Jennings trusted her, but caution was still needed.

The next two weeks produced little information. The equipment for COBRA was ready and packed for delivery. Where it was being sent to and why was still a mystery. Jennings ascertained that, in addition to the prime minister, both Banton and Barrett were guests at the lunch at Lloyds. Jane told them that Appleby would be in Scotland on 1st and 2nd June speaking at a Bar conference. Nothing assisted them in identifying the location from which the assassination attempt would be made.

Banton's speech at the CBI conference received wide publicity. He concentrated his attack on future immigration and the unions. He supported the rights of immigrants who were in the country legally but added that people who were in the country illegally should be rooted out and despatched whence they came. He called for a moratorium on all new immigration. He then turned his attention to the unions, "The Barons of the Working Class" as he called their leaders. He attacked the power of the union leaders and called for greater accountability to their members. The members of the CBI gave him a standing ovation. The majority of the press praised his vision and courage.

The next morning Victor Barrett was interviewed on the *Today* programme. He gave his support to many of Banton's expressed views but his presentation was softer. Gordon Carritt was on the same programme and neither defended nor attacked the home secretary's opinions. An opinion poll published after the speech showed that the government's standing had improved three points, and this was mostly due to Banton. The newspapers took this up and started to speculate on the possibility of an early election. Dowie, a most astute politician, let the stories run.

The days seemed to disappear more quickly than jelly at a children's party. Saturday 2nd June loomed nearer and nearer in the calendar. Banton's speech at the Welsh Conservative Trade Unionists' Conference received wide publicity. He had concentrated on law and order. He had rallied the delegates with phrases such as "Crime must be punished not rewarded" and "If the judiciary will not enforce the law, Parliament must make them".

"There is just one week left." The worry showed deep in the brow of George Pinter. "I am going to have to talk to the PM's office. I've known his press secretary for years. We have got to stop this happening."

"We still don't know whom we can trust." Jennings's voice reflected his anxiety. "We have until the end of the week before we have to do that."

*

The Australian reinsurance season was in full swing. The time difference between London and the Antipodes was always a major problem. It was just before 6 a.m. when Jennings turned into Leadenhall Street. He had already spoken with four clients Down Under and was now looking for a warm café and a hot breakfast.

The lorry turned into St Mary Axe. Jennings stopped and stared after it. It swung into the rear of the Commercial Union building.

Emblazoned on the side was PORTERFIELD INDUSTRIES (AIR-CONDITIONING) LTD. Jennings followed and watched as the driver pulled open the rear doors. A fork-lift truck arrived and pushed its nose into the dark recesses of the lorry's back. It lifted something and reversed. Jennings caught his breath. Carried proudly on the front of the truck was a metal drum measuring some eight foot by four mounted on a pallet. On each end were dials and controls, and across the side was declared PORTERFIELD INDUSTRIES. The truck disappeared behind the building towards the service lift.

Jennings looked up at the building and knew. The top floors of the building were where the services were located, services such as heating and cooling. The top floors were about two hundred feet high and directly opposite the entrance to Lloyds. He watched as the rest of the equipment was unloaded.

Later that morning he visited Commercial Union. He exchanged a cheery greeting with the commissionaire. "Early morning today, Charlie," he said.

"Bloody right," came the reply. "New air-conditioning being fitted. I had to be here at bloody six to supervise the bastards bringing some of it in. There is a load more arriving the same time Friday."

That evening Jennings and his group sat together in Woldingham planning their tactics. It was Monday, leaving them only four days.

The following night Jennings was a guest at the Guild of Insurers' dinner at the Guildhall. As is usual the after-dinner speakers from the industry were both self-satisfied with their own performance and highly critical of everyone else. It was always left to the guest of honour, replying on behalf of the guests, to salvage the evening.

Banton was a highly skilled orator. He made the points he needed, but mixed them into a perfect cocktail with humour and irony. By the time he sat down, the diners were eating out of his hand. He had massaged their egos by telling them how valuable they were to the economy of "Our Great Country". He drew huge applause when he said that insurers were paying the unnecessary cost of crime because there was no proper deterrent. He offered active support to differential premium pricing based on culture and creed. "If people cannot police their own communities, they must pay the cost of their failure." The statement brought a burst of applause. "The law-abiding must not pay to help finance those who have no respect for the rule of law." Some diners were on their feet cheering. The combination of a brilliant orator, an audience hearing what it wanted to be told and three hours of flowing wines and spirits totally captured the gathering.

Jennings looked around the magnificent room. 'If only they knew,' he thought.

Nearly all the newspapers the next day praised young Banton for his courage and forthrightness. Two had opinion columns stating that Banton simply had to be the next prime minister. *The Record* had endowed him with adjectives such as 'far-sighted', 'a true patriot' and 'a giant among the minnows'. If the reaction continued to grow, he would be beatified after his next speech.

Chapter Forty-Nine

Reigate Hill Hotel,
1st June 1973

"What have you got Tony doing tonight?" she said as he slipped the brassiere from her shoulders. He cupped her breasts in his hand and ran his tongue around her nipples.

He looked up and said, "How can I speak with my mouth full?"

His hand ran down her body and caressed the soft hair that nestled at the top of her thighs. She sighed with pleasure and searched out his manhood. She felt it hard and throbbing. His fingers explored the source of the juices that ran from her body. He moved to climb on her.

"Not yet," she whispered. "I want to taste you first."

He shuddered as her lips closed around his erection and her tongue caressed him. She felt him getting harder and squeezed his scrotum. He moaned with pleasure as she mounted him and thrust him deep inside her. They began to gyrate in unison, their orgasms rising simultaneously.

They lay in each other's arms, completely spent.

"What did you do with Tony tonight?" she asked again.

*

They had met seven years ago when he was Chief Superintendent King and her husband a mere sergeant in the Surrey Police Force. Since that time Leonard King had arranged for Tony Hacker to be allocated duties which left his wife free to gratify his needs. She had been an enthusiastic partner in this.

As King's career blossomed so did Hacker's. It was a necessity to make Hacker's working time coincide with King's free. When King had moved to the Metropolitan Police, so Hacker followed.

It was at a New Year's Eve ball that Hacker had first introduced his wife to his superior officer. She was immediately attracted to him, mostly for the power he exuded. She had always been attracted by wealth and power. It was a combination of the natural confidence the strong exude and their ability to manipulate and control people that attracted her.

Her first sexual experience had been when she was fourteen. Allan Jennings's family were both wealthy and powerful. He also had the advantage of being physically attractive. She was well developed for her age and decided that he would be the ideal person to deflower her. The first time they had fumbled clumsily with each other's clothing and eventually consummated their relationship on Limpsfield Golf Course. The consummation was brief and untidy. Whilst the experience was not exactly fulfilling, it had given her a taste of her own potential power over men.

King had asked her to dance at the ball. Whether by design or accident, the band were playing *Love Me Tender*. She had consumed several Tia Marias and was emitting signals while they danced. Her breasts pressed into King's chest and her thigh into his groin a little more than would be expected for social contact. He had no control over his erection and tried to disguise it. She pressed closer and whispered, "Don't worry about your keys digging into me – I quite enjoy it." As they left the crowded dance floor he felt her hand squeezing his inflamed member.

Three days later King knocked on her door under the pretence of wanting to see Hacker. He was, of course, not there, as King knew he was attending a particularly nasty motor accident. She had smiled and told him that her husband was out and invited him in for coffee.

"Shall I bring my keys with me?" he asked.

"I think you should – I would like to see them," was her reply.

They had made love on the floor in the hallway.

King was a superb lover. He was like an artist with her body. He knew every part of her which aroused sexual pleasure. She had never known multiple orgasms until she met him. She, in turn, found every possible way to kindle the raging fire within him.

For the first year their relationship was only sexual. They would meet and make love, each driving the other's arousal to new heights. When she became pregnant, King did not know whether the expected child was his or Hacker's and cared less. The pregnancy interfered with but did not stop their relationship. The difference was that they talked of other things, not just matters of the body. They both knew that their liaisons would have to remain secret. "If I am caught fucking one of my sergeants' wives, that would be my career up the Swanee," he had once told her. Whilst she accepted it, her appetite was voracious and she wanted him every day.

One night he told her there could be a way if she could wait. He told her of COBRA and his involvement. He was transferring to the Metropolitan Police as assistant commissioner and he would soon be on the Council of COBRA. As he unfolded the story a fire began burning her loins. She stroked his penis, wanting it inside her again.

"I want to help you. I will do anything you want."

It was then that he had recruited her as an agent for COBRA.

She was a quick learner and became an expert shot and particularly adept with explosives. She could also break into and hot-wire any vehicle in a matter of seconds.

*

"Tonight, my darling, your husband is supervising the security arrangements for the PM tomorrow."

"Is tomorrow the day?" she asked, stroking the inside of his thigh.

"Tomorrow the new order of things will begin and I can take you for my own. Whatever your husband's friend does will mean nothing."

She took his hand and pressed it between her thighs. "Just the thought of it makes me want you again."

He felt his erection growing. As she pulled him on top of her he whispered, "The rest of the council think my top agent is a man. I'm so glad you're not."

Chapter Fifty

2nd June 1973

Hubbard sat in the corner of the breakfast room consuming a fry-up to satisfy the greatest hunger. Bonner sat across the breakfast room ordering scrambled eggs on toast with coffee. Hubbard finished and made for his room, threw his belongings into the overnight bag and zipped it closed. He opened the briefcase and checked the Browning. The bill was paid and he made for the small hired Vauxhall, which was innocuous and would attract no attention. It was parked in the far corner of the car park, partially hidden by a tree. He had a clear sight of the Range Rover.

Just before ten Bonner appeared carrying a plastic bag, which contained what looked like a cardboard box. He eased his bulk into the car. It glided smoothly on to the London road.

The drive proceeded at a leisurely speed attracting no attention. Hubbard followed at a discreet distance, keeping the Range Rover in sight but not appearing to tail it. The traffic was variable. He wondered why people seemed in such an impatient hurry to go shopping. They meandered through the City towards Lloyds. They went past St Helen's Place and along Gracechurch Street. Bonner turned into Eastcheap and parked. Hubbard pulled into Philpot Lane and stopped. He could see the Range Rover in his mirror. The time was eleven o'clock.

*

Every bone in his body ached. He had been cooped up in a tin can for fifteen hours. His watch glowed in the darkness telling him it was seven in the morning. He rolled over on to his stomach and reached for the two levers. They both gave to light pressure and the dull daylight stung his eyes. Climbing clumsily from the container, he rubbed his eyes and looked around. His eyes became accustomed to the half-light and stopped tingling. He pulled the bag from the canister that was his bedroom and walked to the front of the building. Two hand-held clamps were pulled from the bag and attached to the tinted glass pane. It lifted out easily and the bright morning sunlight flooded in. The man was now totally focused on the job in hand.

The movement and sudden shaft of light stirred Cross. He was twenty yards away, hunched up among the jigsaw of piping and tubes which service modern buildings. He had been there since the previous night. The Lloyds pass had gained him entry to the building. The police search had been cursory, accompanied by the comment, "I'm not climbing over all this shit."

Cross watched while the man went about his business. He had set up a tripod in front of the square of brightness where the glass had been. The FN, its polished wooden stock catching the light, was being cleaned and oiled with a care that verged on reverence. A Parker Hale sight was affixed and the weapon mounted on the tripod. The assassin spent twenty minutes adjusting the tripod until satisfied with the height and angle. Cross could not help but admire watching a professional at work.

The man was tall and angular but moved with the grace of a big cat. When he was satisfied with his work, the pane of glass was replaced. Cross watched, not moving. His injured leg ached from lack of movement. Saliva filled his mouth as he watched his prey pour coffee from a flask. The aroma seemed to fill the whole floor.

Coffee finished, the assassin set to work. He removed a pane of glass from the other side of the storey, facing away from Lloyds. A length of rope, some two hundred feet, was carried across and one end secured to a metal stanchion. An abseiling figure of eight was fixed to the rope. The man seemed satisfied with his work and replaced the glass. The aroma of coffee tormented Cross's nostrils.

Cross now knew the whole plan. After the shot the rope would be thrown from the back of the building but the killer would return into his stainless steel hiding place. The police would appeal for witnesses who had seen the culprit abseiling down the building and absconding. There would, of course, be none. The air-conditioning unit would then be found to be faulty and removed with the killer inside.

The hit man rechecked all his labours and then poured the dregs of his coffee. The time was now ten o'clock.

*

The bar in The East India Arms was buzzing as Pinter pushed his way through. Numerous press photographers were demanding an assortment of drinks from the overworked bar staff. Pinter saw the snapper from *The Record* and forced his way through the crowd.

"What are you doing here, George?" the photographer asked cheerily. "I thought this was just a snapshot to fill a bit of the paper tomorrow."

"An old friend of mine is at the lunch and I'm going to have a few beers with him later," Pinter replied truthfully. "I'll come along and see Dowie arrive and then back here to wait for Allan."

The bar became noisier and noisier as more alcohol was consumed. Pinter wondered what sort of photographs some of the collected throng would produce. The careers of most of those assembled were either on their way up or down, for it was not the sort of assignment for current top lens men. Just before twelve the gaggle began to diminish as some left to book the best pitches. Pinter watched as they departed.

*

The Saturday morning rail service left a little to be desired. It is a fact of life that train times are designed so they will never fit in with any appointments. It becomes a necessity to arrive an hour early or ten minutes late for everything. It was a bright clear morning as Jennings ambled across London Bridge. He turned into Eastcheap and down to the Chez When Club. The owner always had an eye for trade and had opened on this Saturday to allow some of the doyens of the market to loosen up before the lunch. Jennings joined a crowd in the upstairs bar. His watch told him it was eleven-thirty.

*

The man was engrossed in rechecking the set-up of the rifle as Cross eased himself upright. He stood for a moment and let the blood recirculate around his legs. The Browning rested comfortably in his hand. The weight of the silencer made the pistol feel slightly lopsided.

"One move and I'll cut you in half." The voice startled the man from his labours. He turned and saw Cross. "Move away from there and lie flat with your arms and legs spreadeagled," Cross ordered.

The assassin obeyed. Cross took the magazine from the FN and checked that the chamber was empty. He dropped the magazine on the floor, pulled back the bolt and cocked the rifle.

"Get up, take your gloves off, and go and pull that trigger."

The man stood and followed the instructions. He was quick. As he stepped away from the rifle he turned and launched himself at Cross. He seemed to move like a panther. Cross's leg still impaired his mobility and he felt a hand gripping his throat as he was pushed backwards. He swung his arm and felt the butt of the pistol striking flesh and bone. He fell backwards with the man, now limp, on top of him. He pushed him off and staggered to his feet. The unconscious body lay motionless on the floor.

Cross checked his pulse and found that there were still signs of life. He carried the limp body across the floor to where the rope lay and tied the hands and feet. He took the figure eight, wrenched it apart to look as if it had broken and put it back on the rope. He went back to the FN and adjusted the tripod to suit his own height.

*

The group was now getting more than lively. They left the Chez When and went along Philpot Lane towards Lime Street. Hubbard saw Jennings and indicated the Range Rover with his eyes. Jennings glanced over and recognised Bonner's brutal features. He winked at Hubbard, who smiled. At the back entrance to Lloyds a police officer inspected everyone's invitation before allowing them entry. They made their way to the Captain's Room where pre-lunch drinks were in full flow. Jennings knew what might happen but the tide of events was now in the hands of others.

*

Pinter stood with *The Record*'s photographer as the first of the guests began to arrive. Each was greeted by the chairman of Lloyds and then made their way into the Lloyds building. The exceptions to this were Banton and Barrett, who waited discreetly behind the welcoming party instead of entering the premises.

Hubbard took the machine pistol from the briefcase as he walked behind the Range Rover. Bonner was leaning across the seat reaching for the plastic bag when the passenger door was flung open. His eyes stared down the 35mm barrel, and a voice ordered him to sit up. Hubbard slipped into the passenger seat and dug the pistol into his ribs. "Drive and I'll tell you where to go."

*

The prime minister's Daimler glided to a halt in Lime Street. The chairman moved towards him as he alighted from the car. Banton eased himself closer to the welcoming group. He knew that a photograph of his ministering to the stricken premier would grace every front page across the world the next day. If he could get a smattering of blood on him, that would be even better. He glanced up at the Commercial Union building. He saw the flash from the muzzle of the FN. A bullet travels faster than the speed of sound so he did not hear the report of the rifle. Before the sound arrived the soft-nosed bullet crashed into his chest tearing at his vital organs. He was thrown backwards but was dead before he struck the ground.

Cross ran to the rear of the floor, untied the unconscious man and pushed him and the rope through the window. He eased backwards inside the air-conditioning drum, pulled the two handles and locked them.

Pandemonium broke loose as Banton was hurled backwards. Two Special Branch men grabbed Dowie and practically carried him inside the building. The photographers rushed forward hoping to get the most gruesome records of Banton's demise. Barrett was immediately on his knees beside the stricken home secretary for his photocall.

Inside, Dowie was ushered into the marine floor by the Special Branch officers. The domed room echoed with the din of orders being shouted. No one heard the spit of the round as it left the silenced weapon. As James Dowie fell, a neat hole in his forehead, they heard a shout of "Armed Police!" followed by the report of a pistol from the non-marine gallery above them. They looked upwards and saw the peaked cap of a senior officer running along the gallery, shouting, "Get up here! I've got him!"

In the Captain's Room one or two heard the muffled sound of police and ambulance sirens but took little notice and ordered more gin. Half an hour later it was announced that the lunch had been cancelled.

It took Jennings an hour to get away from Lloyds. The police were taking the names of all those attending and requiring proof of identity.

Pinter was in the corner of the East India bar nursing a drink.

"All went to plan?" Jennings enquired.

"It all went to plan with the exception that they had a shooter inside. James Dowie is dead." Pinter's voice was disconsolate.

The colour drained from Jennings's face as Pinter told him of the events of the afternoon. Cross had played his part, carrying out the shooting of Banton as planned. That would have spiked all the plans of COBRA and given them time to expose this insidious organisation by leaks and innuendo. James Dowie would still have been prime minister and COBRA eaten by its own cancer.

"How did they get Dowie?" Jennings asked.

"It's only a rumour, but inside the building there was a police officer or someone disguised as such who shot him. He was then shot by another copper before he could escape. The shit about it is that, so the stories go, the hero of the moment was none other than Leonard King. He's the one who shot the assassin."

All the television channels had extended news programmes that night. There was massive coverage of the press conference given by King. He gave details of the location of Banton's killer and how he had perished when his equipment failed while escaping.

"The second assassin was a serving police officer. I am sad to say that he was from my own force. I was overseeing the security operation when I saw him on the gallery in Lloyds. He fired one shot which killed the prime minister. I called for him to drop the weapon and he pointed it directly at me. I had no alternative but to shoot him."

"What are the names of the two men?" one old hack shouted.

"I am unable to release that information at present," King replied.

"Were they working together?" was bellowed.

"It is too early to speculate on that."

The morning papers were full of theories about the double killings. These ranged from communist plots to fascist plots with a sprinkling of anti-racist and pro-racist groups thrown in. Pinter became more angry the more he read differing versions. Each paper selected as the plotters those who were opposed to their own political views. He longed to put forward the true story.

All the papers decided that the two assassinations were connected whereas the first was actually designed to stop the second. One paper decided that, since one assassin killed himself with faulty equipment and the other got himself shot, the only culprits could be the IRA.

*

Cross strained his ears. For the last thirty-six hours the floor on which his bolt-hole lay had been awash with 'scene of crime' officers. The container had been moved more than once. He had heard them taking fingerprints and tapping the outside. Now all was quiet. His watch told him it was four in the morning. He eased the handles together. They moved silently. He pushed the handles until the opening was a few inches wide. There were no lights and no sign of life. He opened the front, crawled out and closed the canister behind him. His eyes were accustomed to the dark and he could see that the window had been reseated. All signs of frantic activity had gone.

Silently he crossed to the door. Light seeped in around the frame. He listened for an hour and heard nothing. He opened the canister and took out his briefcase. The stairwell was brightly lit and unoccupied. Cross walked down ten floors and went through the doors to the floor itself. The toilets were where he had been told and he entered. He opened the briefcase. It felt good to wash and shave after being sealed in the container which had seemed to shrink by the hour. He now had an understanding of people who suffered from claustrophobia.

The lightweight suit was, fortunately, of the highest quality and the creases soon fell out. He donned a clean shirt and the suit, crammed his old clothes into the case and closed it. He went into one of the cubicles and waited. At nine-thirty he heard someone tunelessly whistling *I Belong To London*. He flushed the toilet, opened the door and to his relief was confronted with Jennings's smiling face.

For the next two hours Cross sat next to Jennings while he persuaded the underwriter that each offer he had was even better than the last. As they left the building they offered a cheery goodbye to the commissionaire on the desk.

"I'm bloody starving!" Cross had not eaten for nearly three days.

Over a pile of sandwiches in the Marine Club Jennings recounted the tale of their success and their failure.

"Banton was never intended to be the man to replace Dowie!" Cross exclaimed through a mouthful of pâté and bread. "I wondered why the bastard was using the FN! That meant that there were to be *two* shots – one for Dowie and the other for Banton."

"That fits," commented Jennings. "It seems as if there is a climate being created for Victor Barrett to put himself forward."

*

Bonner's leg was raw from the shackle that held it. It was three days since he had been confronted with the Browning held in a massive hairy paw. The basement was damp and cold. The thickset man had brought him meals but said nothing. He knew he was in a house in Surrey but nothing else.

The door above him opened and four men descended the stairs. Two looked familiar but he could not think why.

"How nice to see you again, Sergeant-Major." The tallest one spoke.

Slowly Bonner's memory began to function.

"I think that our roles have been reversed."

The memory sprang to the front of his mind. Jennings was his captor.

"I just wanted to say goodbye." Jennings spoke again. "My friend, whom you have already met, wants to talk to you about COBRA." Jennings indicated the violent-looking man with the hirsute hands.

Bonner's fear began to attack his bowels.

"If I were you, I would tell him everything you know, otherwise he can be extremely spiteful." Jennings saw the fear in Bonner's eyes yet felt no sympathy, only pleasure. He knew that Hubbard had Pentathol, but Bonner didn't.

They picked Bonner up and tied him to a chair, leaving the fetter attached to his ankle.

"Goodbye," Jennings repeated and the three left him alone with the evil-looking monster.

*

"He knows bugger all!" Hubbard spat out the comment. "His targets were Banton and Dowie in any order but he does not know why. All the instructions came from Marden. He has no idea who Carter is, except that he arranged for the tour of the area. I'll get rid of him tomorrow."

Pinter raised his eyebrows but decided to make no comment.

"The police have just announced the identities of the two assassins of James Dowie and Marcus Banton," the cultured voice of the BBC newscaster announced. "They are Joseph Starkey, a former member of the SAS, and Tony Hacker, who was a serving police officer with the Metropolitan Police." Jennings sat bolt upright in his seat. "It is not presently known whether the two were connected with each other, and inquiries are being pursued." The report continued with the usual BBC attempt to make ten minutes from a five-second piece of news. Several experts were asked their opinion, and all offered differing and incorrect views.

Anger raged inside Jennings. He remembered Starkey offering help and aid at Pai Ling yet all the time he had been one of them. His anger would have been brief except that Hacker was also said to be implicated. He could not believe it. The television showed film of Tony Hacker's modest house six doors away from The Haycutter. The press were encamped outside. He could imagine Penny trapped in her own home, imagining the worst of her husband but unable to give credence to it. Hacker and Jennings had been friends since childhood. Jennings knew him better than even his wife. Hacker had to have been a fall guy.

"I'll have a wager that bastard King shot both Dowie and Tony," Cross's voice broke through Jennings's inner turmoil. "There were two people on the gallery. One who we *know* was conspiring to assassinate the PM, and Tony. We end up with one dead and the conspirator alive. King shot Dowie and then Tony, planted the first gun on Tony and became the bloody hero."

It was so obvious that Jennings had not considered it. He walked across to the telephone and dialled. Hacker was ex-directory, and perhaps the leeches of the press had not yet discovered the number.

"Will you leave me alone!" a defiant voice answered.

"Don't hang up Penny, it's Allan," said Jennings.

"Oh Allan, thank God it's you!" He could hear the tears in her voice. "They're banging at the door and ringing the phone all the time. They won't leave me alone."

"Where are the children?" Jennings asked.

She told him they were with friends and she was alone.

"Are the press out the back?" he asked.

They were not. He told her to pack some clothes and wait.

Penny Hacker was upset but it was the machinations of the press not the news of her husband's involvement in the assassination which caused her grief.

*

King had arrived at her home at ten the evening Dowie had been killed.

"What are you doing here? Tony will be home soon," Penny had cried, wishing it were not true.

King gently pushed her inside and closed the door. He took her in his arms and she had responded.

"Tony won't be home," he had said. "The plan went wrong. The policeman who was shot was Tony."

Her immediate reaction was shock and then sadness. She had lived with Tony for nine years and at one time had loved him. Slowly, she realised that without Tony her body could always be satisfied. She felt King's strong arms enveloping her. She pressed against him and could feel the hardness growing in his groin. The flames of passion ignited inside her as the zip slid gently down her back and her dress fell to the floor. Before she realised it she was naked. She dropped to her knees and undid his belt. He was hard and tasted salty. She wanted more inside her. He heaved with pleasure as she took more of him.

They lay on the floor, where they had first made love. His tongue explored every contour of her body. Her first orgasm was with his tongue, her second as his hands caressed her. They coupled and the third rose like a Titan rocket and burst through her whole body.

They lay together and she cried. Penny's tears were of sadness for her husband and happiness for herself.

*

Jennings left the Jaguar across the green and went over the fields to the rear of Hacker's house. One newspaperman was there.

"You've found your way round the back as well?" he asked.

Jennings fist caught him squarely on the chin and he found his way into never-never land. He opened the camera, pulled out the film, threw it away and then climbed over the fence. Penny was by the french windows. When she saw him, she opened the windows and fled up the garden. She fell into his arms, her body racked with sobbing. He held her gently, remembering times past when he had held her passionately. They fled across the green, leaving the vultures to pick at the empty shell of the house.

Penny's hands were still shaking as Jennings handed her a second brandy. "They're saying that Tony murdered James Dowie." She seemed numb with shock. "Tony wouldn't do that – he couldn't!" Her voice was insistent. "They said £50,000 had been put into his bank account in Switzerland. We don't have a bank account in Switzerland."

Jennings wanted to know more but this was not the time or place. He put his arm around her and said, "We know that Tony did not do it." Penny looked at him as if wanting more reassurance, her eyes red with the anguish she appeared to be suffering. "Tony was murdered, not a murderer, and I promise you that the guilty ones will get their just desserts."

"That's enough for now," Gwen interrupted. "Penny doesn't want you all fussing around her. You men go into the study and leave us ladies alone."

The four men obeyed. They thought that Penny needed to both talk and cry and that they were probably an impediment to one or both.

That night Penny Hacker lay in bed caressing her own body and imagining her hands were King's. As the little death gushed through her she smiled.

*

"What do we do now?" Cross asked.

"We stop the bastards." Jennings's rage was rising. "And I don't care what we have to do."

"Sit down, Allan." Pinter's voice was placating. "We do have to stop them but in cold anger not flaming rage. First let's understand the position we are in at the present." He went to the cabinet and poured them each a drink. "It seems obvious to me that certain members of COBRA had a different agenda from the rest. The hit man was not just to take out Dowie but Banton as well. We know this by the fact that the FN was used. That means that, contrary to what we heard at their meetings, the hit was set up to put Barrett in the frame. We also know that Appleby, Barrett and McHenry met away from the manor on a regular basis. These are the three we have to stop. Without them, the pack of cards will collapse." The others nodded their agreement. "We have to find a way of knowing Appleby's movements – he is the key to everything. I am afraid that means we have to extend our trust beyond the four of us and ask Jane Salisbury to help. She can give us specific details of Appleby's appointments. The question is, are we prepared to trust her?"

They talked around the thought and had to accept that without her help they would be fighting with only one hand. Cross telephoned her saying that they needed her help. He arranged to meet her the next day.

Chapter Fifty-One

The markets had been in turmoil since the assassination. The pound had weakened against most other major currencies and the stock exchange index had fallen over two hundred points. Quentin Stone, the Foreign Secretary, had taken the role of acting PM until a ballot of the members of the parliamentary party could be arranged.

No one was prepared to put their name forward before the funeral of James Dowie, but much was being fed to the press, and campaign teams were being put into place. There seemed to be three main candidates plus one dark horse. Stone was the man in place and was seen by many as a safe pair of hands. The problem was that the election was now less than two years away and Stone was a very dry ex-career diplomat who had less charisma than a rocking horse. The second was Martin Feltrim, who had charisma enough to charm the population of India. His problem was that he had the brains of a rocking horse. He was currently the defence minister, which suited him as the joint chiefs of staff told him what to do and he complied. The third candidate was the Chancellor Roy Hoare. He was popular in the country and in certain sections of the party. His politics were to the left of the party, which weakened him somewhat. Also, he did not have the Eton/Harrow, Oxbridge pedigree, nor was he a career politician, having previously made a fortune from his own manufacturing business.

Victor Barrett was the dark horse. At the outset there seemed little apparent support for him within the parliamentary party. The mogul who owned *The Daily Record* had different ideas. *The Record* started with small references to Barrett as a possibility and over a short period this developed into full-blown support for him as a candidate. The paper bemoaned the loss of a man of the calibre of Banton but added that the country was lucky to have Barrett as an alternative.

On the day of Dowie's funeral, Jennings was in his office fuming over the latest missive from *The Record*. It was praising Barrett's reticence and loyalty and calling upon him to come forward. As he threw the paper in the direction of the waste bin the telephone rang.

"Allan," - it was Jane's voice - "can I see you for lunch? I have some news for you."

They arranged to meet in the Chez When.

"Appleby has a meeting tonight at Gatefield Manor." Jane was dressed in a perfectly cut Dior suit complemented by a Gucci shoulder scarf. Her hair shone like golden flax in a silken breeze. Jennings easily understood why Cross was totally besotted by her. If it were not for Pansie, he could be the same.

"The car is picking him up at four this afternoon," she continued. "That means that he will get to the manor about five."

After lunch Jennings telephoned Hubbard and told him. The Listener had been brought back to Woldingham and had to be put back into service.

"*Despite the attempts of Marden's associates to completely botch our plans*" - Appleby's tone was severe - "*we are fortunate that we are still able to continue to our objective.*"

"*I cannot understand what happened.*" Marden was valiantly trying to defend himself. "*Starkey was my best man.*"

"*If that is the best you can produce, I suggest that your recruiting is defective,*" Appleby sneered. "*Not only did he kill the wrong man but he then proceeded to throw himself out of a window. Perhaps the latter was the right decision. Apart from that, where the blazes was your back-up?*" The anger in his voice was unmistakable.

"*I don't know - he's disappeared,*" whined Marden.

"*A lot of your people do that!*" The barb was snapped back. "*I wonder whether you should take a leaf out of their book, Mr Marden. The council have decided that you are no longer fit to be a member. I am asking you to leave.*"

Hubbard was enjoying listening to the bickering develop. He raised the binoculars and watched. Nobody left the building.

"*Now that is out of the way, shall we get down to business?*" Appleby's court voice had returned. "*As I said, the whole thing is not such a disaster as it may have been. We achieved the objective of removing Dowie, thanks to the foresight and planning of Mr King. Unfortunately we no longer have the services of Marcus Banton. However, you have, no doubt, observed the editorial tone of* The Daily Record. *It is my opinion that Victor will be elected, provided that he* is given the same support Banton would have received. Please carry on, Victor."

"The situation is", Barrett began, "Hoare, Feltrim and Stone will declare themselves tomorrow. I have a campaign team in place but presently well hidden. I will wait for the underlying support to become more vociferous, and reluctantly put myself forward the day the nominations close. I will do this on the basis that I am answering a call, not pushing for power. From that point it will be necessary for Mr McHenry and Mr Webster to show support for my candidacy from both commerce and industry. With the markets fluctuating in the right pattern and support from the major industries I am sure I can win."

Hubbard saw movement at the rear of the building. Two men were carrying a large bundle across the yard. They opened the boot of Marden's car and tossed it in. They got into the car and drove off.

"Moving the markets to coincide with opinion changes is not a problem. We have already demonstrated what we can do." McHenry sounded confident.

Webster confirmed that implied support would come from the CBI.

The meeting closed and they retired for dinner. Hubbard switched to the monitors in the dining room, knowing he would only hear social chatter. A light indicated that the equipment was also monitoring the large office and Hubbard switched to listen.

"Just a quick word." Appleby's inflection sounded conspiratorial. "I think that matters have gone better than expected. They appear to accept that Banton's demise was an accident. Our strategy is running very nicely. The only thing I cannot understand is why Starkey only took Banton. I presume he was briefed for both. It's lucky that you suggested the back-up, Leonard."

"Better to be safe than sorry," replied King. "Pity about young Hacker though – he was quite a good copper. As far as Starkey is concerned, I most certainly briefed him to make both shots. The only reason I can guess at is that the weapon was faulty. We did find the magazine on the floor not on the FN. I can only speculate that when things went wrong, he panicked."

"Let's not leave the other gentlemen alone for too long," Appleby's voice interrupted King. "I suggest that the four of us meet here weekly to review progress. Is one week from today, five o'clock acceptable?"

King and two other voices agreed.

"So it is still all systems go." Hubbard turned off the recording and looked at the others. "Turn off Banton, turn on Barrett and still get the same result. They intended to take Banton out anyway."

"We have to find a way to stop them. I thought of going to print with the story but it looks like the bloody owner of the paper is in with them." Pinter was exasperated.

King's dismissive remark about Hacker had cut Jennings to the heart. To hear the death of his oldest and dearest friend dismissed as a minor inconvenience tore at a nerve that was still raw. He vowed to himself that whatever else happened King would pay for what he had done. "We'll find a way," he said grimly.

The next morning the papers carried two stories. Hoare, Feltrim and Stone had put forward their names for the ballot; Wing Commander Marden, the head of Air Force security, had been killed in a mugging outside a Soho strip club. The latter story was relegated to the inside pages.

The bookmakers installed Stone as the 7/4 favourite. The stock market fell fifty points. *The Record* carried a leader comparing the assets and liabilities of the three men. They also compared them with those of Barrett, and, to no one's surprise, Barrett was better. The other newspapers were enamoured to varying degrees of the different candidates. Apart from Barrett, no candidate had the full support of any of the national daily papers.

As the week progressed more people jumped on to the Barrett bandwagon. *The Times* wrote a leader telling him to step into the race to give the members of Parliament a true choice. *The Daily Express* followed. It said it supported Stone but the contest needed Barrett to reflect the balance of the party.

Nominations closed the next Friday at midday. Barrett called a press conference for ten that morning. Pinter waved his press card and pushed his way into the overcrowded room at the Palace of Westminster.

"Thank you for attending, ladies and gentlemen," Barrett started. "Over the last week I have been under considerable pressure from both inside and outside the party to declare myself as a candidate for the leadership. I have resisted that pressure. My position as chief whip is as a servant of the party leader. I have served in the whips' office under three party leaders and I have never wanted anything else. The colossal leap from being servant of the leader to being leader is something I could never have envisaged. That is until today. I have been approached by too many of my colleagues in Parliament and friends outside urging me to offer myself as a candidate to ignore their entreaties. I therefore – and I have to say it is with a degree of reluctance – will be tendering my name for the forthcoming leadership election."

The political editor of *The Record* leapt to his feet and started applauding. Others joined in until over half of those present were on their feet. Pinter sat stoically, his mind boiling with anger at this affront to his intelligence.

The statement was followed by the usual torrent of mostly irrelevant questions from the media. Television was, of course, given precedence. Barrett handled the press like an expert angler playing a trout. He complimented the abilities of the other candidates while at the same time subtly undermining them.

The news of Barrett's candidacy reached the financial markets in mid-morning. The FTSE shot up over one hundred and fifty points within an hour. The pound strengthened against all major currencies. Leading bookmakers installed Barrett as joint favourite.

The pollsters all made a great deal of money. Every paper, every television channel wanted their own poll of how the leadership election would go. The first ballot was set for Monday 25th June. As the days passed, various polls were published showing different results. They were living proof that a normal politician knows a lot about politics but little about telling the truth.

Whenever a poll favoured a candidate other than Barrett, the financial markets waned. In one day *The Express* published a poll showing Hoare as the likely winner, causing the markets to plunge fifty points, and in the afternoon the BBC produced one favouring Barrett and the fifty point drop was retrieved with interest. McHenry and his following were manipulating the markets with the efficiency of a Japanese electronics worker. The whole situation was getting beyond the influence of Jennings. A decision had to be made.

*

Friday 22nd June

The Listener was stationed west of the house with a clear view of the west wing. It was the type of summer evening of which Englishmen dream when they are away from home. The sun was easing below the distant horizon, throwing sensational shades of orange and yellow into the dying sky. The flowers were blooming. The Listener was surrounded by a carpet of tall foxgloves, each reaching for the flashes of light that filtered through the trees. The flowers knew that their day in the sun was coming to an end and would soon close their petals to sleep through the night. In the morning the sun would reawaken them and they would arise resplendent. Jennings's and Hubbard's mood did not allow them to appreciate the splendour of nature's panorama.

The first to arrive at the manor was King. He had booked into a small hotel in Caversham that lunchtime. He and Penny had ordered a meal in the room. All afternoon they had made love. He could still taste and smell her as the BMW glided along the drive and came to a silent halt. She lay, naked, waiting his return to fulfil her again.

Jennings watched through the binoculars, wondering why the Metropolitan Police used foreign cars. King alighted, waved the driver away and made his way into the manor. He was presently followed by Appleby, Barrett and McHenry. Jennings knew that this was the main conspiracy. The meeting room light flashed, showing that voices were activating the recording machinery.

"*I believe that we are nearly there, gentlemen.*" Jennings heard a smugness in Appleby's voice which had not been there previously. "*I think that Victor should tell us how successful our plan will be.*"

"*I am delighted at the response from my fellow members.*" Barrett's voice was self-satisfied. "*Every time the markets have moved my support has increased. I am now totally confident that we will win on the first ballot. I will then be magnanimous and give cabinet posts to my rivals but ensure that, within a short time, they receive bad press. As a man of honour I will have to dismiss them and bring in people who are sympathetic to our views. Thus our object will be achieved.*"

Jennings listened, his stomach sickened by the sound of the Dom Perignon cork bursting from the bottle. He heard the fizz as the wine moved from bottle to glass. It sounded like interference on the radio, but was just a fine wine escaping from captivity. He looked at Hubbard, who simply nodded. The transmitter was set to receive. Jennings had heard enough. He switched to another waveband and carefully set the dial. He pushed the switch to TRANSMIT.

Appleby raised his glass. "COBRA and our future," he intoned.

The glasses of champagne never reached any of their lips.

There are many types of explosive. The term 'explosive' simply refers to the ability of a compound to burn at a very rapid rate. The fastest burners are known as high-explosives. The general perception is that everything which explodes is a high-explosive. This is not so. Semtex burns so rapidly that the energy release seems instantaneous. It is not. It may detonate in a microsecond but it is not without delay. There are low-explosives which, to the human eye, appear the same, but burn in several microseconds. The release of energy from a high-explosive is immediate and is followed by a highly volatile shock wave. The shock wave will drive away anything in its path. The low-explosive will shake any obstruction until it collapses. The release of energy is like an earthquake. If the epicentre is close to the surface, the energy of the blast is released in violent and rapid movement of the ground. If the epicentre is deep, the result is a slower movement of the earth over a greater area. Often a deep epicentre will cause more damage and loss of life than a shallow one.

Jennings had chosen both explosive and site perfectly. The instruction from the transmitter was received by the detonator. The detonator fired the Ammatol. Ammatol is a slow-burning, high-intensity explosive. It was often used to attack warships. It would not simply hole the vessel, it would break its back.

It was neither a bang nor a rumble which Jennings and Hubbard heard. The shock waves were not violent enough to blow out the walls but were enough to make them collapse. The walls of the room were integral to the structure of the west wing. They fell inwards, bringing the whole edifice with them. In effect the west wing imploded.

Hubbard watched as the building fell into itself. "Nice one, Allen," he commented as he packed away the equipment. "I don't think Mr Barrett will make the count."

As they drove along the country road away from the manor they heard the wails of the approaching emergency services. Jennings looked out of the window and saw the foxgloves beginning to gently nod into their night's sleep.

As they passed through Caversham they could have seen a light burning in room seven of the Crown Hotel. Penny Hacker was sleeping, her legs spread asunder, waiting for King to lie between them. She was dreaming of the afternoon. King was inside her, driving ever deeper and deeper. She writhed on the bed, pushing her hips upwards, wanting his whole being inside her body. The telephone burst sharply into her private world of gratification.

King's driver had returned to collect him at the manor only to find that part of it no longer existed. He had driven King and Penny to the hotel earlier in the day and knew that King intended to return there. As he related to his mates later, "I had to phone up his bit of skirt and tell her to get her knickers back on 'cos he wouldn't be back to give her another one."

That night Penny Hacker's mood ranged from unmitigated despair to raging anger.

The news of Barrett's and the others' demise broke late that night. All the daily papers held their front pages and dispatched their best to Gatefield Manor to stand around the huge gates hoping to grab a snippet of information ahead of their rivals.

The morning papers were full of the story and gave glowing testimonials to the public and private works of Barrett, Appleby, King and McHenry. After the furore of the previous week the financial markets seemed to show little interest. The index fluttered for an hour and then settled down to business as usual.

On Sunday night *The Times* received a telephone call giving the code word of the Provisional IRA and claiming responsibility for the bomb. This came as no surprise to anybody, with the exception of the IRA. They knew that it was not their work, but decided that the publicity was too good not to take advantage of it. They said nothing.

The elders of the Conservative Party met and decided to defer the election of the new leader until after the remains of Barrett had been interred.

Chapter Fifty-Two

The theoretical objective of a stag night is to take the prospective groom out on a night to remember and do all the things which will be debarred once he has donned the marital chains. What actually happens is that it is an excuse for a lot of adult males to go out together and behave like children. The impending marriage of one of the party is an excuse rather than a reason for the escapade.

The bowling alley at The Haycutter had been selected as the venue, and its door proclaimed 'Private Party'. As all of the regular customers were invited, the occupants of the bar had simply shifted to the bowling alley.

Much as he tried, Jennings could not do the expected thing and get drunk. Too many spectres haunted him that night. In two days' time he was to be married to the woman of his dreams. It would be the happiest day of his life but neither his father nor his oldest friend would be there to share that happiness. In his mind's eye he could see the brigadier and Tony Hacker, arms around each other, leading the singing at the stag night. He made the customary speech, making sure that it did not last longer than the consumption of one pint. It would be bad form to leave someone with an empty glass for the toast.

Hubbard and Cross had thrown themselves wholeheartedly into the celebrations. They were deep in conversation, with neither understanding what the other was talking about. George Pinter had been cornered by Rittle and his eyes were becoming glazed. Whether this was caused by the Glenfiddich or Rittle was anyone's guess. Jennings rescued Pinter and saw Rittle proceed to capture Rasher from the golf club as his next victim.

Pinter raised his glass and said quietly, "To the man at *The Times* who thinks I have an Irish accent."

Hubbard now had the bit between his teeth and called for silence. He proceeded to ramble on about what a fine man Jennings was, what a wonderful person Pansie was and how he would do anything in the world for them. Jennings suggested that the first thing he should do was to stop making speeches.

Hubbard held up his glass and said, "To Allan and Pansie." As everybody raised their glasses Hubbard grabbed Cross and Pinter and dragged them across to Jennings. "Just the four of us," he garbled. "Let's drink to the headless snake."

*

Jennings was sitting in the lounge nursing a large cognac. Pinter, Cross and Hubbard had finally succumbed to the demon alcohol and staggered to bed. His thoughts were far away in times gone by. Rittle sat opposite – his mouth was operating, but Jennings was not listening. Suddenly Rittle's voice forced its way into his musing.

"I could not be certain it was you until that arsehole toasted the headless snake."

Jennings looked at Rittle and could see hatred in his eyes.

"This country would have had a real future but for you and your interfering friends. You and your so-called high morals – you're as big a bloody prig as Charles was!" Rittle spat the words.

The realisation struck Jennings like a thunderbolt. "It was *you* who killed my father!"

"No, but if I had been asked to, I would have done," came the simple reply. "He knew of COBRA and could have destroyed us. You, on the other hand, have murdered the only person I ever really loved. William Appleby was worth a hundred of your bloody father."

As Jennings got to his feet he saw the Walther in Rittle's hand. He had always thought that the Walther was an effeminate-looking hand-gun and often wondered why Fleming had chosen it for James Bond. In the pudgy hand of this toad-faced womanlike man it looked truly ridiculous.

Rittle rose and told Jennings to sit.

*

Pansie needed the feel of Jennings's warm body holding her. Her hen party had finished long ago, and Gwen and Penny were in the land of slumber. She had heard someone come upstairs but Jennings had not appeared. She wondered whether the party had been too good and if now he was sleeping in an easy chair. She slipped into her *négligé* and padded down the stairs. She heard voices raised in the lounge. Through the frosted glass door she saw the silhouette of a short pudgy man with his arm pointing.

"All that shit about you defending me and making a deal was crap! You knew that I was not intended to come out of Colchester!" Jennings's voice shouted.

"You were a mistake and an embarrassment. Then you joined up with others to cause more trouble. Had it not been for you and your meddlesome friends I would have been the Master of the Rolls by now. Now, by the time we've regrouped, it will be too late. You've destroyed my dream and my life. I intend to make you pay for it." Rittle raised the Walther. "You and your father are the same. Your so-called moral standards and just pretentious bullshit." He moved towards Jennings, the baby pistol pointing directly at his head.

There was a sharp report from behind Jennings, and Rittle pitched backwards, the pistol flying from his hand. Pansie stood in the doorway, the Luger in her hand. Wisps of smoke danced from the barrel. The Luger dropped to the floor. Jennings took her in his arms and Pansie sobbed, "He was your father's friend. How could he do it?"

Hubbard and Cross appeared, the sound of the shot having penetrated their dreams.

"The bastard was one of them," Jennings said, indicating the prone body of Rittle. There was a small hole in the centre of his forehead.

"Great shot, no mess," muttered Hubbard, matter-of-factly, as he leaned over the remains.

A sudden and unexpected happening has an immediate sobering effect. Thousands of people were drunk just before the San Francisco earthquake, but everybody was sober after it.

"You two go to bed, I'll sort this out," he said, picking up the telephone.

*

They lay in each other's arms. He clung to her tightly, not wanting to let go. So much had been lost. They made love as though their very existence depended on it. He fell into a deep sleep. He dreamed. There was no fire, no shattered bodies, no phantoms to haunt his sleep. Only his father and Tony Hacker in a country hostelry with the others from the patrol. They were drinking his health and wishing him happiness. Their pain had departed. His would always be with him, but part of it had been assuaged.

The next morning all signs of Rittle had gone.

Penny Hacker had not been asleep. Her door had been ajar and she had heard everything. She suspected that Jennings had been involved in her lover's death and now she *knew*. She clenched her teeth. She would not cry: sorrow would be replaced with anger. She closed her eyes and pictured King exploring her body and she his, knowing that she would never again experience such pleasure. She started to stroke herself, gently at first and then with more and more urgency. As her orgasm burst, a voice in her head screamed, 'I'll make the bastard pay!'

Chapter Fifty-Three

The ghosts that surrounded Jennings were no longer sad. His father stood behind him beaming with delight. He wore the dress uniform of the Lancers. Beside Jennings was Hacker, resplendent in Metropolitan Police number one dress. Six stood in the first pew proudly wearing their beige berets, the cap badges proudly declaring 'Who Dares Wins'. They were all smiling.

The old Norman church was filling rapidly. The guests, who were also business friends, were ushered to the bride's side of the church. Pansie had no relatives, so they balanced the horde which was Jennings's so-called nearest and dearest.

Peter Huber had organised a trip to London to coincide with the wedding. "I can't miss the wedding of the worst broker in the world and the best underwriter. You must be a helluva fuck to persuade her to take you," he had roared down the telephone when he received his invitation.

As Huber glanced through the order of service she sat beside him. At a wedding people are normally happy. This woman seemed distant. His sociable nod to her was ignored.

The organ broke into the bridal march, and the congregation stood and looked to the rear of the church. Jennings saw her. Her dress was pure white satin decorated with lace and pearls. Beside her was George Pinter. He could have been no prouder than if the bride had been his own daughter. She reached Jennings's side and the bridesmaid lifted back her veil.

Beside Jennings was the most beautiful woman he had ever known. He looked into those huge hazel eyes now misted by tears of happiness.

"With this ring I thee wed, with my body I thee worship and with all my worldly goods I thee endow."

A voice said, "I now pronounce you man and wife. You may kiss the bride."

Jennings held Pansie close, never wanting to let go.

As they walked down the aisle they smiled and greeted their guests. All returned their silent salute with one exception. She looked down.

Outside, there was the usual gaggle wanting to either take or be in photographs. Peter Huber stood slightly apart with a few reinsurance people. He noticed that the strange woman was standing alone and seemed agitated.

The photographer was yelling instructions and getting only nominal co-operation.

"Bride and groom's family please," he shouted.

People shuffled about, tall ones standing in front of small ones. The photographer rushed about moving everyone so that they would all be in the memento.

"All the guests please," was the next order.

Huber, who was over six feet, took up his station behind Pansie. He saw that woman elbowing her way past others. She stopped behind Jennings. Huber was about to offer to move so that she could be seen when she reached inside her bag and pulled out something shiny. Her words were only audible to those directly in front or beside her. "Your father and now you, you bastard."

She moved her arm back to strike and Huber saw that she held something pointed. As she struck he instinctively grabbed her wrist and twisted her arm behind her back. She kicked and screamed as he tore the syringe from her grasp.

Jennings turned to see the source of the commotion behind him. He saw his best friend's widow, her eyes flashing with hate, trying to escape Huber's vice-like grip.

Huber held up a syringe and said, "I hope it's a joke and this contains just bromide."

Epilogue

Penny Hacker was charged with attempted murder. The syringe contained a cocktail of drugs, any of which would have been lethal on its own. She employed an excellent barrister who pleaded insanity. He was eloquent enough to have her institutionalised rather than imprisoned. She was found to be cured within three years. She subsequently used her talents, which she had developed over seven illicit years with King, wisely and now owns a very exclusive gentlemen-only club in Soho called More Than a Penny For 'em. Whilst Jennings knew she was responsible for his father's death, his inner torment had been sated. His new life had begun and the old now truly consigned to the past. She, however, retained a passionate hatred of Jennings.

The establishment has its own way of dealing with internal problems. It closes ranks and then quietly metes out its own justice.

Roy Hoare was elected as leader of the party and prime minister at the second ballot. His first appointment was George Pinter, to head his press office. The next move was to reorganise the security services. Both Leach and Piper suddenly disappeared and were subsequently reported to be in South America being feted by a rather nasty right-wing dictator who had received considerable assistance from the Association for Democratic Conservatism. Both were executed following a coup in that country.

Jim Cross was seconded to MI5 as its new controller. John Hubbard was made responsible for all security matters at Number 10 Downing Street.

Corby, Lannin & Davies merged with Manning Steele International to form the largest reinsurance brokers in the world. Jennings was appointed chairman, which meant that Cameron Carter became surplus to requirements. Jennings ensured that he was unable to find any company in London that would employ him. He went to New York and became involved with some rather dubious characters and then was sentenced to serve twenty years in the state penitentiary for racketeering.

Gordon Carritt resigned as leader of the Liberal Party. He took the Chiltern Hundreds and retired from politics. Two months later he died in a tragic boating accident.

The Inland Revenue discovered certain irregularities in the records of Porterfield Industries during a regular audit. Robert Webster was indicted on ten counts of tax evasion and four of fraud. He was sent to prison for six years. He was murdered in prison three months later. The murderer was never found.